BOYD RITCHIE HAD BEEN JAILED IN TARKINGTON FOR RAPE. WHAT HE WAS GOING TO DO TO TARKINGTON MADE RAPE LOOK LIKE CHILD'S PLAY.

Sexual assault was just the first step in Boyd Ritchie's timetable of terror.

Torture, mutilation, and bizarre murder also had parts to play in his exquisitely designed schedule of vengeance.

Men, women, children, all were on Boyd Ritchie's list—and not one of them would escape the ravenous, rapacious night he had lusted for so long . . .

THE LONG DARK NIGHT

"Chilling!"—*Publishers Weekly*

"A sure bestseller!"—*Newsweek*

"The big suspense novel of the year!"
—*Best Sellers*

THE LONG DARK NIGHT

Joseph Hayes

A DELL BOOK

Published by
DELL PUBLISHING CO., INC.
1 Dag Hammarskjold Plaza
New York, New York 10017

For information contact G. P. Putnam's Sons,
New York, N.Y. 10016.
Dell ® TM 681510, Dell Publishing Co., Inc.

ISBN: 0-440-14824-3

Reprinted by arrangement with
G. P. Putnam's Sons

Printed in the United States of America
Previous Dell Edition #4824
New Dell Edition
First printing—June 1977

Revenge is a kind of wild justice, which the more man's nature runs to, the more ought law to weed it out.

—Francis Bacon

Recompense to no man evil for evil.

—New Testament

Vengeance is mine; I will repay, saith the Lord.

—New Testament

Revenge, at first though sweet,
Bitter ere long back on itself recoils.

—Milton, *Paradise Lost*

Part One

It was almost, but not quite, dark when he emerged from between the two granite pillars of the cemetery entrance: a slight boyish figure, not tall, moving with an easy swiftness, an air of confidence, no urgency, head tilted to one side although he did not dart glances in either direction, wearing a black turtleneck sweater, slim tight slacks, also black, and dark tennis sneakers. Covering his narrow head, which he had shaved completely bald, was a knitted ski cap, also quite black. He climbed into the metallic-gray three-year-old Chevy Vega parked along the curb, turned on the motor but not the lights, although there were no houses along this treelined stretch of street, which was almost a road, on the edge of town, and completely deserted. The motor had a hollow powerful roar, even though he was careful not to rev it, the sound incongruous in the small car, which now moved slowly along until, at the corner, its lights came on as it turned, gaining speed, and proceeded downhill toward the pleasant glow in the sky over the main section of town where the lights were coming on.

Behind the wheel Boyd Ritchie was surprised that, after the years of intense self-discipline that had brought him—incredibly and finally—to this place and this point in time, he would still have to warn himself, actually to force himself with a severe wrenching of will, to stay calm. Control, iron unswerving self-control—only that had carried him this far and only that same inner choking-down of emotion could possibly carry him through the night. It was a long time till morning and in those hours, those precious satisfying hours, he would live a lifetime. It had been that thought—the dreaming, the plotting—that had sustained him during the long days and endless nights. Exactly two thousand, four hundred and ninety-two of them in that gray stinking clanging hell; then, since parole, exactly two hundred and fifty-one of them, existing and working in Londonford, twenty miles away, and spending almost every evening here in Tarkington while he began to carry out, bit by careful bit, the scheme that would, tonight, now, soon, bring him back to life. The cold excitement was in his blood, stifled but throbbing as he drove. Almost eight years—he'd make it up, make it all up, in spades, in this one night that stretched ahead with such wild dark promise.

It was a quiet time of evening, with little traffic, the streets dim, lights gleaming behind windows. The town of Tarkington, snug and safe between two Berkshire hills that were almost mountains and hemmed in by a long curving neck of lake at the north, was taking a breath between the day's work and the evening's relaxation and pleasure. Even now he could feel a sort of nostalgic envy mingling with his hatred: they'd cheated him of this, too, even this simple a thing that they took for granted. He passed the Wharton Mills, factories now, grim and high and shadowy, dull gray frame buildings behind high steel-mesh fences. Well, by morning they wouldn't even exist. By morning the whole goddamn town would be a different place. And not so snug—and far from safe, ever again.

Like Judge T. H. Stuttaford—even dead, he had had his debt to pay and now he had paid it.

The car moved inconspicuously at a normal rate of speed—not too slow, not too fast—along one of the four streets running around the path-patterned rectangle of trees and grass which here in New England was referred to as the Common or, in smaller towns, the Green. In the grubby towns where he had grown up in southern Illinois, it would have been less tidy, probably with a dirty courthouse set squarely in its center, and would have been called the Square. Here the courthouse—a neat granite structure of three stories with ivy climbing its walls—stood solidly along one side of the Common, its stone front in sharp contrast to the spanking white of storefronts, the Victorian and Colonial houses, and the churches with imposing Doric columns. As he passed the courthouse, which also housed the jail, Boyd Ritchie told himself that it was too early to think of Theron Diehl. It was not yet time to remember the bruised ribs, the paralyzed neck, the swollen flaming testicles or the feel of the barrel of that old Colt .45 held against his cheek while that gentle Texas voice drawled: *Wider, son, wider, 'less you want the bullet t'shatter your teeth, too. Less a-course by now you're 'bout ready to confess.* Plenty of time for Theron Diehl—now Chief of Police Diehl—later. Time tonight for all of them.

He reached and flipped on the radio. It crackled for a moment, then erupted with a voice, unmistakably Yankee, giving instructions to a patrol car in that nasal twang that Boyd Ritchie had, eight years ago, come to despise. The town was too small for the police to bother with codes; this had saved him the trouble of having to learn any. All he had had to do was to install a radio with a police band: now he could stay tuned in all night to whatever action the hick-pigs decided to take.

He lowered his foot on the accelerator, careful not to allow the powerful engine to reveal its power. But it was there, that power, in case he needed it. He'd installed the Z28 short-stroke motor himself, just as he'd modified it and changed the ring gear and pinion assembly in the Vega's differential to accommodate it. He could rev it up to nine thousand RPM if he ever let it out and there wasn't a cop cruiser in five states that could come within gun range of him. And even if they could, no bullet could ever penetrate the glass on all sides which he had also set into place personally. What made the joke complete was that they had taught him all this. It was what they called learning a useful trade while paying your debt to society. He had learned well.

He allowed the Z28 a trifle more freedom climbing the hill toward the college. It amused him, now driving the Vega, to consider that only a few professors and a handful of students, possibly, would even know who Lope de Vega was. No one else in town, probably, would ever have heard of the Spanish poet and playwright who, for some unaccountable reason, now had a compact American automobile named after him. Or if they had heard of him, they had forgotten. As he had, really. All that shit meant nothing to him now. They'd made sure of that, too. The college was actually a university but the old name had remained: Tarkington College. According to the brass plaque on the cornerstone of the administration building, which he had inspected in the course of his research, the institution had been established in 1879. Passing it now, its buildings imposing and white on both sides, he wondered, again, what he might be doing now—who, in fact, he might *be* now—if he had been allowed to attend for four of those eight years that now lay behind him; if he had been allowed to carry out the plan that had originally brought him to this part of the country. From the top of the hill he could see the last red streaks of sunset in the distance: faint but somber and somewhat glowering in those last few minutes before total darkness would take over. He did not have to search the sky for a moon: there would be no moon tonight. In this latitude, on this date, the sun would set at five twenty-four. Twilight would last—had now lasted—for one hour and thirty-three minutes. Darkness would set in at six fifty-four. The college clock in the tower was now chiming the quarter hour. Nine minutes until dark.

He turned a corner, a by-now familiar corner, on a residential street and slowed. Howells Street. He felt his mouth twisting into a small, thin smile, no mirth behind it. Howells—another literary name. 1127 Howells Street. And there was Professor Fletcher Briggs himself. Everything and everyone on schedule, as predicted. Like clockwork. And at the sight of Briggs, he went sick, faint, as he always did, even when he only thought of him. As if his guts had been shot away. Taste of metal in his mouth.

The tall figure—very spare and rawboned—was walking from the front door of the rather large but faded Victorian house toward a blue MG sports car parked, as usual, in the driveway, behind a tan and brown station wagon. Even if he had not known this was Fletcher Briggs, he would have recognized the walk: a sort of off-kilter slouch, wide shoulders folded forward slightly, his whole body and its movements almost defiantly casual and unconcerned. Well, he wouldn't be so goddamn casual and unconcerned later. But much later, because Fletcher Briggs was to be the last. The last because he deserved the most—and was going to get it, in spades. Because Fletcher Briggs had been the one who really pulled the double cross. The only one who had even pretended to be on his side, his court-appointed lawyer who had lied, lied, promising him a fair shake when all the time he'd been playing their lying game and—

Fletcher Briggs hesitated at the door of the MG. Did not get in. He glanced up at the dark, crisp foliage over his head, then at the dark sky, and then he turned and started ambling, in long but unhurried strides, along the sidewalk in the direction of the campus.

A slight miscalculation. Very slight. Professor Fletcher Briggs invariably drove back to the campus. Well, there had to be a few of those. Whether Briggs rode or walked back to his office really didn't affect the overall scheme. Still, this was only the beginning and if any of his other victims gave in to some casual change of mind, some random impulse—

Boyd Ritchie sped on, face clenched now, allowing the motor a dull growl. The bastard. The prick. He always drove back to the campus at night. Not that Boyd Ritchie hadn't prepared himself against chance and accident. Nevertheless, he found himself cursing aloud.

Tonight was going to go his way. All the way. Nobody was going to change that. Nobody. This was his night.

But he knew he had to play it cool-ass. He'd lay odds, any odds right now, that Fletcher Briggs didn't know where his daughter, named Peggy, was at this moment. Or where his son, named David, was. But *he* knew. And that's what put him in control. He knew. Just as he knew why Fletcher Briggs was going back to his office. Good solid citizen, husband, father, professor of law, respected and respectable—hypocrite. Like all the rest. Phony. He knew where the lying prick was heading, and why; he even knew her name, all about her. He knew more about everything and everybody than anyone in this whole goddamn town tonight. That's where the power was. He was God tonight. He was the only god there was. And by morning—dawn at four ten, sunrise at five forty-three—they'd all know who was calling the shots.

Now that he was shuffling his way through the crackling leaves, Fletcher Briggs wished he'd driven after all. The impulse had been a foolish one: he thought walking would afford him more time to think and now that's exactly what he did not want. Also, he'd hoped the physical exertion would settle him down after the scene with Willa. The scene that had not been a scene, really. Willa didn't go in for scenes, never had, but sometimes, damn it, he wished she would. Sometimes he wished she'd explode, shout, storm at him; possibly then whatever was really disturbing her would crash its way to the surface so he could react, possibly even handle it—at least come to realize what it was. One minute she could be soft and feminine, her old self, quick and alive, vivid in the peasantlike clothes she'd come to wear in the last couple of years since she'd decided to go back to college and take the sculpture courses. Her soft, pale, oval face in the candlelight they always ate dinner by was still lovely: dark eyes sunken deep and peering out at him, luminous, and her black hair, only beginning now to be flecked with gray, parted down the center of her head and falling in two long braids behind. But beneath all that, what? In an instant, out of nowhere, something cold and hard would glint through before she could contain it, bottle it up—if indeed she really tried or wanted to.

"What David needs," she had said tonight, "is something you—"

"Yes?"

"Something I'm awfully afraid you can't give him."

And then she had broken it off, stood up from the table and gone into the kitchen, her eyes again soft and now contrite—while he sat there thinking about David and wondering what he could do and even whether it was really necessary to do anything. Hell, David was sixteen now. If she was referring to the pot, they were all smoking that stuff. Or worse. And he was damned sure David wasn't on anything else. Still, David had been more and more withdrawn of late, his dark eyes, very like Willa's, avoiding, evading, occasionally looking slightly blurred. Another stranger. Remote.

Fletcher Briggs had somehow, slowly, begun to feel that he lived in a house with three strangers. And Willa had managed, in her own quiet way, to make him feel that it was his fault—managed to inject the slow poison of doubt and guilt. She seemed to have the idea—and when Willa latched onto an idea, it was, in her view, the only valid idea extant—that Fletcher's failure or refusal to assert himself, take action of whatever kind, was actually a reflection on his manhood. Just as in recent months—or was it years now?—she had often made him feel the same when he made love to her. Not always: at times she could be as relaxed and soft and giving, as excited and satisfying as she had been over the years. But more and more often she would lie passive, if not stiff, staring away or her eyes closed, detached, distant—so that afterward he would feel depleted, miserable, angry at her, at himself, at life itself. Which? Did it matter?

He quickened his steps. There was a wind on the hill, sharp and cutting. He thought of Annette. He thought of the half-empty bottle of scotch in his desk drawer.

What had happened between himself and Willa over the years? And how had it happened? Somewhere leaves were burning. All his life he had loved the smell, savored it; there was nothing quite like it in the world. Now the odor was bitter in his nostrils and all he could think of was that winter was coming. Another winter. Where had it all gone? The excitement, the promise, the hope and the stirring in the blood that told you you were alive—how had all that withered away? When? Where the hell did the flavor and taste of it all go. Did Willa feel this, too?

He needed a drink. Lately he seemed always to need a drink. Only a quiet secret nip now and then, to keep his spirits at a functioning level. True, the nips were becoming more frequent. He'd never been really drunk, not since he was himself a law student, not since he'd been married, even at parties. He was certain that Willa knew nothing of his drinking. Just as he was equally certain that, in time, he would be drunk, quite drunk, and often, and not only at parties, and that Willa *would* know.

A familiar sense of helplessness came over him. Discontent, but muted. Not anything like despondency or despair, only a kind of rueful melancholy that he had not yet learned to fight, if he ever would.

Hearing the familiar chimes in the clock tower striking seven o'clock, he was walking on campus from one circle of light to the next between the swaying lamps, which had just been turned on, when he caught sight of a girl on another path in the distance, walking arm in arm with a boy. For a sharp and oddly painful second he was positive it was Peggy. At once, though, he knew that he was mistaken. The girl had Peggy's very long reddish hair, slightly paler than his own, that half covered one side of her face and she was tall and slender, like Willa, but—

"How am I to know where she is?" Willa had asked in a teasing tone that held only a kind of faint scornful challenge.

"All I'm asking is why aren't they here for dinner, at least one of them, at least once in a while."

"Ask them. Am I my daughter's keeper?"

Her tone, although soft as usual, had rasped his nerves. "Yes, damn it, you are."

"And you're not? What have you done, Fletch—abdicated?"

It had been a fair question, and to the point, so it had provoked him into silence. All he could think of doing then was getting away. That's when he had walked out of the house without saying good-bye.

The Law School building was within view now and he saw the lighted window of his office on the third floor. Annette. The persistent guilty fear returned with a taste of gall: did Willa know or suspect anything? Would that explain her moods? No, he insisted to himself, no, because those moods had been the reason he'd allowed himself, after twenty years of marriage, to become involved with anyone else. Therefore, his mind mocked, the moods had to precede his act. Therefore. But he wasn't so damned sure.

He was walking fast. Willa had never understood, in spite of all his words of explanation, why, six years ago, he had decided to give up a promising law practice for an associate professorship. Regardless of all her reassurances to the contrary, he had always known that she considered it a retreat. And so it was, in a sense: he granted that. A retreat into the world of theory and scholarship *about* the law, where idealism could still, if only in theory, have some validity—a rejection of the deceit, avarice, accepted trickery and cynicism of professional law. Hell, yes, he'd had enough of it: deals and betrayals of the law by men sworn to uphold it, the whole unholy corruption of using the laws for personal ambition, twisting and distorting and breaking the law for selfish gain, political or financial or both. Not retreat—refuge, sanctuary.

And, possibly for this reason, this impulse in himself, he comprehended, to a degree, why the young people, his son among them, tried to find their own shelters, sanctums.

Closer now, he saw a shadow move across the light of the office window. He had never discussed his decision with anyone but Willa—and then, much later, with Annette. Herself a graduate student and his assistant, Annette had understood at once and they had talked about it often. They could talk. They did talk. And it had been this talking, this mutual understanding of the basic problems that had, at least partly, trapped them both into the relationship that, now, caused them both to avoid any contemplation of what might lie ahead, if anything.

But now, in a few minutes, that would be over, all of it, once and for all. His decision had been made some time ago. He could not go on trying to escape by using Annette and by risking the pain and anguish that Willa would certainly feel if she ever knew. Despite all its complexities, contradictions, and confusions, his relationship with Willa was worth more than that. But would Annette understand? How could he explain it to her when he didn't quite comprehend it himself?

He entered the dark building, climbed the stairs, his steps echoing. What made it all so ironic—as what the hell wasn't?—was that now he'd come full circle. Idealism to retreat to skepticism—and now to something very close to cynicism, if not philosophical despair. The simple and appalling truth was that he was no longer able to define his values—and, therefore, himself. Unable to relate to the realities of a society that made little if any sense, his personal life so askew that he was not sure that he could ever, by whatever effort of will, set it aright again, doubtful even of the ability of the rational mind to determine, to decide and then to act to control or order even his own small destiny or even his own personality—hell, he was as adrift, and frightened, as everyone else and not even sure that that mattered anymore. Yet, when pressed by some insistent student or even by Annette, he would still insist that minute by minute a man chooses what he is and is to become. Without the choice, how could there be any justification for law itself?

He opened his office door. Annette had poured his drink; it was on his desk. She didn't smile. She only sat on the couch observing him somberly while he went to pick up the paper cup.

Then she said: "I was curious to see which one of us you'd go to first."

The heavyset man in his thirties, who had tilted his hat to the back of his head instead of removing it, kept glancing across the booth between sips of his rye-and-ginger, and each time he'd see her thin but very pretty face turned from him, sort of studying the almost empty room. It wasn't much of a bar, he knew, nothing to what she was used to, but holy hell, wasn't that part of the reason she was with him—because she had to get away once in a while from all that dull social crap? At least, that's what she'd told him, and more than once, too.

"Relax, baby," he said. "Nobody you know's going to come in this joint. You're in Londonford, baby, more'n twenty damn sweet miles from home. And for another, your kind don't frequent these crummy dives 'less they're slumming with us factory hands, right?"

"I wish," she said thinly, blowing smoke, "I wish you would stop reminding me of our—" She hesitated. "Why must you harp on it?"

"All right, okay, I'll harp on something else—"

"Now please don't start all that—"

"What's the goddamn harm in calling the police?"

"I said, let's not—"

"We both heard the explosions. You admitted that."

"I told you all the way here from Tarkington: what I heard was a car backfiring."

"And what about that light in between the trees?

What was that, some kinda ghost?"

"I don't see why, if we're going to make love in the back seat of a car like a couple of adolescents, you have to park on a road looking down on the cemetery. You must have something morbid in your nature."

"Well, I don't imagine things. If there was nothing going on in that graveyard, what's the harm in—"

"And if you're going to make love—to *me,* at least—why the hell can't you keep your mind on what you're doing?"

He polished off his drink. He realized he was stiff all over. "Holy hell, baby, all I want to do is what I think's my duty. I don't have to give my name to the police. Or yours."

Her eyes, sharp and icy and direct, were on his now. "If you do," she said, "we're through."

"No broad gives me orders, baby," he said very quietly.

Without a change of expression, her tone still level and cool and low, she explained again: "You know what'll happen to . . . to my whole life, if Phil ever finds out about us."

"I got a wife, too, remember."

She stubbed out her cigarette and then made a small gesture of dismissal with one hand, shoulders shrugging. "The police won't make an investigation on the basis of an anonymous phone call anyway."

But he knew the gesture and the shrug had more to do with him and his marriage than with any damn phone call. He stood up. He saw her narrow eyes widen. He picked up two dimes from the change on the table. He did not speak.

"I meant what I said. Whatever it is, it means nothing to us. It's not our business, so why get involved? I mean it." But there was no plea in her tone, none.

He turned then and strode heavily but stiffly to the phone on the wall. While he was speaking to the operator and then to the police in Tarkington, he saw her stand up—very slim, very elegant and desirable—and gather her things together and stroll out, chin high, without a glance.

On his way back to the booth he moved slowly. He felt one sharp pang of regret, very quick and over at once. By the time he was seated again and had signaled the barman for a double this time, he knew that she had been looking for an excuse. Probably she'd been looking for it for a long time now.

As he lifted his fresh drink to his lips, he realized that the stiffness was gone from him, gone completely. Something very like relief had moved in to take its place. He looked around: this was his kind of joint. He lifted the glass to toast the empty place across the table. Maybe he'd been looking for an excuse, too.

In the evenings it was Vincent Stegner's pleasure, after a supper he prepared himself and ate alone, to sit on the porch of his home that he insisted upon calling a cabin and listen to the sounds of the woods that enclosed him on all sides. Summer was best, of course, but even in the fall there were many natural wonders to be heard and observed and absorbed if you tuned your mind to nature instead of to that infernal contraption with its unnatural blinking eye that seemed to intoxicate or actually drug the universe in recent years. Being an old man now, although still active and vigorous, Vincent Stegner could well remember when man's interest in man came from observing man himself rather than his invented and distorted shadow. Also, nature had its own peace. Not that it did not have its own violence and cruelty—a man had to accept that—but certainly nothing like the repetitious vile mayhem that was purported to be, and accepted as, the action of man on the television tube.

The headlights came as a surprise, but not as a cause for alarm. It could be Coralie Wharton come earlier than usual: this *was* her night to visit him. But he didn't recognize the sound or appearance of the car in the darkness: it looked to be a small Chevy or Ford maybe, dark in color or maybe dark gray. It stopped and the lights went out. He didn't stand up.

"Mr. Stegner, sir?" a voice called, a young man's voice from the sound of it, pleasant and friendly. "Mr. Stegner?"

"That's my name."

"Then I've found the right place!" He sounded very pleased indeed. "You don't know me, sir, but I'd like to take a few precious minutes of your precious time if you'll allow me. Since you don't have a phone, I had to drive—"

"I got time a-plenty, son, but if you're sellin' something, I don't need it."

The young man, approaching, laughed—a genial sort of sound, refreshing really, and welcome. "You can't know that, sir, now can you, till you know what it is I might be selling."

Vincent Stegner stood up from the wooden rocking chair, his arthritis troubling him slightly, and went to the open door leading inside, reached and turned on the living-room light as well as the one on the porch. The young man who stood at the porch steps was indeed young, slight of build, a certain buoyance in his stance, head tilted to one side, and he wore a dark turtleneck sweater and one of those knitted caps that seamen wore in the old days, and his eyes, a very bright blue, looked merry—playful, if it came to that.

"May I come in, sir?"

"You can come in, but I ain't buying and that's that."

As he led the way inside, Vincent Stegner was puzzled for the first time really: the young fellow was carrying an attaché case—well, if he was a salesman, that was natural enough—but he was also wearing gloves. On a nice warm fall night like this.

"Workin' kinda late, ain'tcha?" Vincent Stegner asked, studying him more carefully, hearing the echo of caution in his own voice. Because the gloves were thin and flesh-colored and appeared to be the rubber sort a woman might wear in the kitchen.

"Well, you know what they say, sir—the late bird might not catch the worm, but it's the best time of night for rats." His grin was full and bright. "I've come, Mr. Stegner, to sell you some life insurance."

Vincent Stegner laughed, shortly, relieved. "Life insurance? Why, young fella, I'm seventy-four years old, my wife died years ago, I got nor chick nor heir—what the hell'd I want with life insurance? I'm afraid you've had yourself a ride way out here for nothing."

The young man didn't seem to hear; he was strolling around the large high room. He was wearing dark tennis shoes—now, what kind of salesman would wear a turtleneck sweater, a knit cap and tennis shoes anyway? "Mr. Stegner, you've got yourself a very neat layout here. Look at this now. Look at those solid beams. That cathedral ceiling. And weathered barn siding. All the latest conveniences, too. Why, man, they told me in town you lived in a *cabin.*"

"It used to be a kinda ski lodge, I guess. Now looka here—"

"You must be a wealthy man to be able to afford all this, Mr. Stegner." The young man was standing still now, quite still, head to one side, polished blue eyes fixed on him.

Vincent Stegner felt a tremor of anger along with the apprehension. "I don't think that's any of your business, whoever you are."

"No offense, sir, no offense. I was just thinking that a man in your . . . financial position does need life insurance." Without moving he paused, then added: "Not knowing how long he's liable to live."

Before Vincent Stegner could reply, the strange young man stepped to the window and picked up a pair of field glasses from the windowsill. In an abrupt gesture he tossed them across the room so that, in an automatic reflex action, Vincent Stegner caught them before they crashed to the plank floor. Then the young man placed the attaché case on the long rustic trestle table and snapped it open. "Use the glasses, Mr. Stegner. Maybe you'll need them to recognize me."

Then, again before the older man could speak or move, he reached to his head and in one quick, startling motion he turned bald, absolutely bald, and he was holding the cap in one hand. He smiled faintly and tossed it into the attaché case. "Use the glasses, sir, they'll help." In the next instant, again as if he had not moved a muscle, his head was covered with tight waves of blond hair.

It was then, much too late, that Vincent Stegner recognized him—and remembered. He saw the playful mocking smile go out of the eyes and then, although he did not actually see it move, one hand, balled into a tight hard fist, smashed him across the side of the face, a blow so hard that his denture plates erupted from his open mouth and clattered to the floor and he himself, for all his bulk and weight, staggered sideways a few uncertain steps without going down.

"Oh, Mr. Stegner," Boyd Ritchie said, his tone and manner solicitude itself, "what did I do to you? It's that terrible temper of mine, Mr. Stegner. You remember my temper now, don't you? You remember what you saw me do when I lost my temper, don't you?" And when Vincent Stegner did not answer because of the pain and the blood in his mouth, he barked: *"Don't you?"*

"I only know . . . what I saw . . . with my own eyes."

Then Boyd Ritchie took a single step. His foot came down on the dentures on the floor; there was a crushing sound. Boyd Ritchie stepped back and looked down, once again all chagrin. "Now look. Look what I did to your expensive teeth, Mr. Stegner. And what do you know, they don't even bleed."

Vincent Stegner spat blood, defiantly. "What'd you do, break out?"

"They can't keep a man in prison forever." He was smiling good-naturedly again. "Not even old Whitey. That's what they called me, even the hacks. Old

Whitey. That's how I got my parole, Mr. Stegner." His voice had taken on a singsong quality. "Being good old Whitey to everyone. Anything anybody wanted me to be—that's what I was. That's called good behavior." He shrugged. "They wanted sex, I bent over. Or anything else. Inmates or guards. Good old Whitey was everybody's everything. How I survived. Playing the game. Playing all the games." He removed the blond wig slowly, nodding his shaved head. "Now it's my game. I played their game, and yours, now it's my game."

The smile was no longer there. Vincent Stegner, sick now and cold, stared at the smooth hairless skull, wanting to turn his gaze away. He considered, for an instant only, trying to make a break for the door. Then what? He'd never make it even to his car. Into the woods then, in the pitch-dark—

"And now, sir, I must show you my wares." With a flourish Boyd Ritchie whipped the attaché case around so that Vincent Stegner could glimpse its contents. "What have we here? Ah-hah, many magical things."

Vincent Stegner, with the pain climbing his face and into his skull, thought of his hunting rifle in the closet—the gun he had never used because he could not bring himself to kill a living thing. He spat blood again, aware that his jaw had already swollen out of shape. Boyd Ritchie was like an actor—yes, that's what he was, one of those actors playing a part and enjoying himself to the hilt. And now, through the fear, came rage. Vincent Stegner made up his mind that, somehow, he would have to kill Boyd Ritchie before—

"A shotgun, of all things. A short shotgun. But not for you, sir. For someone else. Someone you know well. And look here—adhesive tape, picture wire, rope. And—cowboy boots—for a cowboy I know. And out there in my car, a trap, man, an animal trap, for an animal I know. Not you, sir—some *other* animal." He reached and his hand came up with a plastic bottle of clear liquid. "Acid. For the face. Eyes. Insides." And suddenly his face became stern. "This court will now come to order! Mr. Stegner, will you please take the stand?"

"There never was no trial and you know it." The words came out blurred together, but each word shot the pain deeper into the bone of jaw and head. "You admitted you was—"

"Mr. Stegner," Boyd Ritchie bellowed, "take the stand!"

And it was then that Vincent Stegner realized that it was hopeless. He felt helplessness seep into every crevice of his mind and body, the slow poison of despair. Nevertheless, he said, "All I can tell you is what I already told the police and the prosecuting attorney. I told Mr. Heckman I saw what I saw and I know what I saw." It didn't matter what he said now. Nothing mattered.

Boyd Ritchie moved closer, bending down. "And what was it you saw?" His voice purred and his eyes were lit with some private joy. "Please—tell the court what was it you actually saw."

"I saw you swim out to the boat." His cheeks, in spite of the swelling on one side, felt as if they had collapsed inward, but that didn't really matter, either. "On the lake. I saw the girl drop anchor, and then you swam out."

"Coralie Powell—wasn't that her name then, Mr. Stegner?"

"I don't remember." But at once, because of the sharp something he saw leap into the young man's eyes, Boyd Ritchie's eyes, he wished he hadn't spoken. "I saw you swim out and then beat her up on the deck."

"Through your field glasses."

"I told the district attorney, I told the police, I even told your lawyer what I'd have to testify to if—"

"Why'd I beat her up on deck, Mr. Stegner? Sir?"

"Why, like she said, to force her to go down to the cabin with you."

"For what, sir? Why? Wasn't it cooler on deck?"

"You couldn't rape her on deck."

Boyd Ritchie nodded gravely. "Or fuck her, either, with you watching. How did you just happen to be watching Coralie Powell on her boyfriend's boat? Through glasses?"

Damned if he'd whine and whimper. He didn't know why he was repeating all this, sticking to it, even now, but he seemed to have no choice although he knew, in a kind of distant stupor, that he had no chance. "She was the best-looking female for fifty miles, all sides, and she didn't wear practically nothing on that boat, that's why."

Boyd Ritchie suddenly looked sad, disappointed. He lifted the plastic bottle. "Mr. Stegner, sir—in this court I set the rules. And unless you tell me why you told this story to the police and to the prosecutor, Mr. Heckman, I'm going to make you drink this. I may even use it on your . . . private parts. I may even pour some up your lying ass."

Vincent Stegner, staring at the bottle, was not breathing. He gave it up. It was over—why should he suffer more? A leaden lethargy had settled over him, settled all through him. He moved his gaze to the death mask with the shaved skull. There was no sound or movement in the room or, seemingly, for miles around.

"Mr. Stegner, sir. I know what you told the police. I know what you told my attorney. You claimed to be an eyewitness. Now, what I want to know is the truth. What you really did see. If you tell me the truth now, just the plain simple truth so I can be absolutely sure, I'm not going to kill you. Do you want to live, Mr. Stegner . . . sir?"

It wasn't really hope that prompted him to his decision; he didn't anticipate escape, or even mercy. But if he was going to die anyway—

"Like you said, I saw her anchor the boat, young Wharton's boat, and I saw her wave at you. And you swum out and climbed aboard. Like it had all been arranged between you. You sat around and played around on deck—"

"I didn't beat her up?"

"Then you went below together. Down into the little cabin."

"Take your time, sir, take your time. The truth comes slow. Then what—?"

"He came out from the other side of the lake, over by the club, in an outboard."

"He?" The voice was pleading, quiet. "He?"

"Paul Wharton. The one she was engaged to. Then you came running out onto the deck, like maybe you or the girl seen him coming, and you dove overboard and swam toward the woods."

"And he followed me—"

"Looked to me like he tried to run you down with the outboard."

"Then he followed me into the woods—"

Vincent Stegner hesitated. Some small hope had by now penetrated the torpor, the stunned fear. So he shook his head. "He turned around in the outboard and headed out to the boat."

"He *didn't* follow me into the woods and beat the shit out of me?"

"You know he didn't, don't you?"

"I only know what everybody said. What everybody believed. What you said you were willing to testify to . . . sir."

"Wharton went out to the large boat and climbed on and he beat her up pretty bad, on deck, ripped off her swimsuit and practically threw her down into the cabin, went in after her."

"Assaulted her on deck, then raped her in the cabin—"

"Maybe, maybe. All I know is now I told you what I really saw. The truth."

"When I was arrested and they brought me in, I was pretty well beaten up myself. If Wharton didn't do it, who did?"

"I don't know." He couldn't take much more. He was old. This wasn't happening. "I don't know, please go away now, I told you what I—"

"Just one thing more. Mr. Stegner . . . sir. Please. Why would you go to the police and tell all those lies?"

In the woods an owl hooted, and in the quiet they could hear the sounds of frogs from some pond in the distance.

"Why? You see, sir, I've had almost eight years to wonder. I've put it together seventy different ways. Who paid you to go to the police?"

"Nobody."

He saw the young man stiffen; he saw the plastic vial move. "Please, sir—"

"She didn't pay me. Exactly."

"The girl?"

"Coralie Wharton—she's Mrs. Wharton now." And while the young man didn't nod, Vincent Stegner suspected that Boyd Ritchie probably knew more about the Whartons and everyone else than even he did. "She saw me watching her, so she—well, she came to me. She said she needed someone to prove that she'd been raped."

"It's what they call a corroborating witness, Mr. Stegner. Without you, you see, it would have been her word against mine if there'd been a trial. You see, if it weren't for you, man—well, we wouldn't both be here tonight, would we?" Then he seemed to lose control; his eyes darkened and his mouth twisted and he lifted his voice. "You lying bastard, tell me who paid you!"

"Nobody. Then. But later, after they got married—"

Boyd Ritchie made an impatient slashing gesture. "I know she's been paying you, I know that. But she didn't have any money then, until after she was married."

Vincent Stegner decided to take his chance, get it over with. "There are other ways for a woman to pay a man."

And then Boyd Ritchie's face twisted into a cold grin. He nodded. It was as if he had had to have his suspicions confirmed in order to go on. "Thank you. The witness may step down. Case dismissed. The defendant is found not guilty."

Boyd Ritchie was poised, dangerous, eyes glittering and every muscle and nerve alive.

"I told you the truth," Vincent Stegner said, hearing a whine in his tone. "I told you now what I really saw."

"You, Mr. Stegner, sir, see too much." Body tensed, hairless head tilted, he regarded the older man. "That's your trouble, sir. You see too much. You even see things that are not there."

He knew then: he'd been tricked. The young man was going to kill him anyway. "Get it over with!" he shouted. "Kill me, damn you!"

But Boyd Ritchie was shaking his head, that grin flickering again. "Man, where I've been, I've met killers. All kinds. What good's killing? I'm not going to kill anybody. That's too easy. For me and for them. If a man's dead, he never suffers for what he did." He lifted the vial again, its pointed nose directed at the old man's face. "There are a lot of things better than killing. Everyone should get his own—what's coming to him and him alone. Open your mouth, Mr. Stegner, please. Open your mouth, sir, so I can see your lying tongue."

But he refused. He clamped his jaws together. He'd rather be dead. He fixed his eyes on Boyd Ritchie's and waited.

"I'm not going to kill anyone, Stegner."

Then, amazingly, he seemed to change his mind. He replaced the cap on the vial and tossed it into the attaché case. Then he reached, and when his hand came out, he was holding a roll of thin copper picture wire which glinted in the light. He extended his other hand, one finger pointed to the binoculars still clutched in Vincent Stegner's almost lifeless hands. The old man managed to pass them over.

"These the same ones, Stegner? These the ones you saw everything with?"

Stegner could only nod, with the pain lodged in his

jaw and the inside of his mouth raw and tasting of blood.

Boyd Ritchie smashed the field glasses against a corner of the table. There was a metallic crushing sound and the clatter of broken glass. He stooped and picked up a glittering sharp-edged lens.

Then he said, softly: "It won't matter if you yell, Mr. Stegner. If it hurts too much, you can yell, it won't bother me.

Before he replaced the telephone, Theron Diehl hesitated, then heard the click, the inevitable click, of the extension in the bedroom. He sat a moment at his desk in the small room that had been converted into his den six months ago when he had decided to write the book. The manuscript pages, scribbled, not yet typed, were stacking up, neatly, in a wooden tray; in fact, the desk and room as a whole reflected Theron Diehl's rigid sense of neatness and precision. He drank off his second bourbon-and-branch of the evening (he allowed himself three, every evening, no more, no less) and crossed the narrow hall to his wife's bedroom.

Nell Diehl was a small-boned, delicate woman, her thin, tall body like a long wrinkle of the bed's covers, her pointed dark eyes riveted now on the television screen, as usual, her forehead furrowed, as usual. Without turning her small head, she said: "Y'goin' to leave me, aren't you?" She spoke in the drawl of east Texas and her tone was at once pleading, pathetic and querulous.

"Ben said it's important, Nell." His voice was very deep, even softer than hers, and very gentle. "He knows better'n to roust me if it isn't." He ignored the television screen, as he always did, and ignored the fact that she had heard every syllable of the telephone conversation. "I don't really reckon it *is* all that important at that, but—"

"Y'goin' to leave me alone. Again."

As chief of police, Theron Diehl hadn't been summoned back to the courthouse during any evening or night for months, possibly longer. The *again* reverberated in his mind. "I could step next door and ask Mrs. Emmett to come over."

"Mrs. Emmett's out, they got a sitter tonight. And *she's* got a boy in there with her." It always astonished Theron Diehl that his wife, with the television going all day and with all the Bible reading she did, could know so much of what was going on all over the neighborhood. "And, Theron, y'oughta know by now I wouldn't have that woman in my house. She's like all the rest. Y'know I cannot abide pity, Theron. *Y'know* that."

"It's only some jackassery down to the cemetery, Nell. I shouldn't be gone long."

"If it's that, it can't be important. And you oughta know I don't rightly relish the way Mrs. Emmett looks at you. She thinks I don't know what evil goes on in some minds. Same as you think, too. As if I can't imagine the way the womenfolk of this town look on you."

Theron Diehl stepped to the bed, stooped from his great height, kissed the tight parched skin of her forehead without speaking. Then he went into the hall and, at the hat tree they'd had shipped all this way north, took down his pearl-handled Colt .45 revolver and holster and buckled the belt around his lean hard midsection, the handle of the old gun riding high on his left side for a cross draw, the way he'd worn a gun all his life.

Her voice drifted to him like a small, plaintive, petulant wind: ". . . your way to desert me, leave me alone in this empty house again . . . not enough you drag me up to this freezing country . . . cold standoffishfolk—"

And drawing on his blue uniform coat, Theron Diehl, without so much as closing his eyes, had a brief but momentarily painful vision: Nell as she had been as a girl, her bright, gay eyes in a flushed, intense, lifted face, while the fiddles cried and the banjos thrummed, her body in the wide-skirted country dress lithe and slender and inviting.

". . . cemetery, my foot. It's what you menfolk cook up between you to fool us wives . . . women or poker or both—"

Ready, thinking of the third bourbon that he wouldn't have now until he returned, Theron Diehl stepped into the bedroom door again, ducking his head in that way he had. "Nell, now you put those thoughts outta your head now, hear? I'll be back soon's I ever can. But, a-course, you want it, I can sit a spell with you now."

Then her eyes met his: sad, faded, resigned. "No, Theron. I wouldn't want to deprive you of your pleasures, sinful or otherwise. You jist go. I got my Bible t'read. I'll be here when you get back." Her pale, thin lips curled in a self-mocking smile of sorts. "I don't reckon I'll be goin' anywheres."

He turned away then and went out to the black patrol car parked in the short driveway. Oakwood Drive was a street of small frame homes, one of the older real estate developments, the houses very similar and built close together. Except for the distinctly Colonial design of some of the houses, it could have been a street in any one of the several Texas towns where they'd lived until nine years ago. He'd chosen this house because of the creek rippling away and gurgling out back. It was a good sound, a fresh country sound. He didn't bother to turn on either the dome light or the siren and as he drove past the sign reading BROOKFIELD KNOLLS, he turned off the squawk box so he could think.

Although nothing that had been said by either of them tonight was substantially different from the thousand variations of the same over nearly forty years of marriage, he couldn't put Nell out of his mind as quickly and easily as he usually could. He had never told her what the specialist in Boston had said and he sometimes thought perhaps this had been a mistake in itself. *What we can say with some degree of certainty, Mr. Diehl, is that there's nothing organic at the root of her trouble. You've asked me whether she can walk. All I can answer is: not so long as she thinks she can't.* The doctor had then gone on to suggest psychiatry, but Theron Diehl had never mentioned this, either. He knew what Nell's answer would be. She herself always contended that her faith would make her well, but so far he could see no improvement. So he had done all that he could do: adapted himself and lived with it. Besides, he didn't hold much with mind doctors himself. If she could walk and then didn't want to, there just wasn't any excuse, that's all. None. Let her muscles atrophy then. That was the doctor's word—atrophy.

Annoyed by his thoughts, he was driving slowly, forcibly putting Nell out of his mind. He couldn't imagine anything that could have happened this evening in this town that would require one-tenth of his knowledge or energy. He sometimes felt that he, as a police officer, was atrophying also. It was a dull town, really: with a rare exception about once every eighteen months, the so-called crimes were routine, nonviolent, open-and-shut. It had been for this reason that he had decided to write his book: *Memoirs of a Texas Ranger.* The only real excitement left in his life lay in re-creating on paper those crimes and criminals and especially the police work that had gone into solving those crimes and bringing the felons to justice. He'd written just this evening: *We still live on the frontier whether we want to admit it or not. On the frontier things were handled quick and that is as it should be. Quick and brutal if necessary. In those days we would collar a criminal, someone we knew was guilty before any jury got in the way, and we would move him to one jail, then to another, all over the state if necessary, so his lawyer couldn't catch up with him with legal papers. Some of the times we would take him to some old ranch house out in the middle of sagebrush country. We had a favorite spot near Houston called the Windmill; many a prisoner now behind bars remembers the Windmill. Now a man, any man alive, can take just so much and sooner or later, depending on how much guts he has to start with, he will reach a point where he does not care anymore. Then he confesses. When his eyes are shut and his ears perforated and his groin is swelled up almost the size of a basketball and his fingers are twisted and stomped about off his hand and his neck muscle's been worked on so he can't straighten his head up—they always confess. Today, though, with all the bleeding hearts and the coddling and all the talk about legal and constitutional rights and so forth—*

That's when the phone had rung. Writing that paragraph had excited him: he still had a long ways to go before hanging up his harness. He hadn't yet made up his mind, though, whether to reveal frankly—although he was damned if he was ashamed of it—why he'd been forced to retire from the Rangers, why he'd come all the way up here to New England, where neither one of them ever felt at home, to take a job on this hick-town police force. He'd never in his life get used to the sharpness of the accent, the aloofness of the people, their exaggerated sense of personal privacy. Not if he lived to be a hundred. But he had found a certain compensation: to walk or drive through Tarkington and to nod coolly but pleasantly to its citizens, catching the open idolatry in the young ones' eyes, the quick if not particularly friendly admiration in others', the envy in the men's glances at his tall, lean figure and silver-haired, silver-mustached, fatherly image, and the carefully concealed but still evident sexual desire in the women's eyes. Nell had sure as hell been right there. There wasn't any gainsaying that the town was damned proud to have an ex-Texas Ranger for its police chief. Hell, the people took a certain satisfaction even in the fact that he always wore a Stetson and high-heeled Western boots with his uniform. Now he had to weigh his own personal gratification against the possibility of how those same folks might react if he wrote down and had published why he'd had to retire from the Rangers. At least some of those smug, law-respecting (so called) citizens, whom he was actually protecting if they only had sense enough to realize it, might feel the way his superiors had felt back in Texas. Did he want to take that risk? He'd only done what he saw it as his duty to do. That's all he'd ever do. He'd done no more to the suspect than he had, with official approval, done to many another before that. How was he to know the bastard had a bad heart? But even then they wouldn't have asked for his resignation, if he hadn't gone off half-cocked in the first place. *You made the wrong assumptions, Diehl, and you took action on them, precipitous action. And not for the first time, we all know that. We have evidence the dead man's innocent. You moved too fast.* Well, anybody could cut a big gut, who said he'd do it again? But before he made the mistake, another mistake, by telling it all and plunking down the three thousand in savings that the publisher out in Chicago wanted to guarantee publication and distribution, he'd have to reach a decision, a wide decision, about how to end the book.

He turned now in the direction of Cemetery Hill and flipped a switch on the dashboard. "This here's Chief Diehl. I can talk now. Didn't want to disturb my wife earlier 'case she happened to overhear. Now, would y'all oblige a ignorant old man and inform me please what the hell can be goin' on in a cemetery if it's not kid shit?"

"Chief, I haven't been out there myself, naturally, but I hear it's pretty gruesome. Ben's there waiting for you. He's got all the poop."

"You can be more specific than that, damn your hide!"

"It's Judge T. H. Stuttaford's grave. Somebody desecrated it. Honest, that's all I know at this time, Chief."

Judge Stuttaford—why the hell hadn't they said so? He sighed and turned on the dome light and siren.

Might as well get to it. He was still convinced, though, that it was kid stuff—hell, young people today took downright pleasure in desecrating everything and anything. But if Judge Stuttaford's grave was involved, it was important enough to bring him in on it, only right and fitting. But just what the hell did that word mean—*desecrate?*

On the police band of the radio in Boyd Ritchie's car, he could hear only the dispatcher's voice, not the replies from the various patrol cars on duty. The discovery of Judge Stuttaford's grave had, by some fluke that puzzled him, come much sooner than he had anticipated. It really didn't matter, and as far as he could conjecture at this point, it shouldn't interfere in any way with his overall design for the night. There was no way for them to connect him with it; he'd made certain of that. He'd even left the label in the coveralls he'd worn in the cemetery—the name of a store in Iowa, which would further muddy the waters in case the waters needed it. He wanted his identity revealed in time—old man Stegner would make sure of that once he was discovered—because that was part of the excitement, the satisfaction, but he didn't want it known soon enough to interfere in any small way with his schedule. Still, how could anyone possibly have stumbled across or otherwise been informed of what he'd done, with such pleasure, in the cemetery? Another of those small happenstances that, while possibly threatening the success of his scheme, also added a certain zest to it. He had pitted himself against all of them, hadn't he? He had to win against any odds they could throw at him.

Young man, your attorney, Mr. Briggs, has entered a plea of guilty to felonious assault in the second degree. (He recalled the judge's eyes glittering, lips quivering.) *To assault an innocent young girl—not only physically and brutally but sexually as well—is to de-*

stroy life just as surely as, perhaps more cruelly than, murder itself . . . one of the most unsavory, heinous crimes that a human being can commit against another— (He remembered the dry, thin mouth twisting in disgust, contempt.) *I am inclined to agree with the prosecuting attorney, Mr. Heckman, that such an assault is a form of human perversion and that you, sir, are a pervert.* (The judge reminded him of his ancestors sentencing women to be pressed to death by the laying on of stone.) *You came uninvited and a stranger to our civilized community and you have maimed forever one of our fairest.* (The pale, watery eyes stone-hard and vindictive, the voice rising.) *Boyd Ritchie, this court sentences you to ten years in the state penitentiary without recommendation of mercy or parole, and the court regrets that this represents the maximum sentence allowed by law for the charge to which you have pleaded guilty. Court is adjourned.*

Boyd Ritchie remembered his shock, profound and shattering. He had turned in the courtroom to see it reflected on Fletcher Briggs' face: the lawyer who had been appointed by the court to defend him looked every bit as stunned and incredulous as he himself felt. Then he saw the prosecuting attorney, Wallace Heckman—and he, too, was frowning in amazement. Then it came to him: they were playing the same game. Even when the judge had asked him whether he had been promised anything for entering his guilty plea, he had lied, like them, as he had been instructed, so that he, too, was guilty of conspiracy. Now that the maximum instead of the minimum sentence had been imposed, both attorneys continued to act out their phony roles, the hypocritical bastards.

And Fletcher Briggs the worst, the rock-bottom worst. As usual, the thought of Briggs made him go all sick and faint, with that paralyzing shot-away feeling in his guts. It had been Briggs who had said: *I can't advise you. I can only report that they've offered us a deal. It's called plea bargaining or negotiating a plea, and it's done all the time. It's simply an arrangement between the prosecution and the defense, presumably without the knowledge of the judge. If you'll plead guilty to second-degree assault, then the confession you signed—under duress, you claim, but duress that we're not going to be able to prove—that confession will not be entered against you, the entire charge of rape will be dropped entirely and you won't serve more than eighteen months of a two-year minimum sentence. With luck the judge might even suspend the sentence and place you on probation. If we fight it out before a jury, there's not only the confession to deal with but the girl's word against yours, the fact that you're an outsider in a small, tightly knit town, and there's a corroborating witness against you now, a man named Stegner, who swears he saw you and the girl on the boat through binoculars. He doesn't claim he saw the actual act, but a jury will probably add it up as the same thing.*

Very simple. No sensational trial, no expense to the state, the defense attorney off the hook, the prosecutor getting credit for another conviction, no embarrassment to the girl or her rich fiancé on whose boat the alleged crime was committed. Called copping a plea in prison; as Briggs said, done all the time. A royal way to get screwed. Rigged, fixed, a frame—they had gotten together and given him the shaft. And they were all in on it: the judge (now dead), the prosecutor (now a Congressman and going higher) and the defense attorney (now a professor of law). Well, the rage that had set in then, the consuming hot fury that had changed everything in his life, had over the years turned to a cold, calculating wrath. And tonight *he* was the one to do the rigging, the fixing—the sentencing.

Wearing a shaggy red wig instead of the yarn cap, a thick mustache, also red, glued to his upper lip, with a worn tweed jacket with leather elbow patches over his own dark turtleneck, and wearing a pair of built-up shoes that added at least three inches to his height, he was behind the wheel of the Vega, which was parked in a row of cars along the curb on a residential street called Emerson Terrace. The row of cars had been an unexpected piece of good luck, something else that he'd had no way of foreseeing: a dinner party was in progress in a house about twenty yards down the street and across from the Wallace Heckman residence, which was classic Colonial, white, all-American as hell. He could hear shrill laughter from the party and he wondered, in a vague and idle way, whether he might have lived in a house like that on a street like this if things had gone differently almost eight years ago when he was only twenty years old. But there was no time for that tonight. The excitement had been growing in him, expanding—a breathless elation and anticipation that threatened to explode. He found himself, eyes riveted on the Heckman house, gripping the wheel. Clasped between his teeth was a pipe identical to the one that Fletcher Briggs habitually smoked.

Pervert. Wallace Heckman had repeated the word bitterly several times in his speech to the judge, but he had not resented it then because Fletcher Briggs had previously explained that for the sake of the court record and so there could be no suspicion of a deal at a later date, the prosecuting attorney would have to make a vigorous appeal for a lengthy sentence in the name of justice. The use of the word "justice" had amused him then, even before sentence had been imposed. And then the first few weeks of his stay in prison, when things began to happen, the memory of its use had enraged him. Until he had learned the game, their game, learned it the hard way, the very hard way, and had then played it for all it was worth. Which was plenty. To deceive, to play innocent or stupid, above all, to do what was expected of him even to the extent of learning to speak the prison lingo—hell, if it hadn't been for his willingness, he wouldn't be out now. Good behavior. Model prisoner. The whole phony bit. And here he was on parole in spite of the judge's goddamn recommendations. He'd outwitted that old motherfucker, too. And the big joke was that he hadn't been a pervert *then*—

"Dennis, you're only eleven years old."

That was the way she always put him down—*only* eleven years old. No use reminding her he'd be twelve in less than four months. She knew that anyway. She was his own mother, wasn't she? He wasn't always telling her that she was old—she was at least forty, although she never told anyone, even on her birthday. He often wondered whether her short-cropped hair would be gray if she didn't have it dyed that bright blond color.

"I already told Freddy I—"

"I said not tonight, Dennis, and I meant it. The sitter's already arranged for."

"Fuck the sitter."

"Dennis!"

That got to her; a word like that always got to her. It was really funny: here she was, always cool, always acting as if nothing could reach her, let alone shock her, and all you had to do was spit out a word like that and those brown eyes would almost pop out and go rolling across the floor. And look at that chin—wow, harder than the granite in the abandoned quarry west of town.

"What's the hassle, old man?"

Dennis hadn't heard his father coming down the thick-carpeted stairway. Now he was standing in the door between the living room and hall and smiling in that teasing way, as if anything Dennis wanted had to be unimportant.

"Dennis," his mother explained when he didn't answer, "Dennis has his heart set on spending the evening at Freddy Stahl's. He doesn't see why he should go to bed at ten and he just said something unprintable about the sitter."

"What I *didn't* say was: all she does is bring her cassettes and play them all evening and *eat* and smoke all your cigarettes and so fuck her."

His father's broad, blunt-featured face didn't sober; he laughed. "Where are you learning those big four-letter words?" But he didn't act as if he even expected an answer: that was the way he was. He turned to Dennis' mother. "You sure you won't come with me, Kay? If you'd change your mind, it'd look better all around and—"

"No, thank you very much, my sweet." She brushed past him and into the hall and stood adjusting her tight dress on her slim, athletic body in front of the full-length mirror on the closet door. "I get enough creamed chicken and peas and, God knows, enough rah-rah-for-our-party speeches while we're in Washington. Spare me on the home grounds."

Dennis sprawled on the sofa, half listening, wondering when, if ever, they'd turn their attention back to him. It was getting late.

"You'll be in for a lot more of same if I'm tapped for lieutenant governor next term."

"Which, of course, you fully expect to be."

"You're always complaining how much you despise Washington."

"I complain because I like living here. Tarkington. And I don't relish the idea of living anywhere else, no matter what honor's attached to it."

"You'll have to admit the lieutenant governorship's a step in the right direction."

"*Whose* right direction?"

"Mine, damn it, Kay." His father's voice, deep and resonant in that barrel of a chest, sounded annoyed as hell now. "My direction, Kay. You'd better make up your mind to it."

"Is that an order, Representative Wallace C. Heckman, sir? *Another* order?"

"Kay, I don't want to get excited before my speech. Let's knock it off, shall we?"

"Because, Wally, you may as well know: I'm getting

very very tired of always taking orders. Of doing everything *your* way."

Dennis opened his eyes. They were facing each other in the hall. Well, nothing new about that. They were always at it. Who's in charge around here? And the old man always won. Fuck both of them.

Then his father came into the room, walking in that springy halfback way he had, on the balls of his feet. He was wearing one of his dark speech-making suits, not a tux, and even if he was getting bald on top, the gray hair coming to a point on his forehead and the heavy sideburns and thick brows made him look pretty young for an old guy of forty-five. "What do you do over at Freddy's, old man?"

"Well, they've got this cool playroom in the basement"—which was true—"and we shoot pool and run the electric trains"—which was one hell of a lie. "You or Mom could pick me up on the way home."

"Well, buddy, we seem to have conflicts tonight. Your mother's getting this golfing trophy and I have to go to this banquet. I don't have any choice if I'm to make a living for all of us. But I don't see why you shouldn't do what you want to do." He lifted his voice. "Don't you agree, honey?"

"If I'd have agreed, I wouldn't have told him he had to stay home. But go ahead, Dennis—whatever your father says. He's the one who has to be loved."

"A low blow," his father said, winking at him and going into the hall again. "*You* love me, don't you, honey?"

"I love you whenever I get to see you without all those voting fans around—which isn't often." But she picked up the telephone and dialed. "I'll tell Karen we'll pay her anyway. It's the least we can do."

"You know, Kay, I sometimes get the definite impression that you really don't want me to land that lieutenant governorship."

"Your impression in this case could be correct. Especially since *that* would mean running for governor in four more years, then what? The United States Senate? Higher?" Then she was speaking into the telephone.

Dennis saw his father snatch his dark-blue topcoat from the newel post, heard him mutter, "To hell with it," and then saw him disappear out the front door, which didn't slam exactly but closed with a bang. His mother's voice continued on the phone, and outside, the Buick started and ripped out of the driveway. Fuck him, too.

Then his mother was calling. "Do you want me to drop you at Freddy's?"

Christ no! "I don't mind walking. It's only a couple of blocks."

"Well, you be careful, and you do *not* have permission to leave Freddy's house. Is *that* understood?"

"Why would I want to leave it?"

"Lock the front door. And I'll come by for you a little after ten."

By the time he heard the motor of her shiny new Opel GT fade away down the wide quiet street, all the wild expectancy had come back. He tore upstairs to get his sweater, ran stumbling down again, flew out the front door, slamming it. How the sweet hell could he *leave* Freddy's house when he wasn't going there? Chew on that one for a while. He was going farther, much farther, across town, to meet Freddy behind a bar located just off the college campus—a favorite hangout for the students where three or four girls, wearing practically *nothing,* took turns dancing in wire cages, wriggling and weaving all over and kicking their bare legs, so that most of the time he felt like jerking off right there on the limb of the old dead elm where he and Freddy had a grandstand seat to see through the large rear windows. With any kind of luck at all they'd have an hour and a half there tonight. He hoped to hell Freddy didn't forget the cigarettes.

He was hurrying, bent forward, and every fourth step or so he'd skip. The whole evening, wow. He was beginning already to fill with that odd fever he'd only recently discovered in his body—that shot-away good emptiness in the stomach and that other feeling, farther down, like a soft hand caressing your balls until they were tight and hard.

He passed the Thornhill house: one of those dumb square dinner parties. A car started up from the curb across the street and its lights came on. It went in the opposite direction, and then it made a U-turn, the headlights sweeping along the street, catching him and throwing his shadow out in front of him on the sidewalk.

But the car didn't pass. Instead, it drew alongside. He glanced. The driver was idling the motor, the metal-gray Vega moving as slowly as he was moving. The driver had shaggy hair and a mustache, both sort of red, and he was smiling around a pipe.

"Want a lift, Dennis?" he asked through the open window.

"No, thanks."

The man laughed. "I'm a friend of your father's. I just left the dinner party back there. Hop in."

"No, thanks. Thanks just the same."

The man laughed again, pleasantly. "You may have heard Wally speak of me. Name's Fletcher Briggs. I used to be an attorney, too, but now I teach at the college. I'm on my way back to campus now, Dennis, if you want to save yourself a walk."

Dennis stopped, squinted into the car. He'd heard his father speak of Fletcher Briggs—yes, he was almost sure he had. And the Explorers Bar was at least a mile and a half away. The man leaned toward him and opened the door slightly. "Last chance, kid." He revved the motor, which had a kind of hollow sound.

Dennis made up his mind. They always said never to accept a ride from anybody he didn't know. Another one of those dumb rules. Fuck their rules.

Once in the front seat of the car, he was even more confident. This dude looked like a professor all right—right down to those crummy leather patches on the elbows of the old tweed jacket. The car shot forward as if, all of a sudden, Professor Briggs was in a hurry.

"What do you teach?" Dennis asked because he felt he had to say something.

"Law. The philosophy of law. I teach all about justice, Dennis. That's my specialty—justice." Then he laughed.

Dennis himself didn't see anything hilarious about that, but this dude was like all teachers—just a little nuts to start with.

The car made a turn and increased its speed. Dennis said nothing.

Then it was going faster still and made still another turn. The motor didn't sound like a Ford's. It sounded more like a racing motor.

Dennis looked at the professor then. He was leaning over the wheel, peering ahead, pipe between his teeth, and his eyes, in the light from the dashboard, looked bright and excited and pleased. As if he were looking forward to something and was now in a big hurry to get there.

"This isn't the way to the campus," Dennis ventured, feeling a clogging in his throat.

"What? What'd you say, dearie?"

"I said . . . sir . . . I don't think this is the way to the campus, is it?"

"We're not going to the campus right away, Dennie. We're going to the Explorers Bar. Isn't that where you're going, Dennie?"

How the hell did Professor Briggs know this? How could he? And nobody ever called him Dennie.

"This isn't the way to the—" But he stopped himself. It was hard to speak. It was hard to get his breath. "I think I'll get out here, sir."

"You'll get out when I tell you to, Dennie baby. And when you do, you'll do what I tell you to do. And if you start to yell, I'll close your mouth so you won't be able to open it. I'll close it with something you never had in it before."

"But," Dennis blurted, "this isn't the way to the Explorers Bar!"

"We'll explore anyway, Dennie. You and me." And then, when Dennis uttered a sound: "If you start yapping, baby, I'll push you out on the pavement. And right now we're going exactly sixty-two miles per hours." His voice was very low, very gentle. "I think you'll enjoy exploring with me more than being wiped up from the pavement. Fact, I think you might enjoy it more than you can imagine."

The fleshless skull had been placed on top of the marble gravestone and in the harsh flat glare of the floodlight, with the dome lights of the cars revolving and flashing red and blue and with the radios crackling and heavy masculine voices conversing in indistinguishable monotones as the search spread out, with the shadows moving between the other varishaped stones, flashlights probing—the whole scene had the eerie unreality of an alcoholic nightmare. The skull seemed to be perched there, itself observing, its bony whiteness reflecting the lights, its dark, eyeless hollows staring as if in mockery of the living's foolish goals and pursuits, a ragged row of gold teeth glittering.

Theron Diehl had been staring silently at the skull for some few minutes now, as if it were a human face, as if Judge T. H. Stuttaford, in death, had finally attained the mesmeric dignity and power that he had only striven and hoped for on the bench.

Finally Diehl shifted the wad of chewing tobacco from one cheek to the other, spat, and asked: "How'd y'all get wind of this, first place?"

Officer Ben Hutchinson, at his elbow, said: "Phone call to headquarters. Male voice. Refused to give his name. Reported some activity and noise in the cemetery. Call originated in some nearby community, not in Tarkington."

Diehl didn't bother to turn or nod. Young Ben Hutchinson was of that new breed of law enforcement officers that Diehl never hoped to understand—efficient, granted, but soft underneath, as polite and obliging to suspects and criminals as to the public or as to the criminal's victims. "How do you know it wasn't from Tarkington?"

"The call was made from a pay phone. The operator was heard to ask the calling party to deposit twenty cents. That narrows it down some. If you give the word, we'll put the phone company on it."

"Hold your horses. Pr'ly kid who called was same one did this. Wants to bug us. Isn't that the up-to-date word—bug?"

"Chief," Ben Hutchinson said, "I don't know what this is all about, but it's no prank."

"Y'don't say?"

"No, sir. The bones are strewn in all directions. Like whoever did it took some kind of pleasure in it, or was sore as hell, or both."

"Maybe then, son, you'll explain to this ignorant ole man how that proves it's *not* kid stuff?"

Diehl noted that when he turned to face Ben Hutchinson, the younger man's eyes met his directly, without flinching away. "To get to the casket, sir, whoever did it had to dig down, expose the concrete casing, drill into it—it looked to us like some kind of acid was used, too—and then plant the nitro or whatever explosive they used. Just to get to the casket. It was a neat clean job, Chief. Like an expert."

"Expert what—grave robber? Son, kids're smarter'n be-Jesus these days—criminal ways, that is."

But Ben Hutchinson, damn him, was shaking his narrow, fine-featured head. "Will you step over here, sir?"

Diehl followed, taking a final, almost involuntary glance at the skull, which seemed now to be leering. On a sheet of canvas, with a spotlight trained on it, lay a collection of items, all carefully separated one from the other in a meticulous pattern. A spade. A hand drill with bit. A crowbar. Ordinary overshoes with brown earth caked on the soles. A pair of mechanic's coveralls.

"Fingerprints?" Diehl asked.

"Preserved, sir. Where possible. But there won't be any." Ben Hutchinson reached out one foot and touched a rubber glove, dirty now but the color of flesh. "Didn't want to get his hands dirty. Other one'll turn up around here by morning, for what good it'll do us."

"What the hell will they think of next?" He looked out over the cemetery; beyond, the lights of town could be seen through the trees. "Comes from too much television. Officer, y'reckon this is what the younger generation'd call one of those caper things?"

Ben Hutchinson's voice, which still had a boyish timbre to it, sharpened only slightly enough for Diehl to catch it. "Is that what we're to do then, Chief—treat this whole mess as some kind of sick morbid joke?"

Diehl eyed the young man in the way that he knew had always commanded respect in some, fear in others. "What they want us to do, son, is take this horseplay here serious. Don't you know that's just the thing they take delight in?" The word "son" usually kept these young colts in their proper place.

"Why'd they pick on Judge Stuttaford's grave then?"

Diehl took a deep breath. This young fellow was just about to get on his nerves. "How the hell should I know? They liked that epitaph mebbe. *The right as God gives me to see the right*. Sentiment like that's reason enough for some young punk these days."

"You may be right," Ben Hutchinson conceded, but neither his tone nor his eyes gave a whit, and Diehl felt again that prickling of irritation that this particular officer managed to rile up in him. "For the record, Chief: the coveralls and overshoes both have Iowa manufacturers' labels. Not much to start on."

This Ben Hutchinson seemed to think of everything. What was he trying to do now, remind his superior officer that he hadn't inquired about these items? "It'd be a fair start if we were conducting a criminal investigation—which we are *not*. There's no evidence of robbery. Hell, considering the price of gold, the judge's teeth alone'd be worth the trouble if that was the motive."

"What then?" another voice asked from the shadows. "We got a family of werewolves in town, Chief?"

Diehl recognized the voice before Gavin McQuade came into view. A small, gnomelike man, about thirty-five or forty years old, who walked with a limp and had the face of a prune, McQuade was one of those who had no respect for anyone or anything. Snide son of a bitch wouldn't trust his own mother, and probably with damn good reason.

"How the hell'd he get in here?" Diehl demanded of Ben Hutchinson.

"Press pass, Chief," McQuade said cheerfully, but scowling as usual nevertheless. "I don't know about the wilds of good ole Texas, Chief, but up here in these here parts, suh, we got what is called the freedom of the press. So, welcome or not, suh, heah is Gavin McQuade, Esquire, to ask whether you-all have got a statement on this here ghoulish party we are attending. I asked the judge, but he's not talking tonight."

Then Diehl had to decide whether to make an issue of it: order Ben to throw McQuade out or play the little crippled bastard's game. He decided. "Ghouls and vampires invited, McQuade, stick around."

"I thought I might. Scared to go back to town without a police escort anyway, what with all those demons and goblins about. Well, Chief, how'll I satisfy the morbid appetite of the curious civilized general public? What's the official line to be?"

"The official line," Diehl said, forcing himself to grin pleasantly, "is that a routine investigation is being conducted and if and when we have anything that is in the interest of the public to know, we'll damn well let the public know."

Gavin McQuade's face became even more pinched than usual and his darting blue eyes sparkled merrily in the strange light. "I often heard you Texas Rangers take a lot upon yourselves. You keep up like this, you'll get yourself a job in the White House."

Diehl ignored that. "Meantime, McQuade, let's stick to *your* version of this episode—werewolves, ghouls." He moved off, hearing McQuade's cackle of a laugh. Damn reporters—always thought they had special privileges. Cynical bastards, too.

Ben Hutchinson followed to Diehl's car. "Chief, do you want me to assign someone to inform Judge Stuttaford's widow? It'd be too bad if she learned about this from the paper or the TV."

Here Ben Hutchinson was again—reminding his superior of his duties and obligations. Diehl forced another smile. "Tell y'what, Ben: I'm gonna leave that pa'ticular little chore to you." That should hold him. "I don't reckon there's anybody I'd trust more to carry out such a kind and delicate mission."

Ben accepted this without a nod or change of expression. "I was thinking, sir, of making up a list of all the men the judge sentenced over the years. Who knows? Maybe one of them, holding a grudge, has broken jail or—"

But Diehl cut him off. "Christ, kid, a list like that'd take days to compile. Weeks to investigate. How many men y'think I got? An' for what? Nobody's been exactly injured tonight here. Whoever it is, he's had his jollies and it's over. Let's not dignify this picayune mischief by treatin' it like some major crime. An' more, son, more, hear me now: if anyone did a thing like this to pay off some old score on a dead man, he'd have to be deranged."

There was a pause that Diehl didn't appreciate. Then Ben Hutchinson, eyes straight and steady, said: "Yes, sir. That's my point exactly. And if he's capable of this on a dead man, who knows what he might do?"

Diehl considered this. He was thinking of the

manuscript pages on his desk at home and of the third bourbon of the evening. What was there to consider? This Ben Hutchinson was turning into even more of a pain in the ass than Diehl had suspected. "Bring in all that . . . uh . . . evidence y'got there. I'll take a peek in the morning."

"Whatever he left, he left on purpose. To throw us off."

"Christ Jesus, I am tired to the bone of hearing every small-time troublemaker called smart or shrewd. Next, you'll be telling me he left them Iowa coveralls jist to make me send a man all the way out there to investigate." He was shaking his head as he opened the door of his car. "Wall, if this here fiend strikes again, son, y'all be sure to call me at home. But only if he commits a punishable crime against a living soul, not a corpse. Hear?"

He took a final look at the skull on top of the gravestone and climbed into his car. In some ways the judge looked better after two years underground than he had behind the bench. He supposed they had to make a big deal of a thing like this, not having any real crime to deal with in a quiet, dull little town like this.

Part Two

The autumn colors of the trees and shrubs and fallen leaves moved hazily in his vision as he drove, without any hurry, no urgency, along the Lake Shore Drive. Except when his headlights caught a dark glitter on a curve, he could not see the lake itself, but he was aware, in a vague and pleasant way, of its presence on his right. It was here, really, that it had all begun. On the lake. The thought was a distant one that didn't seem to penetrate his relaxed mood. He felt empty, depleted, yet satisfied. There was a vast quiet inside Boyd Ritchie now, a tranquillity all through him—the kind of peace and serenity that he knew would stay with him always, once the night was over. He had told himself all along that this would be so; now he was certain.

The motor purred. The night stretched ahead. In a way he wished it would never end. In fact, he reminded himself, it had only begun.

The dial of the dashboard clock read eight forty-one when he turned between the twin stone pillars into the parking area of the Lake Club. The clubhouse was brilliant with lights, which illuminated the docks and boats and were reflected on the surface of the water. The music was muted and mingled with voices. He chose a shadowed place between two large Cadillacs from which he could command a full view of the glass-door entrance, which was decorated with hanging white ropes and nets. He turned off the engine and lights. So far there had been nothing on the radio to indicate that anyone had any knowledge of the Heckman kid. He himself had removed the red mustache and the wig, and he now wore a dark windbreaker over the turtleneck and the stocking-type hat of black yarn which clung tightly to his shaved head. If anyone questioned him here, he would say only that he was not a member but that he was waiting for a certain young lady, whose name he was not free to give; she was to join him when she could get away from her boyfriend inside. He didn't anticipate being questioned, but if he was, he would simply drive off and wait elsewhere for Mrs. Coralie Wharton to leave the club, as he knew she would within the next half hour or so. If by the wildest sort of chance anyone should get suspicious and take his license number to the police, they would only discover that the Vega was registered in the name of Fletcher Briggs, a most respected citizen and member of the local faculty. Up you, Briggs, yours is coming.

Idly then he began to wonder, not for the first time, where he might be tonight and what he might be doing if that cunt hadn't happened along the way she did that afternoon almost eight years ago. Sometimes, when he passed those pleasant houses on the nice streets or tried to imagine what it would be like to sit inside a club like this eating and drinking and dancing, he felt an overwhelming nostalgia. Longing. And for something he'd never even had, or ever would.

It was hard now to picture himself in that time. He'd hitchhiked from Illinois to be interviewed by the college because there was a scholarship available and his high school record plus one year in night college made him eligible. He'd been filled with a sense of well-being, exuberance; the future seemed full of promise now that he was away from the sickly coal towns where he'd spent his life. Then along came this girl in a white Cadillac convertible and damned if she didn't stop. It had all happened so damned fast then: her dropping him in a woods along the shore of the lake, his waiting, following her instructions and wondering what the hell he was into. But unable to bring himself to walk away. Unaware then that there was anything at stake beyond perhaps a fine time on this lovely rich girl's private boat on the glittering lake. When the boat had actually appeared and she had waved and he was swimming out to it, he'd felt vulnerable as hell, leaving all his clothes except a pair of swim trunks hidden in the woods, but nothing could have stopped him then. She was on the deck waving and waiting, blond hair flying in the wind as it had in the car, her skin browned and soft and inviting. What a wild piece of luck. And then he was on deck and she was kissing him, her firm flesh quivering, gray eyes glinting almost black with desire, and her mouth muttering with a harsh urgency that only stirred him more: *Hurry, come inside, oh, please, hurry, hurry.*

The Cunt. In the dark car tonight, he could remember his own wild passion, the stunned incredulity he had felt, but now it all seemed to have happened to someone else altogether. The thought of her body meant nothing to him now; if anything, filled him with a faint revulsion. As if what had happened and all that followed from it had happened to someone else altogether—someone named Boyd Ritchie, a boy who believed in the future as much as he believed in the present. If what he had done in the rocking hot quiet of that boat's cabin had been rape, then he was damned if he knew what rape was.

And he knew. Now he knew. He wondered, keeping his eyes on the door of the club building, whether the gang rape in his first week in prison had been the beginning of the change. In this mood of detachment he could contemplate even that with an amused equanimity. They had held a belt around his neck, choking him, and they had fucked him until he passed out, and afterward, when he woke up in the prison hospital, where he had spent three weeks, he had had to have seven stitches. But he had begun, then, to learn. He had decided that a state prison was populated by people who are not too bright and who fall into three basic categories: impulse criminals, like most murderers; chronic convicts and habitual offenders, who can't seem to function outside without getting caught, largely owing to their own stupidity; and a small number of competent working criminals. He had decided to associate himself, if with anyone, with the latter group. And a damn lucky decision that had been, too. That's how he had met Fleming.

Fleming was a flaming little queen, but if it hadn't been for him, Boyd Ritchie might have been able to plan and carry out tonight's project but he would not have had the means to get away later. Now he had more than ninety-one thousand dollars wrapped in an old rucksack, in with all the other camping gear, in the back of the beat-up old Ford van stashed on the other side of the lake. When he was finished here tonight, sometime before it was light, he'd row over in the small boat he'd hidden in a marshy inlet on this side of the lake. By then the fuzz might be watching the roads, might even have roadblocks set up or copters up above, but who'd see a single rowboat out on the lake in the dark? Afterward then, in the van—which he had painted with bright colors in a wild psychedelic nonpattern—he'd take pleasure in going through the roadblocks, if any, or past the state police cruisers, in the most conspicuous vehicle he could imagine. He'd be laughing all the way to the border. Screw the lot of them, stupid pigs. He'd be free then. Finally. And it'd be time for his life, which had not begun, to begin.

It was too bad about poor little Fleming, but the score had come to only a few thousand over a hundred grand, hardly enough to share if he was to buy the cars, clothes, disguises, ID's and so forth that he had to have. Fleming specialized in robbing the homes and offices of lawyers, doctors, dentists, and other law-abiding citizens likely to be salting away cash. *Most of them don't even dare report the robbery because of the Internal Revenue:* the idea, repeated thousands of times, invariably caused Fleming to chuckle. But Fleming also was—or had been while alive—an experienced and expert safecracker, the best, and when he spotted a potential big score out there in the Iowa City area, he'd phoned Boyd Ritchie at his rooming house in Londonford, as had been arranged, and had announced, in that squeaky little voice of his: *I got Kelsey's nuts out here. And I need me a jigger I can trust.* Which, in the lingo he'd come to understand and of necessity use, it meant Fleming had a job in mind, a job on a safe that was an absolute cinch and offered the possibility of a really big take, and that he needed a lookout to pull it off. So, careful to cover himself at the rooming house and not to be observed breaking parole, Boyd Ritchie had driven the old tan Maverick, which he normally drove, to Boston, bought his airline ticket in the name of Floyd Richter, wearing a wig of straw-colored crewcut hair, and had flown out to Iowa City, met Fleming, and together they had pulled the job on a small-town bank, a job that had probably not even been discovered until Boyd Ritchie was back in Londonford working in the garage again. He had known, of course, what two nights with Fleming would entail, but after having had to be so goddamn careful in and around Tarkington and Londonford, that part had been a relief, too: a happy preview of freedom to come. And he had learned how to use acid to cut into concrete, how to use nitro safely (although Fleming would not use it on bank jobs because even possession was a federal offense and Fleming was nothing if not cautious) and how to muffle the sound. And the two days had given him opportunity to buy the overshoes and coveralls with the Iowa manufacturers' labels, labels which he had not removed because he knew this would confuse the Tarkington pigs when discovered in the cemetery. And by now he was sure they had been discovered. Just as he was sure that nothing had yet connected him with that job or with what he had done, with such personal pleasure and relief, to young Dennis Heckman. No sweat. Clockwork. Let them live it up in the Lake Club, steaks and music and booze flowing—he'd only just begun and he had all night.

Police Lieutenant Ben Hutchinson knew why Chief Diehl had assigned him this rotten chore. In a way it was his own damned fault: he knew better than to cross Theron Diehl, but there were times when he couldn't seem to help himself and, God help him, those times were becoming more and more frequent. Bad as he needed this job—what with two kids now, another due in less than four months and himself not skilled and not trained for anything in particular—he knew he had to knuckle under to Diehl. Had to. Nevertheless, it galled him; it did something to his pride, or manhood, or something. And so did this.

"Mrs. Stuttaford, believe me, I hate to be the one to bring you this news. But Chief Diehl thought it'd be better if one of us told you personal, rather than have you learn about it on the television or in the newspaper."

Mrs. Stuttaford was in her mid-seventies, Ben Hutchinson guessed—an enormous woman with small slits of pale eyes embedded in great hanging pouches of pink flesh. Sunk down in a huge upholstered wing chair facing the television, which leaped with color and music and dancing, at which she continued to glance every second or so, she seemed to be immobilized by her own weight. Ben Hutchinson, uniform cap in hand, couldn't help remembering how tall and bone-thin and sunken-cheeked Judge T.H. Stuttaford had been, almost cadaverous even in life.

"Who did it?" Mrs. Stuttaford's voice was surprisingly high-pitched, almost childlike—but only curious, no trace of anger or shock in it.

"We're working on that, ma'am. Naturally. We hope to find out that fact."

"It could have been anybody. It could have been me." Then, to his amazement, she laughed—a piping flutelike laugh, not pleasant. "Or one of those other poor souls he sentenced." She returned her attention to the television screen. "A great many souls hated him. Insofar as I know, nobody loved him. For my part, I hope you never find out. Would you mind turning the volume up slightly, Officer? Thank you. And thank you, too, for driving out here to tell me like this. You seem like a kindly young soul, but I'm afraid you've wasted your time. Don't fret about me. Good night now."

Kay Heckman, hearing her own voice shaking as she spoke, had tried to fill him in as they went up the stairs together, but she wasn't sure Wally was even listening: he was scowling and, she knew, fuming inwardly because she had called him home from the dinner before he'd had a chance either to eat or to speak. Now that they were in Dennis' bedroom, both standing, facing the child who lay stretched to his full length on the bed, face pale and set but tearless, she knew that her husband would have no more luck in breaking down that grim, stubborn silence than she had had. Seeing Dennis again, she felt her inner terror expand—that dazed, vacant stare, without focus, that unnatural stillness. Oh, God, let Wally reach him; let him at least try. But gently, please, gently, Wally.

"Now, Dennis, old man, let's get a few facts straight first, shall we?" The irritation was still in his tone, but Kay recognized this as his courtroom voice, the one that had broken down many a witness: cajoling, quiet, friendly—but firm and demanding.

"Your mother tells me that she received a phone call at the golf club from a woman—what was her name, Dennis?" No answer. "A Mrs. Deming, I think she said—does that sound right?" No reply. "This nice lady said she had found you wandering along the street as if you didn't know where you were going or where you lived. But you must have told her your name. Did you?" And then, when there was only silence although Dennis' eyes remained open, Wally's voice dropped and he stepped closer to the bed. "Why wouldn't you tell your mother what happened, Dennis? Did anything really happen?" He glanced toward Kay, who shrugged, as the pressure inside threatened to rise into a shout in her throat. "Son, we're your parents. Your friends. We're trying to help you." Then, whether out of genuine emotion or for its shock effect, Wally was almost but not quite yelling: "You're going to tell me what's the matter or we'll go on like this all night!"

"Wally," she heard herself say, "maybe he's just sick. Physically sick—with something that makes him act this way. He seems to be in pain. I think we ought to telephone Dr. Farago and—"

"Kay, I'm handling this. Please." Then to Dennis again, softly: "Old man, if you've done something you're ashamed of, anything—" But he broke off. Had Wally seen what she had seen? *Had* that been a flicker in those still, dead eyes, or had they both imagined it? "If we promise we won't blame you, no matter what, you won't be punished—" And now the head turned away completely, the eyes closing. Wally shot her a swift glance, without himself moving a muscle. "All right, buddy—it's a deal. You let us help you and we'll forgive you, whatever it is." But the room was still again. She could hear Wally breathing. Only that. She saw his heavy shoulders slump just slightly; then she saw them stiffen into determination. "By God, if you won't talk to me, maybe you'll talk to Dr. Farago. He'll get to the bottom of this!"

"No!" It was not a shout, more of a screech torn from the boy's throat. And now he was sitting up, his face twisting. "No!"

"You don't give me any choice, son."

"If . . . if she . . . Mom, will you go someplace? Someplace else?"

Bewildered, the pressure collapsing suddenly into utter weakness, Kay felt as if she might erupt into tears, something she had not done in years. She refused to meet Wally's eyes, turned and went into the upstairs hall, closing the door gently. She started down the stairway, realized that her legs had gone weak, so she slumped down onto the top step, resting her head on her knees.

Then, although it had not been her intention, she discovered that, by not moving, she could hear the voices from the bedroom.

"Now"—and there was a note or relief in Wally's tone, almost a playful, teasing note—"now, buddy, what is it that you think you've done that's so horrendous?"

"I didn't do it. I didn't do anything. I . . . fought."

"You mean you had a fight? Son, when I was a kid—"

But something stopped him. Silence.

Then: "Dad. I can't say it out loud." Pleading: "I just can't."

She heard the sigh of bedsprings: Wally was sitting on the bed. And then there was only quiet again, not the sound of a whisper. The stillness stretched itself out unmercifully. She was not breathing again. It was as if her brain itself were knotting in her head. What, what, for God's sake, *what?*

Then, the eternity spent, she heard Wally's voice, but not, at first, his words. And then what sounded like whimpering. Her impulse brought her to her feet, but she didn't step to the door.

"Now . . . are you listening, Dennis? I want you to describe this man. Tell me everything you know, or saw, or can remember about him."

Man? What man? Oh, God, what was she doing out here? Why did they put her through this? More whisperings: now she could not make out Wally's words, there was only an exchange of brief questions and briefer answers, all indistinguishable. She ran down the stairs; she went into the living room; she looked around in panic, as if she'd stumbled into a strange house and wondered how she'd come here. Then she went into the kitchen, turned on a faucet, ran her wrists under the cold stinging water, saw her face reflected in the dark window—set, ravaged, suddenly middle-aged, if not old. Oh, God, what's happened? And what's coming, what's going to happen next?

She had not heard him come down the carpeted stairs. Behind her, he said, "Do you have a sleeping tablet you can give him?"

She turned. He was almost a stranger to her. His eyes had contracted into fierce, sharp points; his jaw was clamped, rigid; and his shoulders were heaving up and down.

"Wally," she managed to say, "Wally, you've got to tell me. He's my son, too. You've got to tell me, damn you!"

His square chin lifted. "I wish I didn't have to."

"Tell me! What? Tell me!"

His tone was low and hard. "He's been sodomized."

"Sodom—"

"Raped. Forcibly. Not threatened—raped."

"My God."

"I not only have a full description of the man who did it and of his car—I have his name."

"That doesn't matter now, does it? Have you called Dr. Farago?"

Wally came closer. She had never seen that face before. She had never heard that voice. "He doesn't want that. He says he doesn't need it."

"What does a child know? He may be injured!"

"Kay, it's bad enough, privately. He's ashamed. He may even feel guilty, I don't know—"

"Guilty? How could—"

"Imagine what his life'll be like if his classmates get wind of this. His life'd be a living hell."

"His life might be ruined anyway. A kid that age, his most impressionable—oh, God, of course we have to get a doctor's opinion! What are you thinking of?"

"Of him, Kay, of Dennis."

She knew, in that instant, as the words echoed in the

room, that they held truth, yes—but did they hold the whole truth?

"If Farago comes, he'll have to inform the police. A crime's been committed. He'd have no choice."

"Wally," she said, knowing, "Wally, you can't think of yourself at a time like this."

He turned away then, no change of expression on his face, his body stiff and his hands doubled into fists. "I don't need the scandal or the disgrace, and neither do you. But most of all, Dennis might not weather it." He was stalking toward the hall and she followed. "He's a damned sensitive boy and a thing like this could scar him forever. I am thinking of myself, and of you, but I'm thinking of him, too. It's possible to be motivated by more than—" At the front door he whirled to face her. "I'm telling you, Kay—this time I'm telling you flat out. Give him a sleeping pill and let him lose consciousness. He's been through enough, and Farago and the police would only put him through more—"

"But what if he's hurt?"

"Don't call Farago or anyone else!"

It was then that she made up her mind. She said: "You're not going back to that meeting now. Surely you—"

"I'm going to kill a man," he said quietly. "At least I'm going to come as close as I can."

He went out. The door closed. She stared at it. She had made up her mind anyway, but now she was even more convinced of what had to be done. If he knew who had done this thing and if he was going to kill him or almost kill him, the police would have to come into it anyway. Wally, for all his training and discipline, was not thinking straight.

She went to the telephone in the hall and picked it up very carefully so that Dennis, in the room above, would not hear. Throughout her married life she had allowed Wally to make the decisions, give the orders—usually in a subtler way than he did tonight. She dialed. But that part of their life was over now. She knew what had to be done and she was doing it. That amazed her. But what amazed her more was her calmness.

The lethargy had deepened into a kind of torpor. Apathy. Boyd Ritchie was tired, physically tired. He had had more sex tonight than he had had since his return from Iowa. And of a much more satisfying sort tonight, too. His body was sluggish; it felt heavy. After he had made sure that both of the Whartons' cars, his Mercedes and her Jag, were in the parking lot, he had been sitting here allowing his mind to wander drowsily. But he knew that as soon as the Cunt came out of the Lake Club, he would be alert and alive again. He also knew that she would come out alone. Meanwhile, he didn't feel like exerting that iron discipline that he had taught himself in his iron bunk—time enough for that later when it would be needed. Now he was a hawk—no, a falcon—wings folded, waiting, storing up strength for the attack on his quarry below. Hunter. Silent. Unseen. Unsuspected. The image pleased him. A bird of prey. Powerful. Biding its time. And it was not his doing but theirs: *they* had decided he would always be outside looking in. Then let them take the fucking consequences.

It had been Fleming, out in Iowa, who had said, with that sweet, infectious, innocent chuckle of his: *If you pull this off and get away with it—notice I say it—why, luv, you'll go down in what they call the annals of crime. Nobody ever thought up nothin' like that before, I bet. I wish I could just be there to see it. Do I never!*

Well, it was too bad in a way, but Fleming would never know. He wouldn't even know about that big *if* of his. Hell, it'd be in all the papers, all of them, every state in the country—that much was for sure. But poor Fleming, he'd just never, never know.

Thinking of Fleming made him a little sad now. Not

regretful, exactly, but sad. Whenever he got into one of these moods, so many things seemed sad. He hadn't intended to kill Fleming, not after he got the call, or while he was driving to the Boston airport, or on the plane. He wondered now when the idea came to him out there. Was it after they'd counted the money? Well, he didn't know where, when he was finished in Tarkington and was probably wanted all over the world, he could lay his hands on anything like that sum. And half of it would take him just half as far. Facts. Mathematical facts.

But maybe, just maybe, even at that he wouldn't have killed Fleming if he hadn't made the mistake of bragging about what he had in mind back here in Tarkington. It was as if he'd been compelled, as if he didn't have any say or choice in the matter: he simply had to tell someone, anyone, and at the time Fleming seemed the logical person, the only one. Not that he'd debated much about doing it; it just happened. And then Fleming had got so excited—maybe if he hadn't got so excited. Whatever, telling Fleming, even more than the money, had caused him to kill the only person he had, up to now, ever killed. It made good sense. If Fleming was picked up, say, or accused of the bank job, no telling what he might have said, what deals he might have made to get a lighter sentence or even get off altogether. Boyd Ritchie simply couldn't take the chance, that's all. He'd had some experience; he knew what copping a plea could add up to. And he knew how tempting it looked.

That was the reason that, in the almost-deserted parking area of the Iowa City airport when the plane for Boston came in and it was time for him to go inside, he had opened the rear door of Fleming's old Olds, taken up his attaché case, which contained his share of the score, and had then picked up the wire he had planted earlier, looped it quickly around Fleming's neck and pulled, hard, feeling the wire as it cut into the neck muscles, then pulling it tighter and tighter with both gloved hands, until Fleming stiffened for a long moment, then collapsed, head falling forward and sideways.

And then the elation came—an engulfing pleasure so intense and overwhelming that it left him weak, spent. It left him feeling, on the plane, just as he felt now, tonight, after the violent and depleting paroxysms with that Heckman kid. He had not slept on the plane but had gazed blindly out the window, lost in a cataleptic stupor that had been like no bliss he had ever known before. He had seemed to be part of the clouds out there; he had seemed to have no connection with the lights of the prairies and the towns and cities below. It had been a pleasure so exquisite that it was almost pain. And at least part of it had sprung from the awareness of all that he carried in the attaché case beneath his seat—even from the amusing fact that sweet old Fleming had taught him how to use the nitro. He'd run the risk of a luggage search at the airport, but risk was the name of the game, his game. And after he was back in Londonford, working daily in the repair garage again, he had searched the newspapers, watched the television news daily: not a word about the death of an obscure little ex-con whose body must have been discovered in time in his car in the parking lot of the Iowa City airport. Not a goddamn word. Poor sweet old Fleming.

What brought him out of his reverie and back into the present was the emergence from the Lake Club's glass doors of the tall, slim figure of a man with hair so black that it seemed to glitter in the light; he walked swiftly, very swiftly but with controlled dignity, to a very dark blue Lincoln Continental parked at the ready near the entrance; he climbed in and started the motor at once. Leroy Farago, MD. Twice divorced. Crotchety but firm bedside manner that, like his appearance, appealed to women who needed a male, preferably a handsome one, to give them hell and make it stick. Trusted, generally admired, ethical to a fault—a gentleman. And a bastard. He drove off, turning on the headlights, gunning the Lincoln's fine strong motor. Some emergency: heart attack, stroke, asthma, ingrown toenail, some shit, any such shit. Boyd Ritchie had studied the good doctor's comings and goings as he had the others'. Well, Farago didn't figure in tonight's scheme, although maybe he should. He'd been the one to examine the Cunt and to report that, yes, in addition to other bruises on the face and especially the body, there was evidence of semen in the vagina as well as internal bleeding, indicating forcible entry. But you couldn't expect *him* to know who'd committed it—the hitchhiker, Boyd Ritchie, or the chick's fiancé, Paul Wharton. Farago had examined Boyd Ritchie, too, after his arrest. Oh, hell, yes, he'd been beaten up some, mostly in the rib cage and the neck muscles; sure, he'd been kicked in the balls, not once but several times, so that his scrotum was about the size of a soccer ball.

You couldn't reasonably expect the examining physician to know or guess that this had been done not by the violated girl's angry fiancé, as the police and Paul Wharton himself claimed—although Paul Wharton had been wearing tennis shoes at the time—but by Theron Diehl, late of the Texas Rangers, who had been wearing high-heeled sharp-edged Western boots. How could you expect the good doctor to know that Diehl had been using his own police methods—don't leave exterior evidence if possible—methods not likely to be used by an enraged fiancé who happened also to be a collegiate boxing champion more likely to go for the face? The only one who had even thought of this discrepancy had been Fletcher Briggs—who had claimed to believe the accused but had pointed out that it would be the hitchhiker's word against not only the police but against the richest young man in town. As Boyd Ritchie had learned and as he now knew, Fletcher Briggs had been playing games, too.

One minute after nine. She'd have to leave soon. Not to join Farago—although that's what her husband would undoubtedly suspect. He had his reasons, too: solid ones. Boyd Ritchie knew of Paul Wharton's jealousy: its original source and its present roots in reality. But Coralie Wharton limited her visits to Dr. Leroy Farago to the daylight hours of the good doctor's Wednesdays-off. Now it was getting close to Vincent Stegner's bedtime—although the old man would not sleep tonight. What would the Cunt do when she discovered him? That was an easy one; Boyd Ritchie had the answer to that one. In fact, he was relying on that answer, just as he was relying on Paul Wharton's jealousy later. And he hadn't been wrong yet. So far, so good.

It was time for action again. His thoughts had slowly brought him out of the quiet lassitude. He could feel the blood beginning to pump again. Then the anticipation returned, the dizzying intoxication of looking ahead.

Alone in the smooth, heavy luxury of his own automobile, away from all eyes, Leroy Farago discovered, not for the first time, that he still could not relax. Relaxation, he had also discovered and had tried to tell some of his patients, was only a matter of degree in today's world. In his office or at the hospital or at the club, even in bed, alone or with the loveliest company, he maintained a cool façade, as much self-protective as professional, which he hoped gave no slight clue to the tension that had once seethed safely deep inside but recently kept threatening to reach the surface.

He was relieved somewhat now to be away from Coralie's eyes: beseeching, accusing, hating. If the bitch didn't like it, she could get out. Just say the word—as he had told her. But she was trapped and knew it. (Lately he'd almost reached the conclusion that everyone on earth was trapped, one way or the other.) She had to have the barbiturates to get to sleep, the amphetamines to get going in the morning, and tranquilizers to carry her through the day. The syndrome was familiar to any physician. As was her desire—no, need now—for more and more of all of them. He'd warned of the danger of an overdose, but he knew that patients, or even addicts, rarely OD on purpose; usually they lose count, lose control, reach for more, of one kind or another, or mix them. Her damned migraines: he had played along, but he doubted that she really believed she was fooling him. About those or as to why she had to obtain the drugs direct from him rather than by prescription. *Paul goes over every bill like we were poor. He can't know, Lee. Don't you see?* Hell, yes, he saw. That was Dr. Leroy Farago's trouble, or one of them: he saw too damned much. And didn't give a healthy shit in hell. About anything. Or anyone. Nothing. No, not even those Wednesday afternoons with Coralie. They were *his* drug. Coralie and a dozen or so others: he took ass where he could get it, get it safely. And Coralie could pretend he was taking advantage of her because of the pills. *Sometimes I feel like a whore:* she'd said it more than once. But he knew she enjoyed it as much as he did—more so lately. Aye, there's the rub. Leroy Farago, prize stud, ladies' delight, was losing it. Oh, so far he was still able to get it up. But for how much longer? And, after all, what did it really matter anyway? It mattered, although not desperately, because laying some female was all he had left. If he'd ever had anything else. He didn't enjoy drinking. His work bored him shitless. People having a good time bored him more, and his patients bored him most. One more detailed and graphic description of a stool of human feces and he might blow his lid right in his office. Using his considerable skills to cure or save those patients often seemed the most boring irony of all. Now even sex had begun to bore him. At age forty-seven.

If there was any satisfaction left, it was in power. The power to cure. And the power, for instance, to force the most beautiful and generally desirable matron in town to do anything he demanded, no matter how bizarre or degrading—the more degrading the better.

He'd had Coralie Wharton's number for years. Since before she was Coralie Wharton, in fact. From the very beginning when she'd come to his office for the first time to ask him to examine her because she had been raped. She'd been young then, very young and beautiful, even with the swollen splotches of purple on her face, filled with fear and misery. Until she had his verdict: yes, she could prove she had been raped. Then the relief had taken over and then the complicity had settled in. He had allowed her to realize that he had his own doubts. *I wouldn't like to be cross-examined in a court of law. But I'll make up a statement in case the authorities should ask for it. Do you understand*? She had understood. Later, when she'd got strung out on the barbs and then the speed, he'd allowed her to believe that he provided the "medicine" because of her sexual favors—without reminding her that she had become more insistent and dependent on those Wednesday afternoons than he had ever been. And by now they'd lost all flavor entirely, their excitement and satisfaction. Like everything else.

He was damn glad to be away from that club! Even if it meant facing work for an hour or so. What he would discover at the hospital now—it was *always* an emergency!—would only add to his sense of tedium and oppression. Wally Heckman's kid—some kind of accident. Well, a U.S. Representative, especially one on his way up, enjoyed certain privileges, priorities. Damned if he'd ever been able to figure out why exactly. But he'd known Wally and Kay for years, and they were both his patients, like most of the better people in town, but they were among his healthiest. And, who knows, there might be *some* interest: his answering service had mentioned something about Mrs. Heckman requesting that the police *not* be informed. He'd demanded to know what the hell that meant, but all the girl could report was what Mrs. Heckman had said when she asked him to meet her at the hospital as soon as possible. How old would that kid be by now? Too young to be driving a car. What then?

"You're being pretty obvious, aren't you?"

"Obvious?"

"Well, I'd think you might allow a *reasonable* length of time to pass between the doctor's grand exit and your picking up your purse and hightailing it out of here. If only for the sake of appearances."

Paul Wharton was watching his wife's gray eyes very carefully. They didn't waver. Only a familiar expression of disgust crept into them. Contempt, maybe.

"Paul, Paul dear, I explained: I'm getting one of my migraines—"

"And only Farago knows what to do when his favorite patient—"

"I'm going home, Paul. Our home." Her hands clutched the green beaded bag on the table between them. "If you don't believe me, you can phone there later. You usually do anyway. But I warn you: the first thing I'm going to do is take a pill for the pain and another to sleep, so don't be surprised if I don't answer."

"Why should I be surprised?"

He hated himself, really. Whatever contempt for him was in her eyes was also in him for himself. Poison. This empty shaking sickness that he knew he had to handle, somehow handle. God, she was lovely. Even now, even angry and possibly in pain, possibly about to betray him—again? again?—she was still lovely, desirable. He had the fleeting impression that he was going to stand up now, step around the table, take her into his arms, strip her right here and—

"Paul, I'm warning you, I'm telling you, not tonight, I can't take it tonight." She closed her lustrous eyes and her smooth brow wrinkled and she smoothed her flowing blond hair. "If you don't believe me—if you won't—then why don't you come along?"

That did it. How did she know how to do it so well,

in such a neat stroke? Remorse filled him, relief. He felt a pang of joy in his chest. He heard the voices at the other tables. Their friends. And here they were at their own club, having had a fine dinner, with Coralie vivacious and laughing through most of it, even teasing the waiter about the salad—while all the time there had been this gnawing at his innards. And when Farago had stopped by the table to say good evening, briskly, in passing, everything then seemed to have gone out of him. Now, though, seeing how her face had changed in the last few minutes, changed as it often did, the life going out of it, the intense paleness setting in, he knew that she was suffering, actually suffering, physically, while he—

"I'm sorry, Coralie. Christ, how sorry. Honestly."

She nodded without opening her eyes. Her lashes were long and beautiful. Everything about her was beautiful. The cleavage of her long green dinner gown hinted at softer pleasures—his, too, all his, as he damned well knew. "You're always sorry," she said. "But it's all right. I tell myself I should feel complimented. I don't know. There's so much pain now, I—" She broke off and looked into his eyes, pleading. "Take me home then, Paul. There's plenty of booze there, you won't be lonely."

No. If he did that now, it would be an admission of the jealously—which now did not exist, which now was a thing of the past, forever. But he was not drunk—on his way, a little tight, but not drunk. "I said I'm sorry, Coralie. Forgive me. Do you feel well enough to drive?" And when she nodded, her stare as direct and honest, as ingenuous as any husband could ever ask, he added: "I promised Julian Rafferty that I'd talk over his new proposition about the mills later."

"Not mills," she snapped. "You always refer to the company as the mills—because your mother did. It's Wharton Manufacturing."

It seemed a small point. He frowned. She had always hated his mother; he put it down to that. He reached across the table and took her hand in his; hers was limp and cold. "I'll try to remember, dear."

Her hand tightened on his. "Now *I'm* sorry. It's the medicine talking. Skip it."

The medicine? But she'd just said she had to go home to *take* the medicine.

"If I don't get home soon, you'll have to drive, Paul. I mean it, I *mean* it!"

Then an idea came to him, an idea that had tormented him many times over the seven years of their marriage. Too many times. He would follow her. Tonight he would go through with it and then he would know, once and for all.

"I'm a little vague," he said, although he wasn't. "I'm a little vague as to why we had to bring both cars this evening."

She withdrew her hand and he glanced down to see it turn into a white fist alongside the evening bag. He saw her breasts rise and fall. "Then you're drunk already. Mine was being repaired, remember? You dropped me off at the Jaguar garage on the way here and I—" But she cut herself off sharply and stood up, tense with anger and possibly pain, but the lines of her body still flowing and soft under the tight gown. "I'm going. I've had enough of this."

If she had not needed her own car tonight—to go wherever she now planned to go—then why had she so cleverly arranged to have it repaired today rather than yesterday or tomorrow? That clinched it then: he'd let her go, then follow.

"I'm sorry," he said again, but this time he knew he was lying. "I take it then you won't be awake when I get home."

"Oh, bright, bright. You catch on very fast tonight."

"Then I'll wake you," he said, and saw her face go tight.

"Please don't."

"Then I won't wake you. But I'll have you anyway. Don't wear anything when you go to bed."

"Bastard."

"Thank you."

He knew now, he was certain, and the poison was leaping in his veins, hot and ravenous. He didn't speak.

"You won't be able to do anything by the time you get home. You'll be lucky if you don't go off the goddamned road."

She whipped about and walked away. She was the most beautiful woman in the place. In the town. And now she was on her way to someone else. Farago? Someone he didn't even know? Some clerk, or factory hand, or garage mechanic? By God he'd know soon. Then what? He watched her disappear, head high, hair glowing, every sensuous step mocking him. God, how she could humiliate him. How many others in the room knew, had guessed long ago, were now smirking over their drinks and their steaks? He stood up then and followed.

Going down the wide single flight of carpeted stairs to the huge stone-walled foyer, he wondered what he would do if—no, *when*—he really knew for sure. The last thing he'd want would be a divorce. There was still the Wharton name to think of in this town—whether she cared a damn about it or not. Why *should* she care, considering the background she came from? He arrived at the large glass doors leading outside. He was not hurrying. The truth was—and he admitted it—he might kill her. Or the man. Or both. If everyone already knew what she was really like, what she'd been doing to him—and to the Wharton name—then he could probably get away with it.

Kill? He must be drunk, after all. *Kill?*

He saw the low-slung white sports car hurtling out of the parking lot, saw it turn south in the direction of town. And he stopped without opening the door. What was he doing, what the *hell* was he doing, what was he thinking of? He knew his own rages; he knew the intensity and blindness of them—and what he was capable of.

Then, through the glass door, he saw another car,

this one without lights, move swiftly toward the stone posts, then between them, and he saw the lights come on as this other car, some nondescript sort of cheap car, turn south, too. Following Coralie? Then what was he doing, why was he still standing here? He'd been right, there was someone, someone waiting, and she'd planned it all, lied and—

He was going to be sick. The lights blurred. He wasn't tight, not really, but filled with nausea, weak. He couldn't bring himself even to move. He reached and placed his palms against the glass door for support. The glass was cold. What he needed was a drink. Another drink. But how could he make it back up the stairs? Julian Rafferty—something about the mills. He had to go up those stairs. He had to do it because if he followed Coralie now, if he were able to drive and follow her, why, then he would finally know.

And he didn't want to know. He couldn't live if he really knew.

What if the Cunt, for some reason he couldn't know about, decided not to go out to Stegner's place tonight? Doubt had begun to shadow his confidence, gnaw at his anticipation. What if, for the first time, tonight of all nights, she happened to make up her mind to say fuck-you to the old man? The white Jag, thirty yards ahead on the winding road, was traveling fast. Whether she went out there or continued into town and went home, what would it change? Nothing.

Like hell! She *had* to go because this was his night, he'd planned it this way, tonight, goddamn it, everybody had to do what he—

Without giving a signal of any sort, the long-nosed sports car made a sharp right turn onto Highmeadow Road.

And fierce elation burst through him. Joy like frenzy. He gunned the motor, made the same turn, careful not to squeal the tires. He'd been right. He rolled down the window and the chill fall air struck his face, filled the car. He was always right!

He continued at a safe distance. If she realized she were being followed, she might think it was her husband and change her intentions. So he decided to change his plans, slightly—to drive ahead and wait, out of view, at Stegner's. He swung left, sped past, not even glancing. Even if, later, she realized she had been followed, even if her mind were capable now of reading the plates and remembering the description of his car later—by then it would be too late anyway. For her.

Then, for no reason, the uncertainties returned. Had he thought of everything, after all? Suppose just for instance, that when she got a look at Stegner now, she decided to-hell-with-it-all and then, instead of turning and running like hell, she tried to help him, called the police regardless? Suppose, just suppose, she didn't think, or care, about the questions the cops would ask—like what the fuck was she doing way out here? Suppose, in a state of shock, it didn't even occur to her what the consequences could be—for her? Her goddamn marriage, the goddamn scandal, all that Wharton bread—

Something close to panic had set in. He had to choke it down. He couldn't afford it. So far, so good, goddamn it, so far, so good, and that's the way it had to be, had to go on.

Yeah, but if Stegner was able to talk to the cops—hell, even if he didn't, they'd be able to put it together, even that dumb Diehl'd be able to add it up: Judge Stuttaford, Fletcher Briggs, Wallace Heckman, now Coralie Wharton and Vincent Stegner. They'd get to his name in time. And if they did it too soon, how the hell could he get the rest of the job done?

He could no longer see the headlights of the Jaguar in the rearview mirror.

Why the hell had he wanted to make sure the Cunt discovered Stegner anyway? To punish her more? To prove he was right about what she'd do? Was this his first, maybe his fatal, miscalculation?

If that pillhead gave in to terror, or despair, or shock, or if she was too full of drugs to *think*—

She wouldn't call the police. She was too smart, that bitch. She couldn't: she'd know that. It wasn't in the cards. He was dealing, he knew, he'd stacked the goddamned deck, it wasn't in the cards!

If that blond bitch, who'd started it all, if she double-crossed him again—

When the heavy old-fashioned brass door knocker sounded—clump-clump-clump—echoing through the whole house, Willa Briggs considered not answering it. But when it hammered again, at once and with an insistent urgency, she muttered a "damn" and set down the clay figure which had been frustrating her anyway, wiped her hands on a cloth, and left the attic that Fletcher had converted into a studio for her, going down the two flights of stairs without turning off the Mozart. She wondered whether she should take off the smudged smock, decided it didn't matter. The big old house felt so empty that she hesitated in the hall, but only a second, and then flipped on the porchlight and opened the front door.

The man who stood there in the overhead glow looked vaguely familiar: a husky, well-dressed man with a receding hairline and thick gray sideburns. "Mrs. Briggs?" It was a hoarse mutter.

"Yes."

"My name's Heckman. I've come to see your husband."

Then she recognized him: Wallace Heckman, the Congressman. She'd seen his picture in the paper often enough. "Won't you come in?"

He stood stolidly a moment, as if deciding, then stepped inside with, she noted, a smooth, athletic grace in spite of his bulk. "Is Briggs home?"

Not *Mr. Briggs,* or *Fletcher,* or *your husband*—just that: Briggs. For an instant she had the impression that

Wallace Heckman was drunk; then she decided that, rather, he was struggling for control. "I'm sorry," she said, "he isn't. He'll probably be in around eleven. If it's anything really—" But she stopped. Abruptly she knew. "What's happened? It's one of the children, isn't it?" She heard the breathless rush of the words. "Which one? What's happened?"

"It's not one of your children," Wallace Heckman growled. But before the relief could reach her, she became conscious of his eyes: a red-rimmed stare, furiously brilliant, ferocious. "It's my child."

His grimness unnerved her. And what he said made no sense. "Fletcher's working tonight. In his office. I'll telephone him."

"Never mind," he barked, the hard muscles of his jaw quivering, and in his eyes now, unmistakably, something savage, something cruel and almost, yes, demented. "This is personal. Between him and me." And before she could move or respond, he pivoted, opened the door and, without a word or nod of thanks or farewell, went outside, leaving the door open.

She simply stood there. Feeling the wind. Stunned. This was crazy. Whatever was happening was as wild and mad as the deranged look in that man's eyes. Yet there was misery there, too—a desolation. She heard the motor of his car.

She heard the mockingbird in the eaves trying to imitate the sound.

She had to warn Fletcher. *Between him and me.* The man was dangerous in this state, absolutely murderous. She shut the door and went to the phone on the table. She dialed the university number. No answer. What time was it? Past nine thirty? The college switchboard would be closed.

Then there was only one alternative: she had to alert him. And, not so incidentally, to demand to know what the hell, precisely and exactly, was going on.

She threw her striped cape over her shoulders and went outside, paused in surprise to see his MG still in the driveway. He must have decided to walk after the minor and decidedly polite contretemps, to walk off his annoyance and frustration or whatever it was he had felt.

Rather than move cars around to release her Country Squire wagon, she decided to take his MG. He always left the key in the ignition: another of his small annoying habits. And as she got in, she wondered again why a man as tall as Fletcher would enjoy curling himself in this small sporty convertible. Unless it was part of an image, an image of himself that he—

God, what a shrew. Not yet forty—but the fatal natal day fast approaching—she was turning into a genuine, forty-carat hellhag, even in her own mind. Would she, in time, become a bully and a shrew?

Like Hotspur. Her mockingbird that had adopted the Briggs family and the big broad porch for its home. She had dubbed him Hotspur because he was so cantankerous, so primed for battle always, the scourge of every animal in the neighborhood, large or small. Only the size of a robin, though thinner, he would zero in on the rump of any cat that unhappily strolled into view and he could sound like any other bird, including a crowing rooster or a cawing crow, and could imitate anything from a barking dog to a coughing neighbor or creaking fence gate. Fletcher often teased her because of her amusement and fondness for the bird that had either ventured or been blown out of its latitude.

Fletcher. Fletcher had the kindest and most gentle eyes of any person, man or woman or child, whom she had ever known. She had fallen in love first with those eyes: intensely blue and slightly uncertain and even now, still so very young and vulnerable.

She bore down on the gas pedal. Fletcher could never have done anything, anything, that could conceivably rouse the vengeful fury that she had glimpsed on Congressman Heckman's face.

* * *

"You're usually so good, Fletcher. Damn good. But not tonight. Other things on your mind, right?"

"Sorry, Annette . . . Curious: I never think about it that way. One person being good, another worse, or better."

"That's not romantic, right? Well, Prof, you can't have everything."

"Do you want me to turn the light on?"

"I thought you were the romantic one. This way, we've just enough light from the window to see each other and not enough to make sure we know it's only a dreary faculty office and I'm lying on your damn couch which, if I never mentioned it before, has a broken spring. You want to know something?"

"I thought I knew everything."

"With your clothes on you look bony."

"That's a comfort."

"It's a compliment, idiot. You're not. Bony. Give me a cigarette."

"Annette, you said you understood."

"I lied."

"It was your idea, this—a way of saying good-bye, you said."

"Tell me, do you ball her?"

"Who?"

"You know who. Her. Your ever-loving."

"Willa. My wife's name is Willa."

"Right on, man, and excuse my ass."

"You mean do I make love to her? Yes, I do."

"Even since you and I—wow. Oh sit down. It's not my business, right?"

"Annette, do we really have to?"

"We don't have to do anything. Free will. Basis of the Protestant ethic, as well as Anglo-Saxon law. Right?"

"Right!"

"Oh, stop growling. You didn't really want to screw me tonight. You don't want to screw me anymore, ever. What am I supposed to do, slash my wrists?"

"Annette, I've said I'm sorry. It's not much, I know, not enough, but—"

"Oh, don't go on laying on the nine-tails. That's one of your problems, you know. You feel so *responsible.* About everything. It tears you up inside. You see too damn much, feel too much."

"Sometimes I think you're really older than I am."

"That's *my* problem, man: I was born old."

"Shall we get dressed?"

"Why not? Take it from me, I feel at least a century older tonight. Oh, Fletch, I'm sorry. I'm not trying to—you don't know how grateful I am really. True. Grateful to you. So please forgive me. Please?"

"Things are getting kind of turned around here, aren't they? If anyone should ask for forgiveness—"

"I did do one thing for you, didn't I? I did make you feel . . . young again, didn't I?"

"As if the search might be worth the candle, after all. Yes."

"And now?"

"I don't know. God's truth. Sometimes I think maybe the damn candle's gone out."

"Oh, Fletch—no."

"Maybe there aren't any answers, after all."

"And that's what hurts you, isn't it? Hurts you deep and hard. That's why you got into this teaching bit in the first place."

"All cowards run when reality gets too overwhelming. Run and try to get a perspective and then rationalize and philosophize. But they keep running all the same."

"There's nothing wrong with teaching. Someone has to, right? And if you can communicate your ideas and if they're good ideas—"

"Good. Solid. With one flaw: they don't apply to that jungle out there. Maybe we all ought to do what the kids are doing. Go out to the desert, escape to the mountains, gaze at the sky, get stoned on grass—"

"Fletch . . . maybe, even if there aren't any final

answers, what matters is to go on looking for them anyway. Not like Diogenes looking for an honest man, more like Sisyphus pushing that damned stone up the mountain. Maybe that's the way to stay alive, to keep from ossifying into some stale, sterile pattern like the organization freaks."

"You know, you *were* born older than me. You'd make some man—hey, hey, are you crying?"

"Me? Sure. Why not? I cry often. Oh, hell, I know what you think of me. The new liberated woman. And how Jesus-bitten wrong you are, Professor. The one thing in the world I really want, I know now I really want, is someone, a man, to take care of. Maybe even kids later. Can you believe that?"

"I think I've known it for some time, Annette."

"So, you see, I owe you a thanks or two. For splitting. Maybe someday I'll be able to thank you, but right now—"

"Shhh—"

"What?"

"Listen."

"I hear. There's someone in the building."

"Is the door locked?"

"Now it is."

"Don't talk. Don't move."

"But—"

"Do what I say!"

Was she really turning into a shrew? Oh, not your standard conventional type, not Willa Briggs: better a bitter silence than a shout. All the way to the campus, fighting the stick shift on Fletcher's MG, she had asked herself that question over and over, in fear. Bleak and morbid thoughts again: another of those moods. Explaining but not excusing why she'd been so polite-bitchy to Fletcher after dinner—as if whatever was happening to David and Peggy, *whatever* it was, were his fault more than hers. But she had been fighting one of those depressions again, still was. Her elderly doctor, the only person with whom she'd discussed the matter, had suggested her "little blue spells" might be tied in with her time of life, possibly a precursor to an early menopause or even a handsome young woman's quite normal fear of growing old—well, thank you, Doctor, thank you very *much*. Anyway, that was all too pat, too easy. Everything in her nature and upbringing insisted that a human being can analyze and comprehend and then act not only rationally but correctly. *Properly* is the word, isn't it, Mother dear? But what if two people trying to live together came down to a matter of emotion rather than thought? And what if then the ship, without reason and conscious control, was rudderless long before the journey was over? At the mercy, as it now appeared to her, of whatever seas and weather it chances upon. And why—will someone, Mother, Doctor, will someone please explain *why* she couldn't talk all of this over with her own husband?

The bell in the tower was chiming and the window of Fletcher's office on the third floor of the Law School building was quite dark. Unaccountably dark because if he had walked home, she would have seen him, or if she had been too abstracted by her own damnable self-pity to see *him*, *he* certainly would have have recognized his own car on the street. Of course, someone might have given him a lift.

The faculty parking lot was deserted except for one large car, a two-tone black and gold. She slowed the MG, stopped. Hesitated. Then, as she was about to drive on, she saw a figure emerge from the door of the building: a bulky figure, a man, shoulders hunched forward, set and angry. And she remembered, as she saw him get into the black and gold car, the expression on Wallace Heckman's face in the front hall. The big car shot heavily forward, motor thundering, and disappeared down the curving, tree-arched campus street.

Where was he going now? Should she follow? All of a sudden she felt like a perfect fool. And then alarm shot through her. What is he had found Fletcher in his office, what if the lights were off because—

She leaped out and ran toward the building. Chiding herself: it was no jungle they lived in but a civilized town in the most civilized part of the country. Wallace Heckman had been upset, but perhaps he was a man who overreacted—as she herself was obviously overreacting now. Then, as her momentum carried her to the steps, a light came on above.

She stopped. She looked up. She must have been mistaken earlier. Fletcher and Wallace Heckman must, then, have had their confrontation, whatever it was about, and it was over. Thank God.

But why then had the light been out? And why was it now on again?

A shadow moved, indistinctly, above, and then the light went out.

It had all been for nothing. There was nothing to worry about. She retraced her steps to the little car. Slowly. Still baffled. But relieved. There'd be some quitc simple explanation; Fletcher would tell her. A pleasant shock of anticipation passed through her. She'd surprise him when he came out by throwing on the lights. She'd save him the walk home. They might even drive around awhile, perhaps out into the country. She felt the tautness inside give away, go slack. Instead of getting behind the wheel, she took her place in the passenger's seat—possibly the idea of a ride in the country would occur to Fletcher. It would be better that way. She began to wonder what it would be like to make love in a car again rather than in the very comfortable but overfamiliar bedroom. She smiled: imagine Fletcher, at six four, trying to make love in the bucket seat of a little MG. With the stick shift between. She might mention it to him, playfully, just to see that boyish glint dart into his eyes: he always seemed, for some reason obscure to her, to enjoy making love more if she suggested it. Which, for some reason even more obscure, she could only rarely bring herself to do, even when she desired him most intensely. Ladies don't, do they, Mother? It's not ladylike, not truly feminine. He also responded with quick gaiety when her own sense of fun flashed between them.

The door of the building opened. And, instead of one, two figures appeared on the steps of the Law School building.

Two.

A very tall, angular man and a small girl, not too slender, wearing a very short pleated skirt. The tall man wore a tweed jacket with patches at the elbow and he smoked a pipe and he moved with slow casualness.

The girl waited while the man turned and locked the door. Then they came down the steps together. They walked along the footpath leading around the side of the building.

She felt an almost overpowering impulse to flip on the headlights, to flood them. Although she knew who the girl was. And she knew, too, that it was perfectly natural for his teaching assistant, a graduate student in law, to be helping him, even at night, alone in the building.

With the lights out?

Everything seeped out of Willa Briggs. Everything. Forever. She was not even certain she was still sitting there. Or who was sitting there. If anyone. She felt nothing now. Absolutely nothing. As the two figures disappeared around the corner of the building.

Tonight she'd give the senile old bastard the money and tell him where to shove it, and nothing else, nothing else tonight. With all the money she'd paid him over the years you'd think the foul-breathed dirty old son of a bitch would at least have spent some of it to have this driveway, or wagon trail, smoothed out or even paved.

She had no time tonight: she'd try to explain and he'd sit there with his wrinkled old face tilted sideways and grin, with his knowing rheumy eyes on her, waiting. No time, you asshole, no time! Paul might go home early, might even be on his way there now. For a while, after leaving the club, she'd been convinced he was following her at a distance. Then, after she had turned onto Highmeadow Road and the car had passed her, some cheap old Ford or Chevy, she'd been momentarily relieved; but convinced all the more that she had better get back to town as fast as possible. If Paul ever learned about this—the money, just the money, not to mention the rest—he'd explode completely. Like a volcano. That's what it was like, anyway, her whole goddamned life, like living on top of a volcano, day after day and night after night. And when Paul exploded, she knew what it was like. It had happened to her only once, that afternoon on the boat before they were married, that day when he'd tried to run down the naked boy swimming to shore, tried to run him down with the fifty hp outboard that could have chewed him to bits. He'd gone berserk when he failed. Until then she'd never known or seen or suffered such blank savage fury; even her father, that mean bastard, had never been that wild, even at his drunkest. If Paul ever learned, ever began to suspect where all her allowance money had really gone, month after month, leaving out the rest, leaving out the important part, he'd kill. Someone. Stegner. Her. Probably both. Kill. And if he ever had any inkling of the other ways this slimy old bastard made her pay—

She brought the car to a stop in the darkness under the trees. The porchlight was on and, inside, the large high-beamed rustic-paneled living room was lighted. Oh, he was expecting her; he knew she'd come, had to come. She sat behind the wheel trying to smother the hate inside—which, at this point every time, seemed to turn her blood to acid and her bones to liquid. She was sick all through. Again. Weak and sick. It seemed to get worse every time. Yet she had to move and had to get out, go inside. If Paul telephoned the house—she had tried to cover herself on that—but if he went home and discovered she hadn't come in—

She opened the door of the car and stepped out. Reluctance pulled at her muscles, drew at her nerves. She had stopped asking herself why she was doing this. In the beginning she had been thinking only of herself. Hell, yes, she liked being Mrs. Paul Wharton. And she liked having clothes and money and a Jaguar all her own. She'd been hungry once, hungry and worse, and she'd made up her mind when she met Paul that she'd never be that way again. Then, later, as Paul's really pathetic jealousy and insecurity began to reveal what a sad uncertain boy he was underneath—well, call it pity, call it love, maybe it was both mixed together in a way that she couldn't understand. All she knew now was that he'd always suspected what had actually taken place on the boat and that if he ever were to be told the truth, and by the one witness who had been willing to swear, even in court, that she'd been attacked—

With an effort of will she moved toward the light beneath the shadow of the high sloping roof. Her shoes scuffed through the fallen leaves. Yes, but what if, instead of this obscene pilgrimage every month, she were simply to explain it to Paul, force him to see, to understand? She'd been young, impetuous; driving his car on a bright summer afternoon, feeling free and alive, she'd given in to a sudden impulse, a whim, a quick physical desire. But in more lucid moments, she knew she could never explain it all: how she'd gone to Farago to get medical evidence, how she'd bribed the old man, using her body, then how—all to convince Paul, to keep from losing him—she'd even given in to his angry demand that she file formal charges with the police. She had known then, whether he knew it or not, that he'd been testing her, pushing her that last step toward convincing him. As he still did every tense and terrible day and night. Testing *her* even though he knew, had to know, that whatever brutality had been committed on her had been done by him in that first rage on the boat. Knew that those wounds, inside and out, were the very ones that would convince anyone that a crime had been committed. The irony was not so much that he had never been able to believe her since, possibly *because* he knew who had committed whatever crime, but that she, except for Farago and this old man, had been a faithful wife. More faithful than many she knew. Faithful *because* of what had happened. But the marriage that she had dreamed would bring her freedom had brought her slavery—and not to Paul's jealousy alone but to Farago and this filthy hateful old man and their disgusting and bestial demands. As the years passed, she had become more aware of the ironies and they had become more and more sickening, not in the least amusing—appalling, insufferable.

She was on the porch now, hesitating again. Not tonight. She couldn't face it. She only wished she'd taken more of the pills, the downers, a fistful. She shuddered, picturing the other nights, the other scenes: her standing in the light and taking off her clothes, slowly, one by one, very slowly, while the old man sat staring with hooded, glittering, watery eyes, a trickle of saliva running down his chin. And then, because he couldn't do anything else, the unspeakable things he demanded of her. She was convinced that he spent most of his time between her visits sitting in there thinking up more ways to—

She opened the door and went inside.

And saw him.

An apparition, unreal, incredible.

Then she saw his eyes. Or the two white holes where his eyes had been.

She began to scream. She knew she was screaming, loud, over and over, but she heard no sound. Only his voice, or what was left of it, uttering some horrendous inhuman noise, part whimper or moan, part plea. He knew she was there: he knew she was coming, he had heard the car: he could not possibly see her. Or anything. Ever again.

Still screaming soundlessly, beginning to retch, she

turned away. Now what? What should she do? What could she do? She stumbled outside and off the porch. Then she was vomiting over her gown, into the leaves, her entire body heaving in pain-filled paroxysms.

Paul. He had found out, and he had let her come here to see for herself what he was capable of.

But then . . . what would he do to her?

The courthouse was familiar to Wallace Heckman, and at night it had a particular atmosphere: relaxed, quiet—offices closed, courtrooms empty, janitors at work. He was seated in a private room in the police headquarters on the second floor, a cubicle reserved for interviews, interrogations, any private matters that might come up. The anteroom, though, which was the hub, seemed to have more activity tonight than he recalled from the days when he had been prosecuting attorney. A few minutes ago Lieutenant Hutchinson, the young officer whom he didn't remember from the old days, had informed him that a squad car had picked up Fletcher Briggs, who had not objected and he was now on his way to headquarters. Did Heckman think Ben should inform Chief Diehl? He'd already been disturbed at home once tonight and unless the matter was of great importance, the young man made clear he'd just as soon not summon his superior again. Heckman had shaken his head: he was handling this.

He himself had searched all over town, including the Faculty Club, but he hadn't wanted to make inquiries that would stir too much curiosity: for Dennis' sake this thing had to be kept quiet, damn it. Then he had phoned Kay—and the phone had rung ten times, and when he had dialed again and the result was the same, he knew: she had taken Dennis to the hospital. Even though he'd told her not to, had made clear she should not, damn it. He'd had to decide then whether to go to the hospital, try to convince Leroy Farago not to make a police report regardless of what he found, or to go to the police himself. He'd compromised by phoning the hospital and asking the doctor to call him at police headquarters and then he had come here and convinced young Hutchinson to have Fletcher Briggs picked up without his lodging a formal complaint against him. Wallace Heckman knew his way around, always had, and he was going to do all he could not to pull this off with as little further damage to his son as possible. This is where he belonged, anyway. He was a man dedicated to the law, sworn to uphold it. He had been taught, and he believed, that only law, however imperfectly executed from time to time, had allowed man to survive. *Ergo* . . . regardless of the savage rage in him, regardless of the aching jungle lust for revenge, he must not lose control; he must, if possible, allow the law to handle this matter.

But when the thought of what Fletcher Briggs had done tonight came to him, he had to wonder just how far we had come from the irrational depths, the primordial swamp. What he was doing now, what he had to do, was to keep his mind diverted from the doubts that kept slithering into it, as they had ever since he learned. *I didn't do it. I didn't do anything. I fought.* Yet there were no bruises, none visible anyway. But if he hadn't been forced, would he have told his father anything? Christ, what was he thinking, imagining? That the boy had responded? Had even helplessly enjoyed what—

"There's a call for you, Congressman. Line two."

He hadn't been conscious of the office door opening. "Thanks." He picked up the phone and punched the lighted square button. "Wallace Heckman. Hello?"

"Wally?" He recognized Leroy Farago's quiet, calm voice and found himself clutching the telephone. "I've just completed a very preliminary superficial examination." Pain climbed from the grip on the telephone up his entire arm and into his shoulder. "Wally, it's not good news, I'm sorry. Are you alone? Can we talk?"

"Go on with it, Leroy."

"He was hysterical. I've given him an injection and

he's resting now. Now listen, Wally, and try not to get too excited. I'd say he was attacked in three different ways. Fellatio. On him and—I had to ask some questions as well—on him and by him. And, of course, buggery. There's some damage to the rectal tissue, but minor." And when Wallace Heckman could not speak "Wally?" His breath tore painfully at his chest; a hand clutched his heart, twisting. "Wally?"

"I'm here" was all he could manage: a whisper.

"I'd like your permission to admit him to the hospital—"

"What the hell do I have to say about it? Didn't Kay do that already?" Damn her, damn her for not—

"Kay's told me how you feel about what I'm going to suggest, but I'd like to bring Dr. Rosenbluth into the case. He's a psychiatrist and—"

"No."

"Listen anyway. He's a down-to-earth type and, in my opinion, the best man this side of Boston."

"No."

"Wally, you're an adult and you can stick to any ideas you want to believe. You can be strong, you can believe we're all captains of our fates, whatever bullshit carries you through, but this is a child, your child, and something's happened to him."

"Don't tell me something's—" Then he sat back, his mind working again. "Leroy, how about a deal?"

"Doctors don't make *deals,*" Farago's voice said, wearily.

"That's your brand of bullshit. Now you listen. I'll let you bring in Rosenbluth if you'll forget to file a police report."

"I can't do that and you know it. A crime's been committed and—"

"If you file a report, that'll be aiding and abetting that crime!" His voice was rasping, a growl. "You're a physician, not God."

"If you're not reporting it to the police, what are you doing at police headquarters?"

"I'm handling this. Is it a deal, goddamn it?"

"No deal. I'm thinking of my license, yes, but I'm thinking of Dennis, too."

"Who the hell do you think I'm thinking of?"

A long silence. He could hear Farago breathing.

Then: "I'll hold off the report. He's sleeping now, so I wouldn't want Rosenbluth in till morning anyway. You hear me, Wally? I'll think it over."

"Thanks, Leroy." A whisper.

And a soft friendly whisper in return: "Go to hell."

Click. The line was humming. Slowly, very slowly, he set down the telephone. And stared at it. This wasn't really happening, of course. He didn't really believe any of this. If this was happening at all—and of course it wasn't—then it was happening to someone else. Some stranger.

Stranger. The idea had been haunting him for what seemed not to be forever: that eternity since he'd left the house. Did he really know Dennis at all? Was his son really a person to him, a human being? And if not, why not? Because he, Wally Heckman, had not loved? Because he had not given enough of himself, his time—

"Hello, Heckman. I've been told you wanted to see me." It was Fletcher Briggs. In the doorway. Tall and slightly slouched, dead pipe between his teeth, reddish eyebrows cocked, no hat. "But no one would say why. Or, I might add, what right you have to send for me this way."

Ben Hutchinson was standing beside him. "He's been told nothing, sir. Like you instructed."

"Thanks, Lieutenant. You may go."

Ben Hutchinson seemed to take a long time to think this over, while Briggs' eyes studied him. Then the officer said: "I don't think so, Congressman. You see, I may have overstepped my authority already—"

"I'll agree with that," Fletcher Briggs said.

"I'm sorry, Congressman." Hutchinson shook his head. "Anything said in this room's confidential.

What's the legal word—privileged. But I've got to know what's going on before I can take on any more authority here at headquarters." He closed the door and leaned against it.

"It's a point," Briggs said then. "You haven't been prosecuting attorney for almost five years, *Congressman.*"

"Shut up," he said, very softly, seeing Briggs' eyebrows arch higher as that slow mockery, which Heckman remembered from the courtroom, entered his blue eyes. "Briggs, where have you been all evening?"

"Well, let's see. After I had three brandies with the Sikkim of Sakarta, we decided to hunt polar bear with spear guns. Where have *you* been?"

Wallace Heckman recognized the tactic, shook his head from side to side, feeling the muscles pulling at his spine. "It won't wash, Briggs, so I'd advise you not to take that tack." He had never much liked Briggs, in court or out, that joking superior detached attitude of his, and after he'd copped out and taken that teaching job, a slap in the face at the rest of the profession, too good to take his chances in the legal arena with the rest, he'd all but forgotten him. "Briggs, a little boy—" He had to clear his throat. "A boy in this town aged eleven years was assaulted this evening, and he's given a description of his assailant. Red hair, mustache, pipe, jacket, elbow patches, height."

"Assaulted? How assaulted?"

His throat was dry, very dry. "Homosexually assaulted."

Now Briggs was frowning, his rusty brows becoming a very straight line. He took the pipe from his mouth. "Heckman, we're entering Kafka country. Are you accusing me—"

Without being aware that he had moved, Heckman was standing up, shouting: "He introduced himself to the boy by name. Your name!"

There was silence after the shout.

Then Briggs made a popping sound on his pipe and

shoved it into his pocket. "Heckman, I don't have to answer a charge like this. Or defend myself. I feel like a damned fool doing it. You don't know me well, but I'm a married man, I have two kids of my own."

"Nobody," Heckman said, "nobody knows anyone else when it comes to things like this. How do I know how a pervert's mind operates?" He saw Briggs stiffen, his shoulders straightening, but he didn't make a move or reply. "I'm going to ask you again: where have you been all evening?"

"Look, Heckman. You have no official right to interrogate me." He glanced at Ben Hutchinson. "You make note of that, Officer." Then his eyes narrowed at Heckman. "I was in my office in the Law School building on the campus."

That did it. Now he had him. "I went there. There was no light. No one answered my knock. And the door was locked."

He waited. And what he saw—that swift startled look, that quick guilt that he had learned to catch when he trapped a witness—sent his blood surging. Without volition, abruptly certain again, he moved. Around the corner of the desk. A long step. And then he felt the bone of Briggs' face against the bones of his fist and heard the little wooden sound that a fist makes and saw Briggs staggering sideways, saw him totter and finally, losing his balance, start to fall to the floor.

Officer Ben Hutchinson was in front of him as he took another step. The young man's hands gripped his upper arms, held. He struggled to free himself, discovered with amazement that he couldn't. Behind Hutchinson, Briggs was steadying himself, one hand running over his cheek, his eyes dazed and blinking, brows drawn together, tight. Heckman whirled away, turning his back on them, breaking the young officer's grasp, and suddenly he was breathing hard, his heavy shoulders heaving. It had done no good. It was not enough, nothing was enough, nothing he could do would ever repay Briggs for what he had done tonight. Not even killing him.

It was Briggs' voice he heard then, behind him. "Heckman, you listen to me now. I'm going to chalk that up. I'm going to put this one behind us because of your condition. But now it's my turn. I'm going to ask some questions, and *you're* going to answer." The voice, harsh but shaky, came closer. "What kind of car was I driving?"

Car? "A Chevy Vega. Several years old. Metal-gray. With a motor that didn't sound like it belonged in it! Souped-up. More like a racing engine. How much more detailed could you want it?"

"I drive an MG sports coupe, *blue,* and my wife has a Country Squire wagon, tan and brown." Briggs took a deep audible breath. His tone was hard. "And every time I go out to commit a felony, I make sure I wear the same clothes I wear in the classroom and I always, repeat always, give my name first. It makes it so much cozier, especially in homosexual assault."

What was he up to now? Heckman turned, slowly. Briggs stood there—no taunting now, silent, grim. And Heckman felt something collapse inside. Christ. But without the conviction, the certainty—had it been only a blind obsession? Then what did he have to hold him up, to sustain him?

"You told him your name," Heckman insisted, "and said you were a friend of mine." His own voice sounded baffled—not like his voice at all.

"A friend of yours?" He saw Briggs cast a suspicious glance toward the young officer at the door, who was staring. "Heckman, who was this kid?"

Briggs had guessed. He knew. Heckman caught a gleam of compassion in the other man's eyes, a quick realization, sadness. Even regret. "My son," Heckman said and sat down, the fight gone from him, his body gone flaccid. "His name is Dennis." Still, he didn't understand. It didn't make sense.

"Good God," Briggs breathed. Then he came closer.

"Heckman, I was in my office all evening. I was with a girl. That's why the door was locked and the lights were off. The girl will tell you if you still don't believe me. Does that satisfy you, Wally?" The sudden use of his first name startled him. "I wouldn't tell you this, tell anyone, if it weren't true, would I?"

Heckman simply couldn't figure it out, though. He had to ask: "But . . . but why the hell would anyone use someone else's name?"

"I don't know." Slowly. Very slowly. "I'm damned if I know. It doesn't make any—nothing makes any sense."

Ben Hutchinson cleared his throat. "Can I interrupt? I've just been standing here thinking. We've had two very strange crimes in town here tonight. Both about as weird as we've had since I been on the force. I'm only wondering, mind you—it's just an idea—I'm wondering if there just might be any connection."

"What other crime?" Briggs asked.

"Well, it sounds farfetched as hell, but somebody tore up a grave in the cemetery early this evening and strewed bones all over the place."

"Whose bones?" Briggs asked.

Coralie Wharton drove the white Jaguar along Elmhurst Street, which was wide and curving and tree-lined with large old houses, all meticulously maintained, set well apart one from the other by expanses of shrub-studded and manicured lawns. The spasms of retching had become less frequent, but she was quivering in every nerve and muscle.

The house itself, which she knew would never look really familiar to her, appeared serene as ever: an old red-brick structure, tall and narrow, imposing, covered with thousands of strands of ivy. She turned the long snout of the Jag onto the driveway of white gravel which gleamed blindingly in the flare of headlight beams. The wide sliding doors of the garage, which had once been a handsome carriage house, were open.

And Paul's maroon Mercedes sedan was not there.

Then perhaps, perhaps, it had not been Paul, after all, who had done those horrible things to the old man. How could he have, how was it possible for him, why had she ever imagined such a thing when Paul had been with her through dinner? And if Paul had done it, he'd be here now, waiting for her. But if not Paul, then who? And for what reason? Someone who had not known she would go there tonight? Who did not expect him to be discovered—

She left her car in the driveway. The gaping darkness of the carriage house, when she turned off the lights, made her shudder even more violently as she hurried along the curving white-stone path to the front entrance, thick double doors carved in relief and framed by stately high white pillars.

Inside, she was tempted to give way, to collapse onto the sofa in the drawing room off the center hall. How she had managed to make it all the way back to town, simply to keep the car on the road, was a mystery. A goddamned miracle. The image of old man Stegner on his knees, begging, eyeless, bleeding, had leaped onto the windshield over and over, as onto a motion-picture screen so that at times she could not see an approaching car or the road itself. She was going up the graceful curve of stairway now. The sounds still echoed in her mind: the rasping, raw squawk and the wretched whine in that voice that had already been used up. In the car the sounds had filled her head so that she couldn't hear the roar of the motor. The bastard deserved it. She went into the large bedroom. The son of a bitch slimy old man had it coming and somebody gave it to him. She didn't care. He deserved it. She didn't care a damn. But she seemed to be crying for some reason.

She discovered the pills in her hand. She realized she was in the bathroom and there was water running so she must have turned it on. Hadn't she taken a handful on the way home? Found them in her purse with one hand and swallowed them dry. so they gagged her, and then realized that she didn't know which kind she had swallowed and if they were the wrong kind, the morning kind, then she'd never get to sleep, then sleep wouldn't come all night, if ever, and that image and those sounds would drive her insane. She washed down four of the green and yellow capsules: she knew those were the night ones. So if she took the wrong ones in the car, this double-dose would offset the effect. Leroy. For all she knew—she often suspected—he had hooked her on purpose. So he could have her the way he wanted to have her, so he could force her to do it his way, any way he—

Oh, sweet Christ, how long would it take? How long to turn off her mind? She stripped off her green gown, which reeked of her own vomit and stale perfume, and then took off all the rest, as Paul had ordered her to. Let him. She'd be asleep. Let him if it gave him such a kick even when she was asleep. Nobody had ever fucked her because he wanted to fuck her, just her, a person, not just a body, Coralie herself, whoever she was. No wonder then she'd wished so often that she'd been born ugly or deformed, anything so that she'd know when someone really wanted to—

She heard a sound. What? Downstairs? The front door? Oh, God, what if Paul had come home this early! Before she had a chance to sink into that oblivion that had to come soon tonight, had to, had to. She stood tensely listening for a step on the carpet of the stairway. But if Paul had come in, he'd pour himself a drink first, a real blockbuster. Because Paul had to be bombed, really bombed, just to get it up lately—

She made it to the bed, ripped back the blanket and sheet, fell across it, then twisted her body until she was covered. Had she locked the front door? Had she even closed it? She wished now that she had not always insisted that no servant live in the house. But she couldn't bear to be spied on, watched. By anyone, ever. The way that old man with his field glasses had—

She could see Stegner stumping up the stairs with his dangling wire-bound hands extended, bloodying the carpet, but he wouldn't make it, he couldn't make it, the joke was on him tonight, not a chance, you dirty old man, with your ankles wired together, never make it—

She rolled, wondering why, and flipped off the lamp on the bedside table. Darkness. At last. It enveloped her. It allowed her to close her eyes. It wouldn't be long now. No sound on the stairs. No sound anywhere. Quiet, blessed quiet, and more to come. She tried to burrow down to reach that other, that deeper quiet. In which she would, at first, begin to float. In a noiseless, pale, gliding, fishy world as if the sea enclosed her, silent and over whelming and welcome, filling her mind, blurring out that other world beyond so that everything would become dim and dead and meaningless—

There it was again. A sound. When there should be no sound now. In the house? Or outside: a night bird batting its wings against the walls? Or was this only another of those cruel jokes that her medicine played? She lay quite still. Her muscles and flesh felt limp and lifeless. It couldn't be the old man. He couldn't have come this far. He couldn't have come this far on his knees. And it wasn't Paul: she'd hear the clink of the decanter and he'd come swaggering up the stairs, never quite staggering, and he'd come in and turn on the light because he always said he had to look at her to—

Shock. That was it, of course. It wasn't the pills, only shock settling in. The pills hadn't had time to work. Yet she didn't know how long it had been since she took the ones in the car, if she had. Or since she took the ones here, in the house. That's what happened: time got scrambled. Minutes could seem hours, or hours could seem seconds, and there was never any way of predicting or knowing. How long now since—

There was someone else in the room. In the dark. She forced her eyes open. Darkness. She felt like screaming. But her mouth was dry, her throat locked. She strained to penetrate the darkness. The stillness. Whoever it was was not moving. Or breathing. She couldn't scream, couldn't, any more than the old man could scream after he had run out of sound. Then she heard a sound. It was her own heart. Thumping. As if to break out of—

Like the shocking, shattering report of a gun going off at close range, light exploded in the room. It blazed with a dazzling blinding radiance, razor-sharp and merciless.

"Hello, Cunt."

Had she heard a voice actually? And was there light or were her eyes closed and she was only imagining—

"We meet again."

"Who?"

She shut her eyes against the brilliance, but she could still feel the stabbing at her brain. She uttered a low moan. Why couldn't she *sleep?*

"Paul?" Was it Paul after all? He'd been here all along, waiting—

"No, baby, not Paul. Paul comes later. We're going to wait for Paul. Together."

He was talking gibberish and she had to find some way to scream. If she could open her mouth. If she dared open her eyes—

"Look, Cunt. Look, I said. . . . Please."

And then she did open her eyes. And looked into his face, the face she had tried to forget, the light turning his blond hair into a halo of shimmering silver. His lips were curled into a smile. A pleasant smile. It had to be one of those hallucinations Leroy had warned her about, had to be, the DT's of addiction, he called them, she'd had them before but nothing like—

"You ever think about me, baby?" The voice was gentle, even kind, and he leaned closer so that when he spoke the stench of his breath caused her stomach to heave, but she couldn't breathe, so she couldn't scream, if you can't breathe, how can you—

"I thought about you, baby. Plenty. Years and years."

It was no hallucination. It was real. And she was helpless to so much as turn her face away.

"Nobody to watch us now, Cunt. Old man's not looking now, is he?" His tone had taken on a singsong quality, with glee in it, a high-pitched strain of elation. "He didn't recognize you back there, did he? When you turned around and left him. That wasn't nice, Cunt, that was not nice at all. After all he did for you."

But what else could she have done? If she had called the police, how could she ever have explained what she was doing out there? To them? To Paul? To anyone? Now her mind seemed to be working again. If only he'd turn off the light, take his face away, let her sleep—

"Think baby, just think. If you'd gone to the cops instead of coming home, we wouldn't have met again, would we?"

Then she knew. *He* was the one who had done those horrible things to the old man. And now—

"You . . . you're going to kill me, aren't you?" Her voice came to her through a haze. "Yes. You are." Even though it reached her from a distance, it sounded quite natural, though, and reasonable. "Yes." And the idea calmed her somehow.

"No way, baby, no way. Not my style."

But he turned and reached to her vanity table and picked up an object that, at first, she couldn't recognize. A gun. She knew he was lying then. A rifle with a short barrel. No, a shotgun. Her father had owned one. Drunk, he had threatened, terrified the entire family. Her father had never killed anyone. But she was going to be killed now.

"No, baby, no way." He was speaking very quietly, almost tenderly. "I'm going to give you what you always wanted."

More gibberish. She wished she would—

He stepped in, fast, reached and tore back the sheet and blanket. She lay naked, huddled, quivering, almost fetal. She heard a small sound, very indistinct, that she knew she herself must have uttered because she felt a blade turn over in her throat. Her muscles were lax now, though, every nerve limp, and she hoped again that perhaps she was passing out. Oh, God, if only she had more pills, if only she could sink into—

He stood above her. "Only thing you ever wanted from me. Only thing." His tone was musing; he seemed to be trying to prolong his own pleasure. "Only now, no way. It's not where my head's at, Cunt. Even with you there like that." Then he leaned closer again, whispering: "You did that to me, too."

He straightened. He lifted the shotgun. She saw, or perhaps only imagined she saw, a smile flickering along his lips. He lifted the gun so that its dark metal caught the light. "I sawed off the barrel. Hope it's long enough."

More gibberish. She felt her mind drifting . . . floating.

There was a sound: a sharp snap. And he was holding the gun in both hands, the stock at a right angle to the barrel. She knew. He shoved a shell into the chamber. She had seen it done. He snapped the gun together.

She had to move. Find some way to move. She couldn't lie here while he killed her. But he had said he wasn't going to—

"Only thing you ever wanted from me." He came closer still, his face blurring. She heard a click when he cocked the gun. "If you don't do anything wrong—like scream—I won't pull the trigger, okay?"

But she couldn't move. Couldn't.

"Now . . . spread your goddamn legs . . . Cunt. . . . Please. . . . 'Cause you got a real thrill coming. Like you deserve."

* * *

"Didn't anyone else hear it?"

From the way they were staring at him, you would have thought he'd taken leave of his senses. The three of them continued to play their cards. He damn well knew what he'd heard.

"Do you mean to tell me, all three of you, that you didn't hear someone scream?"

His wife said, with patience: "We all heard *something*, sweetheart. Probably the TV from next door."

All the old houses in Elmhurst Street were spaced far apart, with lawns and gazebos and hedges and trees between. "Then why don't we hear the TV now?" He wasted a high trump card just for the bloody hell of it.

"You know *her,*" his wife said, with only a single sour scowl at his card. "I don't think she knows what she's doing most of the time." She cast a knowing conspiratorial glance around the table, a glance that darted past him as if he weren't there. "Personally—and I speak from experience—I think she's inebriated nine-tenths of the time. Although it may be something worse. Who knows these days? But they're both boozers. I can remember him, that Paul Wharton, coming home so crocked he couldn't make it into the house at four in the morning. And I mean when his parents were alive and he was just a *child.*" Then her eyes did meet his. "Your deal, sweetheart."

He gathered up the cards. He wished she'd stop calling him sweetheart. "If it was the television, why can't we hear it now?" he persisted.

"Oh, for God's sake. She turned it off, that's why. Let's concentrate, shall we? We *are* losing, you know."

It had been more of a shriek, or wail, than a scream. "You couldn't find an actress to make a sound like that on television."

"I'll tell you what, sweetheart," his wife said, studying her cards. "Next time you're dummy, why don't you go next door and see for yourself? That *is* what you want, isn't it?" She was being sweet. At times like these she was always very very sweet. "If he hasn't come home yet, maybe you could tuck her into bed."

"Maybe," he said, regretting the words before they were spoken, "maybe it'd be a pleasure."

That did it. The sweet smile broadened coldly and she looked quickly at the Gilberts, man and wife, who were careful to concentrate on their cards, and then directly across at him. "It's what you've been wanting to do, one way or the other, for seven years, isn't it?" Then she bid four no-trump and lit a cigarette. "You've had a lech for that blond floozie ever since Paul Wharton married her." She blew smoke furiously.

She had never before spoken this way, at least not in the presence of company or friends, and she had never been quite this crude before. So he knew that he'd goaded her too far. Call it what you will, lech or yen or desire, he had it and had had it, and he'd known that his wife was aware of it. That Coralie Wharton was one hell of a fine-looking woman, or girl. But tonight all that had nothing to do with what he had heard or with his concern. He should say to hell with everything else and he should go over there to the Wharton house and find out for himself what, if anything, was going on. That unearthly shrill cry had been one of pain, almost animallike in its intensity, and he realized that he was trembling inside. He had lost track of the bidding.

"Well," his wife challenged, "here's your chance, sweetheart. You're dummy this hand."

His impulse was strong. Whether she believed him or not, it had nothing to do with Coralie Wharton as a woman. It had to do with the simple human, civilized obligation to respond to someone crying out in anguish or terror. But he only sat there, wishing that they hadn't agreed—at *her* suggestion naturally—to drink nothing stronger than coffee or tea at these weekly bridge sessions. He sat there knowing that if he stood up, no matter what he might discover at the Wharton's, she'd make life a living hell, or worse, for months. How could a woman be so damned jealous when she didn't give a damn about him as a man anyway and hadn't for years? Oh, to hell with it.

Part Three

On her way home from the campus Willa Briggs had made up her mind, very firmly, that she could not allow this thing to throw her into a tailspin. The incredulity remained, the shock, yes, but underneath she was not really surprised—it was as if she had been expecting something, perhaps not this but something, for a long time. Well, whatever she did now, she must not permit herself to react in some irrational way.

She was wandering around the house for some time, room to room, without aim or reason or destination. Outside now, Hotspur was beginning his nightly serenade. Bold and brazen during the day, at night he put forth such pure and varied tones that she had often listened by the hour with quiet delight. Now the singing worked on her nerves. And so did the house. They had bought it when Fletcher decided to give up his practice to accept an associate professorship at the college. It was much too large for the four of them, really, and not the sort of house they had ever talked of living in: gabled and furbelowed and tricked out with Victorian gingerbread, a monstrosity really, but a monstrosity with its own charm and dignity and one they had come to love. How then had they come to live in it—in spite of all the books and theorizing and philosophizing, all those *words*—like two mute strangers? She had never been able to explain why she had reservations, at least, about his making the change of careers in midstream; it was only something vague, some question as to whether he was going into teaching because he wanted to or because he was running from something. And he had never been able to explain either. How the hell had they, two educated and civilized human beings, come to this? To tonight?

She was bending down to take up a cigarette from the box on the living-room table when something flashed inside her, a cold and hot and blinding thing that made her go rigid. She found a match. She lit the cigarette. Her hand was not trembling. Wasn't her hand supposed to tremble? She drew in the smoke. It tasted dry and nasty. She coughed. She had given up smoking two years ago. What was it she had said at the time? *I'd like to live as long as I can and since all reasonable evidence points to—*

How childish. How stupid. What difference did it really make?

And reasonable—what was reasonable? Was it reasonable for Wallace Heckman, whom she had never even met, to come into her home, murder in his stare and stance, and—

She hoped Wallace Heckman found Fletcher.

She was drifting up the stairs then. In the upstairs hall she stopped. She stood looking into her bedroom. Their bedroom. Hers and Fletcher's. The cold hot blinding thing flashed in her again. She went weak this time. She had to put up her hand and place it against the doorframe for support. But the frame itself threatened to waiver and sink, as if the sinking were some sort of contagion starting and spreading, some ancient fault in the whole structure that would bring it down around her.

But what if she were wrong? What if there were some perfectly ordinary and logical explanation for what she had seen? Or rather, what she had not seen. What she had perhaps imagined. What if—

It was then that she decided—although she wasn't just sure that it hadn't been decided for her in some way—to confirm her dread, have done with it, find proof positive. She went into the bedroom and then, very carefully, replacing every item one by one after examining it and whatever might lay behind or beneath it, she searched down the room: clothes, drawers, closets, every scrap of paper, an empty battered briefcase on the closet shelf—everything he owned.

Nothing.

Before she had half finished, she herself had begun to feel guilty. Foolish.

Nothing, nothing.

She caught sight of herself in the mirror. *You must learn to stand straight, Willa. Shoulders back. Be proud you're tall. Boys love tall girls.* Lies. More lies. She had lived with lies all her life, always. You didn't even have the guts to tell me the truth when Daddy left you, did you, Mother? Now, *more* lies!

In an abrupt and overpowering fury she ripped off the cape and flung it, saw it float across the room. Then she tore off the smock and the dirndl skirt and peasant blouse that she had imagined, fooled herself, into believing that they made her look younger, fool, fool, and then she was standing before the floor-length mirror naked and examined her own body with slow care. With disdain. But the body remained slim, the breasts lifted and full. Tall. So damned tall. *The more to enjoy.* When had he said that? How many years ago? Fletcher, who towered above her—when, how long ago? She took the dark braids into her hands, one at a time, and freed her hair, letting it fall long and full over her bare shoulders.

Why had she never been able to give herself over to him fully? What was it in her, what—

"Shrew!" she shrieked at her image. "Shrew. *Shrike!*"

She turned wildly and left the room, fast, now knowing where she was going even as she descended the stairs. The living-room curtains were open. Let them look. She started toward the kitchen for no reason at all, then thought of Fletcher's study. She went to the rear of the hall and into the cluttered book-jammed room. There she began the search again. What further proof did she need? And did she need it to convict him, to convince herself completely, or did she need it to torment herself more, torture herself with this utter desolate sense of isolation, desertion?

What she found was a half-filled quart bottle of scotch. In a drawer. A small glass beside it. Hardly an incriminating discovery in itself, what the hell. But then she recalled seeing a partly filled bottle in the closet, his closet, upstairs. He had been drinking more lately: at parties, and afterward two or three stiff nightcaps instead of one, that sort of thing. But there was always liquor in the cabinet in the dining room, all sorts and kinds. Why should he feel obliged to hide it? Upstairs, so he could get at it in the middle of the night? Here, so that he could work at night and on the weekends without making telltale trips to the cabinet? She didn't know. That was the terrible thing, the worst—she didn't have any idea. She didn't know him.

But Annette Beauchamp did, of course. Oh, hell, yes, the Annettes always did. Such tired old, weary old, worn-out games we play. She took the bottle into her hands, wrenched off the cap, poured herself a glass full. Full, why not? Sauce for the gander, and she did mean sauce, very funny. She lifted the glass to her lips, drank deeply, grimaced, then determinedly drank again.

And then it happened. A chill went down her exposed body, a chill so intense that her flesh erupted in bumps down to her toes, quivering. But inside she was hot. The burning deep inside, deep, threatened to consume her. She drank again, draining the glass, thinking of Fletcher alone in his darkened office with the small dark girl with the vivid eyes, kissing her deeply, rolling over on top of her—

She gagged. She was not being very modern. She was being Victorian, like the house. She was just not with-it, as either of her children, who were no longer children, would tell her in a second and without any coaxing, without even any excuse or stimulus, as they called it in Psychology I. Because, today, if ever really, what difference, what godly or ungodly difference, could it make where a man placed his cock? In what? In whose? She was behind the times, lagging as usual, to imagine that the act had any symbolic or ritual value, such as an expression of and climax to some deeper, more significant commitment, such as love.

Love?

She drew back and hurled the glass through the window. She stared at the black stellated hole, only afterward hearing the crash of glass breaking.

As if the act had released something in her, she whirled about and tore out of the room, her bare hip catching painfully on the sharp corner of the desk, and then she was running up the stairs, two and three at a time, her mind catching the demonic picture of herself, naked with hair flying, which muddled the bitterness and panic and frenzy into green depths.

She didn't pause on the second floor but mounted the wide stairway, the one that Fletcher had taken such pleasure building for her with his own hands and tools so they could maneuver the larger pieces down from the attic studio. The long, peaked room was still lighted by the fluorescent tubes in the wooden trough that he had also constructed. How many years since she had gone down to answer the knock on the door? She hesitated only briefly. She was not a sculptress, she was not an artist, she was only a woman, not a girl, a woman, approaching middle age and trying to fill in the emptiness that she kept denying was there, and her sculpting was as phony as his drinking, as drugs, as adultery, and procrastination and all the deadly sins.

First, she hoisted the largest piece—an ambitious abstract figure on which she had spent weeks—off the floor, using the block and tackle that he'd installed for her convenience, and when it was three feet off the floor, she released the rope and it slammed down, sending thunder through the entire house, a shuddering smashing thud, and then the choking gray dust that rose from the shattered pieces strewn in all directions only spurred her into further frenzy.

* * *

"What we require, Chief, are the court records for the four years I served as prosecuting attorney."

Chief Theron Diehl's lined and leathery face held an expression of jovial annoyance, amiable forbearance. "Wall, is that all? Congressman, I think you know that just might take a court order, the request coming from a private citizen without any business pending before the court. I'm not rightly certain."

"Well, I am," Wallace Heckman told him. "You have the authority."

Fletcher Briggs had decided to let Wallace Heckman carry the ball. His jaw ached like hell, he needed a drink and he preferred to stay detached, if possible. Also, he wasn't exactly sure why he was sitting here in the corner of the chief's private office rather than being at home where he'd been going when that patrol car picked him up about a half hour ago.

"Y'all wouldn't be ad-verse t'allowing just a ordinary peace officer t'know what brought him in here, this time a-night, to hear a request like this, would you, Congressman?"

"Two crimes have been committed within a matter of hours here tonight, Chief. Linking together, for whatever bizarre or obscure reasons, the names of Judge Stuttaford, Professor Briggs here and myself. The only manner we can imagine the three of us could ever have been linked would be in the courtroom. *Ergo.*"

"I don't know what *ergo* means, but I got to agree with the bizarre. Now, first, just how the hell did we ever arrive at this unlikely conjecture?"

"The idea was suggested by Officer Hutchinson. And the more I think about it, the more sense I think it makes. At least it's a start."

"Ben Hutchinson—that boy's goin' far in police work, that he is."

"It's a hypothesis on which to start!"

Diehl was smiling crookedly. He sat back and placed the high heels of his Western boots on the desk. "Assumption. That what that fancy word stands for? Wall, police work's not built around assumption, whatever name you give 'em. Now I'd be very much obliged if you'd explain what you meant when you said two crimes? Only one crime was reported to me and that was against private property and a dead man. But if you got any additional information—"

Fletcher waited: what the hell would Heckman do now?

"It's a personal matter."

"Congressman, now you listen, hear? No crime's a personal matter. Every crime, if it is a crime, affects this here community."

"If it means getting the records, I'll tell you. On one condition: that it's not official and that you'll take no action and make no record."

Again Fletcher waited—for Diehl this time. The older man tilted back his Stetson. He smoothed down his heavy silver mustache with a knuckle and his eyes were narrow, pale. "If somebody, even somebody like you, Congressman, reports a crime to me in my capacity as chief of police, you know's well as I do, better, I got to treat it like a crime and take appropriate action."

"There are certain circumstances—"

"Let me hear them."

Wallace Heckman considered; he even glanced, quickly, toward Fletcher. Then his face clenched. "Not unless I have your word first."

Diehl twisted his head, leveled his gaze at Fletcher. "How about you, Professor? You privy to this big secret?"

Fletcher didn't hesitate. He had begun to admire the way Wally Heckman was protecting his kid, regardless of the cost or consequence. "It's not up to me." And it wasn't. And he intended to keep it that way. This wasn't his ball game.

Chief Diehl pressed a switch on a box on his desk, said: "Tell Ben Hutchinson to haul his ass in here."

Then he smiled, amiable again. "That's a right nasty bruise you got on your chin there, Professor. Turning purple. Looks t'me like you mebbe got grounds for filing a assault charge against somebody."

"It's a personal matter," Fletcher said, then heard the echo of Wally Heckman's words as he saw Diehl's smile turn to a scowl.

"How'd you get into this anyway, Briggs? Whatever the hell it is."

"That's easy. A couple of your boys invited me into a patrol car. I could've yelled *habeas corpus*, but what the hell, I was curious."

"Hm. So'm I, Professor, so'm, I." He looked up as young Hutchinson came in. "Son, maybe you can clear up a few muddy matters here. Let's begin with why Professor Briggs was brought into police headquarters. Was there a warrant, a complaint, justifiable grounds for questioning?"

"No, sir. I did it for Congressman Heckman."

"On his orders?"

"Well, not exactly orders. As a sort of personal favor."

"Officer Hutchinson, Congressman Heckman has no more standing or authority around here than John Henry Smith down the street. Is that understood, hear?"

"Yes, sir."

"I take it you showed these gentlemen the evidence we got here of the shenanigans out to the cemetery tonight?"

"I mentioned some of it, yes."

"That's what they mean by the crime. It's none of their business, Officer Hutchinson. Hereafter, use better judgment."

"But it'll be in the paper in the—"

"Shut up." He didn't even bother to bark; he simply said it, casually. "Now let's get to this second crime that brought me all the way down here ten thirty tonight. Y'got any information on that? Its nature, its victim, if there *is* a victim?"

"No, sir, I don't."

"I see. Y'all took them into your confidence, but they didn't take you into theirs, that it?"

"Not exactly that, no. You see, they did take me into their confidence." He didn't so much as take his eyes from his chief's. "That's the reason I can't tell you. I'm sorry, sir."

"You are going to be sorry all the way up your asshole to your nitwit brain, this keeps up. I'll get back to you. Dismissed."

The young man's eyes were burning; his jaws were tight; he turned stiffly and stalked out. And Fletcher Briggs cursed Chief Diehl silently and wondered why he was concerned, it was none of his damned business.

Heckman stepped in and faced Diehl again. "I'm making an official request, as a member of the U.S. House of Representatives, although not an officer of this court, to examine the court files." That was it; that was all. He waited. And Fletcher Briggs felt the pain along his jawbone begin to throb.

Diehl's eyes became slits then. "Y'all really think this here criminal you're so hot on's somebody Judge Stuttaford might've tried, somebody maybe you convicted?"

"All I know is we have to start somewhere. Fletcher and I were opposing counsel on a fair number of cases a few years back, all sorts and kinds, and a good many of them were argued before Stuttaford."

"Police work. Jesus Christ, Congressman, I don't try to tell you how to conduct your business. Why don't you and the professor here—"

"Chief Diehl." It was Fletcher and he was standing up and he hadn't intended to say a word. "Listen. If Heckman's right, if we can zero in on whoever the hell this might be—"

"What then, what?"

"Arrest on suspicion of damaging the cemetery, hold for questioning, get him out of circulation."

"On the half-ass theory he might commit some other crime beside the one he already did?"

"Two," Heckman said. "Two."

"I don't know nothing about the second one, remember?"

The sly son of a bitch. "And you're not going to, either!"

Diehl studied him a long moment. "Examine your own files or your memories, if you're so damn set on that theory. Nobody gets those records without a court order." Then he turned to Heckman, shook his head almost apologetically. "Congressman, much as it pains me t'have t'remind you, I got a duty here and I got to play it the way it lays."

"Shit," Fletcher said.

"I've heard the word," Diehl said, nodding. "It applies to a lot I been stepping around here tonight."

"Chief," Wally Heckman said then, "if you persist in this attitude, I'm going to phone Frank Vorpahl."

"Congressman, this old head of mine's been gone over before. My head's still here."

"Let's hope it's still there when this is over."

Chief Diehl glowered but said: "Why, thank you for that kindly thought, sir. Wall, if the official and current prosecuting attorney overrules me, you can play with those files all night long and into the morning. Only thing is: Mr. Vorpahl's gone hunting up Maine way, Moosehead, I think, some cabin up in the bush, no privy, no phone."

Fletcher said: "Any judge can sign a simple order like that. Tonight."

"Now there," said Diehl, standing up, *"there* is a man quick on his feet with the law. On target, son. Only one thing: there's no judge worth his goddamn salt in this town who'd sign such a order without the very information you ain't willing to give. And there ain't a one, also, who would consider it privileged if a felony has been committed." He came around the desk, the high heels clacking on the wooden floor. "Y'see, a police officer's gotta know some law, too." He turned at the door. "Now. You tell me, no strings attached, and I'll authorize access this minute."

Fletcher waited again: it was Wally Heckman's decision. And he was weighing alternatives. It was clear now, painfully clear, that what bugged Diehl was the fact that he had been excluded: that ego of his was gnawing at him right now, stiffening his back, and his sense of power was being threatened. Plus the fact that by now he knew, of course, that Heckman would not trust him. Any more than Fletcher would. Yet Wally Heckman had something at stake, too: his personal need for revenge. Or was justice the word? Diehl waited. With quiet patience.

Finally Wally Heckman said, very quietly: "Fuck you."

Diehl smiled coldly and went out, leaving the door open. Now the noise from the anteroom reached them: the clatter of a teletype, a typewriter. And two voices:

"Lotta VIP's cluttering up the premises tonight, Chief."

"What do you want, McQuade?"

"A jug of Irish, a loaf of truth and thou."

"Stuff it."

"That's downright poetic, Chief. Odd time of night for you to be around, isn't it?"

"You remind me of a hound dog I had once, McQuade. Always sniffing."

"Only way for the plain simple folks to get the stink. Any developments on the fiend from hell who tore up the nice graveyard? I heard one theory: it was the work of the judge's bastard son who was too retarded to think of it till now—"

The voices receded. Fletcher remembered Gavin McQuade with a certain wry fondness: the wizened little reporter with a limp who insisted on working only at night. Their paths hadn't crossed for some years.

Wally Heckman moved heavily to the door, closed it. He looked around the office as if trying to decide where the hell he was and how he'd come here.

"Now," Fletcher said, "Diehl'll chew young

Hutchinson out some more, then go home, have his Alka-Seltzer and chili sauce, say his prayers and sleep the sleep of the innocent." He moved to Heckman. "Well, Wally?"

"Well, Fletch?"

"You pack one hell of a wallop."

But Wallace Heckman didn't smile. He looked as if perhaps he would never smile again. "Sorry."

"It's only a reflection on your inability to weigh evidence." He really didn't know what to say. And he was experiencing a strange sympathy for this man whom he had never much liked or respected.

"Fuck you. That's what my son says. I don't think I ever said it before."

"Wally, all my files have been destroyed. Don't you have a complete set of yours in your office?"

But Wally seemed not to hear him. "I keep trying to think. It would have to be a degenerate of some kind. Queer. To do what—" He didn't finish that. "Can't you think of anyone like that you might've defended?"

"I'll try, Wally."

"Criminal pervert! Why do they always have to try to corrupt others?"

"Take it easy now. Listen, let's get your secretary, go to your office—"

"My secretary's practically in labor."

"I'll get someone then. I have an assistant who'll help. Between us we should come up with something. It promises to be a long night."

Then Wally was frowning into his eyes. "How come?"

"How come what?"

"How come you're dealing yourself in?"

It was a good question. And he didn't have the answer. So he said: "Curiosity. Diehl's got some kind of hangup I can't fathom. Is he scared of making a decision for fear he might be wrong, or is he being a bastard just to prove he's a bastard?"

"Not good enough, Fletch."

"Well then, let's say this. My name's been taken in vain. Maybe just to stir up trouble and confusion. Maybe just for the hell of it because someone's playing games. But wouldn't it be funny if his using my name and posing as me gave us the clue to *his* identity?"

"I still say it's no skin off yours."

"Look, what do you want me to do, quote John Donne? You open your office and get out the pertinent files. I'll have Annette meet me here and we'll join you in something under half an hour."

"Where are you going?"

Fletcher, outside the office, turned. "To call Annette and my wife, and then have a drink. Maybe that's what you need, Wally."

But Wally was shaking his head, slowly. "I already feel kind of drunk." His face twisted, but it was not really a smile. "But that's bile. Or spleen. I don't think I better mix poisons, Fletch."

The poor guy: he looked beat. Fletcher was on his way through the reception room. Ben Hutchinson was not behind his desk. Christ, how he needed a drink.

It didn't take Boyd Ritchie more than a few seconds to decide to answer the phone. Why not? He picked it up on the third ring.

"Hello?"

"Hello. Who is this?"

"This is me. Who is *that?*"

"Is this the Paul Wharton residence?"

"Yes. Yes, it is. 3223 Elmhurst Terrace. Now isn't that a surprise? You dialed the right number!"

He could hear breathing. He waited. His pleasure.

"Hello?"

"Is there something I can do for you?"

He savored the silence. Again he waited.

"I'm not going to ask again. This is Paul Wharton. Who are you and what are you doing in my house?"

"I'm me. And I was invited. If this *is* Paul Wharton and if it's any of your goddamn business."

"Let me speak to Mrs. Wharton."

"Oh, she's busy. She can't possibly come to the phone now. She's busy, we're both busy, you're interrupting and that's not polite, so don't call back." Then he added: "Please." And he placed a finger on the button, cutting the connection. Then he placed the phone alongside the cradle on the bedside table and released the button.

He looked again at Coralie in the bed. She lay still under the sheet which he had drawn modestly up to her chin. She was unconscious. Whether from the pills she had popped or from the pain and shock—well, what did it matter? Just so long as no one, earlier, had heard that horrendous howl she had let go. After that, he had had to place one hand over her mouth. He hadn't pulled the trigger, of course, but the thrill was the possibility that her husband might walk in at any moment. He had realized then, with her head moving from side to side and her eyes wide and glazed, that he should have arranged somehow to get Paul Wharton home earlier so he could witness this. Afterward she had passed out, gone very still and lifeless, but when he had examined her neck, there was still a distinct strong throb in the carotid artery. He didn't want her to die. Yet. It would ruin everything to come.

Then he had removed the pair of skintight flesh-colored gloves—one of the dozen pairs he had purchased in Iowa—and had tossed them to the floor. One of them was covered with blood and he didn't really like to have other people's blood on his own flesh.

He had already removed the shell from the sawed-off shotgun. Risky. But part of the plan: it was all working so well he couldn't change any of it now. He took a high-intensity flashlight from the attaché case, tested it. He was hungry. The way he used to feel after a good solid screw. With the shotgun, broken, under his arm and the flashlight, not burning, in his hand, he went out of the room. Then he stopped, returned, replaced the telephone in its cradle. It didn't ring. He strolled into the hall and down the stairs.

He had time now. He estimated that, at extremely high speed, it would take that bastard Wharton at least fifteen minutes to get here from the Lake Club. The Chevy Vega was well hidden, parked between a truck and the side wall of a closed service station three blocks away. It would never be noticed.

He fixed the exact position of furniture in his mind, then turned off all the lights in the central hall and living room, and without using the flashlight, he went along the hallway to the kitchen door in the rear. By touch he located the refrigerator, opened it, and in the light discovered a huge chunk of roast beef. He picked it up and, still without any light in the dimness, he found his way to the den, or library, or whatever the hell they called it in these parts. He sat at the desk and chewed at the meat, savoring its pink tenderness.

Probably there was no need for the precautions. That bastard Diehl was too damn dumb to add two and two. Texas Rangers didn't depend on putting things together; they depended on brute force and the certainty that not one man in a hundred, guilty or innocent, could hold out against the punishment they could hand out. He felt his scrotum tighten, harden at the memory. Theron Diehl's time was coming. In the meantime—

He flipped on the desk light and picked up the phone, dialed a number he had filed in his mind, waited for seven rings, replaced the phone. If Heckman was not home, he'd be at the hospital—no doubt that's where they'd take the kid. But when he asked the operator to get the hospital because of an emergency and had been put through, he was informed that Mrs. Heckman was there but that Mr. Heckman had not arrived, although he was expected. The police then? The operator was even more eager to oblige. He was careful not to chew on the meat while he inquired whether Mr. Wallace Heckman was there, explaining that he was one of Congressman Heckman's assistants. The voice of the cop grated on his nerves: carefully level, carefully polite to the citizenry. Motherfuckers. He held on, hearing a typewriter or teletype machine, and then the same voice advised him that Mr. Heckman could probably be reached at his office.

His office? It was almost eleven o'clock. This time he dialed Information, realizing that time was getting away so he'd better rush it. And Heckman himself answered.

"Working late, luv."

"Who is this?"

"This is Fletcher Briggs."

"Like hell!" Growl your balls off, you bastard.

"Then it's somebody looks a helluva lot *like* Fletcher Briggs, luv."

That did it; he knew it would. As he knew that, by now, a guy like Heckman would have wised up to that much anyway.

"Where are you?" Heckman's voice was calm now, tense and low, very steady. "I'll come wherever you are. Alone."

"You'll screw a goose if I tell you to, Prosecutor."

"Who is this?"

They didn't know. Not yet. "I'm so disappointed you don't recognize my voice, Prosecutor. All I got to say to you is this, listen. . . . The kid liked it. The sweet little bugger really dug it, man. That's all."

He set down the phone. While inside the elation expanded. He had never felt so exhilarated. So tremblingly alive. He'd always known—he'd known for almost eight years—that when the time came, it would be like this!

He found himself staring into the face of Mrs. Augusta Wharton: an oil portrait hanging on the wall opposite the desk. He'd never seen the bitch, but it could be no one else. A thin and haughty face, eyes cool as glass, small chin set, mouth wide and straight. The white lace at her neck looked like frozen snow. Even in the painting she looked forbidding, commanding. He had heard her name many times, but all he had been able to learn about her was that she had been the one to suggest the plea bargaining. *As I understand it,* Fletcher Briggs had reported, *Paul Wharton wants a full trial, his pound of flesh in revenge, but his mother's thinking of the family name and she's the one behind the offer to make a deal. Even that's gossip. Nobody knows much about the old gal except that she usually gets what she wants.*

And you helped her get it, didn't you, Briggs? How much did she pay you, you double-crossing son of a bitch, how'd she pay you off? Thinking of Briggs again, he could hardly breathe. Like it was in the cell. Just to think of him was like having asthma, as if he was going to choke or puke.

Too damn bad the old bitch was already dead! If not, she'd get hers tonight, too. He leaped to his feet, grabbed a silver letter opener from the desk, stepped around and began to slash the canvas. When he had finished, he stabbed it into what was left of the chunk of meat on the desk, left it upright in it, muttered, "Motherfucker," and went out and up the stairs without switching off the light.

The Cunt had not moved on the bed. She hadn't even turned her head to the other side. He only hoped that when the time came, he could wake her. It wouldn't be the same unless she was awake.

He turned off the bedroom light. Then he sat down in a soft chair by the window. He snapped the empty shotgun together and placed it across his knees. He looked down through the trees, which were almost bare, to the front lawn and curving white driveway, dim but still visible, and along the sweep of old street with its trimmed hedges, its old-fashioned streetlights, its shadowed high houses. He wondered, again, what it might be to live on such a street.

But as the ache began inside, he forced his mind to think ahead: the parked van on the other side of the lake, the ninety thousand dollars, Canada, Europe. And by the time he'd spent the money—hell, long before—he'd have his connections made. Anyone who could pull off what he'd pulled off here tonight could do anything, and there were always people ready to pay for a man who's willing to do anything. And those same people, those people especially, would by then know what he'd done here tonight. The whole goddamn world would know.

He heard a car door slam and a motor start, then a second car door. Lights came on in the driveway beyond the very straight line of slim fir trees that separated the Wharton property from its neighbors'. A black Rambler pulled out of the driveway beyond the trees and moved slowly along the otherwise deserted street.

"Well, sweetheart, I hope you're satisfied." Even before the sound of the Gilberts' car had receded down the street, she was gathering up the cards and coffee cups and emptying the ashtrays before the ashes could cool. "It's only eleven o'clock."

"Yes. It was curious the way Adelaide's headache developed, wasn't it?"

Her lips tightened, all but disappeared in her fleshy face. "Headache! They were both sick of listening to you bicker."

"As someone said about a dance, it takes two to bicker." He switched on the televison and sat down on the sofa. "Shall we dance?"

She was staring at him and now her eyes had all but disappeared. "I honestly don't know what's come over you the last half hour. And all because of her. That hussy next door."

"Hussy?" He snorted a laugh. "I don't think that word's been used for fifty years. Even in this town."

"Harlot, then—is that better? Or do you prefer common whore? Tart! *Bitch!*"

He considered it, wondering what the hell exactly *had* come over him the last half hour. "I think I prefer wench. No, jade—I really prefer jade."

"If you're still so worried about her, why don't you go over there?"

She bustled off toward the kitchen. The television faded in: a handsome young girl was selling toothpaste, her tongue making a lewd suggestion while her eyes sparkled innocence. He had realized during the evening—or rather, he had allowed the awareness to reach his consciousness and to be acknowledged—that his wife didn't give a damn about him as a man. How long had it been so? If she cared at all, she cared about him simply as a possession—like her ivory collection dating back to her great-grandfather's whaling days, like her priceless china that had been handed down through three generations. A thing. A part of her only insofar as she owned him and no other woman had any part of him, even those parts that she held in such basic contempt anyway. All this had come to him since he had either heard or imagined that scream. Now his mind was absolutely quivering with the knowledge, and a slow burned anger stirred an acrid taste in his mouth.

When she returned, she said: "Are you still here?"

Everyone in the room had heard what he heard. He was not sure he *should* still be here. He didn't reply.

She came to him. "You know why I feel the way I do, don't you, sweetheart? You know why I hate that slut next door."

He had developed several theories now, but he said: "I can't say I do."

"Why, sweetheart—because I love you! That's all."

"Bullshit."

"Wha-what did you say?"

"I said bullshit. I could make it horseshit if that's any daintier."

"You have a nerve. You're trying to—what *are* you trying to do? Using language like that in my house!"

"*Your* house?"

"You know what I mean."

"Yes, I think I do."

"*Our* house. Naturally."

"Naturally." He concentrated on the mayhem on the screen. The sound of shots filled the room. "Your father's house."

"Oh, look at us. Look. Quarreling. And over what? She's not worth it."

"She?" He forced down a smile. "She? Coralie Wharton's the cause of this—is that it?"

"Well, isn't she? Do we ever quarrel?"

"Not often enough, no."

"Oh, don't imagine I don't know how easy it is for you to sneak over there when I'm not here. Or any other time. The way that Dr. Farago does. She can't be that ill that often. You don't fool me. I know what goes on. You can bet your bottom farthing on that!"

He almost laughed. "I haven't bet a farthing since I was in England during the Second World War." But the idea of sneaking over to see Coralie Wharton had not occurred to him. He wondered why. He moved his gaze from the television screen. She was standing still now, looking at him. With malice. He could almost smell the venom burning in her veins. "I'm curious about one thing," he said. "One thing only. What the hell difference does any of this make to you?" Then he held up a palm. "And I don't want any more *shit* about sweetheart-I-love-you."

She turned away. Her broad, fleshy back had never looked straighter, stiffer. "This was once the best neighborhood in this town. Elmhurst Street was always respected for its—you know this is where the true aristocracy of Tarkington always lived. Now look at it—a service station not three blocks away, real estate developments on all sides, a prostitute married to a Wharton and living next door!"

Inwardly he shook his head. All that may have been part of the reason, but the truth was more complex, deeper in her, and more personal. He probably should pity her. But he couldn't.

"We lost at bridge," he said, suddenly sick of it all. "Let's chalk it up."

"I *hope* you heard her scream." Her voice was so low, so muted, that he could not be sure of the words until she repeated them, without turning. "I hope you heard her scream. I hope her husband came home and found her with someone, someone like you, and I hope he killed her in her bed."

He had never heard such malevolence in a voice. He had honestly believed he was beyond shock. He was amazed to discover that he was not. He stood and turned off the television. There was enough violence in the room.

"Perhaps," he said, "I *should* go next door."

"Perhaps you should." She went toward the kitchen, her back rigid and unyielding and challenging.

He probably should pity her just as he probably should have gone over to the Wharton house. But taking any action now seemed a waste and could only cause more damn trouble. It was too late now to prevent anything—if there had ever been anything to prevent. And he had his own problems now. He decided to have a nightcap and think about them. Certain avenues seemed to be opening up. He might as well explore them.

Fletcher Briggs had told himself that he'd have a fast double scotch just to keep his energy from flagging because, as he had warned Wally Heckman, it promised to be a long night. He had asked Annette to meet him here instead of in Wally's office. Excuses. Excuses for sitting at the bar in the Colonial Inn, puffing on his pipe and staring out the small-paned bay window at the courthouse across the Common. He hadn't yet arrived at an answer to Wally's question as to why he was dealing himself in since Wally had been right: *It's no skin off yours*. He'd hoped a whiskey or two would open up his mind, help him remember some case involving, as Wally put it, a *criminal pervert*. The only trouble there was, or had been, that "pervert" and "degenerate" were Heckman's favorite terms in the courtroom, effective with juries, heavy with built-in emotional responses, and he used the words loosely and indiscriminately to describe almost anyone accused of a criminal act. But if you're going to try to zero in on a particular case, such general terms only cloud the issue. Fletcher was damned if he could recall ever having defended a homosexual in court. Not because he himself cared much of a damn what a person's sexual proclivities were just so long as they didn't interfere with the next fellow's. Which, tonight, the person they were beginning to search for had most certainly done. And to a child.

Odd to be here, really. Considering the way he'd always felt about Wallace Heckman. And his ilk—all the others like him. The vast majority. Attorneys who used the law for their own ends without any due and genuine regard for the merits of the case or even the truth about it. Or as he often put it in class, any due respect for the lady with the sword. But tonight he had to admire the way Wally was standing up to Diehl. He remembered now that wide handsome athletic face set, hard, and that terrible thing in Wally's eyes—a festering, a smoldering. A dangerous thing, perhaps, but in his eyes because he loved his son and had to protect him. But how? If he refused to let the police handle it, did he have something else in mind?

As for Diehl—hell, it was all there in *his* eyes, too. The hate. The hard, uncaring resentment at having his authority even questioned, the ruthless use of power hidden under the cloak of ritual and the strict interpretation of the rules of the game—when convenient. The law in action. Every time he came into contact again with the legal profession and the routine activities of the police he was more convinced than ever that his decision to withdraw from the whole damned uncivilized patchwork that passed for the workings of justice, had been a wise one.

Whether Willa would ever understand or not. Although he had tried to explain. Willa. Even her name, echoing in his mind, stirred a bewildering sadness. He signaled for another drink. Even tonight she had managed to imply that he, by some damned miracle beyond the powers of any father today, should not only know where his two children were but what they were doing—perhaps even that he should prevent what they were doing. Whatever the hell that was. He sipped the fresh drink, slowly. Hadn't David said he was going camping? What the hell was a father to do, tag along to make sure he didn't sneak a nubile teen-ager into the sleeping bag with him? Or smoke grass? Or both, or what? And as for Peggy: even when he asked her where she spent almost every evening until almost midnight, she'd only make some charming joke, run her hand through his hair, and be on her merry way. A woman. Seventeen years old, but a woman all the same. And he felt a strange sense of loss. Not for the first time.

And here he was halfway through his second double scotch and aware that it was about time now to tell himself that another would clear his mind for the work ahead.

"Buy you another, Counselor? Or should I say Professor?"

Gavin McQuade slid onto the stool beside him: small, scowling, bony face a mass of tiny thin lines. He waited with bird-bright eyes, head tilted.

"You trying to bribe me, McQuade?"

McQuade turned to the empty stool on the other side of himself and inquired: "What reason would I have to bribe the man?" Then to Fletcher, feigning shock: "Can't one man welcome another back to the wasteland without being accused of a misdemeanor? Besides, what the hell could you know that'd be news?"

Fletcher realized with a pang of pleasure that there were some aspects of the old life that he missed. And some people. "You still covering the courthouse at night?"

"Hell, yes, that's when nothing happens. Give me an

Irish and fill my enemy's cup till it runneth over, please. On me."

"You lazy bastard. Nothing ever happens at night around here."

"Too old to change. I like nights, Fletch. I live at night. If you can call it living."

"How have you been, Gavin?"

"Survival—that's the name of the game. Don't let anyone tell you different. How have *you* been?"

Fletcher wondered: how had he been, really? But, instead of answering, he lifted his glass. "Skoal."

"To Theron Diehl, may he be hanged by a Bible belt."

They drank. Fletcher's head had begun to have that blurred pleasant feeling and he looked at the man beside him again, caught the demonic flicker of the reporter's smile, saw the sallow skin, the widow's peak of hair that gave his face the look of an aging Pan, and remembered something Annette had once said: *You're such a phony. All that sophomoric cynicism you charm your students with—do you think it fools me? Oh, God, why do I always get stuck with you battered beat-up idealists who imagine you can change what hurts you by making jokes about it?*

"Gavin," Fletcher said, "I admit Diehl's a tough baby, but listen, suppose, just suppose now without trying to imagine what, suppose there was a story that might make news but also might hurt some people, really smash them perhaps."

"Diehl has the idea he can decide—all the news *he* thinks the people should have. All the news that puts *him* in a good light. Hell, the man ought to be President."

Fletcher shook his head. "All right, forget Diehl. Let's take an incident, a sensational incident even, a crime—do you think everything should be printed, devil take the hindmost?"

McQuade fixed his gaze on him now, scowling, suspicious. "There *is* something afoot, isn't there?"

Fletcher was thinking of Wally Heckman's face: those wounded, saddened eyes, inflamed and obsessed. "No," he lied. "This is a philosophical discussion; maybe you're not up to it."

"If there's a story, Fletch, I'll get it."

"Not from me."

McQuade shrugged. "Even if *you* want to play God."

"And you'll print it, regardless of its content?"

"Professor, I am an observer of mankind's quirks and foibles, not a gladiator in the arena of human idiocy. Besides, I have to eat and drink."

"So *you'll* play God."

McQuade set down his glass. His softly scornful expression didn't change. "You tell me; then I'll decide. Sure, I'm as good a god as you or Diehl."

"The story is this: the vampire who tore up Stuttaford's grave came from outer space via a Russian sputnik."

McQuade was shaking his head. "The story of Stuttaford's grave's already written. Something else. Well, if I don't get it here, there's always the hospital, the morgue, other jolly haunts."

Before Fletcher could answer, another voice, a more familiar one, spoke, at his shoulder: "Do I get one of those?"

He turned. Her face was close, very close. Teasing. "Another," he told the bartender. "Another double. And an Irish for the leprechaun."

"Until you phoned, I thought they had you in the clink," Annette said then. "Why didn't you stand up for your rights when that squad car picked you up on the street? Come now, give me the straight shit."

She looked heartbreakingly fragile and almost breathtakingly young, but with no hint in her eyes of that wry sadness that had been in them as they walked earlier. But he noted, again, that tart demanding note in her voice, behind the bantering, persistently scatological words, and he wondered, also again, whether he'd ever get used to hearing such words from the young, especially the girls. Which made him a stuffy antifeminist, antiyouth, anti-the-modern-world prig, of course. "I'm taking the Fifth," he said, conscious of the leprechaun's ears beside him. "By the way, this is an enemy of humanity named Gavin McQuade, who thinks he's a newshawk but is really a harmless little sparrow. Gavin—Annette Beauchamp, my teaching assistant."

"Hi," Annette said and climbed onto a stool.

Leaning forward, McQuade studied Annette's face a second or two, then sat back and turned to the empty space on the other side of him, addressing no one: "Teaching assistant. Hear that? The euphemisms an otherwise honest man will use when it comes to sex."

Annette laughed. Her laugh had a musical sound. And Fletcher knew that only Gavin McQuade could get away with this. Knew, also, that others had to know about Annette, or suspect. And wondered, again, how the hell he could ever have come to this.

"Somebody hit you, right?" He felt her finger tracing his swollen jaw, gently. "It's all purple. Does it hurt?" She was whispering. "Oh, my dear, dear, it must hurt like hell, right?"

He had almost forgotten it, but now, as if on cue, the side of his face, which was stiff and puffed, began to pulsate with pain.

"I know. I ought to see the other guy, right?"

Suddenly her repetition of the word grated his nerves. *"Right!"* he growled and stood up. "I'll call the house; then we've work to do." Was he saying this for McQuade's benefit? He placed his pipe on the bar. "And if this figment of some madman's imagination gets fresh, wallop him one."

"It'd be worth it," McQuade said; then he called after Fletcher, who was moving toward the booth in the rear: "We won't be here when you get back."

As he closed the door and picked up the phone, he heard Annette laughing. The girl had one hell of a laugh. He remembered the heady, almost giddy sense of relief he had felt earlier: it was over. Yet now, dialing, he was again in the grip of that melancholy incredulity that attacked out of nowhere recently, and at the strangest times. He had always considered himself an honorable man. But wasn't he really like all the others on all sides? The word was not so much adultery and it had less to do with the legality of marriage than with simple human honesty. But the guilt was the same, no matter what the words: betrayal, deceit. Lies, half-truths. Hearing the phone buzzing at the other end of the line, he watched Annette and McQuade at the bar, the empty stool between them. She was sipping her drink and smoking—her trim young body, the bare legs, the dark hair tumbling. McQuade's thin shoulders were hunched over, head turned toward her. She was smoking a cigarette now, face turned toward him: radiant, smiling. And he experienced again that most ironic and incongruous of all emotions in the circumstances: jealousy. A poison mingling in his blood with the alcohol, all the more bitter because he knew he had no claim and tonight had given up, of his own volition, whatever counterfeit claim he might have had. What the hell was bugging him then? That she wasn't wearing sackcloth and wailing her grief?"

The phone in the house on Howells Street rang five times. Then:

"Yes?"

He didn't recognize the voice. "Hello? Willa, is that you?"

"Yes." Just that. No more.

"Willa?"

"Yes." Again.

"Did I wake you? I'm sorry if I—" But he stopped. It was definitely Willa's voice on the line—but low, empty. "Willa, are you all right?"

"Yes."

"Are you sure?"

"Yes."

"Willa, something's come up. I can't tell you about it

now, but I'm going to have to do some work."

He waited. His jaw was throbbing.

"Yes."

"Will you please stop saying yes?"

"Yes."

"Darling, talk to me. What—"

"Don't call me darling."

"What? What did you say?"

"I . . . I asked you not to call . . . call me darling." Her voice sounded blurred now, indistinct, fading.

"Willa, have you been drinking?"

"Sauce for the gander. That's a . . . joke. Poor little joke. Have you? Been drinking?"

"No!"

"Liar." Very quietly. "Phony, phony liar."

"Will you for God's sake tell me what's come over you?"

"You can put you . . . your cock anywhere you want to put . . . put it."

He couldn't talk. This wasn't Willa. Willa had never used that word in her life. Or any word like it. "You *are* drunk."

"Yes."

Christ! "Willa, listen. I'm coming home. Now. Do you hear me?"

"Stay away. Stay away forever."

Followed by a distinct click. Not a sharp one. She had hung up carefully, gently.

He left the booth, compulsion to move tugging at every muscle now. McQuade was standing up, limping toward the door. He stopped when he saw Fletcher approaching. Annette was staring at McQuade, as if startled by his walk. Wounded sparrow.

"Annette," Fletcher heard himself saying, placing a bill on the bar, "go to Wallace Heckman's office. Essex Building. Trumbull Street. He'll tell you what we have to do."

"But, Fletcher, I don't know—"

"Do it." He heard the rasping in his tone, saw her

dark brows rise, saw the defiance enter her face. "I'll be there later. Just do it!"

He went out, feeling a blast of wind striking at him and hearing McQuade's voice behind: "I'll walk you there, Miss Beauchamp. There are werewolves on the prowl tonight, so I'm told."

Fletcher was already running now, across the Common in a fall of wind-shaken leaves, others catching at his shoes, running toward the taxi stand on the corner that he only hoped would be open this time of night.

This was not the kind of case that Leroy Farago liked to become involved in. But doctors, as one of his professors had tried to impress upon his students, cannot be choosers. Nevertheless, he knew right from wrong, and also he was damned if he was going to risk his license, or even a medical board hearing, for anyone, even a Congressman who appeared to be heading for the governorship, if not higher up the political and social ladder.

"Wally, what are you doing in your office this time of night?"

"I'm doing what the police should be doing. How'd you think to phone me here?"

"Officer named Hutchinson at headquarters said you might be there. I hope that means you've reported what happened."

"Goddamn it, you should know I can't do that! This thing can't become public knowledge!"

"Wally, how can the police help if they don't know? Be reasonable."

"My reason's working very well, thank you. What about yours? Is this a private conversation?"

"I'm in a private office the hospital provides for just such a conversation."

"This call's going through the switchboard then."

"Wally, no one is listening in. I guarantee you. So scrub the paranoia. And listen. I've told Kay: unless I can bring in Dr. Rosenbluth, or someone equally competent, when Dennis wakes up, I'm going off the case."

"But we had a deal. You can't—we had a *deal!*"

"I told you I'd think it over. Well, I have. And that's what I suggest you do, too. Now Kay's told me all about your views on psychiatry. In general, I agree that we should all rely on ourselves, our own strength. But we're dealing with a child—"

"We all get over things. We've all had to."

"Damnation, Wally, we're dealing with a child! You're not really thinking about him at all!"

From the silence that ensued, he knew he'd gone too far. He was not being too bright himself. It should be clear from that high-tension strain in Wally Heckman's voice that he should also be treated with kid gloves. Like a patient perhaps.

Finally Wally Heckman said, in a choked voice: "If you were here, I'd knock your goddamned block off."

Warning himself to be professional, he said: "It's hopeless to try to conceal this thing."

"I'll find out who did it. On my own. I'm working on that now!"

"Then what?"

No answer.

He saw it then for what it was: the vague irrational plan of a man almost demented by an act so horrendous to him that he could not maintain his reason or his control, let alone his professional training. "Wally. Leave it to the police."

"They're doing nothing!"

He heard his tone rise: "How can they do anything when they—" But he choked that off: no use going around in circles. Instead, he said, gently: "Wally, to bring in another doctor, all I need is the permission of one parent."

"Kay will do what I tell her."

"Wally . . . Kay has already given me permission."

Silence again.

Until: "I told her not to take him to the—" His voice sounded baffled, faint. "What's happening? Kay's never done anything like this before. What's she trying to do to me?"

"Nothing. She's doing her best. She's terribly distraught. Wally, she needs you. Here."

"She can go to hell, too."

The words were hard, yet distant, almost inaudible.

Still, he had to say it: "Wally, I really don't have any choice." It had to be said: "I'm filing my report with the police."

Then he waited. He was not a father; he had no idea what the other man was thinking, feeling. Yet he was forced to act anyway. The way he saw it. And since the rules existed, he had only to abide by them. It limited his range of choices, but it also got him off the hook in this case.

But Wally Heckman did not respond to what he had said. Perhaps he was unable to. The shock was silent and electric. He said: "Leroy . . . tell me something—"

"If I can, Wally." He was aware of the blow he'd delivered; he hoped he wouldn't have to land another one.

"There are signs of a struggle, aren't there? I mean, Dennis did fight, didn't he? There're bruises—" The voice drifted off.

"Wally, use your head. A frail eleven-year-old kid against a six-foot man. He was scared shitless. He—"

The voice shouted: "That's not what I'm asking."

Startled, he asked himself, fast: what would a lie accomplish? Sooner or later Wally would come to the hospital. He'd ask to see the records. If it meant this much to him, sooner or later he'd examine his son's face and neck and body personally.

"Well, Leroy?"

"I didn't notice any, Wally. But if you like, I'll put something to that effect in my official—"

The line was dead.

* * *

The tremor in his hands, both hands, was so intense that he could control the steering wheel only by gripping it so hard that the muscles of his stomach tightened into a breathless agony and by now his arms were so rigid with pain that he could feel it all the way up to the base of his skull. He was, in fact, quaking all over. But in spite of all the drinks he'd had at the club, he was certain that he was almost sober now. Sober and filled with a cold fury so devouring that, as he swung the Mercedes into Elmhurst Street, he could not believe that he had finally arrived home.

And I was invited. If this is Paul Wharton and if it is any of your goddamn business.

Not Farago. Not Farago's voice. Then whose?

He turned into the curving driveway without slowing, heard the rear tires scream, saw that only her Jag was there, stomped on the brakes, the wheels spitting white gravel, and leaped out. He thought he was going down. His legs were paralyzed. There was a wind. There appeared to be no lights in the house. He knew now. At last he knew, once and for all—a certainty. She'd lie. If the man was gone now, she'd come up with some lie. But he knew. No more doubts, no more hoping for the opposite of what his mind insisted was true.

The front door was unlocked. He stood in the dark hall, straining to hear. Nothing. Only the wind outside, blasting at his back through the open door. But it was only a distant sensation. Was he still trembling? He couldn't be sure. No sound. Was she asleep? Were they both asleep up there? The coldness inside hardened. No butler, as in the old days. Not even a maid. Her idea, too. *I'm sorry, Paul, but servants terrify me. I don't know how to handle them.* More lies: he knew now, knew why for sure—so she could have the house alone with her lovers.

Without conscious thought now, he began to follow out the plan that had taken shape in his mind as soon as he had hung up the phone at the club and gone out to the parking area. He moved down the hall to his study. The desk light was burning. It reflected on his trophies: the boxing figures. There was a hunk of meat on the desk, which looked as if it had been gnawed at, and upright in it, like a knife, was his silver letter opener. He opened a drawer and reached deep. It was there: the .44 Luger that he had used only for target practice a few times, years ago. He made sure the magazine was in place. He always kept it loaded. He was tempted to have a quick slug of whiskey. No. He had to be steady. Mind and hand. As he was about to leave the room, he saw his mother's portrait over the mantel. He stopped. It had been slashed in such a way that the face was unrecognizable and parts of the canvas flopped forward.

Coralie. Only Coralie could have done this. She had always hated her. Sickened but even more determined now, he went out of the room and, stealthily, slowly, along the hall to the stairway. His body and mind knew every step. He seemed now to be floating in the darkness. He had lived a whole lifetime in this house. The only house in which he had ever lived. He had climbed these stairs thousands upon thousands of times. Could he do now what he knew he had to do, here? His mother's house. Yes. She would approve. She had warned him. She would understand. She always understood.

As he approached the bedroom door, he realized that it stood open. Darkness beyond. Stillness. The Luger was lifted and pointed, his finger tight and steady on the trigger. Was he going to blast without even turning on the light? He didn't know.

He stepped through the door.

And in that instant, light struck, intense, stabbing, gouging his eyes, very close, he went blind, he couldn't even squeeze the trigger, the glare paralyzing his mind as it penetrated knifelike to the back of his skull.

Then the light lifted and in the split second's relief he took a breath, but he saw the beam shoot toward the ceiling and then it came down, in a single sharp motion, and then he was drooping, hearing a thud as the Luger fell to the carpet, then hearing only a vastness as he himself crumpled to the floor, and then the pain smashed at his head, shattering everything into darkness, which stellated into slivers of silver brilliance and sharpness before he knew one brief second of contentment with his cheek against the harsh stubble of carpet, and then a shutter came down over his mind.

"Homosexual assault, Chief Diehl," Wallace Heckman said, "does not fall into the category of what you call malicious mischief."

"Now, Congressman, don't take me wrong. That's only a term. I can sympathize with your concern, seeing it's your own kid this faggot, whoever he is, molested. It's a real sorry world we live in, sorry times."

"You said you had to have a second crime, a crime against a living person, I refused to tell you—well, this is it and I am telling you. That's why I came back here from my office."

"Wall, I'm obliged to you for that—"

"You'll be getting a medical report: that'll establish it officially."

"Hm. And just what is it you're requesting me to do?"

"What do you normally do when a crime has been committed? Get off your ass, start an investigation presumably leading to an arrest."

"On the basis of what we got—and you stop me if I'm paddling the wrong creek—we gotta arrest Professor Fletcher Briggs." He sighed and ran a finger over his mustache. "Looks to me like we're dealing here with a kinda freak. Dresses up like another man, uses another man's name. Some kinda nut."

"Exactly," Wallace Heckman said. "And you never know what a nut's going to do next. What we've got are three names. What we have to do is put them together. My files, which are being examined now by Briggs' assistant, are very sketchy for the years I was prosecuting attorney because I've always operated under the assumption that I'd have access to the court records if I ever needed them."

"Assumptions—very dangerous in police work, Congressman. Y'sure you won't take a chair?"

"Positive. Did you hear what I said? If I am making assumptions—and there's not a damned thing wrong with assumptions in *any* kind of work—and if I'm wrong, let's check it out and *prove* I'm wrong."

Pigheaded. Well, Theron Diehl could be pigheaded, too. When he was being pushed around. "Only . . . supposin' I don't buy your theory? Or did someone tell me it was Lieutenant Hutchinson's theory? Supposin' I still hold to it that what happened to your boy adds up to what they call a happenstance?"

Heckman placed his fists on the desk and leaned his weight forward on them. "Chief, I don't give a fuck what you suppose." The man's eyes were bloodshot and his flesh looked almost gray. "What I *know* is: we're wasting time."

"You're asking me to stick out my neck by taking precipitous action. I'm sayin' there's not one scintilla of solid evidence to tie the two together."

"The hell there isn't. I had a phone call in my office less than half an hour ago from . . . whoever did what he did to my son."

Now, of course, he was lying. Just like a politician wanting to have his way. Who the hell would phone a lawyer's office this time of night? "You don't tell me?"

"He called me Prosecutor. It may have been a slip or he may have wanted me to know. Anyway, that clinches it. It was someone I convicted."

"Wall, I'm certain-sure glad you recalled this bit of information. How come he called you? What was the gist of his message?"

He wasn't prepared for what happened then. Heckman straightened; his eyes darkened, then glazed over. He looked blind. What the hell, maybe there had been such a call, after all.

"Wall? What'd he have to say?"

"Nothing." Heckman turned away: he looked weak. "Nothing else. He was just . . . gloating."

That did it. Now Diehl knew the man was lying. But he wasn't angry or even annoyed. The poor guy was desperate. He'd do or say anything to bolster his case. He even had to admire the tough son of a bitch in a way.

Then Heckman said: "Jeremy Welles is on his way here from Londonford."

That did it: you can't be nice to some people. In the absence of the prosecuting attorney, his assistant, Jeremy Welles, as an officer of the court, could demand access to court records. "You been a busy little beaver, ain't you?" Diehl said, running a finger over his mustache again while he stalled. He didn't relish being stampeded and he was damned if he'd let Heckman get away with going over his head. Still, if Heckman turned out to be right, it'd be Theron Diehl who'd wind up in the manure pile. But he wasn't going to cave in just like that. "What's the big rush, Congressman? We'll apprehend the culprit."

Heckman stepped close again. "Why the hell are you so stubborn? It's just possible that if we can get his name, we can get out an alert and possibly prevent another crime in case this degenerate's on some kind of insane rampage."

Controlling his irritation, Diehl held up a hand. "Don't make speeches at me, kindly. This ain't a court of law."

"It's not. But as a police officer sworn to uphold the law—"

"There y'go tellin' me my duty again—"

"—your duty's to do everything in your power not just to apprehend criminals *after* a crime's been committed but if possible to *prevent* that crime's being committed."

"Oh, cut the horseshit. You're allowin' your personal troubles to foul up the thinkin' machine. What you got goin' is a personal vendetta. That's why you're in such a hurry. What you want's revenge."

That stopped him. The thick shoulders stiffened and the coldness came back into his eyes. "One way or the other," he said.

"Within the law."

"One way or the other," Heckman repeated, his eyes not wavering.

And Diehl was tempted to give him a gun. That's the way it would have been handled down home. But up here, if Heckman could pull it off, he'd be accused of murder. It'd serve the bastard right. Diehl asked, "Are you armed?"

"No." Then he added: "Not yet."

Diehl stood up. The other man's eyes stayed on him. Without a flicker. "Congressman, it's *my* duty now to warn *you*—"

"Shove it," Heckman said. "What are you going to do?"

Diehl buttoned his tunic. "Wall, what I'm *not* going to do is go off half-cocked. First off, I'm gonna haul in any known homosexuals, starting with the ones got police records. Just for questionin', understand. 'Specially any ever convicted or accused of crimes against juveniles. And just to play safe, all suspected child molesters in the area. You approve?"

"It's a waste of time and police."

"Y'just can't please some folks." He stepped to the intercom on his desk and flipped a switch. "Ben?"

"Yes, sir."

"I want all available men to report in on the double. Every officer you can contact, drunk, sober, in the sack or out, hear?"

"I've already sent out that order, sir."

Goddamn. But he winked at Heckman and pulled at his mustache as he smiled. "Wall, now, Lieutenant Hutchinson, that's real thoughtful of you." He felt the irritation tightening through his muscles. "Why, you're not only fast on your feet, son, you think ahead. You even think ahead of *me*."

"I only thought, sir, that with a major crime having been reported—"

"Yes, *suh*, indeed! Wall, next time, in case there is a next time, mebbe you'll oblige this dodderin' old plughorse by allowin' him t'issue orders of this nature and magnitude."

But Heckman stepped in before he could flip the switch. "Lieutenant Hutchinson," he barked.

"Yes, sir?"

"This is Congressman Heckman. Did I receive a phone call here fifteen or twenty minutes ago that you directed to me at my office?"

"Why, yes, sir, that's true. He said he was an assistant of yours and—"

"Thanks." It was Heckman who closed the circuit. "There was a call, Chief, and he addressed me as Prosecutor. Now what are you going to do."

"Not that that's any of your particular business, but I thought mebbe I should take a look-see at that medical report out to the hospial and then have a word with the victim."

"Like hell."

"Excuse me, Congressman?"

"No one's going to interrogate my son."

"Now there you go again. First, you demand action, then you obstruct justice." His patience had been worn tissue-thin. "It's outta your hands now. Once a formal complaint's been filed, it's police work."

"I've told you everything he told me," Heckman growled.

Diehl placed the hat on his head, then adjusted it at an angle. "Kid might tell his daddy one thing, might even make up things, all kinda reasons, mebbe wants attention. Kids—"

"He didn't make up anything. It's all in the medical report."

"Wall . . . y'all know the legal definition of rape. Has to be proved forcible, not consensual—"

He saw the movement in time, just in time. He leaned quickly to one side as Heckman's huge fist grazed past the side of his head. He went low automatically and, since Heckman was wide open, could have brought his own fist up into Heckman's midsection. Instead, he grabbed the other man's arm, twisted it, turning the body, and flung it back against the wall, hard, relieved inside at the action.

Then, his face close, he said, flatly: "I ain't the professor. You said yourself: I'm a police officer." He glared into the furious red-streaked eyes of the other man, who was not struggling. "I could place you under arrest for what you just did. Next time—" He released his grasp and stepped back. "Next time I will. But not till after I kick your goddamn balls off, hear?"

Heckman didn't appear to be breathing. But he said: "You're not going to interrogate my son. You're not going to wake him after he's been put to sleep by a physician. You're not going to harass him in the middle of the night for no reason whatever." He took a deep, loud breath. "And if you do, I'm going to bring charges and bring you into court and publicly expose you for the brute you are and see you're sent back where you came from."

Diehl considered. He'd been up against Heckman's kind before. What you did was: you bided your time. You played it cool and you bided your time. But even as he did it, turning to flip on the intercom again, he hated himself. "Officer Hutchinson. Get the key and have someone show Congressman Heckman into the file room upstairs." The bile was stinging on his tongue. "And while you're at it, give him some of that good black coffee you're always brewin' in the back room." Then he snapped down the switch and faced Heckman, who had not moved from against the wall, and he allowed his mustache to curl up with another smile as he regarded him. "Anythin' to oblige a Congressman, suh."

Heckman took another breath, eyes burning, nodded and went out. The winner. Let him think it. All Diehl had to do was bide his time.

Meanwhile, he had to deal with the fags. He could

usually tell whether a man was innocent or guilty just by studying him some. Or maybe after a few questions. Then give him a little time alone with the suspect, and he'd prove it. He wasn't often wrong. And fags broke easier. And sooner. Just a *hint* of physical violence and *they'd* crack.

He sat down behind the desk again, placed his heels on it, tilted back his hat and remembered that third bourbon, the one he'd drunk while he was home for that short time. If he hadn't drunk it, he could allow himself another. But three in an evening was his limit. Once a man started to make allowances—for himself or for others—he was on the road to hell, and he didn't mean the one Nell was always harping on or that was described in her black-bound book. He settled for a chew of tobacco. Usually he limited himself to a chew on his way to or from the courthouse: Nell couldn't abide the stuff and he didn't think these Yankees up here would cotton to it, either.

He was in a picklement, no doubt about it. If he gave in and went off half-cocked, he was risking his position and the respect these folks had for his judgment. But if he stood pat and *then* was proved wrong, he could be in a worse fix. Was he allowing *his* personal feelings—against the Congressman, say—to clog up *his* thinking apparatus, the way he'd accused Heckman of doing? He couldn't afford a mistake here. He couldn't start over, not again. He couldn't fold up his tent here and move on. There wasn't any place to go—not for a man his age who didn't know anything but police work and didn't rightly relish the idea of ending up his days a night watchman or some such.

He hoped Heckman was right if it came to that. Nobody wanted or needed action, real action, more than Theron Diehl. He hoped that whoever had stirred up this brushfire intended to carry it on. Hell, it was only in the last few hours he'd begun to feel like a peace officer again.

* * *

It had been a steady uphill climb against a chill wind that seemed to intensify as he approached the campus area. The drinks he'd had in the Colonial Inn and the urgency stirred by Willa's voice—at first lifeless and then even more uncharacteristically strident: *Stay away, stay away forever!*—had carried him the first few blocks after he had discovered the sign at the taxi stand which read: CLOSED 10 P.M. He should have returned to the inn then and borrowed McQuade's car, but he had decided, for the second time tonight, to walk instead. He had hoped the night air might clear his befuddled mind. But, Fletcher Briggs knew, there was another reason: he needed time, he had to delay since he knew he dared not evade the scene with Willa that, in his marrow, he must have known was inevitable, had been inevitable all along since he had begun the affair with Annette. *You can put your cock anywhere you want to put it.* How Willa had found out was of little importance—except that the coincidence of its occurring tonight, this strange night that already held so many other unlikely circumstances, was baffling. He couldn't help wondering whether there was some pattern or connection of which he was ignorant. He had passed several open bars and been tempted: only one more quick one to brace yourself for whatever the hell lies ahead and to add some vigor to the flagging muscles of your legs for the final mile of the slow climb. But if Willa was drunk—and she certainly had sounded drunk on the phone—he had to be sober. Or as sober as he could be after his visit to the Colonial Inn. Somewhat breathless, sweat hot against his flesh, yet chilling at once, reluctance tugging at the ache in his legs, he hesitated in front of the house.

His MG was not where he had left it but parked now at an angle, half on the lawn, one door open. Which indicated, he supposed, that Willa had, for some reason, been driving his car. He went inside through the front door—which was also open.

He closed the door and called her name in the hall.

The house was silent. He went into each of the rooms and called her name several times again, more loudly. When he reached the door of his study, he felt a blast of cold air and searched for its source—and discovered a jagged black hole in the window. As if a ball had been thrown through it. But there were no shards of glass on the books below: whatever had smashed through the pane had been hurled from the inside. Christ. Then he saw the bottle on the desk. Almost empty. The bottle he kept hidden in the drawer for his quick nips while he worked at night and on the weekends.

"Willa!"

With dread spreading through him, he went up the stairs. The bedroom—his and Willa's—was lighted and empty. Her clothes were strewn everywhere: bed, chair, floor. Her cape of many stripes. The brilliant peasant blouse and dirndl skirt she had been wearing. Bra. Panties. Abruptly it occured to him that perhaps she had changed clothes and left. Yet the station wagon had been parked in the driveway.

He was about to shout again when he heard a sound above his head. Her studio. Of course.

As he went up the wide stairway—the stairway that he had taken such satisfaction in installing to replace the old narrow scuttleway—he went weak with guilt and sadness and a sense of loss, and his steps slowed. But when his head came above the floor level and he saw the studio, he stopped, staring, and felt shock close over his heart and tighten. Havoc. Devastation. It was as if the studio had been laid waste by some invading army or natural disaster, tornado or flood, leaving a dry smell of clay. At his eye level were smashed figures, sculptures without arms, heads like grotesque abandoned skulls, abstractions now contorted into shapeless nothings, mockeries of their own design, pieces and chunks of clay everywhere, and that arid choking smell, as of dust. The long work table lay on its side and, in the dimness, tools glinted through the colorless silt that covered everything.

"You're too late. You missed the party."

At first he thought the words had to be in his own mind: it was not Willa's voice.

"It got a trifle rough at the end, but it was one hell of a brawl while it lasted. But then you had other things to do, didn't you?"

He saw her then, at the far end of the long room, beyond the dangling rope of the block and tackle, a shadowy figure rising wraithlike and tall. A cigarette in one hand. And she was naked.

"I believe there's some liquor left. Would you care to mix a drink? Or . . . would you prefer it neat, like me?"

He climbed the remaining steps and started toward her through the debris. "Willa, what the devil do you think you're doing?"

"I thought I told you to stay away from here."

He stopped. How would it be possible to deal with her in this condition? He glanced and saw a smock lying in the dust. He picked it up, shook it sharply twice, creating a cloud of powder, and approached her. It was then that he saw her clearly: her face and body were covered with gray, giving her the appearance of a statue. He extended the smock, but she didn't move. Her eyes stared out at him as from a mask. So he stepped in closer and to one side and draped the smock around her shoulders.

"Why, Fletcher Briggs," she said, mockingly, in a little-girl voice, "I didn't know you cared." She turned to him and he glimpsed the cold distance in her dark, withdrawn eyes. "Whatever happened to your strong manly jaw? You look all lop . . . lopsided. I do hope it's painful. Too bad, really, he didn't do more."

Instantly he remembered Annette's swift concern at the bar, her finger trailing over his flesh. But he pushed the thought aside and demanded: "Too bad *who* didn't do more?"

"Oh, did I forget to tell you?" She strolled away, kicking idly with a bare foot at the odds and ends of rubble. "You had a visitor. Very *distingué*."

And then a new thought struck him—a baffling, incredible idea. Had he been wrong? Had his sense of guilt caused him to leap to the conclusion that somehow Willa had learned about Annette? If he had been wrong, then—

"Christ, Willa. I know Wally Heckman came by." He felt a sour anger invading his mind. "You can't believe what Wally Heckman suspected." She knew him better than that. Had to. "You can't, damn it!"

She had turned. Her eyes were level, cold, but he saw the bafflement in them. "I'm not sure I know you at all."

"If you can believe that, I don't think you do, or ever have." And to hell with it, to hell with her and everything else. The rage twisted in him. "I don't know where the hell I've been living the last twenty years."

"Join the party. You'd better have that drink."

"I don't want a drink!"

"No?" she mocked. "Since when?"

"Goddamn it, Willa—"

"I think I'd believe anything anyone said about you."

"That I'd sodomize an eleven-year-old boy?"

She gasped and he saw her eyes flinch and, at once, he knew that Heckman had told her nothing, she knew nothing of any of that, and relief flooded the anger away in a single wave.

"*Almost* anything," she whispered, her tone contrite. "No, I'm sorry, no, I didn't—"

"Christ," he breathed, "I'd begun to think everybody's gone crazy."

His eyes were traveling down her body. The smock hung open and loose. She folded her arms. The body he'd possessed thousands of times, had known in every detail, loved. Still loved. And he felt desire take hold, now, at this unlikeliest of times.

"Well?" She tilted her dark head to one side. "Well? Does my body disgust you? Or what?"

The challenge was clear, sharp. But it held contempt, too. For him. Possibly also for herself.

Then, before he could answer, he heard the telephone ringing on the floor below. A moment passed. He didn't want to move. Up here on the third floor the wind outside seemed stronger, whistling, insistent. The phone rang again.

"It might be important," she said, still in that thin mocking tone while he stared at her. "It might be much more important than us."

"To hell with it."

"Oh, answer it!" she snapped, turning away and drawing the smock around her. "It might be about one of the children."

He turned and scuffed his way through the litter and clattered down the stairway and went along the upstairs hall to the phone table. Nothing settled, nothing even spoken. It was as if, in a few hours, the whole damned world had gone haywire.

"Hello?"

"Fletcher?"

Christ, nice timing! "Yes, Annette, what is it?"

"Look, I don't object to doing the dirty work while you go home to ball the wife, but do you have to snap—"

"What is it?"

"You were insulting enough when you left the bar, but—"

"Annette, I'm going to hang up."

"I'm in the Congressman's office." Her tone had hardened and was businesslike, brisk. "Alone. He just called from the courthouse: he broke down Diehl's resistance somehow. We're going to tackle the court records next. His files here are summaries, no details. But there's one case that's puzzling. Aggravated assault. Judge Stuttaford presiding. Heckman for the state, Briggs for the defense. Defendant pleaded guilty, yet Stuttaford gave him maximum. Ring any bells?"

"Sexual assault?"

"Not in the formal charge. Against a female, though. Coralie Powell by name."

He was not breathing now. Coralie Powell—who

had married Paul Wharton. Of the Wharton Mills family.

"What was the defendant's name?"

"Ritchie. Boyd Ritchie. Address: some town in Illinois."

A face flickered in his mind: a handsome young face, blond hair.

"How long ago?"

"Almost eight years. Do I hear bells ringing, Professor?"

Yes. *You gave it to me, didn't you, Mr. Briggs? You gave me the shaft along with the rest of them.*

"Listen. Get over to the courthouse. Ask Heckman what he remembers. Get the complete case record, especially the exact wording of the sentencing. I remember there was something odd there, but I can't remember what. And have the police find out whether Ritchie's still serving time. And if not, where he is."

"You mean maybe I won the gweat big kewpie doll?"

"I'll be in later." Then he changed his mind. "No, I won't be in, but I'll phone in."

"Well, it looks way-out from where I sit, but you're the boss, bossman."

"Get on it."

"Looks like you're safe anyway, right? If you defended someone and lost, he might claim you threw the ball game, but if he pleaded guilty himself—"

"Get on it, I said!" He replaced the phone. And stood there a moment. He was breathing again. Fast. Too fast.

You've been playing games with me, haven't you, Counselor? You're in with the rest of them.

He went to the stairway, forcing his mind to concentrate, to remember. Had he advised the guilty plea? He'd been appointed by the court: he remembered that. But his memory was sketchy. Fragmented. Rape charge reduced. Hitchhiker. Signed confession.

You're worse than they are: you acted like you were

on my side. You were my friend!

Well, he had no time for that now. For the past.

By the time he was in the attic again, he had made up his mind what he was going to do. Call it panic. Call it cowardice. He knew what had to be done. Now. If it was Boyd Ritchie and if he was capable of doing what had been done to Wally Heckman's son—

Willa stood in exactly the same spot as before. Her cigarette was gone out but apparently she had not moved.

"Don't tell me, let me guess. The trustworthy assistant who will assist in *any*thing."

Willa knew. Somehow now this didn't seem as important as it had. In spite of the hurt on Willa's face, the vulnerability behind the loathing, hostile, accusing eyes.

"Darling," he said, and stepped toward her.

"Don't call me that!" she hissed. "Don't ever call me that again, you son of a bitch, you fake, you fraud!"

The wildness stopped him. The hate glittering and smoldering in her dark eyes. And he recalled: *You're as phony as the rest of them. Worse than the rest. You pretended you were on my side.* There had been more shock and sadness than hate in the boy's eyes. No threat whatever, then—

"Darling," he tried again, softly, "please I want to—"

But she sprang at him, fast, her furious fists beating at his chest, then opening, rising to his face, clawing. He tried to grasp her wrists, but her flailing arms moved too fast, he felt her nails gouging down his swollen cheek, he stepped away, grabbed one arm, twisted her away to one side and they stood face to face, her eyes ferocious, but he saw the anguish behind, the deep and terrible hurt, and his heart exploded as he reached again, and this time she came into his arms, managing to break his grip, coming close against his body, her hands tearing off the smock as she thrust herself against him, her face an inch from his now, the flaring hate bright and dreadful, and her body beginning to grind against him, a harsh physical demand, without tenderness, without love, with hot malice and challenge and fury, and then her body rose, hard against him, and her mouth clamped on his, the lips hard and insistent, the mouth opening, and then the teeth clenching on his lips, drawing blood, talons gripping and cutting flesh, and he allowed it, he didn't struggle, he deserved it, he deserved more, he didn't know what had come over her, what was in her, had ever been, but he deserved anything she wanted to do if he could cause her this much pain—

Then abruptly as it had flared, the storm subsided. She pushed him back with her two hands, turned her head, spit his blood, then lifted her chin and glared into his face. She had never looked more beautiful. More desirable.

"Is she better than me?" she demanded in that other voice he had never heard before: raucous, husky. "Is that it? She's better than me. That's all it comes to, all it ever comes to anyway. Well, why don't you try me? Why didn't you ever tell me what you wanted? I'd have done it! *Anything.*"

Her flesh gleamed softly. She was breathing hard. She seemed to be waiting.

He had to break, with a wrenching of the will so powerful that he felt it through his whole body, the impulse to step and pick her up in his arms and carry her downstairs to the bedroom. But there were other things to do. More important things. There was no time to lose.

"Willa, will you talk to me? Can you?"

"Talk? We've been talking all our lives without saying anything!"

"That's not true, damn it!"

"Did we ever talk?" she screamed.

Then she brushed past him, avoiding his eyes, and went down the stairway. He followed, swiftly. They were wasting time, and they may not have time to waste! No matter what, he had to get through to her. The blood was bitter on his tongue, the lacerations on his face stinging.

She was in the bedroom. She had draped the cape over her shoulders and she was sitting at her writing desk, her back to the room, her head down on the top of the desk, dark hair splayed over it.

He halted in the doorway. And it was then that her pain reached him—overwhelmed him. He stepped closer, his whole body and mind aching to take her into his arms, gently, quietly, to calm her, comfort her.

"Willa," he said in a low choked voice, "Willa, I ended it with Annette tonight. Finished it completely."

"More lies." A muted whisper, almost indistinct. "More and more and—"

"I don't blame you for not believing—"

"Ended it in your office?" She did not lift her head, or turn. "In the dark?"

Hopeless. He knew now that it was hopeless to try and time was running out. "Willa, you're going to hear me out now. And you are not going to ask questions. You are going to take my word. If not about Annette, then about what I'm going to tell you."

"Don't I always take your word? Haven't I always?"

"No, you haven't, but—"

"Does *she* always take your word? Without questions?"

"Willa, damn it," he said and stepped closer. "I know you're hurt and angry and I'm sorry, but we can settle that later, it's not germane now."

"Germane." Her voice was muffled in her bare arm. "Your Honor, I object: the question is irrelevant. The question of love. The question of marriage. The question of honesty and integrity. Not germane, your Honor! Not in this lousy, ugly, godforsaken world!"

He had to fight down the crushing sense of defeat. And to go on. "At least, listen. Will you? *Can* you?"

"Order in the court. Silence in the choir loft while the teacher screws the soprano!"

He decided then. He decided consciously and with intent, to voice his deepest fears. "There have been two crimes committed in town tonight. Both the work of a twisted mind. The first, morbid and relatively negligible, but sick. The second, destructive, so destructive that its results will be felt for years. You know now about Wally Heckman's son. The person who committed those crimes—I'm convinced it's the same person—is still free. He's capable of anything. Anything. And I have reason to believe that he harbors a grudge against me. If he commits any other crimes, we may be the victims. One or more of us, and not necessarily me. You. Peggy. David."

He saw her straighten then. Very slowly. But she did not turn in the chair.

"Willa, darl—Willa, do you understand what I'm saying? Your own life may be in danger. Or worse."

"What difference does that make?"

He spoke through his shock. "It makes a difference to me!"

She did turn then; she swiveled all the way around in the chair and smiled. Mockingly. "Fraud," she said softly. "Phony."

He choked down the panic. How the hell could he make her comprehend? Both the danger and that he cared, but especially now the danger. How could he ever break through the liquor and the hate? He couldn't move. He didn't know what she'd do, what rage or worse she might fly into, if he stepped closer. He broke that impulse and said: "Even if you don't believe me now, Willa, you'll have to do what I say."

"Will I?"

"Yes!" he growled. "Damn it, yes, you will! Just this once. Tonight. Maybe never again, but this once or by God I'll—"

But she was up and running, the cape flying behind her, her eyes stabbing his as she passed. "You'll what?" She was going down the stairs. Her voice floated back: "You'll what?"

He ran after her, going down the stairs three at a time, recklessly. He couldn't very well pick her up and carry her, screaming and clawing at him, out to the car and drive her to Boston himself. Even if he could, what about the kids? She was in the dining room, at the liquor cabinet, pouring whiskey.

"Where's David?" he asked, changing tactics—a trick he'd learned in the courtroom. Take her mind off herself and him. "Where does David go camping?"

She drank. "Don't you know?"

"How the hell would I—" He broke off and took a deep breath. "I don't know."

"You might if you'd ever bothered to—"

"Willa," he said tensely, *"listen:* we don't have time for games now. Of any sort."

"But that's what living is, isn't it—a game? Don't get caught." She poured more whiskey—a tumblerful. "This is what one does, isn't it? To keep from facing things. Or to make sure one *can* face things."

It occurred to him then that there might be another way. She rarely drank. If he could allow time and even goad her into getting so bombed she would pass out, he could maneuver her into the station wagon, somehow locate Peggy and David, then drive the whole family to her mother's apartment in Boston. But did he have time? No telling what Boyd Ritchie had in mind, or how soon. Or, for that matter, whether he had *anything* in mind. He might still be in the state penitentiary, for Christ sake!

"If you know where they are, Willa, tell me. David, or Peggy, or both."

Again Willa drank. More deeply this time. She seemed to be considering this carefully. "You know . . . I think I really ought to . . . tell you."

"I think so, too. Right now."

"Yes. I think you *deserve* to know." She smiled crookedly and her gaze, slightly blurred, held a knowing slyness. "I think you've been protected long enough." She took a small sip. "She's at 107 Main Street. Londonford."

"Londonford? But what's she—"

But Willa was shaking her head, the smile fixed, not quite derisive, almost sad. "The second floor. She spends most of her evenings there."

Then he did step to her. "I'll get her. And you'll get dressed and take the MG—I'll need the wagon if I can find David, too—and you'll get the hell out of here, fast. I'll meet you at your mother's apartment. Willa, unless I have your promise that you'll do this, I won't be able to go get Peggy."

"You're awfully eager for me to get dressed, aren't you?" She shrugged the cape off and it fell to the floor. "I can remember when you liked me undressed. All the time."

He ignored this. He had to. "I want your promise, Willa. You'll never have to do anything else for me, ever. You can have a divorce if you want one, later, but tonight I want you to promise me. You've never lied to me."

"That," she said, "is the truth. And that, also, is a joke. Coming from you."

On target. But he couldn't waste any more time. "If you don't promise, I'll have to stay with you. Then God knows what might happen to the kids."

The smile faded. "I promise," she said. "Lord and master." She drifted into the living room and through it toward the hall, glass in hand. "My true and solemn promise. Away to Bostontown and Mama-dear who sees no evil, hears no evil, thinks only evil."

By the time he was in the hall she was going languidly up the stairs.

"Willa," he said, "it's for your own sake. *Believe* me."

"Believe you? Haven't I always believed you? Gird your loins and take up your spear. Farewell, my love. Farewell, my one and only true love."

"Willa!" he heard himself shout. "Willa, I have your

promise. And for God's sake, stop drinking or you won't be able to drive!"

She whipped about on the stairs and flung the whiskey down at him, holding the glass. The liquid struck on his upturned face and dribbled down, burning in the scratches left by her nails.

"Go forth to save me, m'lord. Go forth in shining honor—I mean, armor. Did I say honor?"

She disappeared and he stood a long moment, undecided even now. If she continued to drink—

Then he returned to the cabinet in the dining room, gathered together the bottles there, took them all into the kitchen and poured the contents in the sink. Then he locked the kitchen door and closed the curtains in the living room and went out the front door, making sure the lock snapped behind him. It was colder now. Much colder. And the wind was stronger, with a cutting edge.

Wake up, you lying motherfucker, you brave boxer with an outboard motor, wake up and get the rest that's coming to you! You're not through yet, Wharton, you got a job to do.

He couldn't sit here all night waiting. No matter how many times he stabbed the intense thin beam of light at the closed eyes, the figure collapsed on the floor refused to move. Or to make a sound. What if he'd hit him too hard? Once he'd seen him standing in the doorway with that Luger pointed, he'd lost control. All the rage and hate had come together in that blow, which he'd tried to break at the last second, even as the flashlight was coming down on the motherfucker's skull. Had he blown it? Because if Wharton was dead, the whole scheme was shot. It wouldn't stop him, but it'd ruin the beauty of it. He, he personally, was not going to kill anyone, that was too easy, that was the beauty of the whole plan.

Every once in a while the Cunt on the bed would whimper, or kind of cry like a kid in its sleep, and once when he'd flashed the light on her, she'd opened her eyes. But they didn't see anything. Even the light, probably. They were glazed and sort of blank. And pale—as if all the color had faded out of them. She was off on her own trip. That, or maybe she'd flipped out completely. He didn't give a shit which, just so she was still alive. To hell with hers; she'd had hers. Where she was, she didn't give a damn what came next. What, goddamn it, was coming!

But suppose someone out on the street—walking a dog or window-peeping or coming home tight—suppose someone saw the movement of that light when it went up and down like that. In spite of the heavy brocaded curtains which he'd closed as soon as Wharton pulled into the driveway. There had been a light in the house next door then. Or supposing some dimwit pig started putting it together, adding it up. Like his calling that son of a bitch Heckman *Prosecutor* on the phone. How the hell could he have come this far and then made a dumb-ass slip like that? He still had two more stops—three, really, if you included Diehl's house as well as Diehl personally and Briggs—and he was goddamned if he was going to let anyone or anything, including his own stupid mouth, foul it up.

The smell of blood and the quiet had begun to bug hell out of him. So he stood up and crossed to where Wharton had fallen. Keeping the light on his face, hard and tight, he kicked him, once, in the ribs, hard. On the bed the bitch moaned, but that was all. So he kicked Wharton again. Wake up, you motherfucker, it's not over yet. He went back and sat down and focused the light on the crumpled figure that was now beginning to come to life. He wasn't dead, anyway: that was the important thing right now.

Wharton groaned. And finally lifted his head, then lowered it again. He reached with one hand, touched the hair on top, which was matted with blood. His eyes looked vague, stunned. They tried to stare into the glare of light, blinked, looked down at the hand, which was red now, then peered around the darkness, then closed.

"Welcome home, Mr. Wharton . . . sir."

The head came up again. And the figure tried to stand. Failed. And slumped back weakly, half sitting with its back against the wall. "I'm sorry I had to crack your skull, Mr. Wharton, but you came in pointing a loaded pistol." And now Wharton, planting his feet and bracing his back against the wall, was struggling to rise, his back sliding upward, eyes staring. "Is that any way to greet a guest in your own bedroom, Mr. Wharton? . . . sir." And now the figure was upright, but leaning for support against the wall. The eyes, shuddering, squinted blindly into the light. "I'll have to report you to the Diners Club."

"Who . . . who are you?" The voice was weak and cracked.

So he simply turned the light about, lifted it and held it above his head to illuminate his face and the bare skull in all its bony splendor. "You don't recognize me, Mr. Wharton?"

"No. Where's—"

"I'm nobody. That's who I am. Just nobody your wife took pity on and invited home."

Wharton, as if he had not heard, looked down at his hand again, stared at it as if he couldn't believe it, yet couldn't seem to concentrate on anything else, either. Then he returned his uncertain gaze to the face in the spotlight's beam. "Where's my wife?"

"Scrambling the eggs. She lied, though: she told me she does it with brandy."

Wharton took a step forward, but his legs seemed weak and, when he found himself again pinned in the light, he caught himself. "What do you want?"

"I've had what I want."

That did it. Pay dirt. Wharton, already pale, went white. "Where is she?"

So he flashed the light, swiftly, very quickly, toward the bed. The Cunt's eyes were still closed. Then he fixed it again on Wharton, who was staring.

"She's only sleeping, Mr. Wharton . . . sir. Sleeping and waiting."

"Do you have a gun on me?"

"Now what do you think, Mr. Wharton?" The Luger was in his belt and the shotgun was on the floor, where he'd placed it, carefully. "You shouldn't have brought that Luger upstairs . . . sir. 'Cause now it's pointed straight at your gut . . . sir."

"How'd you get in here?"

"I was hitchhiking. Coralie picked me up. That doesn't surprise you, does it? She often does." He was enjoying himself now. Plenty of time, plenty. "Man, you are one lucky prick. You got to know that. You got the cunt everybody wants. Like the college football team. The tennis pro out at that club that teaches her . . . things. What's his name? Jimmy Shatrow. Keeps 'em drooling in the locker room telling about her." He saw Wharton take another single step: it was enough. "That barman out there, too. Wilbur. The good-looking one. Wilbur Braun." He kept the light focused on Wharton, whose flesh was visibly quivering and whose eyes were now slits as he rubbed the blood from his hand onto the lapel of his jacket. "She's what they call a nympho, Mr. Wharton. Your luck, man. Salesman comes to the door, man comes to read the meter, that hefty brute Whiting who does the lawn." He paused, briefly. "And I'm not mentioning your friends . . . sir. Your dearest and very best friends." He watched the arrows go in. "Like Bill Watts . . . Robbie Dewhurst . . . Matt Durkin."

Wharton opened his mouth. What came out was a shrill high-pitched stream of words that were indistinguishable. Finally a bellow: *"I don't believe a goddamned word you've said!"*

"You think I give a shit whether you believe me, Mr. Wharton? Sir. I was just being what the Bible calls a good Samaritan. You gonna treat me like this, yelling at me, acting like I'm not your friend—hell, man, why should I tell you where she went when she left that Lake Club tonight?"

A pause. Outside the wind had begun to whine around the corners of the high old house.

"She came home."

"Yeah. With me. But before—"

"She came straight home!" It was almost a shriek.

"I'm damned if I'll tell you! You're drunk and you're not listening. I got a notion to take my little old shotgun and go home."

Wharton was breathing hard now, his shoulders heaving. "You better be prepared to use that gun."

"Oh, I am, sir, Mr. Wharton, I am." Then in an entirely different tone: "You better believe it."

But he knew that Wharton believed it.

"She picked me up on the way home from Stegner's place."

"Who?"

"Vincent Stegner. You forgot him already? After all he did for you."

Wharton's eyes looked more baffled than ever.

"The old man with the field glasses, man. The nature lover." His voice was very soft and he could see Wharton straining to hear, as bewilderment began to give way to comprehension in his eyes. "The old kinky gink who saw you beat her up on the boat before you took her down below and raped her."

That did it. More pay dirt. Wharton's brows came together. "Who the hell are you?" His tone was incredulous. "Who—"

"You want to know how she pays off the old man? She uses your money, Mr. Wharton. Sir. . . . Your money and her body. Man, that kinky gink old lech can dream up more ways of using that pretty young body'n you and me together. I watched her from the window. What she did with him. What she did to him. What she did *for* him."

"You heard me! Who are you?" Shrill now. A snarl. "My wife doesn't even know Vincent Stegner!"

"She knows him *well,* man. Well and better. Every month. For years. One night a month. And he knows *her* better'n any man alive. Including you . . . sir."

"Who the hell are you?" The tone was hard but strident, high and thin.

It was time. The time he'd been waiting for. He took the wig from his pocket, worked it onto his scalp, keeping Wharton transfixed in the beam of the flashlight which was held between his knees. When the wig was in place, he lifted the light again and directed it full on his face from below. *His* face. Boyd Ritchie's face. *His.* Look, you bastard, look and may your nuts fall off.

"Holy God," Wharton breathed.

The sound was music, sheer delight, adding to the unbearable elation already in him.

"Too bad you didn't catch me with that outboard, isn't it? Catch me and chew me to bits. Too bad all you did was follow me into the woods and crack a couple of ribs and make mash out of my balls."

Wharton's head was shaking from side to side. "But . . . I didn't. You know I—"

"I know. And you know. And Diehl knows. Yeh. But you *said* you did. To protect Diehl. For favors returned, man. *Noblesse oblige.*"

Wharton had it now. Had it all the way. And he only asked, in a weak voice, slumping against the wall: "What are you going to do to me?"

"Nothing." He was speaking softly now. The ecstasy inside made him almost tender. "I've done all I'm going to do here."

Then he swung the beam of light toward the bed. The sheet was drawn up to her chin as before. Her eyes were open: wide and glassy. The light didn't seem to penetrate them. And she was turning her head from side to side. Until finally her head stopped moving and she huddled herself together, bare arms coming out to cover her face, which was turned to one side. Then she was quiet again.

The light held on her face. He couldn't see Wharton, who was still as death now, couldn't even hear his breathing in the stillness. Slowly then he moved the beam of light off her face, down her body, almost caressing the soft, curving loveliness beneath the sheet. Until it came to the place where her legs joined. Then it stopped. Stopped and held steadily on the splotch of red. On the bedsheet. The red getting darker now.

And, quietly, he said: "This time I did rape her. I really did rape her, Mr. Wharton . . . sir."

He flashed the light to the floor between them. Fixed it on the shotgun lying there.

"With that," he said.

And when Wharton still could not speak, only mutter some indistinct curse or prayer, he added: "She loved it. That's what we were doing when you called on the phone. She loved it. Probably because it was loaded."

The lament faded away. He knew that Wharton was staring at the shotgun on the floor. "She needs—she needs—"

He returned the light to the bed. "She's just strung-out. Pillheads get that way."

"Pillheads?" Wharton repeated the word as if he had never heard it before.

He was certain that Wharton's eyes were darting to the gun on the floor. "Pillheads. Speed. Goofballs. Uppers, downers, alcohol, the works, man. You didn't know?"

Wharton, very still now, didn't answer. Was it shock or was he thinking of what he could do with the shotgun if he had the guts to go for it? He really hadn't known. Blind stupid numskull. But in a way it was beautiful: a dividend. Wharton hadn't even suspected his wife was a pill freak! It was too much, too *much!*

"She looks . . . she looks dead."

He waited for a beat or two. Then he said, "That's what you want now, isn't it, Mr. Wharton? Sir. You hope she's dead now, don't you?"

"Hell, no. I—" But his voice drifted off. He continued to stare at her.

"We could call Dr. Farago. Leroy." He was taking his time now. Not much longer and he'd know. Know what Wharton would do. Could do. "Leroy has more pills. . . . All kinds. . . . That's where she gets them." He let that sink in. Wharton hadn't even turned his head. "Leroy drops by every Wednesday afternoon. To deliver. And collect. Right here. In your bed, Mr. Wharton . . . sir."

That did it. He saw Wharton move, swung the light to him, held it, as Wharton stooped and swooped up the shotgun from the floor, fast, and then without hesitation turned the muzzle on the light and, his face twisting, flinching, grimacing, pulled the trigger.

There was a sharp sound. Not an explosion. A click.

It was too good. He couldn't believe it. It was too beautiful.

"Is that any way to treat a guest?" he asked: almost a whisper. "You could've killed me, man. And I registered the gun in your name, too."

Wharton may or may not have heard that. He was blinking down at the short shotgun in his hands. Then he broke it, held it up, looked through the empty barrel into the light. Then he lowered it. There were tears in his dazed and disbelieving eyes and they began to stream down his cheeks. He lowered his head.

Boyd Ritchie spoke very quietly, in his gentlest tones. "You could have killed me . . . when it's not me you want to kill at all—"

Outside, the wind was beginning to raise hell.

What if he doesn't do it?

Slowly Wharton lifted his head. His eyes were bright and wet. Glassy. There was a low gurgling sound in his throat, a gurgling that turned into sobs as he shifted the gun around in his hands, the metal of the barrel glittering dark in the beam of light, and then he had the barrel in both hands and the sobbing turned into a savage, junglelike howl as he stepped to the bed, fast, raised the gun above his head and brought the heavy wooden stock down. Hard.

There was then only a single sound. As of bone shattering.

Part Four

When things were dull—which was almost every night—Gavin McQuade had the habit of climbing to the third floor of the old Underhill Building to the radio station above the Colonial Inn. Only Jerry Gerrard would be there at night and it was a place to sit awhile, shoot the bull, have a cup of coffee and listen to Jerry talk with the night owls who would keep phoning *Tell It to Jerry* between eleven at night and six o'clock in the morning.

Tonight, shortly before twelve, Jerry—a thirty-year-old two-hundred-and-twenty-pound cherub with a resonant voice that brimmed with sincerity—was involved with an irascible elderly man who was arguing that it was the right of every American, a right guaranteed by the Constitution, to possess arms. And Jerry was saying, into the microphone on his table, as he waved McQuade to a chair, that the Constitution, if the man would forgive his contradicting him, guaranteed the right of the *militia* to *bear* arms, and wasn't that a different matter? No, and that's not the way the man read the Constitution. Then was he suggesting that every man needed his own firearm because the police were not doing their job? The police would do their job and maintain law and order if the Supreme Court and others of that element would let them. What element was he referring to? Jerry, the man said, knew what element, so why was he pretending? Jerry assured him that he didn't know unless the man referred to the criminal element, and the man's voice crackled with the ominous: the ordinary citizen today had to be armed against what the *government* might do. And what was that, sir? "You know what I mean. We've got to be prepared!" Bang: the man hung up. And Jerry leaned back and said, "The shadow knoooows. Well, time for more music." Then he gave the number to call *Tell It to Jerry;* all lines were open. And then he punched a button and the turntable began to play "Eleanor Rigby."

After a gulp of the coffee that McQuade had placed on the table before he sat down, Jerry leaned back in the swivel chair, stretching, and asked, "Will you tell me what the hell I am doing? What an ego trip. Trying to impose my own version of reason and truth on a populace that doesn't give a damn anyway." He said this at least once a week. As he said every night: "Poor ignorant bastards."

He extended a package of Marlboro cigarettes. Gavin McQuade considered a second, then shook his head and watched Jerry light up. They were not Marlboro cigarettes—Jerry rolled them himself. Smoking a little grass once in a while was a way to let down, but tonight, for some reason, McQuade had the feeling that he'd better stay on top of it. Jerry would light up, off and on, until about five in the morning, not enough to get stoned, and then he'd stop completely and air out the studio before anyone else appeared to take over the station.

"And you think you can wise them up?" McQuade asked, more because it was expected of him than because of any genuine curiosity. "And don't ask me why I'm working for a newspaper if I don't believe in truth and all that other crap. If the electorate elects con men, why shouldn't it get conned?"

Jerry snorted. It was a familiar pattern; they'd had the same conversation a thousand times. At least. Odd how many years he'd been sitting here drinking coffee from a cardboard container. Here and in the city room. Until coffee from a china cup didn't taste quite like coffee. He was almost thirty-five years old. Half a life. Or more. And he'd be sitting here having this same conversation thirty years from now. Here or in some other town somewhere, some town just like Tarkington. He listened to the muted music: *Look at all the lonely people, where do they all come from? Look at all the lonely people, where do they all belong?* Jerry played it at least once every other night.

"Gavin, what's happening across the street?" The courthouse was not exactly across the street, but on the other side of the Common, which was a carpet of rust and yellow leaves that were being churned up by the wind. Through the window, but somewhat obscured by the sparse foliage remaining on the trees, he could see the two blue globes of light on either side of the stone steps leading into the stone building. "You've got access to the sanctum sanctorum over there, haven't you? What's cooking?"

"Big night for raids on kids for possession of pot maybe. Gives the fuzz something to do, fills the exchequer when the papas pay off. Christ, wouldn't you think they'd have more to do?"

Jerry got up and went to stand at the window. He always reminded McQuade of a big soft jovial bear. "More than that. The fuzz are arriving from all directions."

"All I know is that some nut tore up a grave early this evening. Diehl pulls the great stone face and—yes, Virginia, there is something else—but all his little officers clam up like the sweet little SS men he's trained them to be. I'll get it off the blotter before morning if they book anybody, so what the hell." He drained the cup, the bitter cup. "Of course, I could raise a stink. People's right to know. But the question is: to know what? Maybe they'll sleep better *not* knowing. We get trapped in all these silly little codes, and when you come down to it, what difference does it make?"

"My, my, what a mood he's in tonight. If you think your cynicism fools me, friend—"

"I'm bushed."

"There's what I'd call a flurry of activity over there.

They're hauling in others, not just fuzz. Who?"

"Way I read it, they're rounding up the queers. So watch it."

Jerry looked at him and the blue pleasantness went out of his eyes. He ran a hand over his sandy crewcut and said, softly: "You can be a bastard, can't you?"

Before McQuade could reply, the music ended. Jerry resumed his seat and snapped a button. It was a woman this time. She wanted to know whether Jerry believed in God. Jerry said he supposed he did; it depended on what she meant by the word. And she said she wished she could believe he really did because if he did, he wouldn't worry and fret so much—about the world, everything. She sits up late every night, somehow she can't sleep the way she used to, and she worries about *him*. He's such a *nice* young man he'd be so much happier if he believed in God and left things in His hands. Obviously touched, Jerry thanked her for calling and asked her to call again.

Meanwhile, only half listening, McQuade was giving himself hell. He *could* be a bastard, no denying it. He'd never mentioned the subject of Jerry's sex life before because it didn't mean a damn thing to him one way or the other. The poor kid was hanging in there, like everyone else, and he suspected that Jerry had this job because he, too, was one of the lonely sleepless people. Christ, what was happening to him? To him, Gavin McQuade, the kid himself? He was turning into a bitter, nasty, saber-toothed middle-aged cynic, that's what was happening to him. And the thought filled him with a slow cold dread that no hot coffee could ever touch.

When the theological discussion was over and after Jerry had started another record, McQuade said: "Listen, if you're really gay, why take me so seriously?" It was intended as an apology.

Jerry studied him a moment or two before he smiled, gently: "Why is it people take so damn much from you, McQuade? It can't be because you're half as charming as you imagine you are."

"Listen to that, will you?" McQuade addressed that invisible presence that seemed to accompany him. "Why does everyone seem so gloomy, so sad?"

A moment passed. He heard the music: *It's a long, long time . . . from May to December—*

"It's all in your mind, Gavin. Like the woman just said."

And it was, he supposed. The aching melancholy was all in his mind.

"If you find out what's going on over there, let me know, will you? I'll pass it along to my listeners."

"And scoop me. That's just about your style, you son of a bitch."

And Jerry put his head back and laughed. His laugh was deep and masculine and usually very infectious. But tonight McQuade was thinking, ruefully, of the girl named Annette Beauchamp. Quite the loveliest and most exciting girl he'd met in years. And because he knew that that was it, the whole thing, the beginning and the end of it, he couldn't shake his doleful mood—what his mother, from Ireland, had called the vapors.

September . . . November . . . December. I'll spend these golden years—

The hands on the dashboard clock had moved to 12:07. Time was getting away. He didn't know how long it had been since he left the Wharton house, walked back to the service station and retrieved the Vega. He'd been driving around the block now for some time, waiting for any sign of action or life in the house on Elmhurst Street. He had been careful to keep his driving pattern various, passing the big white house at irregular intervals, and although only a few lights shone in the windows of the other houses, you never could tell when some nosy neighbor might get suspicious, might even call the police to report a car going by over and over. Why the hell didn't that bastard Wharton do whatever he was going to do?

When Boyd Ritchie, taking the Luger but not the bloody shotgun, had left, Wharton had been in a state of shock—more than shock. A catatonic stupor: body limp, eyes vacant. Supposing that when and if he recovered enough to take some action, he still couldn't think straight? Straight enough to decide on what his alternatives were.

If Wharton brought in the police soon, he had a chance, a prayer, not much of a one, slight. He might already have called them. If he removed his fingerprints from the shotgun barrel and then reported that his poor innocent sleeping wife had been attacked by a sex fiend who had then crushed her skull and that then he, the upright citizen, had come home to discover the remains—well, it might wash. Might. But Boyd Ritchie was relying on two things: that Wharton, if he had been able to hear, now knew that the gun had been registered in his name and that Wharton would be, by now, so overwhelmed by guilt that he would decide the police wouldn't believe his story. Especially now that he believed that everyone in town but himself knew of the Cunt's playing around with every prick in sight. If he was thinking straight at all by now, the motherfucker would probably figure that the police might start lining up the motives for *his* killing his wife. Then it'd be his turn to be faced with the sneering disbelief and suspicion that Boyd Ritchie could remember as if he had faced it only a few minutes ago. Your turn, you bastard, you'd better figure it.

He was passing the house again and this time there was a light behind the heavy curtains in the bedroom window upstairs. What was he doing? Phoning the cops—or cleaning up the mess? Wharton had one safe shot, but he didn't know it, that was the beauty of the whole goddamned ripoff: the bastard didn't know his only chance lay in telling the truth. Because if he did, it wouldn't take Diehl long to connect the Wharton name with Heckman's and Judge Stuttaford's. And since Wharton himself could supply the name Boyd

Ritchie—hell, they'd go for it. But what Boyd Ritchie had to believe now was that since Wharton didn't know about Heckman's kid, or the judge's grave, or how Fletcher Briggs' name had been used, he'd decide that the pigs wouldn't believe any wild tale about a man in a wig fucking his wife with a shotgun barrel and then smashing her skull.

Boyd Ritchie had been right up to now. He'd called all the shots, every goddamn one. Including what Wharton had done to his wife. If Wharton hadn't done what Boyd Ritchie intended he do, the structure of the whole night would have crumbled right there. But he had done it, he had, everyone did what Boyd Ritchie forced him to do.

All the wild fantasies dreamed up in his cell were becoming reality.

He was driving faster now because there was always the chance, an outside chance, that somewhere along the line he'd slip up. What if Wharton now—in panic and unable to think—what if he had already phoned the police?

Impossible. Impossible because he, Boyd Ritchie, had not been wrong yet, was never wrong.

Nevertheless, if any sirens sounded or if he saw any red or blue lights, he'd have to get away from here, fast, and then—identity known—how would he have time to get to Diehl, to Briggs? He was fighting down his own panic suddenly, a metallic taste in his mouth. Then why didn't he split, get the hell away from this whole neighborhood?

Because he had to secure his turf. He had to *know* that Wharton would do what *he* had decided the bastard *had* to do! He couldn't start doubting now, locked in this damned car and passing the house again—no change, nothing moving—he couldn't start doubting himself now.

Wharton had one route to take, that's all. To clean up the mess, get the body out and away. Make up some story to cover her disappearance. If everyone in town knew what Wharton was convinced now they did know, who'd doubt the Cunt'd desert him, maybe run off with another guy? Wharton would have to cover his tracks, make up the lie, bluff it out. Being a Wharton, he'd get away with it. Or at least that's what he'd think. Had to think. And if that's what he decided, he was finished, done, *kaput*.

He could picture him in there now scurrying around, cleaning up, wondering how he could get rid of the body—

But how could he be *sure* that's what the motherfucker was doing?

She was packing for Boston. Coming, Mama dear, coming. She was still packing for Boston because she couldn't seem to get herself organized. She had bathed in the tub in leisurely fashion—what was the hurry, what the rush?—and then she had thrown on her favorite kimono, the silk one with Japanese figures and brilliant colors, but even now she still felt unclean and she still couldn't decide what clothes she might need. Since she had no idea how long she would be required to stay in Boston. Visiting dear sweet Mama darling. How pleased Mama will be. *Do you mean to tell me that he's giving up a lucrative private practice to teach? The man must have taken leave of his senses. What will you live on?* And she had answered, teasing because she had not understood any more than Mama had, *Love, Mother, we'll live on love.* But she didn't add that Mama knew all about love, didn't she? Hadn't it been love, or at least its physical equivalent or concomitant, that had lured poor Daddy from the cultural morass of Back Bay to the cultureless jungle of Florida and its aborginal temptations and satisfactions? One look at her tonight, this time of night, and Mama would know instantly what had happened. Not that she hadn't expected it. One look and she would not have the weakness to say *I told you so* or the strength to stretch out a hand.

Willa slammed down the lid of the suitcase on the bed. And wondered whether she should pack for Peggy and David. And decided to hell with it. To hell with everything. There was a dry no-taste in her mouth, acrid in her throat, and she could feel acid in her blood, corrosive acid. What she needed was another drink. That would solve everything. Or make everything seem less important. Something else she had learned tonight.

So she went down the stairs and into the dining room and discovered the cabinet empty. She was surprised, but already stoned. No, not stoned. That word had taken on a different meaning today. Having not to do with alcohol; having to do these days with pot or grass or hash or whatever the term was. David would know. Peggy would know. She went into the kitchen. And stood staring at the empty liquor bottles on the sink. Every one drained! She heard herself utter a mocking guttural laugh. What a phony.

And then it hit her: desire. Passion. As overpowering and terrible a craving as she had ever known. A raw and terrible physical hunger. So that she knew that if he came back, if he walked in the door now, she'd rip off her kimono and throw herself at him, shameless, demanding. She felt hollowed out, faint, almost sick. All this, she told herself bitterly, because some other woman had had him. And disgust followed. And she knew that, if she was ever to drive alone all the way to Boston in the middle of the night, she had to have another drink. Like him now—had to.

Unloved. The lifelong suspicion brutally confirmed. Unloved because unlovable. Unlovable because if lovable, wouldn't a person be loved? Proof positive. And she had spent forty years unloved. And only faintly, tormentingly aware of it. But why? How had that come about? Very simple: she was not and had never been, as Mama dear had often suggested, really lovable. After all, wasn't Mama always right?

It was getting late. Later. A half hour must have passed since he left. Maybe more. *I promise, lord and master. My true and solemn promise.*

It came to her then. If he had hidden bottles in his desk drawer and in his clothes closet, where else? Why, of course. As night the day. She went down the basement stairs to his woodworking shop. Which was covered with sawdust. But the bottle was there: if he needed it one place, he needed it another. On a shelf below the lathe on the workbench. More than half a bottle. The abandoned workshop filled her with a strange sadness. He'd seemed so happy here, working with his hands, whistling—

But he was gone, He was gone forever. And Peggy and David were gone, too. It had all happened when she wasn't even looking. Talk about future shock—*future,* hell! And now she was alone, completely alone.

Her body off-balance, she retraced her steps: up the stairs to the kitchen, then into the living room. Which had once undoubtedly been called the parlor. Emptiness in the pit of her stomach. A depth and vastness she had never known before. A sense of failure? Someone had drawn the curtains in the living room. Fletcher. Thinks of everything. Darling Fletcher. Modesty is the best policy. After all. After all what?

Her body seemed to tilt to one side as she crossed the hall and went up the stairs. No ballast. No emotional ballast. So, at the mercy of the sea. Without ballast how can you expect to ride out the hurricane, or whatever God or the devil or haphazard dumb fortune hurled at you? No destination, anyway; compass gone haywire, barometer dropping, no stars in view and let's not think about the sextant, not tonight, or about the Plimsoll line, whatever the hell that was.

In the bathroom she poured whiskey into a glass. Drank. It cut through the desert of her mouth, burned her throat, struck her stomach like a blast out of hell. Except, she was always forgetting, there was no hell. How could there be a hell if there was no heaven? And if heaven was an illusion, then hell—

She went weak, her knees threatening to collapse, her legs turning liquid. Sorrow engulfed her like a wave. A forlorn and debilitating sadness. As if she realized, at last, that she had lost something, something precious, lost it irretrievably, forever and ever and ever. Something precious and she would never know it again. And would never be the same again, never be herself again. Never be whole in all the dreary lonely years stretching endlessly ahead.

Mindlessly, she lifted the glass again and drank. Deeply this time. And as if either the gesture or the hot bitterness of the whiskey had shattered the oppressive mood, she felt hate return. Loathing. The lying bastard, the lying hypocritical son of a bitch. Venom gave her strength. Astonished at the intensity of her feelings, she moved into the bedroom. Their bedroom.

Divorce? *You can have a divorce if you want one, later.* But she didn't. Divorce had no meaning in today's world. Why, the tales you hear. And right here in town, too. Right here on the campus, would you believe, do tell. Wife swapping in the biology department. She giggled, she had to giggle, and the whiskey went up her nose, ignited her nostrils, inflamed her eyes. And at least one *ménage à trois* in the English department—or was it the French? And so many AC/DC's guzzling gin at faculty parties that you never knew who was being friendly and who was making a pass. The wolves in female clothing, Mama—and vice versa. Not to mention the students cohabitating, co-showering, cocoiffuring. Why, Mama, today divorce is as meaningless as marriage. But no divorce. Now or ever. She'd forgive him: that was the trick—to say you forgive and by your abiding silence thereafter to play themes and variations on his guilt. Revenge and a just retribution devoutly to be—

She felt a cold shame pass through her. What a vindictive bitch. What a genuine forty-carat harridan she could be. Had she always been? In other ways? In how many ways?

Unloved because unlovable.

She sank down to sit on the bed, spilling a few drops from the glass. She was weak. All over. Every fiber.

She couldn't possibly drive all the way to Boston. The idea was unthinkable. The room reeled. She reached and placed the glass, still more than half-full, on the bed table. She was going to be sick. If she didn't go to sleep now, very soon, she was going to be sick. She stretched out, lifting her legs to the bed. *Tonight I want you to promise me.* Promise what? She had no intention of promising him anything. Or of doing what he told her. He was no longer her lord and master.

She had no lord and master. She was too old. She was very old. She had never had any idea that a person could feel so old.

She shut her eyes and felt a stinging behind the lids.

By that time Wallace Heckman, although he knew he was speaking and operating at top efficiency, had become uncertain inside, uncertain about everything, including the name that Fletcher Briggs' assistant had come up with. The shock of what had happened to Dennis had gone deep and he was aware of this. He didn't like the fluttering deep in his guts, the quavering tension deep down. In him, Wally Heckman—it didn't seem possible. He didn't dare let himself even think of Dennis in the hospital, but he didn't seem to be able to control the direction his mind took tonight.

Damnation, Wally, we're dealing with a child. You're not thinking about him at all! How the hell could Leroy Farago say something like that? At such a time, at a time when he'd come to realize just how damned much he really did love Dennis. And Kay had accused him of thinking of himself, too. What the hell kind of monster did they imagine he was? Well, he'd show them. And he'd show Dennis, too. By the time he was finished Dennis would know how much his father loved him. He'd know it all the rest of his life.

Odd, though: self-discipline had always been a matter of pride with him. But he seemed now to be moving closer to losing that grip on himself—his thoughts and emotions—than he had ever moved before. It was dumbfounding and frightening.

He and the girl, whose name for some reason kept escaping him and whose detached and flippant attitude put him off, had the contents of the file—*State v. Boyd Ritchie*—spread out between them on the long conference table in the file room. He continued to go through the other cases, just in case the girl was wrong, while she continued to study the rather barren facts of the hearing that had sent Ritchie to prison. He hadn't had time yet to reconstruct the case from memory; everything was so damned confusing tonight, unreal, and things seemed to be happening too fast. And he seemed to be doing nothing but waiting. He was waiting now for a report from the state penitentiary, a report that had been officially requested by Jeremy Welles, the assistant prosecuting attorney, who had appeared as promised and was being very obliging.

The police photographs, or mug shots, of Boyd Ritchie lay on the table: a well-proportioned if not handsome young face, eyes bold and direct beneath a cap of waving light-colored hair. Wallace Heckman recalled the face as he recalled the case: vaguely and with a puzzling twinge of discomfort.

Although the room was filled with smoke, the girl lit another cigarette. "He pleaded guilty to aggravated assault, right? But the judge mentions rape in the sentencing."

"Rape was the original charge, now that I think about it."

"He copped a plea then, right?"

"Copping a plea is the criminal's phrase. Plea bargaining is the better one. It's done all the time, you know."

"I know—and in the highest places, too. Whatever euphemism you want to use. If there was a deal, how come Stuttaford meted out the maximum sentence?"

It came back to him then. The old judge had promised him, without being specific, that he would be what he called lenient and then, after sentencing, partly because Fletcher Briggs had been so furious, he had mentioned that promise to the judge, who had shrugged and puffed on his cigar and grinned his sly old man's grin and said: *I must have got carried away. Well, small harm—keep scum like that off the streets for a few years. So he can't violate any more young women.*

"It looks to me," the girl said, "as if the kid was sandbagged."

"Not by me." He heard the irritation in his tone. In spite of her very feminine appearance, she was a tough one, this girl, and she had already maneuvered him onto the defensive. "Not by me."

"Obviously Boyd Ritchie doesn't agree with you."

"Convicted criminals rarely agree with the prosecution." He was shaking inside, hating the girl all of a sudden. "We've no proof yet that it's Boyd Ritchie we're after here. And if it is, he was guilty. Of both assault *and* rape."

"Would he be doing this if he thought so?"

"To do what he's done, he's off his rocker."

"Granted. Possibly. But—"

"I remember now, I'm telling you. We had a confession, a signed confession—"

"Who got that?"

"The police." And then he remembered the charges Fletcher Briggs had threatened to bring to prove police brutality—until Paul Wharton had volunteered that it was he who had beaten up the accused kid in the woods. But Fletcher Briggs had always insisted his client claimed it had been Theron Diehl. "We had a signed confession and an eyewitness," he said to the girl. And he himself, he recalled, had warned the old man—he couldn't remember his name just now—that lying under oath was a felony, yet had been unable to make the man change his story. "We had a corroborative witness."

"Someone who saw the act?"

"Saw enough of it to convince any jury, yes."

"With that and the medical evidence and a signed confession, why not take him to trial?"

At once he thought of Mrs. Augusta Wharton: it had been at her insistence, backed by veiled threats that carried weight in this town, that had prevented a public trial. But it had been her son who had insisted that the charges not be dropped entirely: he had to have his revenge. And now he remembered something that Fletcher Briggs had suggested at the time, something that he had considered outrageous and incredible: *Well, there's always the possibility, given human nature, that Wharton raped the girl himself. If he was angry enough.*

In reply to the girl's cool and logical question, he said now, somewhat harshly: "There are crimes, miss, certain kinds of crimes, that can cause a great deal of anguish, permanent hardship and perhaps permanent damage, to a great many innocent people if they're publicized."

The girl reached across the table then and placed her hand on his, and when he looked up, he saw that her troubled eyes were darker, miserable now. "I'm sorry," she said. "I've been trying to think of a way to say it for almost an hour. I'm terribly sorry about your son. You must love him very much."

Taken by surprise at the gesture, by her words, by her face, he was afraid for an instant that tears would well up into his eyes. Brusquely, he said: "It would have been a sensational case." He didn't want to talk about Dennis or what had happened tonight: he couldn't. "It could only have helped my career if it had been fought out in court and I'd won. As I certainly would have. But there were other considerations." He wanted to stop now; he seemed powerless to do so. "I did what I thought was best. For the girl. For her fiancé. And for his mother. There was nothing to be gained for anybody, anybody except me, from a scandal and—"

But he broke off. Because what he was saying was the truth, yet not the whole truth. Old Mrs. Wharton had lived up to her own code: she had rewarded him, effectively but unostentatiously, by giving him her support, in terms of prestige and very substantial but secret financial contributions, when he was up for election. It had been the old lady's way of thanking him. Had he been aware at the time he allowed the deal to be made that he would be rewarded in time? Had he, consciously or otherwise, curried these future favors?

There was a sound in the hall and Jeremy Welles came in: dark neat suit, handsome face that, although young in years, seemed stamped even now with the casual cynicism of his ambition. "Here it is, Congressman. Hold on tight. Boyd Ritchie was paroled almost seven months ago."

The girl withdrew her hand from the top of his and he could feel her eyes on him as he went tense. "Why don't we have this in our files?"

"Because his parole officer's in Londonford. Which would indicate, unless he's broken parole and left the area, that's where he's been living." He went out and down the hall. "I'll wake up the parole officer."

Wallace Heckman met the girl's eyes. She was frowning. He realized what she was thinking. "Don't ask me what Ritchie could have against Fletcher. He worked like hell, and for practically nothing. Made the only deal that was open to him and in some ways more than his client deserved."

"The question is, I suppose: did Ritchie know that?"

"He should have."

"*Should* and *did* are two different species of fish, right? And he's had a lot of time to brood on it." She stood up. "I think it's time to call Fletcher and fill him in anyway. Just in case."

He knew what she meant. He didn't agree with her, but it wouldn't do any harm to warn Briggs anyway. "Whatever Ritchie might think or believe, whether he was sandbagged or only imagines he was, he's got to be *stopped.*" He wondered why he had said it. It was as if he had banged his fist on the table.

She smiled, faintly. "Justice will be served," she said. Then her smile became more intense and more personal and she said: "Good luck."

He turned and went to the door. And stopped, standing face to face with Gavin McQuade.

"Strange doings tonight, Congressman." It was not quite a question. "Weird and ghoulish acts. Like . . . here's one of our most illustrious solons wasting his night in these dank and hidden reaches." The small lined face looked more pinched, and older, than Heckman had remembered it from his days around the courthouse. "Bless me, are those the well-thumbed records of this court you're hugging to your manly chest?"

"McQuade," he said, hearing the hardness in his tone, "you have no right in this part of the courthouse and you know it." There was nothing shaky or equivocal in his voice. "What Miss Beauchamp and I are doing is none of your business." His mind was certainly playing odd tricks: now he remembered her name, just like that.

McQuade's gnarled features feigned shock. "Is that any way to speak to one of your loyal constituents, sirrr? I'll have you know I represent the people's right to know."

He knew he should play the game. He'd done it often enough. Had even enjoyed it. But now that tremor was threatening. If the press got hold of what had happened to Dennis, if they printed anything, anything, even without using his name—

"Don't you ever sleep, McQuade?" He brushed past the wizened little man who limped to one side.

"Not when duty calls." He heard McQuade chuckle behind him. And as he strode—moving now, in control again—he heard the reporter's mocking voice: "Why, Miss Beauchamp—imagine finding you in this house of ill repute. And at this time of night. Or is it morning? Or do you care any more than I do?"

Heckman clattered down the worn stone stairs and into the reception room of police headquarters. An active place now: several men waiting, eyes averted, others seated across various officers' desks answering questions in low voices. He went directly through a swinging gate to Ben Hutchinson's desk, which, like the others, was behind a railing. Jeremy Welles stood waiting for the officer to put down his phone.

"Thank you, Mr. Gilpin," Hutchinson said, and then: "I don't have that information, sir, but I've a request from the prosecuting attorney's office as to his whereabouts at the moment. I'm sure the Londonford police will cooperate. We need a report as quickly as possible. . . . Thank you, sir." Then to Wallace Heckman: "Boyd Ritchie. Model prisoner, model citizen. No parole violations of any sort. Has job. Unmarried. The parole officer's shocked as the devil."

Wallace Heckman nodded, whirled about, stalked a few yards along a corridor, tapped on the word CHIEF printed on the glass of the door, then went in.

"I've got the name" was all he said.

Chief Diehl regarded him with slow soft scorn from behind the neat desk. Standing with his face against the wall was a very tall, very thin man wearing a frayed sweater. He was quite still. Diehl finally turned his head to the man and sighed. "All right, Bannon. I'm gonna take you at your lyin' word, just for now, 'cause-a this intrusion. Get out."

The man turned. His face was sunken and gray and his eyes were dull with fear. He was about fifty. Or a hundred. "Thank you, thank you, sir."

"Get out and keep your skirts clean."

Heckman stood aside as the man passed him. There was a strong scent of cologne about him, mingling with sweat. The door closed.

"Some freak show we got here tonight, Congressman. Every weirdo in town." He put his boots on the desk top and leaned back, hands behind his head. "All your fault."

"Chief, the name's Boyd Ritchie." He tossed the file folder to the desk.

"Name means nothing to me."

"He was sentenced by Stuttaford, defended by Briggs and prosecuted by me."

"Neat. Nothing more, just neat."

"He's out on parole."

Diehl picked up the folder, idly, opened it, read. While Heckman said: "He's living in Londonford."

And when Diehl didn't glance up, he added: "Not twenty-five miles away."

"You don't say? Seems t'me I been there." Then: "Tell me, where'd you get this information?"

"The assistant prosecuting attorney requested it and Officer Hutchinson obtained it."

Diehl shook his head, almost sadly. "Officer Hutchinson again. Congressman, ain't it bad enough to go over my head without bypassing me t'boot?"

"If you don't want to issue a warrant, Ritchie should be picked up for questioning. At the very least."

"You do like to tell a man how to do his job, don't you? Now . . . just what makes you so dead certain this here Boyd Ritchie's the little cocksucker that outraged your little boy?"

Heckman had to break his first savage impulse: to step, to swing. When he had succeeded, he said in a controlled voice: "I'm *not* certain. Yet."

"I recall the case somewhat. Rape."

"Aggravated assault."

Diehl nodded. "Rape. Never should-a got away with copping a plea. Yeah, I recollect. We had everything on him. The works. If it hadn't been for your professor friend with the bleeding heart—"

"Stop dragging your ass, Diehl. That's not the issue here now."

Diehl was squinting at him. "You look a mite peaked t'me, Congressman, y'know that?"

"The issue here is what you are going to do. And, failing that, what am I going to do."

Chief Diehl took his feet off his desk and reached for a sheet of paper with typing on it. "I got the medical report on your kid. In triplicate. He'll recover. Worse things've happened. Why, hell, man, in Texas—"

"Diehl, I don't care if you fuck cows on the dead run in Texas. I know my rights, and if I don't get them, I'm going to start yelling so loud you'll find yourself dragging your tail back to the wild prai-rie."

Diehl stood up. He towered. "Son, my advice to you

is take it very, very easy. Go slow. You're liable t'allow this thing to crack you up. Your face looks like somebody's been kicking you all over the back lot now."

"Never mind me."

"Y'ever consider real hard what's gonna come about if you do start yelling like you say? You want your kid's picture all over the front pages, here to California?"

That did it. He knew he had been forgetting something. Why was he so damned confused? He shook his head. Could Diehl be right?

"So you simmer down, hear? It's late and we all seen some sights tonight we don't cotton to. Now when you got some hard tangible evidence t'tie this here Ritchie to some crime that's been committed—"

"Is that what you're waiting for—*another* crime? A third one? Is that what it'll take to convince you?"

"I told you, I recollect the case. He raped a female. Same man don't rape a female and—" But something in Heckman's eyes stopped him. "It don't add up to me, that's all. Y'ever hear of false arrest, Congressman? You're a lawyer—"

"I've heard of obstructing justice, too. Every minute we waste here, somebody else might be in danger."

"Who?"

"Anyone connected with the case. Anyone." Then he added: "Even you."

A cool smile flickered along Diehl's lips. "I reckon I can handle myself, Heckman. Even at my age."

"If you don't bring Boyd Ritchie in here in the next hour, I'm going to demand police protection for my wife. She's at Memorial Hospital."

"What could happen to a woman in a hospital?"

"I don't know. Neither do you."

"Y'know I don't have the staff to—"

"Use the men who're harassing the perverts who don't have anything to do with this case!"

"The more you push, Heckman, the less inclined I am to—"

"You'll do it on your own or Jeremy Welles will put out a warrant from the prosecutor's office and you'll carry it out. And if I'm right, you'll look like the obstinate horse's ass you are."

Diehl puffed his cheeks and shook his head again, and his eyes were narrow and dull and furious. But he said, softly: "I'm willin' to oblige, Congressman. I don't buy it, but I'll ask the Londonford police to bring him over here for a little personal powwow just to settle your innards. But not an arrest. Suspicion of parole violation. That's as far as I'll go."

"What about the state police?"

"I said, damn it, that's as far as I'll go! It'll be a goddamn relief to interrogate somebody tougher'n those pansies out there. But I'm *not* sending out a general alarm or arrest. Because he's probably asleep in his bed, like we all ought to be. Does that satisfy you, Congressman?"

"No. I don't want that hospital report to get to the newspapers."

"You don't want." Diehl was speaking very quietly now and his eyes had gone absolutely flat. *"You* don't want. You been throwin' your weight around here all night, Heckman, and I got my gut just about filled to the—" But he stopped and then that flickering smile returned. "Anything you say, Congressman. Anything t'oblige.

He didn't bother to say thanks. Out of the office, he moved through the anteroom: it seemed to be filled with more comings and goings and voices every time he went through it. He heard Diehl's voice crackling, distorted, on the squawk box on Hutchinson's desk: "Will you be kind as to step in here, son?" And then he was in the corridor. But he realized that he was walking in no particular direction. Should he go back to the file room? Why? Then where? What was there to do next? He paused. His head seemed filled with air. Perhaps he should go to see Digby Norton, explain the situation. Being publisher of the Tarkington *Star-Times,* Digby could cut off his reporter McQuade's insistent inquiries. Hell, hadn't Digby suppressed the rape-charge story way back when? It had never reached the papers. Even the sentencing was reported in such a way that the victim's name never appeared. If Digby could do that for old Mrs. Wharton to protect her future daughter-in-law, he could sure as hell do this now when the consequences to Dennis could be—

"Hi." It was the girl. What was her name? "Fletcher's not home. At least, no one answers the phone." She must have stepped out of the telephone booth. "Where do you suppose he'd go this time of night?"

He shook his head. He remembered her name now: Annette. And some French last name. It didn't really matter. "I don't know," he said. "I can't imagine." Vaguely he thought, though, that it was a good idea for Fletcher and his family to get the hell away from here until that perverted—

"Are you all right, sir?" She sounded genuinely concerned. But why should she be?

"I'm fine. They're going to bring in Ritchie. For questioning."

"Then we'll know, right?"

He nodded. Then he looked down the dim corridor.

"Are. . . . Congressman, are you all right?"

What did she mean? "I'm fine," he said. And he was—fine indeed. At last somebody was doing something.

"Well," she said uncertainly, "if you're sure—"

Then she was gone. And he was facing the phone booth. And he knew he should call Kay. But she had not done what he asked—something he had demanded she do and she had refused. But what? He fumbled in his pocket, found a dime, deposited it, dialed. His palms were wet. He could feel sweat under both arms. The voice on the switchboard informed him that there was no phone in the rooms in the children's wing, but Mrs. Heckman would be able to take his call if he would be so kind as to wait.

Waiting again. The whole night, nothing but waiting. He was rigid. Yet the restlessness inside was so intense that he felt he had to move, now, move, do something,

something more than Diehl was doing or claimed he was doing—

"Wally? Wally, where are you?"

"Police headquarters. Kay, is Farago still there?"

"No. But he did stay a long time. No, no one's here. Only me."

"Where's Dr. Rosenbaum?"

"Rosenbluth, honey. Dennis is sedated now. He won't be able to talk till morning."

"You tell Rosenbluth I want to talk to him as soon as he finishes his examination. You understand that? Right away—"

"Wally, your voice. You sound awful. Slow down and—"

"Never mind me!"

"You're shouting, honey. You're—"

"All right!" He took a deep breath and consciously lowered his voice—although he had not been aware that he was shouting. "All right. I must ask the psychiatrist something just as soon as he sees Dennis."

"Ask him what, Wally?"

All I got to say to you is just this, listen. The kid liked it. The sweet little bugger really dug it.

"Wally, are you still there?"

"I have to ask him what kind of permanent psychological damage may have been done." He couldn't say to her: ask him whether there was the remotest chance that such an experience could turn a healthy, athletic kid into a deviate for life.

"But, honey, don't you see, we may not know that for months. Even years."

He went limp. "God." The wetness was running down his rib cage now and he rested his forehead against the cool glass to steady himself. "God."

"I know. Oh, Wally, you don't know what I've been going through." Then quickly, before he could speak: "How are *you,* honey? You don't sound—how *are* you?"

"You know me. I'm in there. I'm on top of it." Then he added: "We'll get him."

"Get him? Do you know who—"

"I said we'll get him."

"And . . . what then, Wally? If he's arrested? Won't the newspapers, the police—oh, honey, maybe it'd be better, better for Dennis if—"

"Why didn't you think of that?" This time he was shouting again; he could hear his voice thundering in the booth. *"Why the hell didn't you consider that when you refused to do what I told you?"*

Then silence. The shout echoed away. More silence. And then the sound of her breathing.

"Wally, why don't you come here? I have to stay, in case he wakes up. Why don't you come, too?"

"I can't."

"But why?"

"I can't, that's all." His mind was functioning again. He straightened. "He has to be caught, Kay. Whoever did this has to be caught and punished, that's why."

"Honey, we can't fret about justice now. Or even about—"

"Revenge. All right, say it. I'm not ashamed of it. I only hope I can get to him first."

"Oh, my God, no, Wally. Stop this. You're scaring me. I'm scared enough. Please stop such talk. Please."

"I'd like to cut his goddamn prick off!"

More silence then. Was she crying? Kay never cried.

But there were tears in her voice when she spoke. "Wally, I need you. I'm scared and I've never been so lonely and I need you."

"I'm lonely, too," he whispered. "But I can't come, Kay. Somebody has to *do* something."

"I see."

"I hope you do."

"I do see. I wish I didn't."

"Honey, you can't take it like this."

"I'll take it," she said in a changed hard tone. "I'll take it any way I damned well please."

"We wouldn't be in this spot at all if you'd done what I told you to do!" he roared. "Now you stay right there, don't leave the hospital, it's the safest place you

can be!" And he slammed the phone onto the hook.

And stood there wondering what was happening to him. To her. To everything.

And he wasn't sure exactly what it was he had to do. Could do. But something—anything.

Then he decided. First, he would phone the security officer on duty at the hospital, introduce himself and instruct the man to be on the alert for any suspicious characters and to look in on Mrs. Heckman every so often through the night. Good. Then . . . then he would drive to the house and get the nickel-plated .25 Smith and Wesson automatic he kept in the bureau drawer. And then . . . then, possibly on the way to the house, he would go over the case carefully, prodding his memory in that way he'd trained himself to do. If Boyd Ritchie was on some sort of rampage for revenge—and he was now convinced—who might be involved? There were Coralie and Paul Wharton, of course. And maybe Diehl, may be. But who else? Fletcher Briggs? Hell yes, that girl could be right—no telling what was in that convict's perverted mind. He came out of the booth and descended the stairs to street level. For openers, what was the name of that old man who had come forward and offered to be an eyewitness if the case came to trial? That information might be in the files in his own office, since the name was not in the court records because he hadn't had to testify. Well, he'd stop by his office first.

It was good to be moving. And to know exactly where you were going.

The two-tone tan and brown station wagon, which Willa usually drove, was moving in a westerly direction—around curves, over hills, through narrow valleys—and it was moving against a wind that stirred the fallen leaves and whipped them against the windshield, often obscuring Fletcher's vision. He had begun to feel the cold. What he needed, really needed, was a drink or two to warm him up, even to relax that tautness inside. But he had not been conscious of needing a quick one back there at the house because he'd been so shocked to see Willa drinking. And that look behind all the other emotions in her eyes: that stricken expression, as of a pain deep within, untouchable, unassuageable. Because of him. Guilt gnawed—through mind, through flesh, into bone, into marrow. How could he ever have known that she loved him that much? Or had, past tense, loved him that much. *Is she better than me? That's all it comes to, all it ever comes to anyway. Well, why don't you try me? I'd have done it. Anything!* But you're wrong, there, Willa, wrong. The physical wasn't the whole of it, only a part, an important part, of feeling alive. Of feeling young. But there was more, too—which he would probably never have the chance now to try to explain to her. There was the talk, the serious discussion, the arguments—Annette's quick understanding, for instance, of the contradictions lurking in the ivory tower. *What good is it to society if you can teach what law should be, ideally, if the theories don't hold when you hit the bullshit ring, right?*

Christ, now he was defending himself! Blaming Willa! He grasped the wheel harder and bore down on the accelerator, passing several neon-glaring country bars, still open. It was not yet half past twelve; in another half hour it would be too late to get a drink. There was no moon: the bastard had chosen his night well, whoever he was. If in fact there actually was anyone. The evidence was thin. What if he was off on a wild quixotic chase having nothing to do with reality?

Boyd Ritchie. Let's see: he'd been sentenced to ten years, hadn't he? All that Annette had to go on was the fact that he'd pleaded guilty and received a maximum sentence. Was that enough? Boyd Ritchie. That was the idea now: concentrate on that to blot out the recurring image of Willa's face contorted by pain and hate. Boyd Ritchie. No parents. He'd hitchhiked from somewhere in the Midwest, to be interviewed at the college. It was coming back to him now, bit by bit. Intelligent kid. Too intelligent to get involved in a rape? It was amazing: he could even picture the boy's face—lean and small-featured, wavy, blond, sun-bleached hair, eyes alert, baffled, angry.

According to the girl, the victim who had brought the charges—he couldn't recall her name now but she had later married the heir to the Wharton interests—she had been on a boat anchored on the lake (hadn't it belonged to young Wharton?) when the kid swam out and climbed aboard, threatened her with a knife, knocked her about on deck, then forced her down into the cabin where he raped her at knife point. It was all coming back to him now, a few details still fuzzy. Young Wharton had then appeared in a small outboard with a powerful motor, Ritchie had panicked, gone overboard, naked (his swim trunks had been found on the boat), had swum for shore, with Wharton chasing him. Onshore Wharton had beached the boat, followed Ritchie into the deep woods, given him a thorough thrashing (there was something about young Wharton having been a championship boxer in college) and had then taken the outboard out to the larger boat to take care of the girl. Ritchie had been arrested a few hours later hiding in the woods and had been packed into a patrol car and driven to the courthouse, still naked (an indignity that he had resented with a passion that he had not otherwise displayed during the entire time), where he had been booked for felonious assault and rape. Because he was penniless, the court, in the person of Judge Stuttaford, had appointed Fletcher counsel for the defense.

Forcing his mind backward now, concentrating intensely as he drove, Fletcher recalled what the accused had claimed: that the girl had picked him up on the road, driven him to the lake, told him to wait till he saw the boat; she had then driven to the Lake Club, where the boat was docked, taken it across the lake, anchored it; he had swum out, they'd gone below to make love, no violence, and then she had spotted her fiancé putt-putting out in the outboard; she had been the one to panic then, had convinced him to dive overboard and swim to shore. Paul Wharton had tried to run him down with the outboard motor, had failed, had *not* followed him onshore and into the woods. The bruises found on his body later by the physician examining for the prosecutor's office, were the result, according to the boy, of a beating administered by the arresting officer, one Theron Diehl, prior to the accused's signing of a confession.

Fletcher remembered now that he had never been able to decide, within himself, whether Ritchie was guilty or not. There were strange discrepancies. For instance, would a boxer concentrate his blows on the back, the ribs, the inner organs and the testicles rather than on the face? What reason would an enraged and outraged lover have to beat up a man in such a way that the bruises and wounds would not be evident when the victim was dressed? And if Ritchie had used a knife to force his will on her (she had claimed he threw it overboard and the witness onshore was prepared to swear he had seen it, but it was never found), why had he needed, unless he was a sadist as well, to use his fists to force her below? And wasn't he too intelligent to commit rape and too attractive himself to be reduced to it? Then why had he pleaded guilty?

Wally Heckman had offered a proposition. It was against his best personal interests, he had said, but the State was willing to make a deal. Since it was, in Heckman's view, an open-and-shut case anyway, to save the victim and her loved ones unnecessary embarrassment and publicity, the State would agree to reducing the charge if the accused would plead guilty to aggravated assault. The presiding judge had already agreed to a minimum sentence, possibly to be suspended, on the lesser offense. It would save the State money and time, the court dockets being clogged as usual, and it would save everyone else, Fletcher included, wear and tear. And very damned important: the defendant would end up without a rape charge on his record.

The prosecutor's arguments had been, or had seemed, conclusive, overwhelming. There was, after all, a signed confession to begin with. There was a medical report of internal bleeding in the vagina, indicating forcible penetration, and there was an eyewitness: a man who happened to have been bird-watching onshore at the time and had witnessed, if not the act, the brutality leading to the act, commission of which might thereby be assumed, and he could corroborate the identity of the perpetrator. If the defense attempted to show consensual consent, it would mean attacking the credibility of a lovely young girl engaged to a Wharton and could be a count against the defendant if the case ever came before a jury. In short, who would believe an out-of-town kid hitchhiking through the area who claimed police brutality, which he could not prove, to abrogate a confession which he had signed? And if he attacked the integrity of a girl whose wounds were quite visible and who was almost a member of the Wharton family—well, more than likely the jury would convict and the judge would throw the book at the kid. Did he want to risk twenty years?

Fletcher remembered distinctly now. He had spoken with the corroborating witness, an elderly gentle sort of man whose name he could not recall, and the witness told a straightforward story that only deepened Fletcher's own doubts. The only reason he could imagine for the girl's lying was that she had to protect her position with young Wharton if Ritchie's version was true—and how could you even suggest that to a jury?

Fletcher himself had not made the decision. In line with his commitment to do the best possible for his client, he had presented the kid with the facts and, in reply to questions, had admitted his own doubts. Boyd Ritchie had added it all up himself and had decided, quite calmly, with a faint bitter smile, not to risk taking the case to a jury. And when the maximum sentence had been pronounced, no one, including the defendant, had been more shocked, outraged, than Fletcher Briggs. He had never liked Wallace Heckman; tricked and angered and betrayed, he had let the prosecutor know it. Heckman swore that he had not been part of it—no collusion! But even now, this many years later, Fletcher doubted him. Much as he pitied the man because of what had been done to his son, he remained convinced, now that he had thought it all through again, that Heckman had lied. Probably to curry favor with old Mrs. Augusta Wharton. Hadn't Heckman run for Congress only a year or two later? And hadn't old Mrs. Wharton, with her considerable political clout, publicly supported him just before she died?

A crossroads sign read: LONDONFORD 3 MI. And opposite it on a curve of road was another bar with several beat-up cars and a few pickup trucks and utility vans parked on the gravel in front. He swung the station wagon across the dark road and went in. Sound struck him first: raucous voices—a general jumble, a high-pitched female cackle from one of the tables, a male bellow at the bar, a blasting rock beat from a machine. How could he be sure Annette had come up with the right name? He went to the bar, ordered a double scotch, then located the phone booth through the smoke. The door of the booth shut out the sickening odors: beer and stale perfume and sweat and disinfectant from the adjoining rest rooms.

He got through to Ben Hutchinson, who said Annette was in the file room, hold on, and then finally, while he remembered that he'd left his pipe on the bar of the Colonial Inn back in Tarkington, she came on the line.

"Where the sweet shit have you been, Prof? We'd begun to think the monster with the cloven hooves had got his claws in you."

"I don't have any time. To answer a question you asked a while ago: I do remember Boyd Ritchie now. Do you have any evidence that he's involved in anything that's happened tonight?"

"He's not in prison, Fletch."

Christ. "Where?"

"He's been living in Londonford for more than six months."

"Londonford?"

"His parole officer's investigating over there and Mr. Heckman's convinced Chief Diehl to put out some kind of order to bring him in for questioning, but nobody knows where he is."

"Where's Heckman?"

"He left here not long ago. In a rather strange state."

"You can go home now, Annette."

"Not on your life, bossman. I've come this far. I got you the name, didn't I? I'm staying for the denouement, preferably bloody."

"Maybe there won't be any."

"Any bets, Professor?"

"No bets." He felt tired now, but a renewed urgency was straining at his mind and muscles.

"Your nice friend McQuade's—"

But he had hung up. Her flippancy, her persistent flippancy, had worked on his raw nerves. But that had been the only feeling she had stirred in him—a detached irritation. He folded back the door of the booth and everything struck at once: the babble, barrage, smoke, stench. He placed two one-dollar bills on the bar and went out into the thin, cold air without drinking the scotch. To hell with it. He had more important things to do.

In the station wagon again he tried to convince himself that he was acting out of irrational panic. Hell, he'd been Ritchie's friend, probably the only friend the kid had had in town. Why should Ritchie hold any grudge against him? But if he didn't, why had he used his name? Christ, how long ago was that now, how many hours? Why had Ritchie even gone to the trouble of dressing like him? And unless he had dyed his hair, he must have worn a wig: Dennis Heckman had told his father his attacker had red hair and a red mustache. Games. Playing games! But morbid and sinister games.

Maybe I can do something for you someday, Mr. Briggs. Like give you the shaft.

You've got to believe me, Boyd. I had no part in it. If it was rigged, I didn't rig it.

No? How much you make outta defending a penniless vagrant like me, Briggs?

I did the best I could!

How much compared to what you can make chasing ambulances? Or advising how to cheat the tax collector?

I can see how you might feel this way, Boyd, but I don't feel any better about it than you do.

Yeah. Well, Counselor, you got ways of getting over it. You know, you almost convinced me you were on my side even if the State is paying you.

How could he have forgotten? Or had he, in some unconscious way, willed himself to forget? Out of what? A sense of guilt?

The same guilt that had prompted him to drop Ritchie a note after he was in prison, a note asking how he was and whether there was anything he needed. A note that had received a scribbled postcard reply: *Screw your conscience, Counselor.*

All uncertainty left him. He was doing what had to be done. No doubt remained in his mind now: the kid had believed over the years that he had been betrayed—and not alone by his enemies but by his one and only friend. As if a brother had been stabbed in the back by a brother whom he trusted. Or as if a son had been sold out by a father. If anything, Boyd Ritchie probably hated him more than he hated the others. The irony being, of course, that what fed the obsession was false—a fact which, once rejected, had no place in the blind savagery of the obsession.

LONDONFORD 1 MI. Ritchie was living in Londonford. Peggy was in Londonford now, this minute. If that cruel, disordered mind had already plotted and carried out one obscenity—

The station wagon was careening around the curves now. Whatever interweaving of fate and character and circumstance had warped that mind and whatever role he himself had played to distort it, he had to put all that aside now. He had to deal with things as they were. Now. Tonight. And he had to make sure that, whatever his justification, Boyd Ritchie did not reach or harm any of his family. He could no longer quote John Donne. Not now. His motives were immediate and personal. When the bell tolled next, it might be for him. And now that came first. God help him, that came first.

The station wagon rounded a curve on top of a hill and he saw the lights of Londonford along the river down below. There were not many of them this time of night.

"Is this Mr. Gerrard?"

"That it is, sir. Jerry Gerrard. *Tell It to Jerry*. Every night till dawn do us part. What do you have on your mind at . . . at twelve thirty-one this dark and windy morning?"

"Jerry, this is Harvey Keen."

"Yes, *sir*, Mr. Mayor."

"First, I'd like to tell your many listeners: I'm one of them. I'm a night owl, too."

"You know when history is made, Mayor."

"I've just come home and I've had three calls already from three of my constituents—"

"Voters. Yes, sir, Mr. Mayor."

"Are you telling it or am I?"

"The airwaves are yours, sir. But I do want our listeners to know: I am speaking with the handsomest, youngest mayor this town ever had. A true man of the people."

"I'm not in the mood for your sarcasm, Jerry. I've had a lousy night. I lost at poker and now I'm getting calls asking me what's going on downtown there. It seems you've been dropping hints of big doings across the Common at police headquarters."

"I don't know about hints, Mayor—"

"Ah, come on, Jerry. This is Harvey Keen. You know the way I operate. I don't want to butt in downtown to find out. Those men know their duty. I've full confidence they'll do it without my help. But what's up?"

"Mayor, I'm going to be honest with you. There's a pall of secrecy that's been dropped around headquarters. But plenty of action. All I know—and even this is hearsay, so don't quote me, please—is that a grave has been dug up and a body desecrated out at the cemetery. But there's more, and worse, or every policeman in town wouldn't have been summoned to headquarters. As one mick to another, Mr. Mayor, there's more here than meets the naked eye."

"Such as?"

"A lot of citizens are being brought in for questioning, all males."

"Meaning what?"

"I've had a lot of calls myself, your Honor. Everybody's asking, nobody seems to know."

"Well, I'll find out. Thanks, Jerry."

"Anytime, Mr. Mayor, and if you do find out something, why don't you call me back? I'm in direct touch with your *constituents* right here."

"If we weren't on the air, I'd tell you where to go. So long, Jerry."

"Pleasant dreams, your Honor. And I've been there, many times."

107 Main Street.

It was a stationery store. The printing on the plate-glass windows read: GIFTS, OFFICE SUPPLIES, PRINTING, ENGRAVING. Like the street this time of night, the store was deserted. Only a nightlight burned forlornly inside.

Fletcher Briggs killed the motor, opened the door of the station wagon and stepped out into the street. He experienced a sharp second of sheer panic: he didn't want to know, he couldn't find out. But then it was gone: he had to get Peggy out of town, out of this whole area. First, Peggy; then David.

The second floor. She's there most evenings. He stood back, the sharp wind cutting and stinging his lips that Willa had bitten. He looked up. The roof of the building appeared to be, from the front, an enormous glass-paned skylight at a steep slant. And the glass looked dark, reflecting only the glint from the streetlight on a post at the curb. He knew buildings like this and located the door, also numbered 107, adjacent to the glass storefront. The door was unlocked and behind it was a narrow, steep and very dark stairway, its wood giving off the musty odor of age. As he mounted the steps, which creaked in the otherwise-silent old building, apprehension gripped him, threatened to suffocate, strangle, and Willa's words clawed at his mind: *Yes, I think you deserve to know.* Deserve? As if whatever he was to discover at the head of the stairs would be just punishment for some crime that he had not even known he had committed. *I think you've been protected long enough.* Protected? From what? What?

At the landing where the stairs ended, there was a dim light above and a door on the left, solid but decorated in wild colors, in an abstract design, and the wall facing him was, floor to ceiling, a depiction of a devil, but a madly merry sort of devil, more mockery than threat, his eyes so all-encompassing that he seemed alive.

Stooping slightly, in the way of a very tall man in very close quarters, he knocked on the door and heard the echo of that knock vibrate through the building. Instantly he thought of himself with Annette on the couch in his office when Heckman had hammered on the door, which he had not opened. It had been that decision, he knew now, that had caused Heckman to go to the police, and if he had not, they would not now, or by now anyway, have the name of the only suspect—

Thinking of all this and of all that had occurred since then, he rapped on the door, harder, angrily. Aware as he did so that he was reacting to his own shame, his own guilt.

Then he heard a voice: "Yes? Who is it, please?" A pleasant deep male voice, polite but reserved. With only a faint suggestion of a foreign accent. "Who is it?"

"It's Fletcher Briggs. I'm Peggy's father."

A silence. No whispers behind the door. A hollow aching silence.

"I am afraid," said the man's voice, apologetic now, "I am afraid, sir, that I do not know anyone named—"

"Oh, cut the crap," Peggy's familiar voice said then. "Come in, Daddy." The sound of a lock turning. "Come into my parlor, said the shy young maiden." The door opened and she stood framed in it: slim, rather tall, fair hair streaming. She reached and the room came alive with light. She wore a floor-length caftan of many colors. He saw defiance in her very level gaze—a challenge, too, and only a suggestion of uncertainty. "Come in."

He stepped through the door. The room was enormous and appeared, at first glance, to be roofless, as if the black night sky itself were a part of it. The sides of the room, running the length of it, were glass, reaching from the floor at identical very sharp angles to meet far overhead. The impression was one of vastness—and, then, of color. Paintings were everywhere: propped together, hanging from wires so that some dangled freely from the long beam above, others stood upright on easels placed at various angles. All seemed to exude violent color in various designs.

"Daddy, this is Eric Lindenberg . . . Eric, my father, who seems to've wandered far from home."

"How do you do?"

Eric Lindenberg had a lush gray beard and a shock of hair that was almost startingly gray, nearly white. A husky man with flesh like burnished leather and penetrating but now guarded blue eyes, wearing a kimono flowing ruby-red to his sandals. Hell, the man was older than Fletcher himself—although not older than Fletcher felt at this moment.

While he had not allowed his mind to conjecture too widely on his way here, Fletcher realized with a shock that what he had now walked into was not nearly so unexpected as he might have imagined it would be. Still, when Peggy suggested wine, he had to struggle with a smoldering anger—almost outrage.

"We were having some. It's very good."

The urgency had come back. "We don't have time," he said, but his eyes came to rest on the sparkling decanter and his need for a drink, a solid slug to keep him going now, was more intrusive and intense than ever. But he had to have a clear mind—for this and for whatever else might lay ahead. "Get dressed, Peggy. You're coming with me."

Peggy didn't straighten from the marble-topped table; she only hesitated once, briefly, before she poured the amber liquid into a glass and straightened to lift it to her own lips. "Daddy, are you ordering me about?"

"If that's the way you want to look at it—"

"Well, don't. Don't start now."

It was like a blow. At home she might joke and tease her way, but now she seemed dead serious, not a girl but a woman.

"You're simply going to have to take my word that it's important." Hadn't he said something like this to Willa earlier? Why the hell couldn't they take his word, do what he demanded without questions? Why couldn't they trust him?

The room smelled of wet paints, incense—reminiscent of but not really identical to the way Willa's attic studio always smelled. He couldn't think of that, or of Willa, or of what she was feeling—he damn well didn't have time.

"Peggy, listen. I'll explain in the car. But it's late. Possibly too late even now. You're coming with me."

He saw her defiance flicker; he saw the uncertainty intensify in her blue eyes; he saw her turn her gaze, with questions in it, in the direction of Eric Lindenberg. Then he saw the man's head nod, just once, decisively. And then Peggy was setting down the glass and moving off. She said nothing. As she passed the bed in the corner against the solid wall, she stooped without breaking stride and gathered up some clothing that he vaguely recognized. Then she was gone, without a backward glance, through the only other door in the room.

All Lindenberg had had to do was nod. He had not spoken a word.

"I hope you realize there are legal implications here," Fletcher heard himself saying—very stiffly, with cold controlled anger. "She's not of age, you know."

"Of age?" The man's total serenity in the circumstances—the way he stood there, at ease, without a gesture, without any visible discomfort, his almost Oriental imperturbability—stirred Fletcher's ire more than if the man had tried to bluff it out, to argue, or defend. "Who is there to say when a woman is, as you put it, of age?"

"The laws of this state define—"

But he broke off because Eric Lindenberg was shaking his head, very slowly. "We are men, are we not? We are men and your daughter is, in your eyes, a child, and in my mind she is a woman. If you wish that we do not enjoy each other physically, as a man and woman, then you must make me respect that desire on your part by some argument other than the laws of this state."

"Listen, damn you. I've based my whole life on law. Law's what holds society, any damn society, together, makes it tick, survive. I didn't come here to argue law with you, I came to get my daughter and—" And? Suddenly he remembered why he had come, what he had to save her from. Not from this man. But from Boyd Ritchie. From a man who was capable of doing what Boyd Ritchie, for whatever reasons of his own, had already done to Heckman's son. Christ, couldn't anything ever be simple? He had spent several years now trying to arrive at some philosophical detachment, but all the harsh and horrible realities continued to impinge, to— "Peggy!" he shouted. "Peggy, hurry up!"

The shock of his own outcry, which he could now hear as an eerie echo, disturbed him. He had to be careful. He felt like a fool. An absolute fool.

"Sir . . . you're distraught. Is there anything I can do?"

The man's impulsive and very genuine concern was reflected in his eyes—which now appeared almost tormented with compassion. Fletcher found himself further disoriented—at sea.

"Anything at all?"

"Yes." His tone was low and grim. "Yes. You can leave my daughter alone."

Gently the man said: "I do not force your daughter. She comes to me because she wishes."

"Next," he growled, "you'll be saying you love her!"

"In my way, yes." It was almost a whisper, a low, sad whisper. "She is a girl who needs love."

What was he saying? What was he implying now? Everything was happening at once. Too fast. Too much for the mind—

"Where are we going, Daddy?"

Peggy was back. She was wearing a floor-length military-looking blue coat. Her hair dangled to her waist. She moved with girlish abandon. He watched her as she approached Eric Lindenberg. He saw her kiss him, swiftly, lightly, on the lips. He felt a stab of something like rage, or envy, or jealousy.

"If you need me—" the man said and had to say no more.

The words stayed in Fletcher Briggs' mind all the way down the narrow stairs, across the sidewalk and into the station wagon. He could not think of the words. Or of: *She is a girl who needs love.* He had no time for all of that now, any of it.

"Where's David?" he asked, driving.

"David? How should I know?"

"Peggy, I think you do know. When he says he's going 'camping'—I can guess what it means, but I can't guess where they go. Now—where is he likely to be? Now?"

"I'm not going to tell you."

"You'll tell me."

"I won't even guess for you unless you tell me what this is all about."

"All right, I'll tell you. Now listen. Listen and don't

ask questions till I'm through."

"I've got a report from Londonford, Chief. The parole officer's name is Albert P. Gilpin."

"Very good, son. Very, very clever of you t'come by it."

"Mr. Gilpin and a Londonford officer inspected Boyd Ritchie's living quarters a few minutes ago. In a rooming house at 2242 North LaSalle. Room in perfect order. Nothing missing. The landlady was upset to be woke up this time of night and said she couldn't understand why the police would care to bother a nice polite God-fearing boy like Boyd Ritchie who always paid his rent on time."

"Lieutenant Hutchinson, kindly spare me the jokes. Get on with it."

"Mr. Gilpin agrees with the landlady, if I may say so."

"Y'can say so, son. Y'can say anything y'want in this here office. Now where was this suspect personally?"

"He wasn't in yet."

"But expected?"

"Yes, sir."

"Proceed."

"We now have a description of his car. A Ford Maverick. I have the data from the license bureau. 1969. Tan color, two-door. Do you want me to put it on the air?"

"Why not, Ben? It's that time of night. Why not put it on the air? Give all those patrol cars something to look for. But just the vehicle, hear? No name."

"Anything else, Chief?"

"What else is there? What more could a plain ole ordinary chief of police like myself *expect* of an efficient fire-eater like you, Lieutenant Hutchinson?"

"Thank you, sir."

"Pleasure's all mine, son. All mine."

Whatever the hell he was doing in there, that motherfucker Wharton was taking his time. It'd been more than half an hour now since that light had been turned on behind the heavy curtains at the window of the upstairs bedroom. Still no other action. But also—no cops. If Wharton had decided to call them, even the hick-pigs here would've showed by now. Or at least they'd have had something on the radio. While it sputtered orders once in a while, none of it had to do with him. Hell, they probably wouldn't know what had happened till it was all over and he was on his way.

Only one small incident had occurred in this interim and he had no idea what, if anything, it might mean. A two-tone black and gold Buick had driven by the house, only once, but very slowly. Heckman drove a Buick like that. But since it had not stopped and had not returned, he had decided to forget it. If it had been Heckman, at this time of night, it could mean that he'd gotten wise. Or it could mean the bastard was driving around looking for his son's assailant. Forgetting it, though, was not easy. Because if Heckman or anyone had wised up and if they had put any of it together, it sure as hell would threaten the rest of the plan. Goddamn them, they couldn't put it together this soon!

Every trip he made past the house, though, added to his risk. He'd varied the pattern so often—even making sure he allowed different periods of time to pass each go-around—that now there was no way for him to approach the Wharton house without taking the chance that someone—like maybe those neighbors in the house next door where the light still burned—might get suspicious. Jesus Christ, was Wharton sitting in there too zonked by it all to do anything but switch on the light and stare at her body?

Or maybe . . . maybe, realizing what he'd done, he'd decided, some way, some way, to cash in his chips completely.

As the Vega crept along Elmhurst Street once again, he had to mute the engine carefully so it wouldn't growl and charge ahead. And then he saw the window. The light in the bedroom had been turned off. But there was light now in the center hall on the ground floor, visible through the fanlight above the front doors.

He was right. Again. Wharton was moving around in there. He'd decided what Boyd Ritchie had known all along he would decide. The motor gained speed and passed the house and turned right at the corner. Wharton was going to try to cover up. Which was like admitting he was guilty of murder. Which, in fact, he was, wasn't he? The Vega made another right turn and he let the motor out a little, reckless now, excited again. What would Wharton try to do with the body? It really didn't matter: he was too stupid, too scared and too shocked, to get away with it. And when he failed and was nabbed, imagine the bastard trying to explain to the fuzz how his wife had been killed. Another right, careful not to allow the tires to squeal. Faster and then another turn; now he was approaching the house again, so he slowed.

All lights off now. The house was dark. But one of the cars had been moved. The Cunt's white Jag was missing and the door of the carriage house was closed.

And as the Vega eased past, almost silent, a side door of the house opened, a shadowy figure emerged, with something draped over its shoulder, something wrapped in a blanket. The figure started along the white path toward the carriage house.

It was all he needed to see.

Puppets. All of them. Puppets on strings. And he was manipulating the strings. They had no wills. He was the only one with a will.

Kaput. Wharton. *Kaput*.

The familiar elation returned. The galvanizing exhilaration. He was still ahead of everybody, always. They did what they had to do, but it was almost as if they did it because, instead of being able to predict their actions, he actually *willed* those actions.

He drove on along Elmhurst. No need to return now. Wharton had chosen his route. Had passed beyond the point of no return. No matter what he did now, where he went, what he tried—the noose was around his goddamn neck. Loose, but hanging there. It really didn't matter what tightened it. Or how soon.

And Boyd Ritchie, with only two to go now and the night still young, had moved that much closer to living. He rolled down the window and allowed the chill wind to blow against his face, which was burning. He almost wished the night would never end.

A mile away from the Wharton house, the radio came to life again and the calm impersonal voice of the police dispatcher said: "General alert. Be on lookout for 1969 Ford Maverick, color bronze and tan—" Then he gave the license number and the registration number, instructing all police to stop the car, question occupant and report to headquarters. Then he repeated the message while Boyd Ritchie's spirits lifted even more. His car. Not the one he was driving. The one he'd stashed, and stashed good so no one could ever find it while he drove the Chevy Vega with the Z-28 souped-up engine. The laugh was on them. Again.

But was it? An electric shock straightened him in the seat. If they had a description of the car, which was registered in his name and which he had not used tonight, and which had broken no traffic or any other laws—

They had his name.

They had to have his name.

But if so, why hadn't they put that on the air?

Who the hell was trying to bug him now?

The man's body was lying on its side on the floor. As if it had toppled from its bent knees. The lids of the eyes were drawn back, but there were no eyes. There were two cloudy milklike bulges streaked with red.

Whatever Wallace Heckman had expected while he was driving out from town, he was not prepared for this. Nothing could have prepared him for this. He stood staring: faint, sickened. Yet he had no strength to move, even to turn his gaze away. It was as if he had been stunned into immobility, his eyes magnetized by the figure of the old man, whose face Heckman had not been able to remember as he drove. If he had been able to picture the old man's face, he still would not have recognized this prone mask, this absurd and mocking horror. He longed to be able to turn away, but somehow he still could not.

The trees outside, almost bare now, seemed to be pressing against the windows, dark and oppressive. And the wind was whining. He was miles from any living soul. With a corpse. How had he come here? His mind refused to function. It seemed deadened, drugged. What had taken him so long? First, he had had to go to his office to look at the file on the case: that's how he had come by the name. Vincent Stegner. But there had been no address, so he had to look up the name in the city directory in the very empty office. When the name was not listed, he had phoned an old friend at his home, Jimmy Cavagnaro, who worked in the Social Security office. Cavagnaro had groused and asked him whether he was drunk, and it had taken time for Cavagnaro to drive to his office. Meanwhile, Heckman had remembered about the gun, so he had driven to his house on Emerson Terrace, but on the way, because his mind was performing very well, he went by the Wharton house. Where everything appeared to be normal: a white Jaguar sports coupe and a maroon-colored Mercedes sedan parked in the driveway, no lights in the house. He'd considered waking Wharton, just to alert him, but had changed his mind when he remembered how that son of a bitch Diehl still refused to believe there was any connection between Ritchie's case and what had already happened in town tonight. Wharton might not believe him, either, especially if he was sleeping off a drunk. So he'd driven on to Emerson Terrace and after getting the small black automatic with the nickel-plated handle from his bureau drawer, he'd phoned the Social Security office and Cavagnaro had grumpily given him Vincent Stegner's address. Then, since it was only a few blocks out of the way, he'd gone farther up the hill to Howells Street. There had been a small car parked at an odd angle with one door hanging open in the circular driveway in front of Fletcher Briggs' Victorian house—the same blue foreign sports car he'd seen there earlier. A few lights were on inside. Everything routine. It was not until he was more than halfway out on Highmeadow Road that he remembered that Annette Beauchamp had said that she had tried to phone Fletcher at home and had received no answer. Then why were the lights burning? Perhaps his mind was not functioning so well, after all. To forget a thing like that in a matter of minutes. He had gunned the Buick then to get here as fast as possible. He had decided to wake the old gentleman, to hell with whether he was making sense or not, tell him what *he* believed was going on, then return to town and follow through on the others, even if possibly he was making a fool of himself.

But now the elderly gentleman's lifeless shell, like a statue that had fallen and refused to break, lay before him in the high-ceilinged rustic room and there was a stench in the air, as of blood or possibly death itself. And he was too appalled to move, although he knew, of course, what had to be done once he found his strength, his will. As prosecuting attorney in the county for six years, he had seen corpses before but, until now, never a murder victim. He had never seen anything like this and he knew, still staring, that he would never forget the sight. This was more than murder—and worse.

How long since the pervert had been here?

It was anger more than revulsion that moved him, finally. He turned away.

He knew what had to be done. Stop at the first house, demand to use the phone, tell Diehl that he had another crime now, this confirmed everything, a man was dead now, he hoped he was satisfied.

The wind cut into him, sharper, colder. He got into the car. Diehl would have to provide security now—at the hospital first. Kay. The big car rocked over the ruts and onto the narrow dark road. Diehl would have to send someone to the Briggs' house, too. At once. And to the Whartons'.

He saw a dark frame house near the road, hit the brakes, and turned, tires squealing, into the dirt driveway.

Gavin McQuade said: "I seen me duty and I done it. All the hospital would tell me was that a Dennis Heckman, age eleven, had been admitted, following what they termed an accident. But even I, with my filthy mind, couldn't have suspected this."

Annette took the single copy that the machine spewed out, glanced at it, reading only the heading: MEMORIAL HOSPITAL POLICE REPORT. She handed the original to Gavin McQuade and then read the copy. They were in a brightly lighted storeroom above the Colonial Inn bar, which was now closed, in the rear of the radio station, separated from the conversation-plus-music program emanating from the front studio. The sound was piped into every room, but it was muted in here: the listeners were telling it to Jerry and Jerry was telling it to them and all was well in Insomniaville, they all sounded wide awake, as if it were midday instead of ten minutes after one in the morning.

"What did Diehl say when he gave you this?" Annette asked, bewildered.

"He said he thought the press should have this. He said he didn't want to be accused of obstructing justice. He also said to make a copy and return the original, and if I told anyone where I got it, he'd deny it and accuse me of stealing official documents."

"What an asshole," she said, and saw McQuade's shaggy brows lift, his mouth tighten in that odd sallow face that somehow filled her with sadness. "Why the hell is it," she asked, "that men your age always get so uptight about language?"

McQuade drained his cardboard container of coffee,

limped to sit on a straight chair. "Men my age are all male chauvinist pigs. We expect women to be women. And, if it signifies, I'm thirty-five."

Surprised, she only smiled. "What would *you* call Diehl for leaking you this?" Somehow she was pleased that he was not older, although he looked it.

"Well, according to me old mother, God rest her soul, I'm an ungrateful cad. This sheet of paper, girl, represents news." He sighed. "She also spent her last years trying to convince me there was no such thing as pure malice." He snorted. "Asshole's a *damned* good word for Theron Diehl."

She laughed; she moved closer and perched on a worktable stacked with pages of typewritten paper. She became conscious, as she usually was not, of her very bare legs. Because of the direct and admiring and unselfconscious way he was looking at them. "But why you? I thought the chief hated your proverbial guts."

"He does. But he must hate them less than he hates Heckman's. And if proverbial means I don't have any guts, you're probably right."

She doubted that. She had no good reason but she doubted that very much. "Poor Mr. Heckman," she said, reading the report again. "Not to mention the Missus and the kid, right?"

"Not to mention," McQuade said, "the whole blooming human race." And she was startled again. He turned his head as if to speak to someone she could not see—his guardian angel, perhaps. "Tell me now, now that I've got the story, what they call the Truth, tell me what the devil I can do with it." His strange bitterness seemed to fill the room with his own particular savor, almost tenderness. He seemed so vulnerable as he turned his boyish eyes in the old man's face on her again. "Well?"

"You have your moral dilemmas, McQuade. I have mine."

He chortled, but there was only an astringent skepticism in it, no genuine mirth. "You may even know the name of the ghoul responsible for—or at least suspected of—this." He flicked the hospital report and waited.

She considered. What *were* the ethics of the situation? Congressman Heckman had said they were going to bring the suspect in for questioning. This McQuade, he'd been around awhile; he might even know him. "Name Boyd Ritchie mean anything to you?"

Her eyes scanned his. He nodded and said, "You smoke too much—did anyone ever tell you?"

"Boyd Ritchie," she said.

"Yeah, I remember. Kid. Accused of rape. Diehl arrested him and brought him in naked." He stood up and walked, in that off-kilter way of his, to the dark window and looked out. His walk roused a certain very odd and very puzzling ache in her somewhere. "Charge reduced. All hushed up, covered up. He pleaded guilty and went up. Could have been a raw deal."

"It looked raw to these inexperienced eyes. I've been going over the record."

He turned to face her. "Bully for you, sis. What're you, one of those bleeding-heart justice freaks?"

"Go shit in the corner."

"My, my, there come those four-letter words again. What are you trying to prove?"

"Can't you stick to the subject, McQuade?"

"My friends call me Gavin."

"Who says I'm a friend?"

He smiled and his whole lined face crinkled into a ridged mask of delight. "I could like you," he said. "I could like you very much, Beauchamp."

"Raw deal—why?"

"How the hell do I know? I smell things. My editor quashed—isn't that the legal word?—my publisher, I should say, quashed the story. I stood still for it." Then he took a few lame steps toward her, head cocked to one side. "A Mrs. Augusta Wharton seemed to be calling the tune." Then he laughed. "What the devil difference, girl? How'd Fletcher Briggs get rung into this?"

"Are you asking how *I* got rung into it?"

"I might be."

She shook the paper in her hand. "Whoever did this to little Dennis Heckman used Fletcher's name. And dressed like him. Down to the red hair and mustache. Down to the *pipe* for God's sake."

"Kook. Some kind of kook."

"A dangerous kind of kook, Gavin. And out of prison as of seven months ago."

"You're worried about Fletcher, aren't you?"

Was she? The question churned up all her old confusion about Fletcher—and along with it now, the sense of loss. "Yes," she admitted, and it was true. "Yes, I am."

"Then you don't think this . . . kook's done all he intends to do?"

"Do you?"

"I doubt it."

"I have a feeling," she said, "a kind of intuition—that by the time it's over, nobody's going to be quite the same again, ever."

He frowned, studying her face. His eyes narrowed, roamed over it. "Maybe that's all to the good."

"You think everyone *should* be shaken up, right?"

"Don't you?"

"I don't know, Gavin McQuade. I don't know."

"You strike me, girl, as someone who's already been shaken up a bit herself tonight."

She considered it. And shrugged. "Only a bruised ego, McQuade. No mortal wounds." And at once she wondered why she had made the admission. The question was, of course, how many bruises the ego could take before they became mortal wounds. "I had a mother, too. She warned me about married men, especially ones with red hair."

Gavin studied her face, frowning—comprehending at once if he hadn't already done so long ago. Then he asked: "Do you want me to drive you home?"

"No," she told him. "Unless you're tired of my company."

His face twisted again. "You'll be tired of mine before morning."

She stubbed out her cigarette and got off the table. "I'll chance it if you will."

She was on her way to the door when Gavin said, "Listen."

She stood still and heard Jerry Gerrard's voice on the radio: ". . . three cars, including Chief Diehl's, leaving police headquarters now at top speed. Well, folks, something *is* indeed going on tonight and if you stay tuned to *Tell It to Jerry*—"

As they moved together, faster now, she heard the sounds from below drowning out the voice: the insistent *wow-wow-wow* of several sirens.

A narrow rock-bottomed creek meandered through the real estate development known as Brookfield Knolls. Kenwood Drive, after intersecting with Euclid Drive, terminated at the creek several hundred yards beyond the corner. A sign reading DEAD END, posted at the corner, created a tree-tunnel cul-de-sac. Beyond the white planks of the barricade, with STOP painted on it in red letters, was a downslope of weeded turf leading to the swift gurgling water and beyond it was a steeper bank rising sharply to the rear yard, unfenced, of the Theron Diehl residence facing Oakwood Drive beyond. Boyd Ritchie had selected the spot some time ago with great care.

But now that he was here, nosing the gray Vega toward the barrier, with his flesh leaping and his nerves jumping, he had something else, something totally unexpected, to contend with: there was another car parked there—a small Toyota, pale yellow.

Its lights were out. But it was not empty: shadows moved beyond the dark pane of window. He saw, or perhaps only imagined he saw, a flash of bare white arm. The night was dense, quiet, with only the pleasant soothing sound of the creek—and the occasional moaning of wind. That sinking shot-away feeling came back—loss, longing. How long since he had sat in a car with a girl? How long, now, since he had wanted to? Cheated, cheated—on top of everything else, they'd cheated him!

Well, go ahead, you horny little bastard, get it over with, screw her and get it over with, stop playing around, get to hell away from here.

Diehl wouldn't be there, across the creek, in the house that was only a frail low shadow in this distance, without lights. His old lady had probably gone to sleep, hugging her goddamn Bible, praying for God to cure her of the paralysis. Diehl wouldn't be there because he, Boyd Ritchie, had planned it that way. What had happened to the old judge's grave would be enough to draw Diehl downtown and keep him there at the court house tonight. Not to mention what had happened to the Heckman kid—if Heckman had had the guts to report it.

And if Heckman had reported it, what was he doing out driving his Buick past the Wharton house? Or had that been Heckman's car, after all? Well, somebody was onto something because they were looking for the Ford Maverick, which he'd stashed so they'd never find it, but it meant they had his name and if they had his name now and were working on it—

He turned around in the seat and lifted a double-strength shopping bag from the rear floor. He placed it on the seat next to him. He opened the bag, removed the protective section of cellophane food wrap from the top of the jug, which contained high-octane gasoline, and felt the strips of cotton sheeting which were stuffed into the bottle's neck. They were still dry.

But he couldn't move with that other car still there. He placed the glass jug of gasoline, still in the shopping bag, on the floor. He took up the flashlight. If he played it over the fuckers, shooting from his car—

But what if the dude in there got tough, what if he

got so heated he jumped out of the car and came across and picked up a stone and smashed in the windshield or window? No telling what—

Then he'd kill him, that's all, shoot him, use the Luger he'd taken from the Wharton house, shoot them both—

Hold it, cool it. That'd wake the whole neighborhood. And he'd never be able to get in, into the Diehl house, and out, fast, and off in the car. Never. Someone would be sure to see the car, they'd be down on him in minutes, seconds, and he still had two to go, Diehl and Briggs, two to go—

Damn them, goddamn those fucking lovebugs, why didn't they go home, why didn't—

The radio was raising hell again. The dispatcher's voice, the only one he could hear even in two-way conversations with other cars, had been silent for a while. But now he heard the words "Highmeadow Road" and he leaned closer, holding his breath, straining to hear every syllable: Car Seven was to proceed to 310 Commonwealth Avenue, where Dr. Wright Scofield would be waiting in front of his apartment house, then proceed to a house well off Highmeadow Road on the left two miles past the intersection with Nutmeg Road.

The radio buzzed. He sat back. Slowly. Highmeadow Road. Where old man Stegner lived. Had lived. Because Dr. Wright Scofield was county coroner.

So there it was. Another kick in the balls. First, they had a description of the old Maverick he usually drove, meaning they already had his name. Now this. But the old man wasn't supposed to die. That wasn't in his plan. Stegner was to stay alive, blind, blind, that was part of the beauty of the plan. Stegner wasn't *supposed* to die, goddamn it! And they weren't supposed to know the name Boyd Ritchie till morning, until after it was all over. It was all happening too fast now, too soon.

Which one of the motherfuckers had come up with his name, which one, how? *He* was the one calling the tune—who was screwing it up like this?

Murder now. Murder One.

But not true: he hadn't premeditated it. Not murder. That was an accident. Anyone could see that that was an—

He had to move now. Had to move goddamn fast.

But if he did, what about whoever was in that Toyota over there? They'd see the flames. They'd move, too, and fast.

And then the goddamn cops'd have a description of *this* car.

He would have to wait them out. He'd come this far, he couldn't change plans now, plans that were working, he'd wait the fucking lovebugs out, that's all. He could do it. He could do anything.

Peggy Briggs was slouched down in the front seat of the station wagon, huddled in her double-breasted military-type coat, watching her father who was in a lighted phone booth alongside the road. She was not really shocked by all he had told her—puzzled, rather. The whole thing was beyond belief. It was reasonable, she supposed, to try to link the two incidents—the attack on the judge's dead body and the homosexual attack on the Heckman boy—and it was reasonable, too, for her father to feel some concern since his name had been used. But to tear around like this, like some grim-faced madman himself, to protect his family—well, from what? Far-out, very far-out. How did he know this Ritchie dude hadn't used his name just to bug him? Suppose, now that he'd had his hurrah with the kid, he had no idea of doing anything else. He could be over the river and into the trees by now.

She watched her father's lips moving; then he placed a hand on the hook to cut the connection and deposited another coin. While she sat out here freezing and listening to the west wind blow. She knew that, as soon as he returned to the car, he'd start the same theme song again: where's David? She'd told him she didn't know—which was only more or less true because she did know a few places where he might be. What was the point of his finding David somewhere, maybe stoned out of his skull? If his own father couldn't locate him, how could the scourge of poor little Tarkington town know where he was? Not that the ogre was looking, if you asked her. She almost wished her father had given her hell about Eric: he didn't seem to give much of a damn about that. Typical. Par for the course.

The light in the booth went out and then he was getting back into the driver's seat. "I spoke to your grandmother in Boston. She was sleeping the sleep of the innocent, so she had to make me feel guilty." It was enough to blow your mind, that he could talk this way now. "Your mother hadn't arrived yet and I'm not sure your grandmother's looking forward to being invaded by the lot of us." Driving now, he added: "I called the house. No answer. David's not there and Willa's on her way."

Why shouldn't she be? Unless she, also, was skeptical of the danger. Why should he doubt that her mother would do what he asked? And if he didn't doubt it, why had he phoned the house? *Only* to learn whether David was there?

The purple swollen ridge along his jaw and his broken lip had startled her when she first saw her father's face in Eric's studio, but he had explained that: Heckman taking a swing. He had not referred to the scratches—claw marks, really. It was only a suspicion flickering in her mind, damned if she'd mention it, but suppose Mother had somehow learned about Annette Beauchamp? Peggy had known for months now and she felt like a hypocrite—like *him*—every time she thought of it. Yes, like him. Here he was charging all over hell's half acre trying to save wife and kiddies from some mythical spook who'd dared to wear his own sheep's clothing—as if that act could make up for it, for any of it. No wonder he was overreacting. She knew what it came down to—guilt.

"If you don't really know where your brother is, tell me where he *might* be."

"I told you: David and I aren't that close these days."

Which was true, but dishonest at the same time. She was tired of dishonesty, all of it, everywhere. He was no worse a hypocrite than she was. Hadn't she been making up hundreds of lies so she could spend that time with Eric? How had her mother learned the truth? And what did it matter now? Lies, lies everywhere, always.

Saying that she and David were no longer close also made her a little sad. As if she'd lost something. But he'd become so withdrawn the last couple of years. He spoke seldom and the few times he had expressed himself, it had seemed more of an attack on . . . well, on everything and everyone. His idea was to live alone, in the wilderness, or in the desert, with a minimum of possessions. And the single time she recalled his expressing himself at the dinner table, he had tried to explain that law, like business, was only more competition, only more meaningless motion to obtain *things*. His values, he said, were different. He was interested in individual survival. To which, she remembered, her father had replied that society had to survive, as well as the individual, and law was one of the ways man had devised to allow him to live with other men, therefore *to* survive. And David had smiled that vague tolerant smile and asked why society, as presently constituted, *should* survive. Then he had given the peace sign with his two fingers and, smiling gently, had left the room. She had been as bewildered as her parents—and remained so. But the thought saddened her now. Even though, thinking of her own lies as well as her father's, she had to admit that she understood at least some small part of what David felt.

They were in Tarkington now and her father had not asked her again about David's possible whereabouts. Whether because he had not or because she was thinking of David's really sweet qualities of gentleness, she said: "I do know some of the places he might be." And she wondered whether her father was prepared for the state David might be in if and when he found him. "It'll mean waking up his friends' parents at this time of night."

"To hell with that. Who? Where?"

She couldn't recall hearing her father speak in that tone before. She slid further down in the seat. "Shall we save the private homes for later? A favorite spot for overnights is on the beach about three or four hundred yards west of the Lake Club. That's for starters."

The station wagon surged ahead. "Then let's start."

"Isn't there a heater in this hog?"

"Sorry. I didn't think of it."

"And how about some music?" She flipped on the radio.

"Is your door locked?"

"It is now." If it'd make the man feel better, why not?

In his early years Albert P. Gilpin had studied for the Catholic priesthood; then he had decided that he did not have what was then called a vocation. In the many years since, he had devoted himself to social work of various kinds until, five years ago, he had taken on the part-time job of parole officer for Londonford and the surrounding area. The compensations for the work, he always felt, outweighed the disappointments. But tonight he had begun to fear, not for the first time, that he might, just might, have been fooled again—conned. He was, he had to remind himself, a law officer now, not a social worker; therefore, he had to look at the evidence, whatever it turned out to be, in an objective and dispassionate way. For instance, the landlady of the decrepit old house in which Boyd Ritchie rented space had, earlier, been shocked that the police, in any form, should be interested in her roomer's doings or whereabouts. She remained convinced, when other elderly women of her sort might have taken some satisfaction in the opposite view, that Boyd Ritchie, *her* Boyd Ritchie, was incapable of any wrongdoing whatever. Well, at that time—less than an hour ago—Albert P. Gilpin had been inclined to agree with her and he had indicated as much on the telephone to the Tarkington police. Boyd Ritchie, since he had come under Albert P. Gilpin's jurisdiction and surveillance, had fulfilled all and every obligation of the parolee in this state. He had reported regularly every third Monday, he had registered his car—a Ford Maverick, 1969, brass-colored, as Gilpin remembered—and he had maintained gainful employment, all of which was required by state law. In addition—and here was the part that was disturbing Gilpin tonight—Boyd Ritchie had impressed him personally, impressed him to such an extent that he had come to believe that this quiet, affable young man would rehabilitate himself in the community, in today's society, to such an extent that he would create for himself a new life and prove that the penal system sometimes did rehabilitate.

But now Albert P. Gilpin had begun to entertain some doubts of a serious nature. Doubts that might, in the end, prove him so wrong that he might have to decide that he was not really fitted for this job.

That the parolee had not come back to the rooming house by twelve thirty, when Gilpin and Lieutenant W. H. Webster of the Londonford police had interviewed the landlady, was not unusual, although it did represent a very slight infraction of the midnight-curfew rule that Gilpin himself had somewhat arbitrarily set up. But there were other things. While waiting at the Londonford police station for Ritchie to phone—*Just as soon as he comes in, Lieutenant, and I know he'll be glad to do it,* the landlady had promised—Gilpin and the lieutenant had kicked around the possibilities, wondering what was happening over in Tarkington to make this matter so urgent. Gilpin had a photograph and description from his files and he studied it while they waited: such a polite young man, quietly handsome in a rather old-fashioned way now with neatly trimmed hair, blond and wavy, and a rather romantic-looking mustache, also blond, his gaze direct and ingenuous, slightly hurt and baffled, if anything, not in the least bitter or defiant. As the clock had moved toward one o'clock and there was still no call, Albert P. Gilpin became more and more uneasy. And then Lieutenant Webster, who was a heavyset older man with a gray brush cut that made his heavy face look even heavier, had decided to phone the landlady: no, Boyd hadn't come in yet, did the lieutenant think something terrible might have happened to the child? The two men were faced with a decision then: to report again to the Tarkington police and to continue to wait or to push on with an investigation on their own. Because Gilpin had begun to feel responsible, if not yet guilty, he suggested: "He works in a repair garage for a man named Don Zeitlin. I've talked with Zeitlin several times. It could be the boy's working all night."

On the way to the garage, situated on a side street toward the edge of town, Gilpin explained to Lieutenant Webster that the job had been arranged for Boyd Ritchie, to utilize the trade he had learned in prison, by Digby Norton, publisher of the Tarkington *Star-Times*. Digby Norton, for reasons still unknown to Gilpin, had taken a particular interest in the parolee as soon as he had been released. And Don Zeitlin was in some manner related to Norton, although Gilpin couldn't recall at the moment exactly how. Anyway, the employer had always commended Boyd Ritchie highly. *He's quiet. He minds his own business. And he's a good mechanic. That's all I ask.*

Nevertheless, when they roused Don Zeitlin from a sound and possibly beer-induced sleep in the living quarters he maintained over the garage in the concrete-block building, he was not exactly in a jolly mood and he didn't give a damn who knew it. But Lieutenant W. H. Webster's quiet presence and uniform made him grouchily cooperative. Yep, Boyd often worked nights down below, but it was on a car of his own and he was always quiet about it so as not to interfere with the television, so even Don Zeitlin's wife, who could be hell-on-wheels sometimes, didn't object. Don Zeitlin was a very fat man with enormous jowls and permanently grease-stained hands and his eyes kept darting around the small, slovenly living room before he got up the courage to offer them a beer. They refused, but he went into the cubicle of a kitchen and took one out for himself and popped the tin lid and drank from the can. The kid might be downstairs there now, working, for all he knew.

"Listen, I was against the whole thing right from the start, see. I knew this night was coming. But listen, whatever you got in mind, my vote's with *him*. I maybe got talked into this by that uncle of Flora's—that's my wife—but that kid's one hundred percent, period. See?"

Albert P. Gilpin was beginning to feel relief: the landlady and now the boy's employer and Ritchie's prison record—well, the Tarkington police were on the wrong track, that was all.

But Lieutenant Webster said: "Seems to me we're talking about two different people. Mr. Zeitlin, what's *your* Boyd Ritchie look like?"

"Look like? Well, let's see. He don't weigh much. He's kinda short. Dark hair. Dark mustache. Hates to get his hands dirty and for a mechanic working—"

"Hold it a second," Gilpin said. "Dark hair? Mustache?"

"Yeh. Black, you might say. Why?"

"The Boyd Ritchie I'm talking about has blond hair, a light mustache. At least he does when he reports to me in my—" Then he stopped.

And the lieutenant said: "The Tarkington people said he might be red-haired or wearing a red wig."

Then the three men stood and looked at one another, frowning.

Until Gilpin said, somewhat hopelessly: "Ex-cons do

that sometime. I mean, he's got to fit his prison description when he reports to me. But otherwise . . . they don't like to be recognized by other people, people on the street, who might remember. It's against the rules, but—" His voice drifted off. It was no use, really. He knew.

So did the lieutenant now. "What kinda car he drive, Mr. Zeitlin? We got it a Ford '69 Maverick, dark gold or brass, maybe tan."

"You got it right, Lieutenant. That's what he drives okay." Then he took a long gulp of beer and said, "Let's go downstairs."

They trooped down a narrow concrete stairway and Zeitlin turned on the lights in the garage. A truck was hoisted on chains, its hood removed. A motorcycle was lying on its side, one wheel missing. Otherwise, there were no vehicles in the garage.

"Holy God," Zeitlin breathed. "That little son of a bitch."

Albert P. Gilpin hated to ask: "What?"

"To think her damned Uncle Digby'd get me into this."

Lieutenant Webster demanded: "Into what?"

"He's got another car. Been working on it for several months. Putting a new engine in it. Some engine, too. Been modifying that. In a Chevy Vega. 1969 four-door. Gray. That sneaky little son of a bitch, what's he done over there in Tarkington?"

"We don't know," Gilpin said. He felt a little lightheaded. A trifle weak in the knees.

"Suspicion of parole violation," Lieutenant Webster said, and he was moving.

Albert P. Gilpin followed. That was the official word all right: suspicion of parole violation covered what he thought of as a multitude of crimes. The only reassurance he could give himself now—and it was a foolish one, he knew—was that they hadn't requested an arrest, only that Ritchie be brought in for questioning. But that had been more than an hour ago.

* * *

If only the phone would stop ringing, stop and not ring again, it had been ringing for hours and now it had stopped again, but now she couldn't drift back, back to where she had been, to that place, that time, was that all a dream really, that place and that time when the promise inside filled her, overflowed, the years stretching ahead, mysterious and filled with all the numberless promises of all sorts, was it her wedding day she'd been dreaming of, was she awake now, her wedding day. I love you truly and forsaking all others, all a lie now, now that she was awake again, if she was, what's a vow, Fletcher, tell me, what does a vow mean, you bastard, to have and to hold, and now he wanted a promise, made her promise, tonight, how many hours ago, what had he demanded, demanded she promise him, that she'd go somewhere, drive somewhere, but she wasn't even dressed, she was wearing only a robe, in bed, on top of the bed, her suitcase there too, but the bile inside was rising, her mouth was dry but the gall was bitter in her throat, filling her head, and another drink would cut straight through it, no wonder people drank, she had never known the delight, but it was not all delight because she was sick, her stomach was closed tight, a knot, but nothing another drink, like the one on the bed table, wouldn't cure, wouldn't relieve, and if she drank it all now, the whole glass, then perhaps she could drift back to that time and that place that she had known once, that exquisite promise that still now lingered in her mind, calling her back, tolling her back, but the whiskey burned and brought tears, and she never cried so they couldn't be tears, some women she knew took sleeping pills, every night, how she'd prided herself she hadn't needed them, or anything like, that smug pride, gone now, she needed, what did she need, she hoped the phone wouldn't ring again because she wasn't going to answer, she refused, no wonder David smoked pot if it gave him this floating faraway feeling, dulled the blinding terrible light, no wonder, she understood now, and why young people retreated to the woods to commune with nature, any nirvana to escape the nirvana she had been living in, the long, long lie, like Peggy, who thought she had her fooled, too, but that was the beginning, that evening when she'd followed Peggy, saw her climb into that gray-bearded man's beat-up jeep, followed her to Londonford, that was only the beginning, that shock, a man Fletcher's age, older perhaps, why should Peggy choose such a man, ask Fletcher, ask her father, but he didn't know, refused to know, he had his own lie to maintain, this time she spilled a few drops on her silk robe, what did it matter, she wasn't going anywhere, even if she had promised, even if she had never lied to him before, that's a joke, Fletcher, her not lying to *him,* she wasn't running home to Mama because she had said she never would, no matter what, matter of pride, she would not be forced and what was a promise after all, except that promise in her blood while she slept, if she could sleep again it would all come back, shutting her throat, entrancing her, all those years ahead that were not there when she was like this, awake, if she stretched out again, if she turned off the light, he could do what he wanted, if he existed, this raper of young boys, of a young girl, let him, what did that matter either, whose cock where and when, it had no meaning now, and if he came and if he killed her while she slept, she'd never know, she'd know only that lovely, lovely brightness in her head and her blood and not anything to come, all problems over, gone, let someone else carry them, let Fletcher carry them, and his guilt, let him stagger under it all the days of his life, he plighted her his troth, didn't he, his truth, which she now knew did not exist, so what, she hated him, she wanted to sleep, why couldn't she sleep again, she hated and she hated herself even more and she was going back to sleep, now I lay me down to, if only she didn't feel so alone, deserted, alone, alone, where were they all, now I lay me down to—

* * *

With all the windows of the Toyota closed, they could not hear the creek that they both knew was out there in front of them since this was their favorite place to park. They could hear only the wind, which was growing stronger by the minute.

"You want to go someplace else?" the boy asked.

"Do you? It's getting late, isn't it?"

"I don't see why we should move. We were here first."

"I know, but . . . it's not the same. It's not private anymore."

"Let *them* go someplace else."

"Are all the doors locked?"

"Sure. Oh hell, I'll make sure. Just for you. Yeah, they are."

"I still wish they'd go someplace else."

"Did you hear that motor when they came in?"

"No. I wasn't thinking about . . . motors. Then, I mean."

"I couldn't help *hearing* it, could I?"

"I guess not. I didn't, though."

"Well, it didn't sound like a Vega, that's for sure. More like a souped-up three fifty. Or a Vette four fifty four."

"You know what I wish? What I really wish. That we could go someplace, like out West, a cabin by some lake maybe, or Switzerland, or the moon. Where there'd be just us. Nobody else."

"Yeah."

"Don't you?"

"What?"

"Wish that?"

"Yeah. Sure. Hey, don't cover up your bazooms. I like to look at them."

"Are you sure they can't see? From the other car?"

"What if they can?"

"I wish you'd say breasts, not bazooms."

"You're always wishing. What's the difference?"

"I don't know. But there is."

"Let's take a snooze."

"You do love me, don't you?"

"How many times do I—"

"I know. But if you didn't—love me, I mean—I'm old-fashioned—I warned you—I couldn't be like this if—"

"Well, I told you, but I'll tell you again. I do. What's the matter, don't you believe me?"

"I want to."

"Well, when you wake up, I'll show you again."

"That's not what I mean. I want you to love me *before* you show me. And after. Not just *during*."

"I'm almost asleep."

"Pop's shift gets off at one thirty. He'll have a couple of snorts, but I have to be home in bed by two."

"Don't get uptight. It's not even one o'clock yet."

"You don't know what he'd do to me if he ever—well, you just don't know. Now that Mama's gone, it's worse."

"You told me."

"I love you."

"Sure. Sure—me, too."

"I only wish they'd go park someplace else."

On the far side of town, up the hill, the clock in the tower at the college was chiming one thirty. It could not be heard at this distance.

Paul Wharton, by now, had lost all track of time. The clock in the Jaguar registered 6:03. But he had himself in control now, his mind was working, and he knew that he had come home from the Lake Club shortly after eleven. Since there was no sign of dawn, it could not possibly be six o'clock. He had no idea how long he had been driving now—first, around the lake and then along the river, all the while forcing himself to keep his eyes from drifting to the still upright form, covered by a blanket, in the bucket seat beside him. The form that, in life, had given him more pleasure than anything he had ever known. What he was searching for was a place where he could drive the car off and into the water, a place where it would not be seen or heard and where, he hoped, it would not be discovered, ever. But in all the time since he had left the house—it seemed like hours—he had not been able to locate or to think of such a place. He couldn't leave the thing or the car in the woods because sooner or later they would be discovered, and he couldn't drop the thing itself off a bridge, for instance, often as he had been tempted, because unless it was weighted, as by the car, it would float to the surface. And he knew that he couldn't touch it. Not again.

How long had he sat back there in the bedroom, weeping and wondering when he would ever stop? While he tried to make a decision that he knew, even in that stupefied state, was the most crucial of his life. His mind had floundered and gone off in various directions, at tangents. He could say, simply, that he came home and found her like this, dead in bed, having been attacked and murdered by some unknown intruder. But if all that Boyd Ritchie had said was true—and, still weeping helplessly then, he had known that it was—and if everyone knew of his jealousy, as they must, the police wouldn't believe him. Not for long, anyway. Even if he wiped the fingerprints from the shotgun, as he had done later anyway, no one would believe for long that he hadn't killed her. As, in fact, he had. He had to keep that fact uppermost in mind. Then, too, he had thought of leaving the house, blood and all, and letting someone else discover the thing in the bed. The maid, Agnes, would come in at eight thirty in the morning. But where could he spend the night, and what story could he devise to convince them that he hadn't come home? He had been sick all the time he was thinking it through, or trying to. The sickness went deep and he had to ignore the clawing at his guts and the tightness crushing his ribs. Inside, all the while, was the feeling that no matter what he did, it was all hopeless. Then he may as well call the police and tell them the truth. Crying like a child, actually sobbing while he sat motionless in the chair and stared blindly, he had known that no one would believe the truth: what had actually happened was the most unbelievable story he could tell. Strangely, he felt no compunction about what he had done. Only that he really shouldn't be punished for it. It had occurred to him, too, at one point, that he might name Boyd Ritchie, accuse him, even say that he himself witnessed not only the outrage but the killing. Who would believe Boyd Ritchie against Paul Wharton? He had the enormous lump on his head to prove that he had been knocked out and Boyd Ritchie had his Luger, still had it so far as he knew. But what if Ritchie was miles away by now, going fast, fading into anonymity several states away? What if they could never catch him? And, then, he still had to think of the Wharton name. And his mother. At the thought of her his sobs had turned into a soft whimper. But his decision, he realized, had been made. He would do what she would have advised him to do if she were alive.

He had worked with a deadly calm then, struggling with the nausea in him, the gut-wrenching need to vomit. For once in his life he had made a decision, a commitment, and now all he had to do was carry it through. He had cleaned the place completely, forcing himself to remove the body, which by then was only a thing, from the bed, which he then stripped down, wadding the bloodied sheets and bedspread into a ball. He had wiped the shotgun clean of blood and prints, remembering what Ritchie had said about its being registered in his name, and placed it on top of the sheets. Then he had taken a quick shower, scrubbing himself clean of blood, tormented momentarily by the scents—her scents—in the bathroom. Then he threw his bloody clothes on the bundle and put on a fresh suit. He packed her clothes, not taking time to be either selective or neat, into her own suitcases. *She must have left me. There's no note, but when I came home from the club, she was gone. Also her clothes. Her car's missing, too.* If everyone in town knew about her affairs —the same knowledge that would condemn him if he made any decision other than this one—then no one would doubt that this was the very thing a woman like Coralie Wharton might do, and just the manner in which she, having once been Coralie Powell, would do it. He had gone down and backed her car—it had to be her car—into the carriage house. He had remembered to remove the meat from the desk in the library but had not moved the slashed portrait of his mother. *She always hated Mother, so I suppose this was just the way she took to show it before leaving.* Upstairs again, before forcing himself to pick up the limp thing, he had wrapped it in a blanket. The bleeding seemed to have stopped, so he threw it over shoulder and carried it down, fighting nausea all the way. A car which he could not see passed on the street as he moved out the side door to the carriage house, but it did not stop or slow or speed up so he had to assume that he was not seen in the dimness. The car sounded like a foreign make with one of those thrumming motors. When he returned again to the bedroom, he remembered her cosmetic kit, which was filled with plastic vials of pills. He gathered it all together, careful not to leave the shotgun, carried the lot to the carriage house and locked it in the luggage compartment of the Jaguar.

He discovered when he started the car that in spite of all his care, there was blood on one hand and a damp stickiness on the front of his fresh shirt. And then he realized that the convertible top was down, so he put it up.

All the time that he had been driving—having no idea how long his search had lasted—he had been filled with an overpowering sense of loss. His head rocked with pain and his ribs ached and caught with each breath, all the way up the river, all the way down on the other side, while he struggled to remember any cliff overhanging the water over which he could ease the Jaguar and its contents. The calm had worn off and a slow panic had begun to set in. What if, after all his careful thought, he had made the wrong decision?

He should have offered Ritchie money. Why hadn't he thought of that? Money, a lot of money, to clear out, to leave them alone. That's what his mother would have done. She would have thought of it.

He was on the outskirts of Londonford, now, passing the dark factories along the river's edge. He couldn't go back to Tarkington; he couldn't risk it and there was no place on that road to offer a solution. He knew the river downstream, too: it was shallow and lined on both sides with either more factories or cottages. Then what? Where? He couldn't drive all night. The hopelessness returned. Despair. He knew he was doomed. He had known it all along. Had he been in such a trauma that he couldn't recognize it? It had all been for nothing.

He began to curse aloud as he turned onto the familiar Londonford-Tarkington road. And then he pressed down on the gas pedal and felt the car charge ahead. He couldn't go back there. He couldn't go home! But panic was driving him, and the pain in his head, and the silent presence of that stiff unreal thing mocking him, winning, winning even now because he was doomed, it had been a damn-fool idea, how had he imagined he could get away with—

He approached a downhill curve too fast, realized it only when he saw the dark woods looming in the headlights and the pavement twisting off to the right. He fought the steering wheel, felt the tires gripping the road, responding—and then felt the thing next to him topple against his shoulder. He uttered a sound. Gagging. A cry.

Then, even though the Jag left the road for a few yards, riding the weeded shoulder, he swung the wheel to the left, throwing the stiff blanket-covered thing away from him and against the door. Where it remained. Inert. Upright.

He was shaking now. Inside and out. And retching as he glanced at the dashboard. Sixty-four miles per hour. Too fast, too fast. And his eyes passed by the fuel gauge. It showed empty.

E.

For how long? How many miles?

The lying bitch. The car had not been repaired this afternoon. They would have filled the fuel tank as a matter of course. And they would have repaired the clock. She had had to make sure she had her own car at the Lake Club. In order to drive out to old man Stegner's place. To pay him off. *Man, that kinky gink could dream up more ways of usin' that pretty young body'n you and me together. I watched her from the window. What she did with him. What she did to him.*

For an instant he thought that he was going to reach out and slash at the blanket-covered thing with the back of his fist.

But he didn't. He stifled the new fury and wondered whether there was a service station open. Wondered and tried to recall—before he realized that he couldn't possibly stop with the thing propped against the door like that. What then? What could he do? If he ran out of gas out here on this deserted road this time of night—

Shuddering, he warned himself that the human system can take only so much. It didn't calm him. He doubted anything could ever really calm him again. He put down the window and gulped cold air and wind. His flesh was shivering, leaping, and his spine was like a rigid column of ice.

It was then that he was blinded. A gust of wind smashed a wall of leaves against the windshield and the road ahead disappeared. He slowed, but not soon enough. The road turned and the long snout of the Jaguar shot straight ahead, the windshield clearing. He saw trees on all sides, in front, and he fought to hold onto the wheel, applying the brakes, as he was jounced up and from side to side and then he heard the metallic crunching of a fender and the car came to a shuddering halt. He felt the steering wheel crushing into his chest, his neck snapped, and then his forehead struck the rim of the wheel, violently.

But he was not unconscious. The motor was dead. He heard the crash echoing through the woods. His mind reached for darkness, longed for it, and he wondered for a second whether he was dying. And hoped, in that same second, that he was.

He could hear a dog barking in the distance, beyond the trees, and when he turned to look, in the dimness, he saw that the thing had collapsed so that it was crumpled partly on the seat, partly on the floor, and the blanket had fallen away and he saw bare dead flesh and the darkened side of head where a face had been.

Ben Hutchinson could breathe again—out here in the cutting night air instead of in there with the smell of dried blood and death. He could still hear the medical examiner's preliminary report to Chief Diehl: "Heart attack. Best guess. And *only* a guess." Dr. Scofield spoke in asthmatic little barks. "No mortal wounds visible. 'Less he bled to death. Which is not indicated. Shock, more likely. May've strangled on his own blood. Or tongue. Vocal cords might be ruptured. Yelling for help. Out here." The voice came closer. "Have to wait for autopsy. Nasty job. Tomorrow." He came out the door, a crisp wisp of a man huddled in a heavy coat, with Diehl towering and silent beside him.

"You're not going to do an autopsy tonight, Dr. Scofield?" Tense and packed with a kind of anger over which he didn't seem to have any control, Ben Hutchinson hadn't realized that he was going to speak.

The little man placed a battered felt hat squarely on his bald head and peered at him. "You think that thing in there's going someplace?"

"How long do you estimate?"

"Since what? Since he was gouged in the eyes? Or since he gave up the mortal spirit?"

"Both." In the headlights from the parked police cars he could feel Diehl's eyes on him, lazily observing. But he'd gotten in this deep, so to hell with that. "Both," he repeated.

"Not dead long. Only a guess. You'll get the PM report in the AM." He grunted a laugh. "Me, I'm going home and back to bed."

To his own surprise Ben was walking alongside the doctor toward one of the cars. "What if we'd come a couple of hours ago, Doctor?"

"If. Young man, haven't you learned? That's one of the smallest but definitely the biggest word in the human lexicon."

He had to know. "Could Vincent Stegner been saved if we'd come out to investigate sooner?"

They stopped at the door of the car, which a uniformed officer held open, and Chief Diehl strolled closer. "Doc, we got us a fire-eater here. Fire-eaters blossomin' all over tonight, you'd think we had us a prairie fire." He spoke with a soft pleasant mockery. "Son," he asked mildly, "what'd we have to investigate?"

"We've known since before midnight that Stegner was an eyewitness in the case. And we could have known a helluva lot sooner. It's now exactly seventeen minutes till two."

Diehl shook his head. "G'night, Doc. Talk to you in the morning." He nodded to the officer, who closed the door after the doctor and then got into the driver's seat to take him back to town. As the car pulled away, Diehl regarded Ben. "People eat fire, they li'ble get burned."

"Chief Diehl!" Congressman Heckman was approaching heavily but swiftly from the steps of the lodge. "Well, Diehl, you convinced now?"

"I am convinced, Congressman, that you have no official capacity here and you better go home and go to bed because you are fast losing control of yourself, hear?"

"Never mind me. You've got your third crime now. How many more do you need?"

"My, my." Diehl pushed his Stetson back from his brow and shook his head. "I am sure gettin' it from all counties this night."

"I'm asking you, Diehl: What are you going to do?" The Congressman looked like hell. His eyes, even in this light, looked inflamed and he seemed to be having a hard time controlling the leaping muscles of his face. "There's no knowing what that degenerate maniac's going to do next."

Ben saw Gavin McQuade drift closer from out of the shadows, limping, his back half turned as if he had no interest in any of this—as if this, like everything else, only amused him. No notebook, no pencil—just those alert ears. Ben glanced and saw McQuade's little dark green VW in the cluster of parked cars.

"Wall, now we got not only a prairie fire, we got us a mad dog runnin' amok. If you want my opinion, Congressman—"

"I gave you instructions. Did you do what I told you?"

"To the letter, Congressman. To the letter. I always follow orders." He tilted his head, smoothing down his mustache. "Anything else now?"

Heckman apparently was in such a state that he didn't realize he was being mocked. "Security for my wife at the hospital."

"I'll detail a man pronto. And?"

"Someone ought, at the very least, to explain the situation to the Whartons."

"Thy will be done. I got just the man. Lieutenant Hutchinson here—he's right competent at little chores like that."

"What about Fletcher Briggs?"

Diehl's patience was running very thin and so, Ben realized, was his own. He reminded himself of Diehl's invalid wife and struggled inside for tolerance as the chief said: "When the professor asks, official and personal, I'll dig up another officer I can spare. Anyone else you think's in danger?"

"Possibly," Heckman said. "You."

Diehl grinned; it was a cold one. "Now I told you before: that scares me. That scares the shit right out of me." In the distance the sound of an approaching siren could be heard wailing above the howl in the trees above. "Wall, here comes the meat wagon."

Then Diehl turned his back on Heckman and strode across the rutted ground in the direction of the car with CHIEF OF POLICE printed on the door. McQuade fell in alongside him.

"Chief," Ben heard the reporter ask, "is it safe to assume there's some connection between what happened in the cemetery and this murder?"

Diehl stopped. "It's never safe to *assume* anything. Coroner hasn't even designated this a murder till he's had his autopsy."

Ben saw Heckman move toward the other two.

"You mean, Chief," McQuade asked innocently, "you mean it might be suicide? He trussed himself up in wire and starved to death?"

"Wait a minute," Heckman called as he approached them. "Wait a minute. You can't print any of this!" His voice was getting shrill. "Chief, you reminded me yourself what would happen if—"

Diehl shrugged and interrupted: "Congressman, you keep yelling for action. You get action, you get the press. Now which way you want it?"

Heckman looked from one to the other. He looked lost for a moment, baffled; then his face took on the expression of a trapped animal—abruptly ferocious.

McQuade said, as if he regretted having to say it: "There've been three crimes, Congressman, in a matter of hours—"

"How do you know that?" Heckman snarled. "What three crimes?"

An expression of abashment crossed McQuade's face. Now he was the one who looked trapped. "Well, two crimes anyway—"

But Heckman exploded. "What do you know?" He was glaring into McQuade's face. "What third crime are you talking about?" Then to Diehl: "I thought we agreed—" Then he whirled, fast, muttering, and grabbed McQuade by the upper arms and began to shake him. "You're not going to print that filth, how do you know, who told you, you're not going to ruin my son's life just to sell a lousy—" But he didn't finish.

Before Ben could move, as he saw other officers approaching, Diehl stepped in, feet planted, and lifted one arm and brought the edge of his hand, which was rigid, down vertically on Heckman's shoulder. It broke Heckman's grip and McQuade, looking startled and drawn, fell backward and lost his balance and went down into the dirt. Heckman was turning sidewise, his face twisting with the numbing pain that paralyzed the whole right side of his body. It appeared for an instant that his legs might cave.

Then Diehl stepped closer. Facing Heckman. And plunged a fist into the man's midsection. The sound of the blow was lost in Heckman's gasp, then his audible openmouthed struggle for breath, as his body doubled and swiveled away, his back to Diehl. Ben stepped closer, but before he could reach the chief, Diehl brought his fist up again and then down on Heckman's rib cage from behind, just above the kidney. Heckman straightened slightly and staggered forward a few steps.

Ben's impulse was to act. To smash his own fist into the gray mustache. But instead he stepped swiftly toward Heckman and caught him before he dropped. The heavy athletic body was heaving in his arms and the face, close now, was ashen. The eyes looked stunned, filled with pain and disbelief.

Then his gaze seemed to clear, to harden. And he lifted his right arm, wincing at the move, and shoved his hand into the jacket of his suit. There was something cold and hard in his eyes—something murderous. And Ben Hutchinson had the abrupt impression that the Congressman might have a weapon of some sort in his right hand inside his pocket.

But when Diehl stepped closer, the haziness returned to the eyes and the stone glitter went away and Ben stood back, relieved but still amazed.

"I'll handle this, Lieutenant," Diehl drawled, but his tone was different and when Ben looked into his face, he saw the look of fear there: Diehl was appalled at himself. He'd been proved wrong, he'd been driven too far, and now he knew he had given in to his own feelings and had committed, before witnesses, an act that he might have to regret forever. All this Ben read in the older man's eyes and face, but even this did not stir in him the quick compassion that he wished for. The chief placed his arm around Heckman and, half supporting the sagging hulk, led him toward his maroon-colored car. "I am truly sorry, sir, but I'm sure you can see that I couldn't allow you, a man your size, to attack that poor little reporter." His tone refused to give up the slight derision even as it seemed to beg for forgiveness. "You probably didn't observe it, Congressman, but the man's a gimp. Now you acted in a fit of anger and that's understandable, we all li'ble do that at times. But I didn't want to add to your personal troubles this night by being obliged to bring an assault and battery charge agin you. I'm sure you understand that, sir."

But Heckman did not answer as Diehl helped him into the driver's seat, asking whether he wanted someone to drive him home.

Ben, confused now and wondering just what the hell would come of this, crossed to McQuade, who had picked himself up and was flapping his hands at the dirt and leaves on his suit. "You all right, McQuade?"

"With Theron Diehl as my protector?" He tilted his head to one side and brushed off his seedy jacket. "How could I be anything but?" Then he turned and began to limp away.

Ben watched, helpless, with renewed fury pulling at his vital organs, hearing the approach of the siren. Meat wagon. God. Diehl had been aching for action all night. The only kind he understood. Earlier, Ben had noted the avid way Diehl's eyes had studied the corpse inside—with a certain pleasure, even satisfaction, behind his official curiosity. The sight of blood. Or death, maybe. God.

Heckman was starting his motor and Diehl was striding toward his own car again, ignoring McQuade as he passed him.

Then Ben heard McQuade's voice: "Ben—"

He moved toward McQuade, who had stopped now and was holding a sheet of paper in his hand. Ben's own voice had an odd hoarseness in it, hardness too. "What is it, Gavin?"

"Do me a favor. Return this to Chief Diehl for me. With my thanks, of course."

He took the paper, but McQuade didn't move away. Behind him Heckman's Buick was jouncing along the rutted driveway between the trees.

"You may read it, Ben."

Ben glanced, holding up the sheet of paper. The light was poor. MEMORIAL HOSPITAL MEDICAL REPORT. And below that: "Patient: Dennis Heckman." He didn't bother to read it. He simply gave in to his hate.

"I guess he gave it to me to make sure the press didn't get it," McQuade said wryly.

Ben turned and stared in the direction of Chief Diehl's car. Diehl was behind the wheel, the door open, holding a mike in one hand, speaking. Then Ben glanced toward McQuade's Volkswagen, watched him climb in, awkwardly. And saw someone else inside, in the shadows—only a figure. Someone who hadn't gotten out of the car.

"Hutchinson! Haul your ass over here!"

Longing to utter an obscenity, get into his car and drive home and get into bed with Myra, who would be warm with sleep, and very soft, and who would make him forget it all, he walked toward Diehl's voice.

". . . what I'm saying, Mr. Mayor. Now you stay right there at headquarters and I'll explain it all to you soon's I get back there."

Mayor Keen's very smooth voice came over the speaker: "What I'm wondering is whether I ought to go on the air myself and try to calm the fears of these people."

"Wall, that might just be a fine idea, yes, sir. There's always a lotta nervous nellies squeaking 'round. I got a few 'round here myself. But we gonna have the perpetrator in the next hour or two: you can take my solemn word on that, Mayor."

"Well, see that you do."

"I'm right on top of it personal, sir."

"I'll wait here for you, Chief."

Diehl replaced the mike. Sat staring a second or two before he turned to Ben. "Jerry Gerrard," he said. "That radio bastard's starting to broadcast news. Got the mayor's balls in a uproar." Then he reached and clicked another lever and when a voice answered, he said: "Anything on Boyd Ritchie?"

"Not yet, sir."

He clicked it off. Ben couldn't believe it.

"Aren't we going to send out a general alarm, Chief? Orders to arrest?"

"No, *we* ain't. Not till we got some evidence t'go with all this bullshit theory I been listening to."

Ben couldn't believe this. "Theory?" He had to control his voice. "Well, if it's theory, this proves it. This ties it all together."

Diehl sighed. "Not for me it don't. But we got a order out to pick him up for questioning, don't we? That's enough for now. I still think we're pissing in the wind."

Ben could not recall when he had hated anyone this way or this much. Ever. "What about hospital security?" But he knew; by now he knew.

"I can't waste men on personal matters now, can I?

With this here big manhunt goin' on."

Ben understood. Or thought he had now come as close to understanding as he ever would. He hoped his anger wasn't distorting it. He understood that Theron Diehl was one of those people who cannot make a mistake and be proved wrong and admit it. Who cannot take orders or threats. Call it pride or vanity or egomania, call it a god complex—whatever you chalked it up to, it came to this: such blank stubbornness was a form of insanity in itself. And dangerous. He understood, but it did not alter his hate.

He was about to turn away when he realized that Diehl was again speaking to headquarters: "That's right. Jerry Gerrard. You know him?"

"I know who you mean, yes, sir."

"Wall, send somebody across the Common and have him in there when I get in."

"On charges, Chief?"

"No charges. Yet. But if he gets fresh, mention interference with police work, obstructing justice, inciting to riot. I just want to have a private little chat with him."

"You . . . well, he's on the air till six in the morning, you know—"

"Sad shit. No privileges. Listen, who the hell is this? Are you questioning my orders, too?"

"No, sir."

" 'Cause I got a gutful of people questioning my orders." He was glaring at Ben, who was motionless and, he hoped, expressionless. "Gerrard's a fag, ain't he? We been questioning fags all night. Do what I tell you." He replaced the mike and waited.

So, as if to oblige, Ben said: "What're you going to ask him—how he managed to assault the Heckman kid while he was broadcasting?"

Diehl regarded Ben from beneath half-closed lids. "Hutchinson, you keep this up an' you and me're goin' to the mat. And you ain't going to get up. Hear?"

The hate was like a hot poison in his blood now. But

he turned away and started to walk.

Until Diehl called after him, as the ambulance, siren dying, moved through the cars toward the porch: "Where you going?"

"To the Wharton residence, sir."

"Yeah. Wall, we got more important things."

That was the moment. Ben thought of Myra and the two boys, Mickey and Teddy. But he knew that, in spite of everything, in spite of his love for them and his own need to keep this job that represented security and more, things he'd never had in this town, position and his own pride—in spite of all of it, he had to keep something more important inside himself that he could not give a word to while he was this cold and still with hate. He said: "I'm going to alert the Whartons of the possibility that they might be killed. Or worse. You gave the order yourself."

He was walking away. He saw the white-jacketed attendants get out of the ambulance and go into the Stegner living room.

He heard Diehl shouting after him: "I'm rescinding that order!"

But he did not stop walking until he arrived at his car. And, behind the wheel, he did not look back.

Paul Wharton's head still rested on the rim of the steering wheel and each time that he had lifted it, the pain, which was steady, would intensify so that it blinded him when he opened his eyes. He was aware that he couldn't remain here in the woods forever. He was aware, more vaguely, that there was something that had to be done. But he was in what his best friend at Groton had called a blue funk. Dazed. Stupefied. And as much unwilling as unable to take any action.

And there was a dog baying. Close to the car. Coralie's Jag. Very close, and the baying was insistent and high-pitched and drawn-out, and it worked on every nerve in him, even penetrated the blue funk. Then he realized that it had begun to rain. He could hear a faint sprinkle, a tapping on the roof of the car. And he was cold. The chill was in his bones, his marrow. And each breath was torture—what had happened to his ribs? They felt as if someone had kicked them. And why didn't that dog stop yowling out there?

He forced himself, bracing for the pain, to lift his head, to open his eyes. The windshield was wet-black, only a blur of headlight beyond it. He had not turned out the lights. In all this time. What if someone driving by on the road, should see the lights through the trees? Now, though, he needed the beam because if he could locate the source of that sound he could blast it into oblivion with the shotgun. He leaned to turn on the windshield wipers—and when they began, he realized that he had also not turned off the ignition. My God, was he trapped here? If the motor wouldn't start, then what? But first, there was something else—what was it? He'd had it a second ago. He had to shoot that damn dog. With the shotgun. But the shotgun hadn't been loaded. How could he forget a thing like that? And he'd stowed it with the bedclothes and suitcases in the luggage compartment, anyway.

The glitter of rain on the glass in front of him dazzled his eyes. And the dog was nowhere in view. Only dark tree trunks, brown and yellow shrubs and weeds, laurel and rusty-red sumac. Yet the sound continued, high and mournful.

He turned his head and his neck cracked. He heard it deep in his skull: a definite sound. *Crack!* And the pain then gathered itself into a knife and stabbed down his spine. As he stared at the thing. In the dim light from the dashboard. It all came back then, not in a flood but more like an explosion that threatened to shatter his mind and body. Why he was here. How he had come here. Why there was such pain in his head. He could see the gleam of bare arm or shoulder or breast, where the blanket had fallen away. And the thing itself rested, as if frozen rigid, at a grotesque angle, partly on the seat, partly on the floor. And in an abrupt paroxysm of hate and revulsion that sickened him, he was tempted to lean across, fling open the door and push the thing out of the car altogether. Let the dog have it. Let the dog do whatever he wanted with it.

But he knew this wouldn't be safe. Not after all the care he'd gone to, all the work and thought. He had to drag his gaze from the thing half-sprawled there to look at the fuel gauge, to make certain that his mind was remembering. It was. The needle stood at *E*. How many gallons would be left in the tank after the indicator registered empty? And how long had the needle stood there? How many miles had he driven before he had become aware of it? His eyes swept past the clock: it still showed 6:03. And then he thought of his wristwatch. Why hadn't he thought of it before? Because he had been too angry at discovering that the Jaguar had not been repaired. Another lie. In a lifetime of lies. He really ought to toss her out to that damned howling vicious beast! But he looked at his watch instead: 2:07. At night. Morning. God, he couldn't go on sitting here. He had to pull himself out of this blue funk and get cracking. He had a five-gallon container of gasoline in the trunk of his Mercedes. He was a man always prepared for emergencies. There had been some reason why he hadn't taken his own car—yes, so that he could claim, later, that she had deserted him. Of course. He had to keep things straight in his mind. What he must do now was drive back to the house, empty the gas into the Jaguar's tank, *then* find a way to get rid of the thing. And the car. And a way, afterward, to get back to the house. He hadn't, he realized now, ever solved that part of the problem, either. He couldn't hitchhike, no buses ran at night, he had to be back in the house by morning. He could ask a friend. But who? He thought of the names Ritchie had mentioned. He didn't have a friend. Not a single friend he could trust. How was that possible? And what time did dawn break this time of year?

One thing at a time, he warned himself sternly. One

thing at a time. To get fuel: that was number one, top priority now. So he leaned, head cracking again but not so intensely this time, and twisted the key. The motor groaned, sluggishly. Panic struck: the battery! He had left the lights on, the ignition, he had turned on the wipers. He tried again, pressing hard, and after two more prolonged rebellious growls, the motor caught and roared once, then began to throb. He threw the gears into reverse and heard, over the wind and the rain and the baying, the sound of heavy metal grating as the left front fender was loosened from the trunk of the tree. Then, after a small jolt, the car was free and backing up. But he couldn't see out the rear window, which was opaque with rain, so he lowered the window at his side and put his head out into the rain, which had become steadier and heavier now and which blew blindingly into his eyes. The cold swept through the small compartment and he felt his flesh quivering as he maneuvered the Jaguar between the trees and onto the pavement, astride the road.

He had to think a long moment before he could determine which was the way to Londonford and which the direction toward Tarkington. Then he whipped the wheel and decided not to think ahead, only to concentrate on the driving. One step at a time.

But he could still hear the dog. It was no longer baying. Its growl erupted ferociously into a snarling bark, loud and repeated and desperate. The animal was running alongside. A demon out of hell. Why had this animal been sent to plague him further? He felt again that overwhelming impulse that he had felt in that split second when he held the shotgun in his hand. To kill! Instead of sending the car charging ahead, he slowed. And the dog, unable to break its own speed, raced ahead and into the headlight beam. Then he bore down on the gas pedal, twisting the wheel only slightly, swerving the long nose of the car, and he felt the impact, a small jolt really, but the caterwauling turned into a yelp, followed by a repeated howl of pain and then the car was speeding along the road and the only accompanying sounds were the motor and muted click-clack of the wipers and the drizzle and wind beating against the windshield and blowing with a faint whistle around the sides and over the low roof.

If he ran out of gas now, before he arrived home—

And then he realized, for the first time, that the headlight beam was lopsided. The left headlight had been smashed against the tree. He was driving a car with one light.

Ben Hutchinson had never before been inside the Wharton home. Or, in fact, any of the several dozen of homes like it in Tarkington. It was as elegant and graceful and impressive as he had always imagined. But he was really not sure he should be in the house now. The front door had been not only unlocked but ajar and no one had answered his repeated poundings on it. He had no warrant to search, but after he had pushed the door open and called several times and since he had been assigned to investigate with the intent of warning its owners of a potential crime of some unspecified nature, but a crime nevertheless, he had felt justified in looking around. There was one car in the driveway, a Mercedes sedan, none in the garage that looked like an old but luxurious stable. And no one was at home at two eleven in the morning. Nothing seemed to be out of place in any of the rooms downstairs with the possible exception of the den—or would they call it a library?—where a drawer of the desk stood open and, to his surprise, an oil painting on the wall appeared to have been cut and gashed—destroyed. He recognized the woman's face: everyone in town, growing up, knew and respected old Mrs. Augusta Wharton. He went upstairs.

In the master bedroom, which was in itself as large as many apartments he had seen, nothing seemed to be out of place when he first turned on the light. But then he saw that the large bed had been stripped of sheets and blankets. Odd. He stepped closer. He saw the blood. Or the stains of blood. Brownish splotches on the mattress. In his brief career as a police officer he had seen the stains of blood more often than he cared to remember now. But usually after automobile accidents, not after calculated violence. Not that he would allow this to convince him that any violence had already occurred here. The blood was dry: it could have been there for months, years. He looked into the closets. Everything seemed to be in order except that one closet was empty—as if, unless it was not used at all, its contents had been snatched up at one time. Again: odd. But not odd enough for him to consider informing Diehl. He found a number of suitcases, all empty, more men's than ladies', but what the hell, the Whartons may have taken a short trip or vacation, how was he to know how many pieces of luggage they owned? Then he discovered a discoloration on the carpet near the hall door. And he touched it with his fingers, then rubbed at the mat—his fingers came up sticky, not quite wet very slightly dampened but not discolored in any way. He supposed, damn it, that he'd have to call Diehl after all.

The idea of talking with Diehl again was repugnant to him. He had pushed the chief as far as he dared tonight, perhaps too far, and he had to consider the consequences of whatever action he took now. He had to consider Myra. He had to consider the boys, Teddy and Mickey. Even the thought of the three, especially of Myra, caused a heart-stopping surge of emotion inside him. He supposed it came down to that old-fashioned, that outmoded simple word that everyone seemed to use less and less lately—love. Had the moment of satisfaction—anger and pride and defiance—back there at the Stegner place been worth it? On the other hand, he had to consider himself, too. Ben Hutchinson, the man. If he had to spend a life knuckling under to men like Theron Diehl, was the job really worth it? Any job?

He didn't know, but he had to swallow that anger and pride now, make his report and allow Diehl to call the next move. He went downstairs and outside through the light but steady rain to his patrol car, and when he had made contact with headquarters, he asked to speak to the chief, all the while haunted again by the idea that if anything *had* happened here tonight, it might have been prevented by earlier and decisive action. He was informed that Chief Diehl was in conference with the mayor and had asked not to be disturbed by anyone, for any reason whatever. He left word that the chief's presence was required at 3223 Elmhurst Street.

Then, with the rain an incessant patter on the top of the patrol car, he sat looking at the house next door, where a light showed in a downstairs front window: should he ask a few questions? If that bleeding had occurred tonight, someone had suffered pain. If anyone had suffered such pain, wouldn't he or she have cried out? Had there been any other unusual activity in or around the Wharton house tonight? The house, although the closest, was still separated from the Wharton residence by an expanse of lawn, many shrubs, a line of narrow conical fir trees and a low stone wall. Did he have a right to bother those people on what small evidence he had—which amounted to little more than a hunch, a feeling inside?

There was a rapping on the window at his shoulder. He peered through the rainswept glass to see Gavin McQuade scowling in at him. Gavin was not wearing a raincoat and his body looked shrunken even more than usual, and soaked.

"Come around," Ben Hutchinson said, with resignation, but at the same time pleased somehow to have the company of this little man with the wizened face and the softly derisive manner that was still lively and vital in some whimsical way. But he knew that tonight he had to play his cards very damn carefully with the insistent reporter, who probably knew more by now than anyone in town. McQuade had as little regard for Diehl as he had come to have, but he couldn't give the reporter any ammunition now that could be used against Diehl or himself or to confuse the investigation.

When Gavin was beside him, blowing his nose, slamming the door and bemoaning the fact that the bars were all closed and "It goes without saying an upright young pig like you wouldn't have a snort secreted in the glove compartment," Ben Hutchinson slid down in the seat and said, "Gavin, I'm investigating a parking ticket, why the hell don't you stop tailing me?" Then he added: "By the way, I spotted your VW around the corner."

"You're a liar," McQuade said jovially. Then turning his head to the other side: "Listen to the man!"

"Who's your passenger?"

And McQuade whistled between his teeth then, his gnarled face knotting. "None of your business, Doctor Watson. Big night in the boondocks, what? *You* wouldn't be inclined to tell *me* what we're doing here, would you?"

"I'd be inclined to tell you to go to hell."

"That's been done tonight. In no uncertain terms. By the Congressman, remember?" He lit a cigarette. "How come there's no arrest order out, no warrant?"

"For who?"

"It's whom, but you pass anyway. For an ex-con named Boyd Ritchie. That's who."

"Gavin," Ben Hutchinson said then, hearing the strained quality in his voice and wondering at it, "what I'm doing here is strictly police business. What you're doing here is interfering."

"You sound like your boss—forgetting the public's right to know. How come he hasn't been nabbed yet? Car description went out almost two hours ago. Town this size—"

Ben Hutchinson knew it was a good and reasonable question, but he'd been asking good and reasonable questions all night and he was not in the mood for any more of them. He asked: "Why do you want to make it any rougher, Gavin?"

McQuade shrugged and blew smoke. "I got my job. You got yours."

"Go quote yourself," Ben said.

And McQuade chortled sourly. "Ben, it's been a long night." He opened the door. "It looks to get longer." He got out into the rain and leaned into the car. "How about your calming down? We don't have many good men. Wouldn't want to lose you." He slammed the door again.

Ben turned his attention again to the house next door. Gavin was right, of course: it was getting to him. All of it. The violence, the murder, poor Heckman's frustration and rage and that wild look in his eyes, the mutilated body of the old man, Diehl's stubborn blindness, or worse, his willful selfish determination to prove himself right and in control, all of it, it was getting to him and if he allowed it to tear *him* apart, what could he do either to apprehend the criminal or to prevent more horror?

He made up his mind: he might as well ask a few questions. Do what little he could while he waited. He opened the door and stepped out. The wind had subsided slightly and as he crossed the wide lawn, already going soggy beneath his shoes, he thought again of Myra. If he decided to chuck it, or if Diehl asked for his badge, she'd simply smile and ask where he thought he could get another job. But if he chucked it, just like that, because of a bastard like Theron Diehl, then wouldn't he be turning law enforcement over to the Theron Diehls of the world? Men who were damned eager to get it into their grasp even though they had no genuine respect for it themselves. Was he going to tell Diehl what to do with his badge without putting up a fight to keep it?

He passed through the row of wet trees and over the stone wall onto the lawn of the house next door—also a large and impressive one, suggesting past glory, grace and extravagance. He went up the steps to the front porch and lifted the old brass knocker.

When she saw him approaching along the wet sidewalk, thin shoulders hunched against the rain, no raincoat of course, walking in that lopsided way of his, Annette Beauchamp felt a constriction in her throat. A choking sensation. She couldn't help herself. When he got into the seat beside her in his VW, she was intensely conscious of his presence—as if something warm and oddly reassuring had entered the small compartment of the car, adding a certain savor. As of cinnamon. Or clove. Even the gentle swish and gurgle of the rain outside seemed to close them in together here. She longed to be able to dry him off somehow. There was something so vulnerable and boyish about this little man, in spite of the way he talked and acted. Or possibly because of it. She suddenly had the impression that they were together in a small tight boat at sea, with a storm moving in.

He took off his soaked hat and whapped it against the wheel, water sprinkling. "Ben summoned the chief, so something's doing." Then he started the motor. "I can drive you home."

"Or what?"

"I'm going around the block and then park across from the Wharton place. It's what they call my beat."

"If you took me home, I could give you a drink to warm up the gizzard." And then she was wondering how Gavin McQuade would make love. He had said he was thirty-five—to whom *did* he make love? And then she remembered how crotchety and indignant Fletcher had become when she asked him whether he balled his wife. Where the hell had Fletcher gone and what was he doing? "Well, McQuade?"

"Can I take a rain check on the offer?"

"Since it's raining, why not? But the offer was only for a drink. Or for a drink only."

He started the car and drove to the corner. "Listen

to that, will you?" he asked the nobody—or elf—that was always perched invisibly on his shoulder. "I seen me duty, I done me duty, and all I gets is a offer for a drink only, the girl says." As he turned the corner in no hurry, he said: "The word's out. See the lights in windows. The populace is up and stirring. Phones are ringing. Lock the doors, lock up your virgin daughters, get out your trusty muskets—there's a maniac aprowl."

"Well, isn't there?"

"A maniac or some poor driven soul who's in as much misery as the rest of the godforsaken—" But he stopped. "I don't like the effect you have on me, girl."

"I could say the same thing, McQuade."

"Thou shall know the truth and the truth shall—" He allowed the bug to drift to a stop along the curb a hundred yards down the street and across the glimmering dark pavement from the Wharton house, where she could see the police cruiser, lights out, parked in the driveway. "Biggest story of my fabled journalistic career probably, and I'm damned if I want to write it." He switched off the lights. "Riddle me that one, pretty lady."

She recalled watching Wallace Heckman attacking him at the Stegner place—lifting him off the ground, shaking him violently. And she recalled her own swift impulse to leap from the Volks and run to where the men gathered, an impulse that bewildered her then and disturbed her now. She didn't need to speak now; really felt reluctant to speak. She understood. In spite of Heckman's rage and fear. Gavin McQuade hadn't decided how to handle the matter of the attack on Heckman's son in his news story. His impulse was to escape. An impulse she comprehended well. Too well.

"If I don't write it like it is, the wire services will. Then what's been gained?"

Impulsively, as she had done with Heckman in the file room ages ago now, she reached out a hand and placed it over his on the rim of the steering wheel. His felt knotty and hard and cold and wet.

He didn't turn to look at her. Nor did he make a mocking remark. She allowed her hand to remain on his.

"A sound. A loud sound, you say, sir? Can you be more specific?"

"Well, at the time, I . . . I'd call it more like a scream."

"And you—did you hear this, too, ma'am?"

"No. I can't say that I did. Nor did the Gilberts, who were playing bridge with us at the time. We heard nothing."

"Only you, then, sir? Out of four people?"

"Apparently that's true. *Apparently.*"

"Well, you needn't sound so put-upon about it, sweetheart. *Apparently* you're being proved right. Isn't that what you're suggesting, Officer—I didn't get your name."

"Hutchinson, ma'am. And I'm not suggesting anything. I'm only doing what I think ought to be done, that's all. And you, sir, let me get this straight—even though you heard this strange sound, possibly from the house next door, this sound that you call a scream, you didn't do anything about it?"

"What could he do?"

"Well, he might have gone next door to investigate—"

"He's not a police officer, young man."

"Or . . . he might at least have phoned the Whartons. Or, sir, you might have called us."

"Nonsense, young man. He couldn't be sure. How could he be sure?"

"That's what they convinced me of, Officer. Or, rather, you did . . . sweetheart."

"Officer Hutchinson, isn't it time you told us what's happened over at the Whartons?"

"We don't know yet, ma'am."

"By that you mean you won't tell me."

"I only mean I don't know."

"Well," she said to her husband then, "well, sweetheart, I suppose you'll just have to pick up the phone and pull some strings downtown and find out."

"I don't have any strings to pull . . . sweetheart."

"Uh . . . at about what time did you hear this sound that might have been a scream, sir? Approximately, of course."

"Approximately? Say, ten thirty."

"Closer to ten, don't you think, sweetheart?"

"No. If I thought that, I'd say ten . . . sweetheart."

"Well. That about wraps it up. Thank you both for your time and I'm sorry that I had to bother you this time of night. Morning, now. But, sir, next time you hear—oh, never mind, it'll probably never happen again. If there are any other questions, Chief Diehl or someone else will be in touch in the morning. Go back to bed now, and thanks. Good night."

"Good night, Officer."

After the door had closed, she heard a heavy exasperated sigh. "Well, I must say."

"I beg your pardon?"

"I said: I must say."

"I know. But you didn't. Say, I mean. For instance, you didn't say that you and the Gilberts did hear something but you decided it was on TV. That's what you didn't say."

"You confused me. And embarrassed me beyond words. Humiliated me in front of that handsome nice young man. By contradicting every word I said."

"I was the one who should have been humiliated. But I wasn't. And that handsome nice young man is only a police officer trying to do his duty. All he wanted was the truth."

"I told the truth. I always tell the truth."

"I know . . . sweetheart. When it doesn't humiliate you."

"And what, may I inquire, were you doing awake? You told him you were up even before he came over and knocked on the door."

"I couldn't sleep. Maybe my conscience was bothering me."

"Oh, what nonsense. If you ask me, all that happened over there was that he swatted her a good one and she probably was drunk and she definitely deserved it."

"That's when she screamed then."

"You've been drinking."

"I imagine we all get what we deserve. Sooner or later."

"I know what's bothering you. You might not have her next door after this—so you won't be able to run over there every time you get a filthy erotic impulse."

"Suppose . . . sweetheart, just suppose that something really dreadful's happened to that girl. Is that all it means to you?"

"It means that to me because I love you, yes. And don't you dare use that awful word again."

"How could you love me? Someone as weak as I am. Every time you impose your will, I give in. Which gives you an excuse to despise me for being weak."

"I really think sometimes that you have a disordered mind. Or does that only come from sitting down here drinking by yourself?"

"Would you care for one?"

"I'm going back to bed. Coming?"

"Not for a while."

"Conscience still bother you?"

"No. It's just stopped."

"My, aren't we cryptic tonight? Well, I don't relish having involved conversations at two thirty in the morning. Be sure you turn out the lights."

"I will, sweetheart."

And he did so, as soon as she was gone. Out the window he saw the dome light atop the patrol car come on and begin to revolve, throwing a weird pattern of blue against the windows at regular intervals. He poured another whiskey. Tomorrow was another day—and it had already begun. A new day. He sat down and crossed his legs and put his head back and closed his eyes. For more than thirty years of marriage she had suspected and accused. Without cause. If her doubts had tormented her because she loved him, as she claimed, he might be able to continue to live with them. But since she herself had no genuine interest in what she called his filthy erotic impulses—well, women she would consider strumpets were everywhere. But of course they were not the luridly painted streetwalkers and whores of her imagination. They were in his office. Among their closest friends. Everywhere. Wenches galore! He laughed aloud. Beginning tomorrow, he would prove her worst suspicions correct. And she would never know. That would be part of the satisfaction, too: she would never even know.

He opened his eyes, saw the reflection of the revolving blue light on the ceiling and wondered whether, if it had not been for that scream, he would ever have reached this mood of almost youthful renewal. How many years had it been since he looked forward to a new day?

Ben Hutchinson had returned to his car in a reckless frame of mind. He had not forgotten his decision and determination to placate Theron Diehl and thus hold onto his job, but what he had just learned next door had caused him to flip on the dome light. It was time for action. He reported in by radio and asked whether there were any developments. Yes. Information from the Londonford police and Boyd Ritchie's parole officer: Ritchie had not returned to his room, he had been living in Londonford using a disguise, which was described, and he owned another car, which was also described, with a Chevrolet Vega high-powered racing motor that he had modified. It all fitted. The scream. Heckman's kid. All of it. No more stalling now. He asked to speak with Chief Diehl and was informed that the chief had again left orders not to be disturbed: he was interrogating a suspect. Who? Jerry Gerrard? God.

As if Gerrard could possibly have committed these crimes when he had been in front of a microphone talking with people all night. Why was Diehl wasting time with him except for some weird satisfaction of his own? And why weren't the state boys in on this? Standard procedure, and long before now. But while they were viewing Stegner's remains, Diehl had said: *We can handle this, who needs them?* And look what he did to Heckman—hell, even Diehl must know he couldn't get away with that. In his own way he had to be as crazy as Ritchie was in his. But whether he was or not, there could be no more ass-dragging now. Something had to be done; they had to go the whole route now before anything else happened. If Diehl wouldn't do it, or wasn't capable—

"I'm at 3223 Elmhurst," he said. "Call the barracks. Get the state boys here, especially detectives and fingerprint men."

"But Chief Diehl said—"

"You heard me. I'm waiting here. Then get out a full description of that car—general pickup order. And a warrant for the arrest of Boyd Ritchie, suspicion of homicide, and a five-state alarm with a warning that he's armed and probably dangerous. Make that *extremely* dangerous."

"But Chief Diehl instructed me—"

"Chief Diehl doesn't want to be disturbed. Well, don't disturb him. I'll take full responsibility. Get on it. *Now!*"

He flipped off the radio and sat back, the urgency and excitement working in him like three or four stiff drinks in a row. The chips were down. And he felt relief at last. No matter what came now, he'd be able to face himself in the mirror.

More than an hour. For more than an hour and fifteen minutes now Boyd Ritchie had been sitting, stiff and cramped and aching, behind the wheel of the gray Vega, which remained parked at the barricade across the creek from Theron Diehl's backyard. Trapped. Stymied. In the dark, with the lights turned off, he had to strike a match and lean far down to see the hands on the dashboard clock. And each time he was struck with that same sense of incredulity: it had to be later than that, *had* to be.

If the couple in the Toyota saw the flare of match, they'd assume he was lighting a cigarette. If they weren't *dead* in there! What the hell were they doing—fucking, sleeping? Or had they OD'd and zonked out? As long as they didn't move, he couldn't move.

He didn't dare get out and carry the gallon jug across the brook and do what he'd planned to do. As soon as they, whoever they were in the other car, saw the flames—and they'd probably be the first to see them—they'd put it together, realize who'd done it. Especially since he'd have to wade back to the car to get away. They'd be able to describe the car to the pigs. This car, not the decoy Maverick the stupid pigs were breaking their asses trying to find. If the Vega was identified by anyone and if all the streets and roads were covered by cops, he wouldn't be able to finish the job. After all. After all he'd done to get to this spot, this night!

Savagely he reached for the Luger on the seat beside him. If he used it now, fast, blast through the windshield, let them both have it, they were the ones doing this to him, holding him here while everything was getting out of hand, two shots, make sure he got them both, then wade the creek, do the job over there and—

He heard himself growl. What was he thinking? What was he letting them do to him? *He* was the one who decided. He couldn't lose control now, this late, he couldn't let *them,* all of them—

Cool it! Hang in there.

He still had things to do after this. Like Diehl himself—personal. He could feel his bag tighten up around his balls at the thought.

Like Fletcher Briggs. Last but not least. Like Fletcher Briggs' dear sweet all-American family. Give them time to get home, all of them, snug in their goddamn beds. And if they didn't get home, he damn well knew where to find them.

He was still going to come out on top. What difference if the old man died? What difference if they blamed him for it? Then, for the first time, it came to him: the Cunt. Why hadn't he thought of that? That's what she did in Stegner's place. She saw her chance and she killed the old man. And they'd blame him—Boyd Ritchie. In a way it was kind of beautiful that way, because *now* she was dead, too. And Wharton was shitting in his pants trying to get rid of what was left of her. Yeah, that was kind of beautiful in its own way.

All the same, if that couple in the Toyota didn't split soon, damn soon, they'd get theirs, he'd think of a way, they'd get theirs, too. He'd play their game, their war of nerves, just so long. They were against him, too, and they'd get theirs. Boyd Ritchie settled all scores.

The rain, which had been only a drizzle until now, suddenly turned into a downpour. Even the goddamn weather was against him all of a sudden. He'd researched the weather, just the way he'd researched everything else, and no rain was predicted for this date. His back was stiff, his muscles cramped. Where had all the anticipation gone? That giddy pleasure, almost ecstasy, that he'd felt earlier. He was in prison again. In solitary. Where was that exultant feeling? Wasn't he still the bird of prey, perched to swoop down? If not, what had all the work gone for—all those days and nights of planning, those long evenings of surveillance—studying their comings and goings, the cautious waiting and watching? Why couldn't he shake off the feeling that somewhere along the line things had stopped going the way he'd planned them? That, for all his work, they were not going to come out the way he knew they had to come out, *had* to!

The radio had been silent for some time now.

Maybe he should change the scheme: drive around to the front of the house, stop the car, run up the front walk, do the job, then split, fast, hoping no one would see him or the car. In and out, fast. But there had been a reason why he didn't want to do it that way. A reason he was damned if he could remember now. His heart was smashing inside his chest like a goddamn time bomb. Why not, *why not?*

Diehl's old lady. Of course! Christ, how could he have forgotten that? Diehl's old lady slept in the front bedroom. If he did it from the front, she could be killed before anyone could get to her. He didn't want to kill anyone. It wouldn't be the same if he personally had to kill anyone. That would detract from the overall beauty of—

But Stegner was dead.

Had he killed Stegner?

No, the Cunt had killed Stegner.

But they'd blame him. They'd always blame him.

Then the calm impersonal voice of the police dispatcher spoke again, his words filling the closed car. And Boyd Ritchie heard his name for the first time tonight.

The Londonford-Tarkington road had been deserted, and until he reached town, he had driven automatically, succeeding to some degree in blanking his mind. The windshield wipers snapped with mesmerizing regularity before his blurred eyes. All the way he was conscious, but only in a distant way, of the thing that seemed to have frozen itself now half on the seat and half on the floor; he didn't glance at it, not once. And with each breath a stab of pain along his ribs and his head a hammering ache, he had been tensed for the first cough from the Jaguar engine, signifying that the gas had been used. If that happened, he did not know what he would do, or could do, so he made up his mind not to consider the possibility. But, on a deeper level, he knew that if that did happen, it was all over.

All he could possibly do now was continue to act, even without hope, and perhaps he would be able to get back to the house and the gasoline in his Mercedes.

But when he was moving along the streets of Tarkington—streets that, however changed, remained familiar and seemed reassuring now in some way—he began to become conscious of something odd, out of the ordinary. Especially at this time of morning. He didn't look at his watch, but he knew that, driving carefully at a normal rate of speed to conserve the fuel, he could not have arrived here before two thirty, probably ten or even fifteen minutes later. Yet there were lights in windows. And there were people on some of the porches. And, even in the rain, a few had come together to stand talking on sidewalks and lawns. He flipped on the radio, twisted the dial to the local station's 1350, heard nothing. Nothing. But that fellow Jerry Gerrard was on till morning. And if not his voice, then music. No matter how he adjusted the dial, there was only static.

Then he remembered the single headlight. The smashed front left fender. How could he have forgotten? And what good was remembering? But if a policeman stopped him to inquire—

It came to him then that all these people knew. They were all looking for him. Who else? Paul Wharton. Who had murdered his wife.

Who else?

Nothing else had happened.

Murder.

He was tempted to turn around. But where the hell could he go? The needle on the dim dashboard had not wavered.

Home. He had come this far. There was no place else to go anyway. Hadn't he tried? Hadn't he searched for a place, a safe place—

But that came later. To search again.

After he had the gasoline—

He'd go insane if he didn't keep things straight. One move at a time.

He turned down Elmhurst. Passing the corner on which he had played as a boy. Passing the houses he had always known.

There was a dark-green Volkswagen parked along the curb across from the house. People in the neighborhood usually parked in their own driveways. And damned few owned Volkswagens. Because of the rain, he couldn't determine whether it was occupied.

Then he saw the car in his own driveway.

A police car.

With a blue dome light revolving.

In his driveway.

Then he had been right. They knew. The whole town must—

He fought down the impulse to increase speed. He passed the house. Nothing seemed to be moving, inside or out. But there were lights on now. He had turned out all the lights. He had made a special point of—

But why was he doing this? If everyone knew, the whole town, the police, if everyone knew—

And if he ran out of gas now—

If he ran out of gas before he could get rid of it and then walk home—

But he couldn't walk home now.

Home. He had no home.

It struck him then, completely: he had no home, he had never really had a home, he had lived in the same house all his life, yet he had never never never—

He heard a sob in the closed car.

But he did not stop. He passed Old Quarry Street, continued on. To where?

Old Quarry Street. Which became Old Quarry Road. Which led to the old abandoned granite quarry where he had swum as a boy.

Why hadn't he thought of it? Why had he thought only of the river?

He felt dampness on his cheeks. Cold. But behind his eyes was a burning sensation.

He was crying. Again.

Weeping tears of helplessness and anguish and hate

and despair. No matter what he did, it would not be enough. Nothing could ever save him now.

But he had to do it.

He made a U-turn and returned to Old Quarry Street. How many miles out to the quarry itself?

And if the motor faltered on the way—

There was music from a radio in the next room, which Peggy took to be a bedroom. The woman had one of those old-young faces that always confused Peggy as to pinning an age to it. She could have been thirty-five or fifty-five. Without makeup and wearing an old flannel bathrobe, her small thin face trembled with startlement and near panic, as if she were trying to prepare herself for tragic news. "Has something happened to Jesse?"

"No, no, I don't know anything about your son. I'm asking whether you might know where he is because my son David might be with him."

Standing in the small disordered living room of her modest split-level house in one of the new subdivisions about ten miles east of town, the woman shook her head, somewhat hopelessly, her expression still one of distress. "I don't know, Mr. Briggs. I don't know where Jesse goes. All I know is he's never home."

"My daugnter and I've been all over—" He broke off and tried to smile and Peggy saw the growing tiredness in the lines of her father's face. Yet he seemed to throw it off even as she watched. "I'm sorry to bother you."

"No bother, Mr. Briggs. I was listening to the radio, anyway. I never can seem to sleep till he—" She took a tentative step. "What's going on tonight? Can you tell me? Earlier I heard on the radio that there'd been a crime and the police were going in all directions. Then, for no reason at all, the station went off the air—no music, commercials, anything. And nobody answered when you phoned in. Now it's just come back on, but the announcer, the one called Jerry, he was too excited to do anything but put some music on and say he'd explain in a few minutes. He sounded so upset, I felt sorry for him. What do you think, Mr. Briggs? Could something terrible be happening? I wish Jesse was here."

"No, no. I don't think you have anything to worry about." And Peggy heard the gentleness in her father's tone, saw the kindness in his very blue eyes as his rusty mustache twisted into a reassuring smile. "I don't think your son's in any danger whatever. I really don't."

"What then? What?"

Peggy knew he couldn't tell her. Or wouldn't. "Let's just say you're safe and he's safe." His voice sounded almost as haggard as his face looked. "I'm sorry we—"

But there was a voice from the next room and the music was no longer playing. "Is anyone listening? This is Jerry Gerrard and this is *Tell It to Jerry* back on the air. I know I promised an explanation of why this station was dead earlier, and as soon as I can gather my wits, that's what I'm going to do. But right now let me tell you that I can now explain some of the action I've been keeping you abreast of tonight. There's been a murder, folks. A murder in our fair community. Earlier tonight the body of an elderly recluse by the name of Vincent Stegner was found in his cabin just off Highmeadow Road. He had been brutally tortured. That's as much as I can tell you now. The police are investigating and—"

But Peggy realized that her father was no longer in the room. She followed him outside into the rain and saw him climbing into the station wagon, so she ran after him, hearing the woman calling from the doorway: "Good luck, Mr. Briggs. Good luck, whatever—"

But her father was driving. Fast.

"I'm out of names, Dad," she said. "Places. They go camping sometimes in Berkshire Park, but that's miles and miles away. I just don't know." She put her head down between her knees. "I don't *know*."

"Easy now," her father said softly. "Easy, kid."

And she felt his hand on top of her head and then she realized that she was crying. "Where are we going now?"

"Police headquarters."

Her head lifted and she felt his hand slide down to behind her neck and stay there as he drove with one hand. "Who's Vincent Stegner?" she asked. "Do you know?"

"He's the eyewitness who helped send Boyd Ritchie to prison."

"Wow." Only a whisper.

"I couldn't think of the name earlier."

"Then that means—" She felt his hand tighten on her neck. "You've been right all along."

"Maybe they've apprehended the sick bastard by now," he said.

But he didn't sound convinced. If they had not, who was left?

Who was next?

There were even more police cruisers on the street now. And more lights in windows; and more people gathered in small groups on the sidewalks regardless of the rain or on porches with the porch lights turned on. She did not mention this. Or her shaking pervasive fear that while she was safe with him, David was someplace else, and vulnerable, and unaware. She was too grateful for her father's hand on the back of her neck. She had stopped crying.

The rain was drumming on the roof now and gusts were splattering against the dark windshield and beating against the window at his ear. But how come it was raining? Rain had not been predicted—not by the radio, or the TV, or the newspapers, or the *Farmer's Almanac*. How come then?

He had no idea how long he'd been slumped here behind the wheel. In a stupor. His mind wandering. Without the strength or inclination even to strike a match and look at the clock again. Numb. Without will.

And in the torpor that held him he kept hearing his name over and over again: *Boyd Ritchie . . . order to arrest . . . suspicion of homicide . . . armed . . . should be considered extremely dangerous.* And his description. *Suspect may be disguised.* And a description of the Vega, a very accurate and detailed description down to the type of motor, but without the license number, because he'd registered it in another name, the joke was on them again, he'd registered it in the name of Professor Fletcher Briggs, the biggest lying hypocrite of them all!

Suspicion of homicide. That meant the Cunt. Wharton had got up the guts to go to the cops after all. To accuse *him* of killing the Cunt. Wharton had crossed him. Another kick in the balls. Innocent again, like with Stegner, like rape, but—

In a vague stunned distant way he knew that he couldn't go on sitting here. But what could he do as long as that fucking Toyota didn't move?

Kick in the balls. Diehl. Diehl was next. Diehl had made him confess. Broken him. The only time he'd ever been broken. By pain. To break a man's spirit by physical pain. To make him admit something he didn't—

That's why Diehl was next.

Diehl, then Briggs. There had to be time for Briggs. Especially Briggs. But time—

If only he could move. He had to do something. What?

He had to do it soon, whatever it was. Because the sun would rise at five fifty-three, then it would be light. Dawn at four ten. He remembered *that. Farmer's Almanac.* His mind was still in fine shape. Exactly one hundred and three minutes from first light to daylight: almost two hours. But he had to row across the lake before he could be seen, or noticed anyway. Before full light. And things to do in between. If only he could think of—

The rain was like thunder. It filled the car—the car they *were* searching for now—and boomed in his ears, rumbled like a violent surf through his skull.

What if it rained so hard and long that it soaked the house over there on the other side of the brook? Drenched it down so that it wouldn't burn?

Burn. Now he had it. *That's* what he had to do first! He sat up straight. Christ, had he waited too long?

It was *their* fault if he had. Whoever was over there in that yellow Toyota. If he was wanted for murder anyway, why shouldn't he kill them for making him wait so long? They were against him, too. This whole town had always been—

But why *was* he waiting? Now?

Why?

He was clutching the wheel.

Some of the numbness seeped away.

What the hell was he thinking of? He didn't have to wait now. His goddamn mind was screwed up! His own mind was crossing him!

There was nothing those fuckers in the Toyota could do to *him*. Not now.

He reached to the seat and pulled on a new pair of skintight rubber gloves.

He started the motor and turned on the lights. He revved it. *Zroom—zroom—zroom!*

Let them see the car. The police already had its description. Up the pigs.

He should have shot those two, killed them when he first thought of it.

He'd do it now, but he didn't have the time.

Pain from his grasp on the wheel climbed his arms, dug into his chest. Galvanizing him. Bringing him back to life. To now. He flipped on the windshield wipers and gunned the motor, really revved hell out of it this time, and in the roar threw it into reverse. It jolted backward and he felt the wheels spin on the wet leaves. He stopped it as he whipped the steering wheel; then he zoomed off. Down a residential street. Under trees. Like a tunnel with yellow and brown and gold above. He leaned forward to stare ahead through the silver sheets of rain that were being wiped away with a clack-clack that he didn't even hear.

He saw lights. In windows. On porches. And the shadow of a person or two. Some inside. A few—what were people doing up and awake this time of morning?

He passed one street, which he knew also dead-ended at the creek, charged to the next corner, took a left turn at high speed, the rear end slithering over the wet pavement. Then the car seemed to leap, or fly, over a steep humpbacked bridge, then to reach the next corner in seconds. He wrenched the wheel and the car turned left onto Oakwood Drive. The house was now two blocks away, on his left.

More lights. More people. Up them, too! He didn't give any more of a damn about them than about whether Diehl's old lady died. What did it matter now? Her or how many others. If she died, it'd only piss the old bastard that much more! Make him more reckless. He had Diehl figured, doped down to the ground—his hate, his pride, his goddamned manhood at stake. He had always known how he was going to get Diehl: he'd make the motherfucker come to *him*. And on *his* terms!

In front of the house, he braked the car at the curb, reached for the shopping bag, lifted out the gallon jug, then climbed quickly out with the jug cradled in his left arm, careful to leave the door open. He could feel the rain drenching him and the marshy lawn under his feet. Behind, the motor was throbbing, ready. He was soaked. Without looking in either direction, with no waste motion whatever, he moved swiftly to the bay window. Stopped. Reached into his pocket and brought out the butane lighter that he had bought in Iowa. Then with his fingers he removed the cellophane food wrap from the cotton strips. The strips were quite dry.

He moved with quick methodical calm. His thumb rasped the flint wheel of the lighter and a thin jet of flame shot up. He didn't hesitate. He placed the flame against the twisted strips of sheet and allowed the improvised wick to begin to burn. When the small flame was steady and climbing, he snapped the lighter shut without taking his eyes from the other larger flame. It was then that something went wrong. The strips of cotton were flaring toward the jug and, in that instant, he realized with a jolt that they were dangerously close. He took a quick step toward the window, shifted and lifted the jug in a single swift movement, and then felt a searing scalding sensation in his left hand as the blazing wick curled and wrapped itself around the tight rubber glove.

He went faint. But he stepped back, as if already retreating from the heat and conflagration, and, stooping, heaved the container through the window. The small panes shattered. And inside, at once, a great mushroom of blinding, engulfing flame rose in a bursting vortex that immediately exploded in all directions.

Then, half-blinded, he ran across the grass splashing through puddles to the car and threw himself into the seat. But when his left hand touched the wheel, the raw flesh inside the right glove rebelled and his fingers refused to close over the rim. They felt as if they might break off or crumble. He had to allow the momentum of the car as it shot forward to slam the door shut. Then he drove with his right hand, smelling for the first time the stench of scorched rubber and skin and flesh.

He thought for a second that he might black out. But nothing was going to stop him now. He didn't look back. He didn't even glance into the rearview mirror. His guts twisted and he thought he was going to puke, but he leaned over the wheel and drove, fast. What he had to do was get out of town now. It wasn't far. Just so he didn't meet any patrol cars. Maybe the state police hadn't been brought in yet. Even if they had, there'd be fewer people out of town, less chance of a cruiser spotting him on a country road.

If only he didn't pass out from the pain. His hand was a swollen, bulbous, useless thing burning and throbbing inside the glove.

It wasn't fair. After all he'd done. It just wasn't fair, goddamn it, to have this happen now.

"Ohmigod, wake up, Christ sake, something's on fire over there."

The boy's shout filled the car, but the girl was still half-asleep, pulling on her clothes as she tried to peer through the rain-clouded windshield. All she could see was a shimmering pattern of orange and red, very blurred, on the other side of the wooden barrier and beyond the creek. She'd wakened when the car alongside had thundered away, zroom-*zroom,* and she'd started to dress at once, chilled clear through, and she'd asked him what time it was several times, but all he had cared about then was convincing her not to get dressed.

Now he was starting the car, turning on the wipers so she caught a glimpse of flickering flame, low, and the dark smoke and the lighted sky: a glaring radiance that reddened angrily even as he backed the car out of the area and turned it onto the cross street. He was hunched over the wheel now, really barreling it.

She asked him, again, what time it was and he snarled, "Going on three," and she felt the panic explode inside. Her father would be wild, he'd kill her.

"You lied!" she heard herself cry against the motor's rumble. "I know I didn't sleep *two* hours. You lied to me! You said it wasn't even one o'clock when—"

But she broke off. It would do no good. He'd never understand. Or really care. Now or ever.

He made a left turn, the little car seemed to leave the pavement and sail over a steep humpbacked bridge, jolting her head against the ceiling, and then she realized he had made the wrong turn, he wasn't taking her home, he was going to the fire! Oh, my God, no—

Another wild left turn, careening, tires sliding, and the fire was ahead on the left. A few lights, a few vague movements on both sides, more lights coming on in windows, on porches. But she had to get home. What could they do at a fire? The sky was violent with color, the pavement and lawns and houses eerily lighted by a flickering scarlet glare. More running shouting shadows and silhouettes in the tinted slanting rain: dreamlike, unreal.

Then she saw the house itself. She felt the car slow down as they both stared and he muttered something under his breath. Tongues of red licked out the front windows, the whole small house was a gaping holocaust, and now she could hear the sound, the crackling and popping, even through the closed windows of the car.

As they approached, she saw a figure emerge from the black rectangle that had once been the front door. It came hurtling out, one arm lifted as if to protect its face, but its long gown already completely afire. Running blind, crazed, a human torch trailing flames and sparks across the porch, onto the lawn. Then, as they passed, she saw the figure give way, collapse to its knees, remain there upright a moment, arms beating frantically and hopelessly at the blaze, its mouth a gaping hole that may or may not have been howling, its eyes already black sockets. And then it went suddenly quiet and toppled forward, lay inert and continued to burn.

She felt the car shoot forward. He wasn't going to stop! "Where are you going?" But she wasn't sure she had really shouted because she didn't actually hear the words. "Why aren't you stopping? That woman, didn't you see—"

He yelled something that she could not understand. She saw his mouth moving.

She heard her frenzied shriek: "Let me out, stop, let me out of here, somebody has to—"

"None your goddamn business. Plenty others—"

He *had* seen the woman. He *had*.

She reached for the wheel, tried to rip it from his grasp, but he held tight and cursed her. So she stretched out her left arm and took hold of the ignition key, twisted it.

The car jolted, snapping her neck, then jerked forward convulsively, coughing, and came to a quivering stop over the edge of the curb. She didn't hesitate; she scrambled out, hearing his voice cursing behind her as she ran. She was saying something, saying it over and over, but it was not until she was almost to the lawn of the blazing house that she heard the words, the incredible words that she meant with every throbbing fiber of her being: "I hate you, hate you, hate, hate—"

The figure was struggling to its knees and the street was alive with nightmare sounds. Doors slamming, voices shouting, and from directly across the street a woman's hysterical scream that seemed to go on and on. She stopped, staring, like the others, and realized that she could not approach the kneeling desperate figure. She could smell the stench of burning hair and flesh, and she could hear the demonic crackling of wood burning, the crash of rafters collapsing, and the awful whooshing roar that seemed to fill the universe as walls gave way. Sparks were shooting furiously, falling, hissing on the wet grass. She stood fixed and stiff. And then she saw the figure—red and black, its face a grotesque inhuman mask—crumple, collapse into a curled shapeless lump of smoking flesh. It lay very still.

Still, she couldn't turn away. Even though she knew that she was watching death for the first time. She heard words, mostly hushed now—doctor . . . police . . . fire department . . . poor old lady . . . crippled—but they seemed to be coming from some vast echoing distance.

A man came running forward, detaching himself from the group of unreal figures standing frozen in the intense heat. He threw a coat or blanket over the figure and rolled it over the wet pink glittering lawn. But she knew. He probably knew too. Yet he continued to roll the limp charred thing until there was no more flame, no more smoke.

She had never seen death before. She shuddered deep inside and wondered whether, after seeing it, she could ever be the same.

She did turn away then, a frail girl soaked and

alone, and started to walk home in the rain. She knew, though, that the chaos she was leaving behind would stay with her always. It didn't matter now what her father said or did. And she hoped she would never see the boy again. She wondered whether this was what it felt like to grow up. She no longer felt young. She felt old. And sad. Very old.

Part Five

And that, as I'm sure everyone recognized, was 'The Impossible Dream.' As what isn't? Well, ladies and gentlemen and any other happy insomniacs who are still tuned in at exactly . . . three oh one on this rainy morning, Jerry promised to explain why he was off the air for almost an hour. The reason that you were spared listening to my voice, my favorite nostalgic music and . . . hah-hah . . . my favorite commercials is very simple. I was over there at the police station across the Common and I was being questioned about—but I've promised not to mention any crimes that may or may not have been committed tonight. Far be it from Jerry to interfere with police work. Suffice it to say that I'm over my mad now, but I'm sure Chief Diehl, that old Texas Ranger in our midst, won't object to my saying: please don't panic, folks, stay off the streets, lock your doors, and report anything suspicious to police headquarters, not to this station, please. . . . Now I think—whew, if you *knew* what I've been through!—I see that both lights are blinking at me so I'll take a call. Hello, this is *Tell It to Jerry*, good morning."

"Jerry Gerrard?"

"Yes, ma'am. Go ahead, you're on the air."

"Jerry, there's a house on fire. On Oakwood Drive in Brookfield Knolls. I live just around the corner. Some of the neighbors saw a car and we think it's arson. I don't know whose house it is yet, but I thought you ought to know."

"Jesus Christ."

"I beg your pardon?"

"I said thanks."

* * *

Boys don't cry, Paul. Do you hear me? Boys don't cry. Yes, Mother. But he was not crying now. He had stopped that senseless feminine crying some time ago now. Although he didn't know how long ago. What, after all, was there to cry about now?

Luck was with him. You may say all you like about character and willpower determining your life, Mother, but luck plays a part, too. Hadn't it been luck that he caught sight of that sign reading "Old Quarry Street"? It may have been his mind that put Old Quarry Street and Old Quarry Road together and it may have been memory that made him picture the abandoned old quarry in his mind, but what had really carried him was a stroke of good fortune—the incredible fact that there had been sufficient gas left in the Jaguar's tank. He had located the turnoff easily in spite of the downpour. The approach was a narrow ledge of gray granite sloping from the country road ten yards or so toward the abrupt brink of the sheer stone cliff that he knew dropped sixty or seventy feet at least to the surface of the dark water that, over the years, had filled the depthless abyss where he had swum as a boy. Where and when had he learned that the granite once taken from this quarry was estimated to be over three hundred million years old?

Time. A car rolling down and charging out over that rainfilled darkness and dropping into that space and water would sink completely, especially if the windows were lowered a few inches, enough to allow the water to gush in but not enough to allow the thing on the seat to float out. A century could pass before it, or the car, would be discovered. No, a million years. You see, Mother, you're not the only one who can think things through. And something else odd, Mother—or as you would say: very peculiar. No compunction. Queasiness, yes, revulsion inside, but you often used to say that once one has made a decision, no conflicting feelings should be allowed to interfere. The idea, you always said, was to make up one's mind and then act. *To shilly-shally is to lose, son.*

Then why was he sitting here in the dark? What was he waiting for? Not for the rain to stop. It was pounding on the roof and the small compartment of the car was filled with a rumble, but the wind had died somewhat so that the deluge was like a heavy booming steady thunder over his head. No, he couldn't wait for the rain to stop. It might be morning by then.

On the far side of the chasm there was a glow that lit the rain, a distant glitter which he could make out only faintly now through the windshield, which was almost opaque before his eyes. Beyond the high steel posts and sagging cables above, which were thrown into ghostly relief, someone had built a campfire. A campfire in the rain? Young people probably. But at this time of night? God, it must be after three. And they were not singing. Didn't young people on a picnic or campout sing these days? He'd always sung. And roasted frankfurters. And marshmallows. And the girls' faces in the firelight had always looked vital and alive, their eyes bright with happiness and promises. In spite of the racking pain in his head and the knifelike stabs in his right lung when he moved or took a deep breath, he felt suffused by a warming nostalgia, pleasant, yet aching, a longing that slowly turned to a pervasive anguish. How long ago all that seemed. And it was gone now. All of it. Time had robbed him of it. Whatever it really was. That stirring in the blood, that certainty that whatever was to come would be an exciting adventure, fulfilling, that someday, surely, he would be whole and complete. He remembered the swimming parties—diving from the granite ledges, plunging into the icy breath-stopping water, then clambering wet and happy in the sun up the walls. Gone. Like everything else.

If you spend your time daydreaming, Paul, you'll never amount to anything. Wise people do not live in the future or the past.

The present, then. Now. So long as that campfire burned over there, he could not back the car up the slope, throw it into forward gear, leap out, releasing the clutch pedal at the same time and let it roll down and then over the edge and plunge into the depths below. Could not because whoever was over there would most certainly hear the clatter if it should crash against the wall and even more certainly would hear the splash. Also . . . also, what if his memory was faulty? He remembered this side of the quarry dropping in a sheer perpendicular wall, but what if there were protruding ledges that he'd forgotten?

He had to make sure. *One considers all the possibilities, Paul. Then takes action.* Yes, Mother. He eased open the door, rain beat in, and the interior light came on. The thing was still slumped and curled on seat and floor, grotesquely stiff, and on this side, the side of head he could see now, there was no face, only reddish flatness that appeared to be darkening. It wasn't Coralie. He was really relieved to see that it wasn't Coralie. It wasn't anybody. And Coralie no longer existed.

What if someone, driving by on the road behind, saw the light? Carefully and slowly, aware of what he had to do but aware in a deadened way that spared him the insane terror that had attacked him when he saw the flashing blue light on top of the police car in the driveway, he slid out and stood up in the deluge. Instantly he was drenched. But he closed the door, with only a clicking sound, and the light went off. Blinded by the heavy smash of rain against his face, he made his way cautiously to the precipice, sensing rather than seeing the abyss below.

He was about to lean forward to look down when he realized that, in the dark and in the rain, he could see nothing down below. Only yawning darkness. What was he doing?

Mother.

He stood there. Why had he—

Mother.

If anyone heard the car smashing against the wall on its downward plunge, or the crash of its submersion, then what? He could picture the long low-slung white car being lifted slowly out of the water, then up inch by inch to the surface, hoisted by those rusty old cables; in his mind he could hear the straining and creaking of the corroded wires and the huge wheels groaning at the tops of the posts, and he could picture the Jaguar suspended in space, dripping. Then they'd know. They'd find not only the thing in the seat but in the luggage compartment the sheets and bedclothes and his own bloodstained suit, even the shotgun.

Luck. Luck, Mother? What the hell can one do against the accident of kids building a campfire on a cold rainy night? Well, what?

Nothing.

Too late.

Mother, why did you die?

Abruptly then he had the impression that he had lost his balance, that he was falling toward, or being drawn toward, the edge. He could feel himself floating out in the dark wetness, floating and then dropping with exquisite slowness, with a cool, serene sense of relief, to the dark welcoming depths, the water closing mercifully over—

Mother!

He was going to topple. Simply fall over and out—

He scrambled, his shoes slipping, away from the edge, clawing the rain, the empty air, his ribs knifing his lung, panic seizing his mind.

Then he was in the car, the door closed, breathing hard, grasping the wheel, eyes shut, head down.

All her fault. Everything. Hate engulfed him. Pill-head, speed freak, addict, bitch, paid whore! Yet he had brought her into the house, his mother's house.

She's not our kind, Paul. She never will be. You knew, didn't you, Mother? From the beginning. *There was a young man once, Paul—I thought I couldn't live without him. But I have. I married one of my own and I survived.*

He lifted his head and stared at the rigid fixed shadow. Remembering the softness. The beauty. Skin and flesh and smile and hair. Her quick wild response and her groans and soft whimpers of pleasure and—

Why had he ever believed her? You never believed her, did you, Mother? Or had he really believed her? Ever? From that day on the boat—

Or before.

He had always known.

He reached in the dark. His hand touched something. Something smooth and cold. Hard. Arm? Shoulder? Breast? But it was not flesh. Not now. It was something else.

He drew back against the door, shuddering. A strange sound rising in his throat. He shut his eyes.

Then it came to him: If he had allowed her to drop the charges—the rape charges—the way his mother had wished, then none of this would have happened.

You were right then, too, Mother. Even in that.

Then why hadn't he? Because Boyd Ritchie had to be punished. For what he had done. But had he done anything? That was the question, the one that had to be proved. And could only be proved by her stating that he had; by her refusing to turn away; by her insisting, for the official record, what had happened, what Boyd Ritchie had done to her.

Which he now knew to be a lie.

Which you, Mother, knew all along to be a lie. And that was why you hushed it up. Why you arranged, however you did, not to allow it to come to trial. Because you knew.

Did you know, too, or did you suspect, Mother, what your son had done, that bright summer's afternoon on the lake? And did you ever have any idea that if he had done as you advised, had thrown her over once and for all, she would have then told *that* part of the truth, also publicly and for the official record? You wouldn't want your son to risk that scandal, would you, Mother?

He felt strangely purged. As if he had somehow

emptied his mind and memory of poisons that had been sickening and tormenting him for years.

Then, opening his eyes because something had changed, he stared at the windshield and realized that it had stopped raining. Just like that. The drumming on the roof was over. The compartment was silent, the thunder gone.

The glowing dial of the clock still registered 6:03. He was trying to look at his wristwatch in the dark when the smell reached him. A smell he had never known before. Not the steamy dampness or the oppressive closeness of the car. Overpowering. Dry and rancid and sickening.

He had never known it before, but some instinct in him recognized it: the foul and fetid odor of death.

He longed to open the door. He didn't have the strength.

He sat limp and lifeless and soaking, staring through the streaming windshield at the dim light of the campfire that shouldn't be there, across the quarry, was it really there, was he imagining it, the light that had to go away so he could do what he had come here to do.

So he could then walk. Before it was light. Walk home. The home he didn't have. Had never had.

How could he possibly walk that far? And what could he possibly say that anyone would believe? He felt a slow, cold despair settle through him. Very quiet. Total.

The odor invaded his head, his mind, his every sense. Slowly. Inexorably. And he was helpless, trapped now in a hopelessness so profound that he had lost all inclination even to move.

The stench would not go away and he couldn't find strength to open the window and the stench would not go away.

Mother, please. Mother. God. Anyone. Please.

Although only one fire truck had passed them on the way, the distance seemed filled with the wail and clang and blare of bells and sirens. Peggy couldn't see her father's face as he eased the station wagon along the curb of the Common, but she herself was startled by the activity in and around the Tarkington Courthouse. The rain had left a sheen on the dull stone façade, and on the pavement and on the leaves covering the grass and on the many cars, mostly patrol cars, some of which charged off, red lights burning, others of which came swinging in to park. Uniformed officers came and went, nodding silent greetings, if any, up and down the steps between the blue globes of light. A van with call letters which she couldn't read was angled against the curb and two men were hauling wires and television or radio equipment out of it. Her first thought was of David—and without looking, she knew her father shared that quick uprush of concern, not quite panic.

She was about to ask whether she should stay in the car when he said, "Come inside," and slammed the door.

He went up the worn steps, fast, his wide but thin shoulders straight: no slouch now, no lounging casualness. And in his gaunt and harrowed face, which she could see while she tried to keep stride, no detached amused irony tonight. He held the door for her and they mounted the inside stairway, which was loud with the hollow clattering of heels but seemed strangely empty of voices.

Her anxiety turned to quick terror. What if they were too late?

But she had concluded, earlier, that David was not in town. Or if he was and could not be found by his father and sister, how could he be located by some stranger? But his father, face grim and jaw set, had refused to accept this. He had refused to give up. He had driven from place to place, house to house, with a dogged urgency. To protect David. As he had found her to protect her. And there was something surprising and disturbing in this, at the same time something heartening that she hadn't been able to get into focus during the hour and half of fruitless frustrating searching.

He had had little to say. Once, some time ago now, he had asked, "How old is Lindenberg?" And she had asked him what difference that could make, until he turned pointed, burning eyes on her and waited. "Eric's fifty," she had told him, and he had not even nodded, had only returned his attention to the rain-soaked road. But she had been left with the impression, which for some reason was hurtful and sharp in her, that Eric's being closer to his age than to her own, *did* make a difference to her father, a painful difference perhaps.

On the second floor he again held open the door, this one labeled POLICE HEADQUARTERS, and she entered a room she had never seen before: a large reception room with desks along two sides, behind a waist-high wooden railing, with benches facing each other across a space where more men seemed to be going and coming in a pattern similar to the one on the wet street below. She could hear masculine voices, a telephone ringing, typewriters clicking, and out of view somewhere, the staccato of a teletype machine. Her father nodded to her, once, briskly: a silent command to take a seat. Which she did.

Then her father stepped to where a man about his own age sat, seemingly in repose, legs crossed: a heavyset muscular man with receding distinguished-looking graying hair, wearing a dark business suit that appeared crumpled, damp and caked here and there with dirt, or mud.

"What's going on, Wally?" Her father spoke in a sharp level tone she had never heard before. "Wally!"

The man lifted his head, blinked twice, then shook his head, smiling very faintly. He behaved as if he were spaced-out, but she somehow doubted that. "I drove by your house, Fletch. Everything A-OK."

Her father's face lost some of its hard severity and his blue eyes took on a bewildered expression, but she knew he was feeling her own relief: whatever was causing this uproar here did not concern David.

"Wally," her father said, softly, leaning down, "Wally, are you all right?"

"Me? Oh sure, Fletch. I'm just waiting. They'll get him. I'm just . . . waiting."

Her father seemed momentarily confused and she saw something she could not recall having seen in his face: bafflement followed at once by a swift naked concern so powerful that he seemed to flinch from the feeling inside himself. His dark red mustache twitched and his eyes narrowed as he seemed to force himself to turn away. Then he strode, without losing any of the stubborn vigor she had seen during the night, through a swinging gate to stand at the desk of a young officer behind the railing.

"Ben, what's the matter with Heckman?"

The officer was young, handsome in a square crew-cut sort of way; he shook his head. "The Congressman's had a few shocks, I'm afraid. He was the one who discovered Stegner's body."

"How was Stegner killed?"

"Heart attack. Loss of blood. They don't know for sure yet." Then he added, more forcefully: "His eyes were gouged out and his hands were practically cut off by picture wire."

Her father didn't react outwardly. But his voice sounded stranger than ever when he asked, "What about Heckman's boy?"

"Still sleeping, lucky kid, far's I know. I guess what's on the Congressman's mind is: what about when he wakes up? Say, you don't look so great yourself. How about some coffee?"

Her father ignored this. "Anything else?"

"You want some advice? Why don't you and your family get outta town?"

"My wife's gone out of town." Then he persisted: "What else?"

"Well, I think some sort of violence took place at the Wharton house."

"Go on."

"The state boys have got a crew in there now and they've already confirmed what I found—traces of fresh blood in various places. We've issued a missing persons on both Mister and Missus."

"And?"

"Chief Diehl's house is burning. It won't spread, but it's going to the ground."

"Christ."

"And you may as well know: Mrs. Diehl was asleep inside—well, she's dead."

But her father said nothing. He didn't seem to be breathing. She felt an impulse to get up and rush to him. How could she have doubted—

"Where's the rest of your family, Professor?"

But her father didn't answer. He asked: "Where's Diehl?"

"In his office." Then the officer added: "Business as usual."

Her father hesitated a second, as if giving himself time to absorb all that he had learned in the last two minutes. Then, without glancing at her or in the direction of the man named Heckman, he stalked along a passageway and disappeared.

She looked around. At one of the desks behind the railing at her back a uniformed officer with a thick, weathered face was speaking with a young boy of fifteen or sixteen: a boy with a sensitive face that seemed clenched now in defiance mingled with fear. She heard him ask, "Why are you asking me these questions?" and she heard the officer reply, quietly: "A neighbor saw a car, a Toyota like yours, speeding away from the scene of the fire. She had the quick wit to take down your license. All we want to know is what you were doing there, almost three o'clock in the morning, that's all."

But Peggy decided to move closer to the end of the bench closer to the passageway through which her father had disappeared. As she did so, she heard another voice, a strained and deep-throated one: "I'm *getting* out, Diehl. But that won't stop me asking why you waited so long to inform the barracks!" Then he appeared, a bearlike sort of man, face set, eyes flaring, wearing a state trooper uniform; he shambled through the gate, snapping it, and then went out into the corridor without so much as a nod to the other officers.

Out of view, she heard a heavy tired drawl: "Professor, just who the hell gave you the go-ahead to stomp into my private office?"

Her father's tone was level and quiet, but firm, and it carried: "Chief, my right's the right of any citizen. I simply want you to locate my son."

"Sure, sure, that's all I got to do tonight. More security, like the Congressman's wife." The voice sounded heavy—tired and truculent. "Why don't you locate him yourself?"

"I've tried." The demand was still there, and no admission of his own tiredness, but she could hear that strange gentleness that reminded her that her father was acutely aware that he was speaking to a man who had just lost his wife. "I'm asking for help now, Chief."

"How come a daddy don't know where his calves are, this time of night?"

"How many calves do you—" But the sudden sharpness in his voice faltered, and then he said: "Sorry, Chief. I just heard about your wife. Sorry."

Even now, even at a time like this, he could feel compassion. But why should she be so surprised?

After a brief silence, the chief's voice said: "Professor, you defended this killer mustang's I recall. Hell, man, I remember: you did best you could. More'n you had to. More'n I thought you *should,* considerin' he was guilty as hell. Now, even if he *has* gone completely loco like they claim, what the hell could he have against you or yours?"

"It's not what he *could* have, it's what he *thinks* he has. I don't pretend to know how that kind of mind works. Maybe it has its own weird kind of logic. What I do know is that I can't take any chances."

The chief sounded like a tired man, near defeat, who could not make another man listen to reason. "If you can't locate your son, what makes you think this nut can?"

"He seems to know every nook and corner, he seems to—listen, he's planned and plotted this thing down to the ground and by now you should know this better than I do. If you can't find Ritchie, at least you can find my son."

"I'll find Ritchie." The chief's tone was hard now, no denying the emotion behind that drawl. "We got arrest orders out. Five-state alarm. He'll never get through the roadblocks. Helicopters on the way, case he does. Gonna be light in a hour or so. Got descriptions of his cars, both of them. Rooming house staked out. FBI's getting into the act. We'll get him, and when we do—"

But her father's voice broke in: "I don't care about that. Any of it. All I care about, God help me, all I give a *damn* about now, this minute, is getting my family out of town and somewhere where they'll be safe. That's all, God forgive me, that's all."

She waited. She glanced across at the young officer whom her father had addressed as Ben. He was looking at her. His face was quiet, expressionless. He lowered his eyes. Had he also been listening?

"I can't spare any men, Professor. I can't spare one man. Town like this's not organized for a crime spree like this, we just ain't got—"

"Diehl!" She heard that note of regret again, that gentle reluctance. "If you refuse even to try to locate David, whether anything happens to him or not, I'm going to take action. I'll start with the press. The governor if I have to. I'll think of others."

"Professor, y'come in here t'threaten me? 'Cause, son, I got my gutful of threats. Ever'body from the mayor to the Congressman out there who's acting like a goddamn zombie. You heard the captain of state police just now. And that radio-shit across the way, who's got *his* coming, he put the description of the car on the air and now every screwball in town's seen it at least twice. I'm tellin' you—I'm not gonna sit still for no more threats."

Another pause. Peggy had to strain to make sure they had not lowered their voices. During which, she heard the kid behind her saying to the officer at the desk: "The motor didn't sound like a Vega. More like a foreign make. Or a Chevy three fifty." And the officer said: "I'll have to have the girl's name and address." And the boy said, "Sure. She'll prove where we was. She'll tell you."

She looked across to where the man named Wally sat as before: self-contained, detached. Was he the Congressman that the chief had referred to? And had she recognized or had she imagined a certain personal note of gratification in the chief's voice when he said he was acting like a goddamned zombie?

When the chief's voice rose again, she realized that she had not heard something her father must have said. "Lemme get this straight, Professor. You are actually asking me to have your son arrested for possession of narcotics?"

"I'm not asking, I'm making a formal complaint, which I'm willing to sign, and I'm demanding it be acted upon."

The chief's tone was almost a groan. "Be reasonable. I ain't got the manpower to track down misdemeanors tonight."

"The name's David E. Briggs. I suspect he's dealing in hard drugs. That's a felony. Arrest him."

"Now, Professor, now believe me, I have had it all. So help me. I got the works this night. Parole officer in Londonford won't believe this Ritchie's capable of anything more'n overtime parking. My own house burnin'. Maybe I should be out there, I don't know. Thought I might be able to do more here. Briggs, tell me honest now—y'ever get to the point you just plain don't know?"

"I've been there many times. Too often. But not tonight."

"I got to be here, you see that, don't you? Bastard killed my wife, I got to be here, I got to handle it personal, you see that, don't you?" It was almost a plea, but she heard the human need for revenge behind it. "Suppose they get a line where he is—who y'think I could let handle that? He's gonna answer to me."

"I do see that, I'm afraid. I wish I didn't. But I don't want to have to feel that way. I'd like to prevent my ever having to feel that way. Are you going to have my son arrested and brought in here?"

Then she heard a bellow. It seemed to come from down the passageway and from the box on the officer's desk at the same instant: "Hutchinson! Lieutenant Hutchinson, haul ass in here pronto. I got another maniac on my hands!"

She watched as the young officer stood up, placed the clipboard he had been holding on the desk top, then walked toward the chief's office. Before he disappeared, he threw a glance over his shoulder. She wasn't just sure what it was intended to convey. It seemed to have a quality of resignation in it.

"Ben"—and now the chief's voice had changed—"Ben, if you was gonna bust a gang o'kids for possession tonight, where'd you assign your men?" The voice had become gentle in some strange way. "The professor here wants us to bust his son."

"It's . . . it's everywhere, Chief."

"Yeah . . . yeah, well, le's be a mite more specific, huh?"

"First, I'd try the beach out by the lake—"

"Covered," her father's voice said, shortly.

"Private homes. Clubs. Poolrooms."

"Covered."

"Well, this time of night—"

"Say it, Ben."

"Another favorite place. Camping overnight. What they *call* camping. There's that abandoned quarry out

Old Quarry Road. They build a bonfire, sit around, get high maybe. I'm always scared one of 'em'll go into the drink."

"I know the place. Thanks, Ben." And then in a different tone: "That's the best you're willing to do, is it, Diehl?"

"That's it, Briggs. And it's a helluva lot more than you got any right to expect."

"If anything happens to my son," her father said then, "if anything happens because you won't cooperate, *you'll* answer to *me*, Diehl." There was a quiet savagery in his voice.

"Get outta here!" the chief snarled.

When her father and the officer appeared, she stood up and watched them walk together, behind the railing, to the officer's desk. Her father's face—fixed, drained, lopsided from the swelling along one jaw, scratched, ferocious—was the face of a stranger. And she wondered at him. At herself. Why had she never seen him this way before? Had she ever looked?

". . . get there, you'll see a kind of stone access lane that dead-ends right at the edge of the quarry. You might turn in there first. If there's any sign of a campfire on the other side, you back up and go on down the road. There's an old work road that curves around to the other side. If they're there after that rain, that's where they'd be, Fletcher."

She had not heard the young officer call her father by his first name before, and suddenly she wondered whether she was listening to something that she should not be a part of.

"Thanks, Ben."

But as her father was about to move, Ben opened a drawer, glanced hastily, almost guiltily, around the room and produced an ugly-looking black revolver which he placed on the desk as he regarded her father.

"I doubt you'll need it. If you tell where you got it, I'll call you a liar. Do you know how to use it?"

"No." But he picked it up and stared at it. "But if I

have to use it, I imagine I'll learn pretty fast."

"Good luck, sir."

The word "sir"—for some reason—quivered in her mind and she felt her throat tightening.

"Thanks again, Ben."

And as they left together, he took her arm and she heard, from behind: "What the hell, I'm not long for this job anyway. I went over Diehl's head and put out the arrest order. If I'd done it earlier, maybe his wife'd still be alive."

As the door closed behind them, she realized that there was more compounded into that than she could unravel, but she saw her father's face lose, just for a second, an iota of its hardness, its grimness, and it seemed to take on, instead, a comprehending ironic awareness, even a sadness, and suddenly he looked wiser, older, more fatherly than she had ever known him to be. And as they hurried to the stairway and started down, Ben's unmasked respect and admiration found a reflection in the mounting emotion in her.

Then their path was blocked by a small man with a wizened face and mocking blue eyes who mounted the last two steps with a pronounced limp. "The professor himself, well, well. Here to prepare his defense before the fiend is in custody?" But then, because of something that he remembered or because of something he saw in her father's face as he stood there, the little man seemed to shrink. "Go ahead, Fletch," he said. "Swing away. I deserve it." And then when her father neither moved nor answered, he asked, with an instant's glance at her: "Anything I can do, Fletch? *Anything?*"

"Yes," her father said, in a low voice that was more powerful than a shout. "Wally Heckman's in there. I don't know for sure what he's thinking, but I have an idea. Get him away from here. He needs medical help. His personal physician's Leroy Farago."

All taunt vanished, the man named McQuade nodded. "It's done. Anything else?"

Her father's shaggy head shook and he was about to

move off when he stopped. "That fellow across the Common. On the radio. He's a friend of yours, isn't he?" And when the smaller man nodded: "Ask him to put out an appeal. To David Briggs. Tell him to come directly here. Not to go home. It's important: he is not to go home in any circumstances. And tell Ben what you've done, will you?"

"Aye, aye, sir." But there was no derision in his face or tone now, as he stepped aside.

Her father took her hand and drew her down the steps in such strides that she found her own long legs stretching to keep pace. He was plugging every hole. On the street he opened the door of the station wagon and stood back. Her heart foundered for a beat or two. Had he ever opened a door for her before? Three times tonight.

And then she heard a voice: "Where the sweet shit have you been?"

Annette Beauchamp was approaching from a green VW parked along the curb behind the television van. She stopped and regarded him, head tilted, eyes playful, yet grave, inquiring.

"Thanks for the concern," Peggy heard her father say as his voice retreated around the rear of the station wagon, "and so beautifully expressed."

Annette Beauchamp wrinkled her nose teasingly and stooped slightly to look at Peggy as the interior light flashed on and off when he opened and closed the driver's door. "Hi, Peggy. What're you doing up this late?"

"Studying human nature," Peggy said and wondered why she should feel this immediate hostility.

"Oh? That should be discouraging. Right?"

"Not entirely," Peggy admitted. Then she said, more firmly, as though she had thought it over: "No."

As Annette Beauchamp arched her dark brows, Peggy's father started the motor. "Why haven't you gone home?"

"No way," Annette Beauchamp said. "I told you,

remember? They'll be bringing him in soon, right? You think I'd miss that?"

"Right!" Over the roar of the motor, she was not certain she had heard what her father had said. But, throwing the shift lever into drive, he said it again, clearly, with surprising harshness: *"Right!"*

Then, as the station wagon careened along the edge of the Common and turned in the direction of Old Quarry Road, she felt a sharp pang of guilt. She had behaved like a bitch. A jealous bitch. And what was he feeling now? Nothing he had said had been definite, but she sensed that his displeasure or anger was directed not so much at Annette as at himself. But for what? For whatever feeling he might once have had for the dark-haired young woman? Well, whatever that feeling might have been, he no longer had it. How could she know that? And what if, for reasons she could never know, her father needed that emotion or some emotion like it? Some emotion that she, perhaps even more than her mother, had failed to offer him—

She felt sadness settle over her as the car sped along the streets. There were lights in many houses now. And more people on the streets. As if everyone, in some way, had become involved. And the sirens continued to wail. But now she could not think of all that. Now she could only wonder in what way she had failed him. If she had been a different kind of daughter, more loving, warmer. If she had confided in him, made some attempt to be his friend as well as his daughter. If she had been able to give him unquestioning love instead of blaming him for treating her as if she were still a—

"How long have you known?" he asked, his face intent over the wheel.

It was as though he had plucked her thought from the air between them. And she knew it would be useless, dishonest, to evade or to pretend she didn't understand what he meant. "Almost from the start, I think."

"Before you . . . before you took up with Eric Lindenberg?"

"Yes. Before." It was an admission whose implications, in that unlikely instant, she comprehended. "Before, Daddy. Yes."

He said nothing. He accelerated.

Then, as if to relieve the burden she knew her admission had added to whatever weight of anguish or guilt he carried, she said: "I won't be going to Londonford again."

And with the words, a sense of loss invaded her. Eric—who had been so kind, so gentle. So fatherly. And strong. But mingling with it at once, relief, too: all the phony lies and tricky mendacity to which the affair had reduced her, all that was behind her now.

On some impulse that she did not care to examine, she moved closer to her father in the seat. So close that her head could rest against his shoulder. She felt herself relax inside as she had not relaxed in years, if ever. Whatever was to come—and the night was far from over—whatever, he would take care of her. He would search her out if necessary, as he had tonight, and he would take care of her. What more did anyone need as proof of love? What more was there?

"Hello, daughter," he said.

"Hello."

They spoke, she realized, as contentment spread through her and nudged at the fears—they spoke as two people discovering their love for the first time.

"Good to have you aboard," he said.

In the long dark night of the soul it is always three o'clock in the morning. The quote from F. Scott Fitzgerald had always stayed in Eric Lindenberg's mind even though he didn't know where he had read it, or how long ago. In the sleepless and often endless nights it would return to haunt him, to add to his melancholy.

He was seated at the front window of his studio, looking down on the wet and desolate street. Londonford. He often wondered how he had come here, but then he wondered that about all the towns and even countries in which he had lived. He was now reaching that point that he knew so well: an invisible line, really, toward which the spirit seemed to move even as he recognized the forlorn and wretched regions into which, at times such as this, he seemed inevitably and inexorably drawn. The rain on the large slanted skylights had stopped a short time ago, but now he remained imprisoned nevertheless in the dark rain-streaked glass with the darker sky beyond but close.

Peggy was gone. It was over.

And depression, his old and familiar enemy, had moved in, had taken possession. Glum and still, he sat sipping aquavit in the gloom.

The time that he had always known was coming had arrived: he was again alone. He had known it, swiftly and fully, when he had heard the footsteps on the creaking wooden stairs around twelve thirty. Followed by the knock on the door, then by her father's quiet, firm, demanding voice.

And although he knew even now that there would be others, probably many others, for whom he would feel a similar mingled tenderness and desire, her going, even though he himself had nodded the assent that sent her off, had left him disheartened and in solitude here in the partial darkness—despondent to the brink of despair. He could faintly see the shadowy paintings, his work, and he saw himself now as a ludicrous figure really: an aging man fighting hopelessly against the inevitability of time, posturing, assuming a romantic eccentricity that even he doubted was genuine, surrounded by work that was only second- or third-rate at best, and would always be, presenting this foolish clownlike image to a small industrial town where he had lived for two years and where he would remain, however long he stayed, a stranger. An outsider and intruder pretending to a superiority and talent of which he had years ago secretly despaired. And tears of self-pity gathered in his eyes as he sat, quiet and somber, in the chill and oppressive dampness of early morning.

Then he decided—more final ritualistic gesture than hope or even curiosity—to telephone Peggy. He knew and yet, as if he had to add to the morose and pervasive sadness of his spirit, he had to be absolutely certain. Once he heard her voice—

He stood up and made his way, a shadow fading into other shadows, to the phone stand alongside the low unmade bed. And as he dialed, he felt himself fading into a gray impalpable world that was itself dwindling and dissolving.

And while he listened to the distant unanswered ringing, he wondered why it was—how it had come about—that he had never really been able to love anyone, even himself.

It was time for him to move on. He had no idea where. The Western mountains. The upper bush of Canada. The fjords of his native Denmark. Wherever, it was time to move on again.

There was no answer.

He replaced the phone.

Farvell, Peggy. My love. My daughter. *God nat,* my child.

The shadows moved closer in the cold air, the solid world seemed to fade and dissolve even more, and he shivered and poured another drink.

The phone had been ringing again. Willa had heard it. The sound had reached her from far away, a vast impenetrable distance. Space. Her mouth was so dry that even her lips seemed glued together. The house was dark and cold and she could sense its emptiness. Her head was a stone packed solid with ache. Her body felt limp and lifeless, without blood.

The phone had stopped ringing now and she rolled onto her side, drawing the kimono around her body against the bitter air, which felt damp, her head burrowing into the pillow. She heard the clear, flutelike serenading by her mockingbird. How sweet of you,

Hotspur. How sweet of a bird to sing in the middle of the night. How lovely and unlikely. And she felt sleep returning. How kind of sleep to return before her mind, her foolish mind, could begin to ask its foolish questions or to—

Suspect is armed. Exercise caution. To be considered extremely dangerous.

You better believe it! Extremely. The Luger was on the seat beside him and his right hand, with which he was driving, wasn't burned and if any cop cars approached from behind or came alongside or if anyone—

What the hell time was it? Where was the clock on the dashboard? Then he remembered: he was not driving the Vega but a Datsun half-ton truck, red. That was the point, wasn't it? Why he had stolen the truck—while they were all out beating their asses ragged looking for a gray Chevy two-door.

Goddamn truck. No clock. And no power. Japanese tincan, it'd never take off the way that Z-28 job would and what about the bulletproof glass in case—

He wouldn't need it. He'd already seen a few cop cars, some state police, but none of them took any interest in a red pickup.

But without a clock, how could he know how much time he'd lost? It'd begin to get light at four ten, but what the hell time was it now? He couldn't row across that goddamn lake in the light!

At first, after leaving the house burning behind him in Brookfield Knolls and driving into the country, being careful to stay within the perimeter of road blocks, which would be only on the main arteries anyway, he had been fighting pain all the way. His left hand seemed no longer a part of him: bloated, throbbing mercilessly, hanging useless along the side of his body where the grinding agony reached up the arm and into his tightened chest and down into his guts, routing them, and up into his head and brain, making him go so blind and dizzy at times that he thought he would blank out completely. And then he had heard the instructions to Car Seven from police headquarters on the radio: to proceed to an address on Commonwealth Avenue to pick up Dr. Wright Scofield and to transport him to an address on Oakwood Drive in Brookfield Knolls. It had been as if things had begun to repeat themselves in his clouded whirling mind, but he knew, he knew: Scofield was the coroner. Mrs. Diehl had died. Tough shit. Murder, though. Homicide. But he hadn't planned that, that had never been part of his scheme, like Stegner dying, it was their fault, not his, they had to keep getting in the way and fouling up his beautiful pattern, well then they could take the goddamn consequences, all of them.

But that sunken leaden panic had returned then. And he had thought about the boat: all he had to do was drive to the lake, stash the Vega in the stand of pines, part of the pattern all along, row across the lake in the boat, while it was still dark, to hell with their roadblocks, fuck their choppers if they had any up there, what could they see in the dark, row diagonally toward the sky-high Colorado blue spruce that marked the spot where he'd left the van—the van with all that bread in it, more than ninety thousand, and the new ID's, and the brown shoulder-length wig and scraggly beard and the open sandals and poncho and patched dungarees. Hell, even if they stopped the van to ask questions, he'd be just another hippie roaming around. Chances were against the pigs even stopping it unless it was just for the hassle—who'd suspect a fugitive from justice, a *killer* now, to drive around in a van painted about seventeen different colors in psychedelic design? Who'd have the guts, the arrogance, the fuck-you contempt to try a snow job like that? Boyd Ritchie, that's who.

But later. He couldn't split now. Because if he did, if he left the job incomplete, then getting away and whatever came after that would be just so much waste, just so much shit. This came first. Diehl came first. Then that prick Briggs and his all-American family.

So he'd driven to the Datsun dealer's showroom-garage-used car lot which was located a couple of miles out of town on Whittier Road, and he'd made the trade. It'd been hell to do, especially that bit with the wires under the hood of the pickup, because he'd had to peel off what was left of the charred glove on his left hand and skin had come off with it, skin and patches of flesh, and he'd dropped to his knees in the dark behind the showroom, writhing in pain, folding the hand, which seemed to shrivel instantly in the night air, into his right armpit as he tried to breathe while waiting for the torture to let up slightly. But in the end he'd switched cars, transferring the attaché case and the bear trap and the other jug of gasoline from the Vega to the rear of the truck, all the while cursing them all, all of them, they'd brought him to this, they'd get theirs back, they'd pay even more now, *more*.

He'd lost time, though—how much time? He couldn't think of that now. In the beams of the headlights, he saw the phone booth he'd selected and had, earlier, checked out to make sure it was functioning. It stood alongside a wooden frame structure that had probably once been a home but had been converted into a grocery. He turned in. The sign over the long front porch was fancy-lettered: THE VILLAGE STORE.

He parked, killing the headlight and motor with care, climbed down, leaving the door open, and the moist night air cut into the exposed flesh of his dangling hand. It no longer felt swollen. It felt dry and charred and shrunken. And instantly he again thought that he was going to pass out. But after a moment's dimness, his mind cleared and he stepped into the booth and reached above with his right hand to unscrew the light bulb overhead.

In the darkness, he deposited a coin and dialed *O*, then asked the operator to connect him with police headquarters, please, there had been an accident. And while he waited, it came to him that luck was still on his side. Diehl's wife was dead. No doubt now that the ripoff would work. Oh, hell, no, he had him now!

When an impersonal masculine voice answered—Christ, how he hated those calm, efficient pig voices!—he asked to speak to Chief Theron Diehl personally and then he added: "If you please."

"Chief Diehl's in conference. May I tell him who's calling?"

Now what? Now what were they trying to do to him? "The name's Ritchie. Boyd Ritchie, you bastard. Now put him on."

"Hold on."

He held. His pleasure. He had time. He knew. He had a minute and a half at least before they could trace a call. Even if they did, he'd be long gone before they could get a car to the Village Store. He'd forgotten the quivering rawness of his hand. He was in control again. The vitriol was running high. He felt a little drunk.

"This is Chief Diehl speaking."

That goddamn drawl. Kindly. Fatherly. He could feel his scrotum tightening. "Diehl, I got no time, so listen. Shit in your pants, you cowboy son of a bitch, but listen. In twenty minutes, look at your fucking watch, twenty minutes from now, exact, I'll be at Hanover Pond. You know where that is? End of Echo Valley Road. You want to see me, you got any scores to settle, personal, I'll be there. Only, listen: you come yourself. You bring anybody, send anybody, you followed by anybody, any sirens or redlights, forget it, it's up-yours, Theron, I'm on my way and you'll sit here holding it. That's it."

"I can make it in less."

"Don't get your balls in an uproar, Diehl. I got other things to do first. *Nineteen* minutes now."

"I hear, I hear, I'll be glad to oblige. Now you, kindly, just hold on now just a—"

"Fuck off!" His contempt was like wild music inside. He forgot completely the pain in his hand and arm and chest. "Go ahead, trace it, you dumb bastard, go ahead. And give my regards to the Missus, man. Tell her I hope it's warm enough for her."

He slammed the phone onto the hook with such violence that it came off, dangled. To hell with it. They could trace the call faster if the line was open: let them. He was on his way.

He returned to the truck, running. He knew Diehl, knew what he'd do, what he'd feel he had to do now. Pride—he was banking on that goddamn phony Texas pride. If Diehl could collar him alone—arrest or kill—then Diehl would be the hero, would have his own personal revenge as well. Well, let him try. The scheme was chiming again.

But driving fast now, he felt doubt beginning to gnaw at the exultant confidence. What if Diehl didn't swallow the bait? What if he'd read Diehl wrong? But hell, he'd read the others right every time. The Cunt. Her husband. He knew, he always knew, he was always right.

He headed the truck downhill in the direction of the Wharton Manufacturing Company. Take Digby Norton—he'd read him right, too. Hypocritical old bastard. Tomorrow the front page of his own paper'd make a fool out of him. And he deserved more, a hell of a lot more. Coming into the cell and telling him the Tarkington *Star-Times* was interested only in the truth, asking questions—then never printing any of it. But he'd get his when he realized how he'd been conned. When it dawned on him how Boyd Ritchie, rapist and arsonist and *killer,* had used Digby Norton's sense of guilt to get what he wanted. The guilt that Boyd Ritchie knew had to be there in a sucker like Norton. Without his help, if Digby Norton hadn't arranged the job in Londonford, none of this could have been pulled off tonight. He only wished he could be around to see Digby Norton's sanctimonious old face when he realized. Chalk up still another one whose account was being squared.

Suckers, all of them. Including Albert P. Gilpin, parole officer, fool. As easy to snow as the warden, as the parole board.

He'd read them all and read them right and he'd read Diehl right, too. Because if Diehl didn't hope to settle the score in person, how come he was still in his office now when his wife was dead and his house burning? Hell, he'd been sitting there waiting for a call like that—hoping for some goddamn way to get to Boyd Ritchie in person.

Ahead now he could see the bulky outline of the mill buildings, shadowy and huge. His heart was quivering and the bitter acid was burning in his veins again. His breath was coming in short gasps. He felt as if he were swooping down—eagle again, falcon—and he warned himself that he had to be more careful with the gasoline this time, he couldn't afford to lose the use of his other hand, not with all he had yet to do before morning. The newspapers would never be able to bury this. They'd all know who did this. All of them, not only this fucking little town that he hated but the whole world that he hated with equal intensity.

And they'd hate him, too. The whole goddamn world. This time they'd have something to hate him for.

And this time he'd enjoy their hate that much more.

Since the Tarkington *Star-Times* was an afternoon publication, its offices were pretty well deserted at three thirty in the morning. Tonight, however, its managing editor and publisher, Digby Norton, more than a little mystified by what he had observed enroute, was in his office: a semicircular room which occupied the top floor of a silolike wooden structure attached to the old red-brick building just off the Common. He was even more astounded, McQuade knew, by what he was now reading, the rundown on everything that had occurred and that was now happening—Gavin McQuade's fact sheets, with the explanation that these represented the substance of the story and as much background as he had been able to dig up so far but that it was not the story itself, which would undoubtedly change with subsequent developments. McQuade had also handed over a copy of the medical report on Dennis Heckman. Now he stood—point of honor for a man who refused to use his crippled leg for any advantage large or small—before the long and cluttered layout table that Digby Norton used as a desk. He was acutely aware of Wallace Heckman sitting upright in a chair with fevered eyes and undoubtedly still suffering from the blows Diehl had delivered at the Stegner place more than an hour and half ago. As well, perhaps, as the heartache and thousand natural shocks that flesh is heir to—and, tonight, an unnatural shock from left field. Heckman had undoubtedly been the one who had summoned Digby Norton to town from his bachelor digs in the country. McQuade couldn't help admiring the big man: he would stop at nothing to protect his son. But Digby Norton was reading the copy of the medical report now, and once he was finished, he would know, as McQuade did, that there would be no way to accomplish what the Congressman hoped to accomplish. In the otherwise silent room the clatter of Norton's teletype seemed terribly loud. And in the distance there was the occasional *wow-wow-wow* of a police siren.

Finally Digby Norton lowered the pages to the table, frowning. "Ho-ly Mother of God," he breathed. And from his expression McQuade could judge the depth of the older man's astonishment and incredulity. He was fumbling then with one of the many pipes strewn across the desk top and shaking his head, dumbfounded. Digby Norton was a huge, balding man, softness going to flab in his late years, with pink skin that always struck McQuade as inconsistent somehow with the grizzled look of his broad, fleshy face and with his normally impatient and gruff voice. "No wonder they love you at the courthouse, McQuade. Don't ever get arrested for double-parking."

"What I try to do," McQuade said, knowing that it

was true yet wondering why it should really seem important now, "is to write it like it is."

"I daresay." But Digby Norton's face had paled. A thick hand came up to move over his forehead. "Jesus."

McQuade decided not to mention that more out of anger at Diehl than for reasons of public duty, he had given Jerry Gerrard the description of the car that Boyd Ritchie was driving and that Gerrard had already put it on the air. "I dug into the morgue," he said, "out of curiosity. Found damn little. One brief story of an arrest for assault, then about three weeks later a briefer one about this Boyd Ritchie pleading guilty and getting ten years. No mention of the victim's name. Or of the defense counsel. Although the prosecutor was quoted—something about justice being served and without additional expense to the taxpayers."

He saw Digby Norton glance toward Wallace Heckman, whose face remained impassive. And McQuade remembered Jerry Gerrard's saying *You can be a bastard, can't you?* And he agreed. Who was he to jest at scars, he who had felt only his own wounds?

"If you're suggesting that a news story was suppressed," the editor said, blowing into an empty pipe, "you're absolutely correct, McQuade. I did it myself. I also managed by devious means to keep the wire services off it, as well as the television and radio know-it-alls. Why? It's none of your business, but I'll tell you. You came to town—what?—maybe four, five years ago. Well, I lived here all my life. I have some respect for the Wharton name, what it represents, what that family's done for Tarkington. I didn't see any reason to muddy the name by splashing it across every front page in New England, maybe even the New York tabloids. I thought, too, that the girl should be protected. The one you call the victim."

"Wasn't she?" McQuade asked, mildly.

And Digby Norton slammed down the pipe. "Look, McQuade, don't futz around with me. You know who I mean. You have it in your fact sheet." He stood up, glaring, and picked up another pipe. "You don't have to prove you're a good reporter. Only with that girl and her husband both missing, maybe dead by now if you're right, don't start digging into the past. I suppressed the original story. You try to print anything about what took place eight years ago and I'll suppress what *you* write."

Before McQuade could remind the publisher that every reporter in the business would soon be trying to learn what triggered tonight's rampage, Wallace Heckman spoke for the first time since McQuade had come into the office: "That's really all I'm asking now, Digby. As a friend. You understood then, you must understand now. You have it in your power to wreck my son's life before it even gets started."

McQuade felt his compassion stirred and he revolted: he'd been tricked and betrayed all his life by that softness in him, that weakness. But the stricken look on Heckman's strong, masculine face, the pleading vulnerability in the way he sat, even his tone of voice, all caused McQuade to return his gaze to Digby Norton. Who shook his large head again, his pale eyes clouding. "Jesus, does the past always catch up? It's as if I knew this time was coming. It's like living through something you know you've lived through before."

"What's so important to the world, to anyone, to report what happened, what that degenerate did to Dennis?"

"Maybe, Wally," Dibgy Norton said, slowly, turning to look out at the wet streets through the semicircle of lead-paned window, "maybe we could leave out the name. That's done all the time. He *is* a juvenile."

Heckman leaped up then. His body seemed to be trembling and there was a frenzied desperation on his face. "Are you blind? People will put it together! You know how people talk in a town this size. Why the hell did Kay—" He broke off and then cried: "Hasn't the kid been put through enough?"

Digby Norton, who looked trapped and miserable and helpless, returned to his swivel chair, sank into it, picked up a pencil, tossed it down, picked up another. "Do you try to kill a story for the sake of people who might be hurt? It's a big question, Wally. It's a very big question." Then he looked across at McQuade. "Well, Gavin?"

Taken by surprise, irked at first, McQuade said: "We could skim over the incident, maybe evade mentioning it altogether. In the *Star-Times,* that is." He couldn't look at Heckman's face; he didn't dare see the hope that he knew was flaring in those inflamed eyes. "But the story's too big. They'll all have a crack at this one. Wire services, Boston papers, New York. The weeklies. Hell, television—they're already on it. And there are hospital records. Most important, sir"—and he had to face him now—"you're a United States Representative. That's news. It'll come out, that's all. I'm sorry, there's no way, I'm sorry, no way."

And the truth shall set ye free. But Heckman didn't look very free to him. The teletype seemed louder. Down below somewhere a typewriter clicked away. And, slightly closer this time, sirens whined with plaintive urgency.

Then Wallace Heckman stood up. He stood there, very quietly, eyes open—but it was as though he were asleep. Sleep: balm of hurt minds, death's counterfeit. "No way," he echoed, but in a voice so hushed that for a moment McQuade couldn't be sure he had spoken. Then he repeated the words, this time as if he were really accepting them: "No way."

Nodding then, he made his way to the door. His step was heavy, slow. McQuade and Digby Norton exchanged glances.

"Justice," Heckman said, and turned. "All my life I've believed in justice." His tone was low and reasonable, without any pleading in it—simply a statement, and to no one in particular. "A man has to continue to believe in justice."

Then he was gone and they could hear his steps going down the enclosed wooden stairwell.

Digby Norton said: "Last man in the world I'd ever—" But he didn't finish it; he didn't have to finish it. "Sit down, Gavin. Times like these I wish I was a drinking man."

"I am," McQuade said, "only there's this publisher I know who prohibits booze on the premises." He heard Norton grunt a laugh. So he sat down at last. "Justice," he said, wondering.

"Don't talk to me about justice," Digby Norton snarled, abruptly enraged. "Or guilt. Would you believe I've known Boyd Ritchie was here all the time? Truth. Kid gave my name to his parole officer, man named Gilpin in Londonford. Told him I was the only person around here who'd treated him like a human being when he was arrested. Hell, all I did was visit him in his cell, at Fletcher Briggs' request. Listened to his story. How Diehl had beat the confession out of him. Only Diehl and young Wharton claimed Wharton had committed the mayhem. I didn't even print his story. How come he picked me as his friend?"

"Might be he picked you as his patsy."

Digby Norton sighed and picked up another pipe, sucked at it, spoke around it. "More like it. I even arranged to get him a job with an in-law of mine. In a garage. So he could make monkeys out of all of us by sending Diehl and company off on wild-goose chases." He tossed the pipe aside. "Looked at one way, that kind of makes me accessory after the fact—or is it before the fact?"

"It appears to me he might have manipulated that, too. Perhaps to make you feel just the way you apparently are feeling."

"Well, if that's it, he succeeded. This is my town, I—" He sighed again, more deeply this time. "Any leads as to where young Paul Wharton's disappeared to? Or why?"

Immediately McQuade thought of the white Jaguar

sports coupe with one light and a dented fender passing by the Wharton house less than an hour ago while he and Annette were parked there and the police were inside. He'd later researched it: Coralie Wharton drove a white Jaguar. Should he have done more? What? Reported it? "No leads yet, so far as I know."

Digby Norton leaned forward. "You're so bright, McQuade, riddle me this: how come the past always seems to catch up? This conversation is what they call off the record, Gavin. The root rock-bottom reason I didn't allow the story to be printed back then was that Paul Wharton's mother persuaded me. Mrs. Augusta Wharton, née Fuller. Sometimes called Augie Fuller. I was in love with her all my life. Was still, when she died four years back. Wouldn't marry me 'cause I was only a hardworking ambitious nobody." His face was twisted into a gentle mask of lines and wrinkles. "Tough old hard-nosed aristocrat. Always got her way. Feared, respected, hated. Never loved, so far as I know. Except by me. To me she was always a breathless young girl running through the woods with her shoes off."

Gavin McQuade remembered a girl like that: Annette Beauchamp reminded him of her, very much. He said: "I'm sorry."

Digby Norton looked startled. "You can't be too sorry and stay in the newspaper business, you know."

"I know. Any more than you can give too much of a damn about justice and stay in the legal business. I'm quoting a friend of mine."

"A lady?"

"Well, a girl. She's waiting downstairs."

"Then what the hell are you doing up here?"

McQuade stood up. "Listening to my boss blame himself for trying to be a decent guy."

"Or for trying to right what may have been a wrong, too late." Digby Norton, who looked very tired and oddly older now, was lifting himself heavily from his chair when the telephone buzzed. He reached, closing his eyes, spoke his name, and then he said: "He's here." He extended the phone to McQuade.

"This is McQuade." And then he was listening to Jerry Gerrard's familiar voice until he said, "Thanks, Jerry," and replaced the phone. "The Wharton Mills are burning and the fire's threatening to spread."

Digby Norton's normally pink face looked gray and bleak and oddly unsurprised as he nodded and swiveled away to look out the window at the rooftops of the town he loved.

The stench had become overpowering. Even with the window open, he couldn't breathe in enough of the damp night air to combat the foul odor, as of something stagnant, or rancid. He was nauseated, but unable to decide whether the noxious smell was in his nose and throat and lungs, whether it actually existed in the car's interior or whether it was only in his imagination or mind. The pain in his side was like a vise gripping his lungs, so that by now he had begun to wonder whether he would suffocate in here with the thing. And his head rocked with an ache that blurred his mind.

The campfire across the chasm of quarry walls had died down somewhat, but it still threw a faint glare that lit the poles and cables in a nightmarish pattern. Several times it had occurred to him, in what seemed to him lucid and rational moments, that if he only had the Luger—he had had it in his hand earlier, where had it disappeared to?—he might place it at his own temple and pull the trigger. Suicide pact. Two married lovers. One with her face caved in, the other slumped behind the wheel of a white Jaguar with a hole in his head. Romantic. At those times, though, he had also wondered whether he was completely sane. Whatever the line was, could he be certain that his mind had not by now passed over it?

He had to get out of the car. He opened the door and stood up, closing it quickly to kill the interior light. His lungs gulped air, each gasp a spasm of agony along one side. He couldn't remember how he had injured his side. It was as if a rib had been broken and was stabbing his lungs. But how?

Even as he walked, bending slightly to one side, to the brink of the pit, the odor of putrescence clogged his nostrils, dryly closed his throat. And in that instant he again had the overwhelming impulse to step farther, to leap out and away from the perpendicular stone wall and to drop through dark air into the darker water that he knew was below. He stood there, wavering, helpless in the clutch of that longing. And this time not terrified into turning and clawing the air back to the safety of the car.

It was then that he saw the sky. Not the sky beyond the quarry, lit by the feeble campfire glow. But the sky off to his right, toward town. It flared with an angry red, shimmered high with a terrible, heart-stopping, hell-like incandescence. The brilliance was streaked with coruscating flashes. At this distance its radiance was so intense that, even as he stared, he couldn't believe what he was seeing.

Tarkington was burning. That was all he could think. The town itself. The whole town.

He knew he should move. But horror held him. Cold freezing terror. The town was ablaze, the world had gone mad, and he had gone mad, too. Stricken by dread and disbelief, he couldn't decide even where he was or what he was actually watching, and he couldn't remember how he had come to this strange place in the dark. What was he doing way out here? And alone.

Then wildness exploded—a livid intensity that carried him, stumbling on the stone, back to the car. Never mind the rancid stink. Never mind whatever it was that had held him this long. The mills might be burning. Wharton Mills. He had to be there. He had to do something. He started the motor and threw the gears into reverse and shot the Jaguar backward, up the stony incline and onto the pavement of Old Quarry Road.

Then he applied the brakes. It was her fault. If nothing else, that much was clear. It was, in fact, the only really clear thing in his mind.

You were right, Mother. You were always right.

With that carrion stench roiling in his brain, he turned his head to look at it. He did not switch on the lights. It still half sat, half sprawled there. Stiffly. Grotesquely. The blanket had slipped and bare flesh gleamed white. He could not see the head. What was left of the head. How had he ever imagined he loved her? He had hated her always. For all she had done. For all he knew she had done. It had all begun a long time ago, years ago, something about a boat on the lake, and he had really hated her ever since even as he lied—to her, to himself—that he loved her. But he had never hated her so much as he did now. Never. Because, in some way, some way that he wasn't clear about, she had brought him to this.

The red sky in the distance came from Wharton Mills. That was it: it was his duty to do something about the mills. They were his responsibility, weren't they? His alone now.

He was about to turn the car toward town when he switched on the lights and saw the lopsided glare shooting down the stone incline and into the dark over the quarry. He was driving a car with only one functioning headlight. But how had that happened? Had she had an accident she didn't tell him about? It was like her to—

The police. The police would be certain to notice a car with only one headlight. They'd stop him, even if only to give him a warning ticket, and they'd throw a flashlight on the thing and then they'd ask questions, accuse him, and what of the Wharton name then, what about the disgrace and scandal and no one to help this time, the way you helped, Mother—

But . . . but there was a way to avoid all that. Such a simple way. He felt very sly now, very certain and even relieved. He raised the window until it was only three or four inches from the top. That was to allow the water to come in. Because if the water didn't come in through the window, it might take time for the car to sink and if the campers over there heard the splash—

But it didn't matter what they heard now. Or whether they heard anything.

As he threw the car into forward gear, he remembered what he had told himself earlier, he couldn't remember when: that a century could pass before the car would be discovered, if ever.

He pressed his foot down, hard, on the accelerator. What did he care about the Wharton Mills? He had always hated them. The way he had always hated Coralie. And his mother.

Yes, Mother, hate, not love, hate, hate, hate—

The car was shooting forward over the stone.

You'll be sorry now, Mother. You'll be sorry—

Then it was sailing out into space and so he let go of the wheel because it was all out of his hands now. He was free. At last. Forever. And he was not weeping. He would never weep again.

He could feel the heavy nose of the Jaguar slanting forward. Everything was happening very slowly. It was in space, in sheer air, and he noted, in a reasonable and relaxed way, that it did not crash along the granite wall after all.

He had been right about that anyway. At last he had been right about something.

Then there was a sound, as of an explosion. He heard it and he felt his head slam against the ceiling and then he heard and felt nothing.

He had unholstered his weapon, the pearl-handled Colt .45, because ever since he had left town, two headlights had been following, no matter how many fake turns he had made; and every time he sped up or slowed down, the lights in the rearview mirror held a consistent distance.

In twenty minutes, look at your fucking watch,

twenty minutes from now, exact, I'll be at Hanover Pond.

As Theron Diehl drove along Echo Valley Road, holding the cruiser back the way you have to handle a spirited horse, he was cursing. He could have made it in ten minutes. Less if he'd used the siren and lights. But that bastard Ritchie had what he called other things to do first.

The headlights of the car behind were set close together. A small car then. A Chevy Vega was a small car, wasn't it? He'd known from the start who was behind him. If Boyd Ritchie thought he could bugger him this way, he didn't know his man.

Theron Diehl had to restrain himself to keep from plunging the cruiser ahead at full speed, rounding a curve, lowering the window, slamming on the brakes, and letting go with his piece. Get it over with. Slimy bastard didn't deserve to be arrested, trial, all that legal shit. And why wait to get to the pond, why give him a chance to get in the first shot? But Theron Diehl had no intention of simply shooting him, killing him. That came later. That came afterward.

He bit off a chew of tobacco. For now he'd play the little weasel's game. For now. He was safe behind the bulletproof glass in case Ritchie should start shooting. Not that he expected that. Ritchie was smart—at least smart enough to know he couldn't get at him while he was in the police vehicle.

In the course of the night he'd recalled the case—and cursed the bleeding hearts and do-gooders, parole boards and social workers and that ilk, who'd allowed a wild one like that to run free again. He hoped they were satisfied now. He had remembered, among other things, what he had done to the depraved cocksucker when they'd found him hiding in the woods. He'd concentrated on the ribs, stomach, kidneys, muscles and nerves of the neck and, of course, the balls. So there'd be a minimum of physical evidence. So that the criminal couldn't abrogate the confession later, claiming police brutality. Which they always did. Which Ritchie had, of course, tried. He'd always worked on the theory that a man arrested was guilty. To hell with all that constitutional crap. He was almost always right, too. There wasn't a man he couldn't get a confession out of, given enough time. But Ritchie had been a tough hombre. The kid hadn't cracked till, after the physical violence, he'd used the old trick he'd been taught years ago: holding a cocked revolver at his cheek, forcing him to open his jaws, wider then wider still, holding them like that for hours on the threat that you're going to put a bullet through his two cheeks, sooner or later, and you don't want to shatter his teeth or jawbone. Well, Boyd Ritchie hadn't wanted that handsome young face torn up, although he'd lasted for hours before he finally broke. And confessed. And if anybody still doubted that he was guilty of raping that poor girl, look what he did tonight. Wasn't that proof that any method of interrogation should be allowable if the suspect is guilty? Look what the shitpoke was capable of even after seven years in the stone country club: homicide. He was a killer. Twice in one night—

The call on the radio was for Car One. He took up the mike. "Wall? Spit it out."

"Chief, the Wharton Manufacturing Company buildings are on fire. Lieutenant Hutchinson said you'd want to know."

"Damn white of him. Fire under control?"

"Not yet, sir. Several houses and a café are burning, whole neighborhood's threatened. Fire department's sent for help from Whittier and Londonford. They suspect arson, sir."

"Mighty damn foxy of them t'think of that. Shows real savvy. Lemme talk to Hutchinson."

"He should be out there by now, sir."

"Connect me, damn it!"

"Yes, sir."

That particular young Montgomery Ward lawman had been nothing more nor less than a burr up Diehl's ass the livelong night. Sending out unauthorized arrest orders, missing persons bulletins on the Wharton couple. Bringing in the state police on his own. Leaking information to that gimpy newspaper vulture. Most likely feeding that radio fag his information—the description of the vehicle that the suspect was driving, for instance—so the queer could broadcast it to the public. Inciting to riot. Obstruction of justice. He'd have young Hutchinson up on departmental charges sure as hell, soon's this was over.

And why was Hutchinson stalling now? Where the blue-belly hell was he?

The lights remained behind. Fine. Stay there, Ritchie, stay close. Keep on trying to rawhide the old man.

As for that Gerrard pansy—he had him. He had him on drug possession: that package of Marlboros from his pocket. He wouldn't have brought charges if the lily-livered tulip bud had been satisfied just to shake and shudder and pee in his panties, almost mewling, and if he hadn't gone back to the studio and broadcast an appeal for the Briggs kid to come to the police station. He'd get another shot at interrogating that hothouse flower tomorrow. And by then maybe—

"Chief Diehl. This is Ben Hutchinson."

"Where the fuck have you been?"

"There's a fire here. At least one injury, possibly serious, maybe more. You had something to say to me?"

"I got plenty. Like when I can't ramrod my own outfit, I'll turn in my spurs."

"I don't believe I understand."

"I believe you do. I'm conducting a private investigation into the death of my wife, so I can't be there to ride herd. What I want is for you to take over down there."

"If that's what you want."

"It ain't what I want that rightly weighs tonight, is it? Only since you already taken over the station tonight, I just kinda thought y'might get a boot outta handlin' things this morning, too. Afore I ask you for your badge when we both get back to headquarters."

The wire crackled then, until Hutchinson's voice said: "I'll leave it on your desk, Chief. With the pin open. So you'll know what to do with it."

The radio went dead. The tangled murderous fury in Theron Diehl expanded.

He looked into the mirror. *Don't get you balls in an uproar, Diehl. I got other things to do first.* Like setting another fire. Well, you won't have anything to do soon, Ritchie. Nothing. Because you'll be dead.

And give my regards to the Missus, man. Tell her I hope it's hot enough for her.

Nell. According to that sweet-faced young filly they'd brought in for questioning, the gal who'd been a witness and whose father had apparently punished her already, and good, for parking in a car with some horny coyote that time of night—according to her, Nell had come running out of the house on her own two legs. *Running* out—a woman who'd claimed to be paralyzed for more than ten years now. The Bible-reading *liar!* Making him fetch and carry. Making him feel guilty if he didn't stay home with her. If there was a hell like the one she never tired of warning him of, he hoped Boyd Ritchie was right: he hoped it *was* warm enough for her. The laugh's on you, Ritchie—you did Theron Diehl a favor, a whopping favor.

If he'd lost anything in that fire, it'd been all those pages he'd worked on for so long. His memoirs. Well, he'd have to write them all again. Only now he had his ending. After tonight he'd have a climax to be proud of. With all the publicity that'd come out of this—Jesus, maybe he wouldn't have to pay the printing costs himself. Maybe—

But first things first. Boyd Ritchie *had* killed his wife. And he had to avenge that. Point of honor. Never mind the relief he felt that she was gone. The point of honor was separate from that. Something you and your kind could never understand, Ritchie.

And after he'd done that, soon, then there'd be nothing but gratitude. Respect. Admiration. Not only here in this town, but everywhere. With all those newsmen coming in—hell, all over the world, most likely. Including Texas. Including the Rangers who'd know he'd played a lone hand, did it his way, a real man's way, the way he'd been brought up to respect. The values, the true and abiding values that he'd always lived by.

He had to force himself to slow the car because the excitement was running high and thin in him now. He knew that feeling. It'd been a long time since he'd had it. The thing that really dumbfounded him was that he was being offered this chance. To wrap it all up once and for all. *Himself!*

You're some smart criminal, Ritchie: following like that, not knowing you're sure to be spotted.

Or did Ritchie intend that he be spotted?

To hell with that. And to hell with whether Nell might not be dead now if he'd begun the investigation and search sooner. That thought had flickered through his mind several times. Well, maybe he had had a hard time making up his mind, but he hadn't wanted to be made the laughingstock of Tarkington, maybe lose his job. No danger now. They'd forget that now. And they'd forget what he'd done to the Congressman, too; he'd blown his skull there, striking a man in Heckman's position. But once this was over now, Heckman would have enough sense not to bring charges against the man who'd rid the world of the shit-heel psycho who'd terrorized the whole community. And if Heckman was heading where Theron Diehl believed he was, where he *hoped* he was—to the booby hatch—well, then, that high and mighty gentleman would have his fangs pulled anyway. And when anyone mentioned Nell—at the funeral, for instance—he'd say that maybe it was a mercy in disguise and everyone would pity him as well as respect his courage: look what the poor man did even while his beloved wife lay dead. And then he'd reveal it all in his book and—

HANOVER POND

The sign loomed before him before he could slow down. He had almost passed it. He braked, hard, hearing the slithering of rubber and seeing the flash of lights across his mirror as the vehicle behind swerved around to avoid crashing into the rear end of the cruiser. He grabbed up the Colt with his right hand, whipping the wheel with his left, and then, glancing into the mirror again, he saw the other vehicle passing behind at right angles, continuing down Echo Valley Road, a very small car, a bug, a Volkswagen, too small to be a Vega, and he remembered that most motorists hesitate to pass a police vehicle even at the legal speed limit.

Ahead he could see the glimmer of pond as his car crunched over the gravel along the rutted path toward it, fast, because what he had to do now was to make a U-turn in the parking area, which was surrounded by trees and picnic tables and benches, and face out to command the narrow entrance, so he gunned the motor, and as he started along the path toward the road, lights came on in front of him, blinding him, headlights facing him, flaring, another vehicle had moved in to block the path, cutting off his exit. When his vision cleared, he could see that the vehicle facing him, only ten yards from his own headlights, was a truck, a small half-ton of some sort, it looked red, he could not see into the cab.

Sandbagged. Bushwhacked.

He turned off the motor and sat there, very still, the Colt in his hand.

Your move, you wily little cocksucker.

The reddening sky behind had been at first a pale pink reflection in the rearview mirror. She had been startled that her father, driving, had not mentioned it since he must have become conscious of it earlier. She had twisted in the seat, removing her head from his shoulder, and then, as the station wagon moved swiftly uphill on Old Quarry Road, she saw the frightful puzzling luminescence out the rear window. As if the sky itself had become a wavering sheet of reds in various shades.

"What? What is it?" she had demanded. "Daddy, what *is* it?" As if he would know. As if he, of all people, had to know and he alone could reassure her.

"I wish I knew," he had said.

And suddenly she had felt overwhelmed, helpless. It must be the way people felt in some great natural catastrophe: baffled, lost, stunned by incredulity.

In silence then they had come to the place where she knew the old quarry was situated. She had even swum here a few times. The station wagon passed the short narrow lane that led between bushes from the road to the stone precipice. Her father turned right on the crushed-stone work road that Lieutenant Ben Hutchinson had said curved around behind the pit, and the headlights probed over the surface of glistening gray stone, lighting two small cars parked side by side at a slab barricade. Beyond she could see now the glow of a campfire, feeble and pale compared to whatever conflagration seemed to be devouring the town in the distance. The whole night, from the time she had realized that it was her father who had mounted those stairs in Londonford and knocked on the studio door, had an unreal quality about it. Dreamlike. Many times she had actually wondered whether she was asleep or dreaming. And this impression returned now, more overpowering than ever.

Her father didn't hesitate or speak. He didn't even switch off the motor as he got out. He leaped the gray damp slab and strode, fast, toward the campfire. Quickly, she followed, unable to keep her eyes from the growing frightening puzzling brilliance of the sky beyond.

Several figures, shadows really, even in the headlights' glare, were stretched out in sleeping bags on the flat granite floor that reflected flintlike glitters from the dying fire. One sat huddled, Indian-fashion, legs crossed. It was impossible, in this light, to know which were girls, which boys. She saw her father stop, glancing, his tall frame upright so that he seemed even taller tonight, his shoulders wide and set.

"David." It was all he said.

"Dad?" She recognized her brother's voice, heard the surprise behind the slow slurring. Then she saw him. He was standing off from the group, near the quarry's edge: short, thick-shouldered, long dark hair tied behind his ears and hanging, wearing tattered dungarees, frayed and dirty tennis shoes and a sweat shirt with the letters *BS-USA* printed on it in red, white and blue. As if peering through fog, he said, again: "Dad?"

"Thissabust?" a boy's voice inquired. "Hey, man—" And it drifted off.

"David," her father said, "you're coming with me."

"Yeahhh?"

"Yes."

A moment. The rain had gathered in small pockets on the surface and the puddles glimmered darkly.

The figure sitting Indian-fashion spoke: "Didn't anybody else . . . nobody else hear it? A kind of . . . a big splash—"

David called: "Can't see down . . . can't see down there. Nothing."

"I heard. I know I heard—"

Then her father demanded: "Is everyone accounted for here, David?"

"Ac . . . counted for, Pop?" He chuckled. "You think maybe it was one of—" He was shaking his head. "She's stoned, that's all. Nobody else heard a thing."

"David. Did you hear me? Let's go. Now."

After a silence, her brother said, very quietly: "No way, man. No way."

At first she was not sure she had heard him. David had never before spoken that directly to their father, that defiantly. For that matter, she realized in a rush, she had never in recent years heard their father issue a direct order. It was a strange time for the thought to strike her, but she wondered, as she had in Eric's studio earlier, whether she had not longed for, even needed, to hear her father speak to her as he had. Then, of course, she had had to bitch it up, just to make him feel worse, by pretending that it was Eric's command that had caused her to leave. She was tempted now to flare out at David—to tell him not to make waves after they'd spent hours searching for him.

"David," her father said, and he did not sound weary or professional or ironic, "David, you're coming with me if I have to carry you to the car." He sounded quietly fierce—cold.

David snorted a laugh. "Yeahhh, man? Car—ry me?"

"We don't have time to waste." It was a flat statement. "Now."

"Who's-at?" another girl's voice asked. "Professor . . . Professor Briggs?"

"Pops," David said then, not moving, "Pops, I am . . . peace. No duel, man. You know? No . . . no battle. You know?"

But her father did not reply. Instead, he crossed the wet stone in long strides and, when he stood only a foot or two from his son, he stopped, as if to give David one more chance.

"David!" It was her own voice. "David, come on for God's sake! You're bombed out of your skull. Why make any more trouble?"

"Peg?"

"Yes." She was suddenly terrified that her father was going to hit him. She could not recall his ever having done so. Ever. "Dave, please. *Please.*"

But David's voice was softly mocking, "Passive resistance, man. You know?"

Her father acted then, but he did not strike out. He reached, in a fast shadowy movement, stooping, and the next second David was over his shoulder, one arm pinioned around the back of his father's neck, the other behind his own back, head and hair dangling. Her father turned and, as if the heavy body were no weight whatever, returned, passing the campfire, stepping past the figures.

"Passive," David was murmuring. "Peace."

"Wheee—lookit," a male voice said.

And another: "My turn next, Pops."

She hurried ahead, the incredulity growing by the second, hearing the girl's voice, plaintive, near tears: "I didn't dream . . . heard it . . . someone down there." And a boy's voice: "Lookit that sky. Looks like morning. Not morning yet. Hey, somebody, what time is it?" She opened the rear door, but her father, when he reached the station wagon, kicked open the front door with his knee, the one she had left ajar, and turning, he heaved his heavy limp burden onto the seat where she had been sitting.

Then he snapped down the lock mechanism and held the door handle. "David, you listen. If you touch the door handle, or this lock, while I'm driving, so much as touch it, I'm going to tie you up in the back with the towrope." He spoke quietly, with a simplicity and directness that gave her, again, the impression that she was listening to a stranger. "Do you understand that, David?"

"Pops. I dig. All the way. Dig, man. You know?"

Then her father, for the first time, lost his temper. "I don't *know* what I know, but you'd better stop asking me!" He slammed the door with such violence that the sound exploded and then echoed over the quarry and into the woods and over the hills.

When they were on the road again, pointed in the direction of the interstate leading to Boston, she sat in the rear seat, trying not to look back toward Tarkington. It was some time before anyone spoke.

Then David said, his voice slightly less blurred: "You are uptight tonight, man. You . . . also tight? Uptight-tight?"

"I haven't had a drink for hours," her father said.

She couldn't stop herself from saying: "Not that it's any of your business, little brother."

"Another . . . another country heard from." His tone was relaxed and he drew out each word. "Another coun-ty. Londonford County."

So he knew. "That's all over," she said. "So shut up about something that's a closed book." It was the best she could do. She knew that her father, if not David, understood.

"Pot always calls . . . kettle. You know? Sorry, Pops. Scrub that you-know. Kettle calls pot . . . Yeahh, man, bombed out. Like you, man. You get high. I get high. . . . End justify means, man? Both same end. Different means."

"Go to sleep, Dave. Just, please, sleep it off." But it was no use. She knew it was no use. "He's doing this for you," she snapped.

"Ahhhh? For me."

"Yes, damn it, yes!"

"Scared I get busted? Big bust on tonight? Get the . . . get the kids, let the Mafia go. Congress. President. Let . . . let 'em all go, bust the kids for pot."

"You don't know what you're saying."

"I think he does," her father said. "Maybe I haven't been listening. Go on, son."

"Cop-out," David said. "Sure. Yeahhh. Cop-out. From what?"

"You tell me."

"You don't care!"

"Try me."

"Don . . . don't care. All care about—not my son. Not my belov-ed boy. Got to save . . . save name. Job. Re-puta-reputation. Position!"

"Oh, for God's sake, Dave, fuck off!" Then, hearing the word here, in this car, she felt a sharp, painful contrition: her father always hated it when either she or David used the mildest of such language at home. "Sorry, Daddy."

"I've heard the word," her father said.

"But not from me."

"No."

"Words," David said then. "Words. Not acts. Not lies. Not . . . cor-rupt-ruption. Facts. Only . . . words offend."

"Lay off, Dave, I mean it. Whatever he's doing now, I told you, he's doing it for you. Us. It doesn't matter what you think." Then, with an urgency that clutched at her whole being, she said: "He cares."

"Yeahhh? Since when?"

"Shut up!" she cried. "If you don't shut up, I—"

But her father's voice cut in. "Peggy." And she subsided, trembling a bit. "Listen, David. We've all made mistakes. Maybe that's what it adds up to: one mistake after another. But that's all in the past now. We'll make others in the future, too. But this is now." His tone took on an edge, a quivering but muted intensity. "No time for all that now. Whether you believe it or not, I do care. And whether you believe it or not, I think there's a danger. I hope I'm wrong. I don't have much evidence. I'm playing a hunch. I'm making as sure as I can, that's all. If it turns out to be lost motion, it's in the best cause I know. But, God damn you, if you don't believe something's going on, look out that back window. Were you too blind to see it from the quarry? Look back there! For all I know, the whole damned town's going up in flame!"

Then David slid up in the seat, turned his head. In the dimness she could see his face. She saw the shock come into it. The puzzlement then. And the disbelief. His eyes found hers.

"Where . . . where's Mother?" he asked, in a whisper.

Peggy hesitated. But, not certain yet that it was true, she said: "She's with Grandmother in Boston."

She glanced into the rearview mirror. Her impulse was correct. Her father's eyes searched hers in the mirror. She saw her own doubt reflected in them—as if she had put it there.

Then he returned his gaze to the road.

A wave of compassion engulfed her. She stared at the back of her father's head: the firm determination in the way he held it now, the shaggy red hair, darker than her own, the urgency in the way he drove. *If it turns out to be lost motion, it's in the best cause I know.* His words echoed in her mind, painfully. It was as if, for the first time, she had moved, in some mysterious way, outside herself. As if she could now see into and comprehend someone else—and care for that someone outside herself even more than she cared for herself. And giving herself over to the compassion for and comprehension of this man, her father, she began to wonder whether she could ever again tell herself that she was in love with anyone until she could feel this way about him. Until she was old enough and mature enough to feel this way instead of longing or demanding that she must herself be loved. Until she could become the lover instead of the loved. Was this the only path to being loved?

Then she saw the roadblock ahead. Yellow and blue lights flashing off and on. A red light revolving. Figures moving. Uniforms. And a line of cars.

"God," David said. "Good God."

Her father eased the station wagon into the line. David turned once more to look out the rear window.

"God," he said again, softly. "I'm a bastard. Not to believe you, Dad. I'm a real bastard, aren't I?"

Her father was reaching into his pocket for his wallet. "I hope not, son," he said. "I sincerely hope not."

Then she heard her brother laugh. Very quietly. And she felt her own face twisting into a smile. And as the line of cars moved forward, she felt very safe. Very secure. And she even forgot her doubts about her mother. *He* was handling it. He knew. No matter what was going on back there in town, he was taking care of everything here.

An officer approached the car and stabbed his flashlight over it and through it and asked, please, to see her father's driver's license.

It's still your move, Ritchie.

According to the lighted clock on the dash, seven minutes had passed since he'd been trapped—if Ritchie imagined that's what he'd done. The silence had stretched into hours. But if the conniving little bastard wanted to play more games, Theron Diehl had time, all the time in the world. His eyes had become accustomed more or less to the twin high-beam headlights of the pickup, which was definitely red and some foreign make, he'd judge a Datsun. How Ritchie had maneuvered it into position like that while he was turning the cruiser around at high speed—well, the truck must have been in among the trees, waiting, and he hadn't seen it because his mind was on that damned Volkswagen that had not, after all, been following him at all. Unless it was a decoy to take his attention—

This Ritchie was capable of anything. And up to now he seemed to have thought of everything. The area here might be mined. But even with that thought, Theron Diehl felt the surprise that he had experienced many times in the old days: he was not scared. It had always been that way. He supposed he really didn't know what fear was. At least it was not a part of him, then or now as his eyes scanned the woods on both sides. The lack had always been his greatest asset as a peace officer, his advantage when it came to times like this. All he could feel now, besides the smoldering anger and the amazement that he'd been tricked into this spot, was a cool animal caution. He wasn't going to be stampeded, even by silence, into trying anything foolish or risky. He was safe in the bulletproof cruiser as if it were a Sherman tank. Unless, of course, Ritchie had some sort of bomb, maybe like the one the fire department had reported he'd used on the house.

But he had the feeling—call it a hunch—that Ritchie didn't want to kill him outright like that any more than he wanted to kill Ritchie outright. Nevertheless, no matter how long the kid tried to string this out, one of the two of them would be dead soon. Possibly very soon.

The games are almost over, Ritchie.

He reached and switched off his own headlights.

Glanced into the mirror: the pond was quiet, glimmering dark and glassy, framed by high pines beyond. He peered into the woods on both sides of the narrow passageway, the trees shadowy in the spill from the truck's lights. Nothing moved.

His place, he knew, was back there in town. For all he knew Ritchie could have him locked in the car and in the lights for some other reason. Some devious reason beyond his ken. Ritchie might not even be in the truck; he'd had time to get out and away before the police vehicle had made its full turn. Ritchie could be off somewhere snickering up his sleeve again. Hell, he wouldn't put anything past that—

Well, he'd hedge his bets just a mite. Damned if he was going to let Ritchie call the tune all the way. He shifted his weight to the passenger's seat and then, very slowly, he rolled down the right window. A risk, sure—all anything added up to when you came down to it. He lifted the Colt and placed it outside the car in his right hand. Calculate your risks; then do what you have to do: it'd been his code all his life. If Ritchie was not in the truck but off in the woods to the right, he'd have a clear shot at Diehl's head. But Diehl had to assume that the kid was in the truck, not in the woods, and that, whatever his game, he didn't intend to shoot Diehl through the head.

He reached with his left hand to grasp his right wrist, steadying the revolver, as he squinted through the windshield, wondering whether he should put his head out the window and into the glare of light. The question was whether he could shoot with any degree of accuracy this way.

Concentrating, adjusting the barrel's aim, he fired. Once. Then quickly, again. Two of the four headlights went out, shattering, and the shots reverberated through the woods. Quickly, he took aim again, diagonally, and fired, twice, in rapid succession.

Darkness. And after the explosions had died down in the distant hills, the tinkling of glass.

In the dimness now, the cab of the truck appeared to be empty.

He raised the window, moved across the seat again, flipped on the spotlight mounted outside the car, maneuvered it by the handle inside, brought it to focus on the windshield of the pickup. Unless he was crouched down out of view on the floor, Ritchie was not in the truck.

Unless he was behind the cab, in the bed of the truck.

Diehl then turned the light into the woods and played it, probing, among and between the wet and dripping trees, first on one side of the lane, then on the other.

Where the hell was he hiding? Or had he gone completely?

Was the whole thing a hornswoggle, just to give him a royal screwing? Hell, Ritchie could be miles away!

Boyd Ritchie was not miles away. He was, however, not in the truck, having abandoned it on the run once he had the exit blocked with the pickup and while the police cruiser was turning around. He was crouched behind a waist-high stone wall beyond twenty yards of woods where he could command a view, between the pine trunks, of the truck and patrol car facing each other. He had seen the four headlights shot out—he granted Diehl his deadly aim and made note of it—and he had been able, by ducking down, to evade the spotlight's beam as it searched the woods.

He was not yet ready to move. Let Diehl sweat. The whole idea was not to kill Diehl; he could have done that with one shot when the asshole rolled the window down. The idea was to break him. Break him completely. As a man. As a human being. The way Diehl had broken him.

That Diehl had made the first move was encouraging: a sign of weakness. The grizzled old bastard might not be as tough as he'd thought. But it would be light soon. And after he was finished with Briggs later, he had to row across the lake with one hand. His left was black now, and raw, so raw that the chill morning air knifed into the meat, and although it was of no use to him, he couldn't force it into the pocket of the dungarees he now wore. The pain was constant, no longer throbbing but stiff and still and hard. But he was going to play this out as planned.

He was going to get Diehl out of that car. He wanted him alive, he knew exactly what he was going to do to the motherfucker and he was going to make sure, if possible, that Diehl stayed alive to remember it. Nothing was going to stop him now, not even the sun's coming up if that should happen. Nothing.

Next, Diehl would call out to him. He had to wait for that. And he'd be ready. The bear trap was at his feet in the dark and it was set, both springs sprung open, its jaws wide, its steel teeth poised. He could handle it in the dark, just as he had set it in the dark, because he had spent hours practicing. He had had the use of both hands then, but he had managed with one hand and one foot tonight, aware of the risk he was taking. He could do the rest of it with one hand, too.

He had one other stop after this and he'd have to make it in the daylight if Diehl took too long to show signs of cracking. And if Diehl didn't show such signs, there was no way he could imagine to force Diehl out of the car. Well, he'd wait a while now, just a goddamn short while, and if his mind, which was not as sharp as he'd like it to be at a time like this, didn't come up with some scheme to goad Diehl out of the safety of that car—well, in that case, he'd have to kill Diehl regardless. That had been the backup plan all along. Diehl really imagined he was safe in there. He wouldn't be so goddamn safe if the whole car burst into flames or blew up.

If anyone thought he could unnerve Theron Diehl, he just hadn't reckoned on the man he was up against.

That man could sit here and chew his cud till doomsday if he had to. No doubt now that Ritchie had planned this, just the way he'd planned everything else. But he wasn't going to get away with it. It was Diehl's job to avenge the town itself, not just Nell and himself. He knew now that his whole career, maybe his whole life, was at stake here. Everything he'd believed in and devoted his life to.

There was no sound. No rain. No wind. If only he could be sure that Ritchie was in the truck. There was no evidence that he was. But was Ritchie the kind to get him out here, box him in, then just tail out?

With his left hand he directed the beam of the spotlight to the windshield of the truck again. Nothing. Then he turned it into the woods again, lit dripping underbrush, shrubs, tree trunks. It probed deep and moved along a low stone wall, which Diehl would have called a fence, then over the gleaming wetness of picnic tables, benches, metal trash containers.

Nothing.

Not a damn thing. Nobody.

He had to know. Was it a flimflam, a bamboozle, a sucker game he'd been duped into?

He eased down the left window, only a few inches this time. Then he shifted the Colt to his left hand, picked up the bullhorn with his right, placed it in the aperture and brought his lips against the mouthpiece. "Wall," he said, careful to drain all strain and tension and rage from his voice, which was amplified and distorted by the instrument, "wall, you little punk, by my calculation this here's Hanover Pond, ain't it? It's your deal." But then he couldn't help adding, "It's your deal, you little cocksucker."

Nothing. The air came through the open slot of window, brushed the side of his face—which was, he realized in surprise, hot, almost feverish.

There was no sound. No response whatever. He could hear only the dripping, the high shrill chirp and buzz of insects, the caterwauling of frogs in the pond behind him.

If Ritchie had the idea he could con him into stepping out of the car and making himself a target pinned in a flashlight, Ritchie was pissing into the wind.

But the quiet, the lack of action, the possibility, however slim, that Ritchie was not even in the area—everything seemed to come together and, for the first time, he was tempted to radio in for more men. Just to make goddamned sure.

Instead, though, he spoke into the bullhorn again: "It's almost sunup, you fart-faced weasel. You called the game, it's your deal!"

At once he regretted it. He heard the quavering irascible tone in the blare of his voice as it died away. And he listened.

Then he heard another sound. A voice. At last. "You got it all screwed up, Chief." A voice from the direction of the truck, no doubt about that. "You're Diehl." There was laughter in the voice, derision. "Who's on first and you're Diehl."

Ritchie was still here. And in the truck. He'd been right!

He flashed the spotlight in that direction.

Diehl felt no relief. He'd been right, but he felt no relief whatever. Only a sort of chill. Which he attributed to the cold against his face.

The only reason that Boyd Ritchie, staying low behind the wall, had answered at all was that he had caught the note of frenzy in the man's voice, even in the distortion of the horn's bellow.

He was holding a miniature microphone at exactly the distance from his lips that practice had revealed would allow him to speak without any suggestion of the mechanical blur or humming that might betray him. So that his voice, passing from the mike along the wire that he had so painfully strung along the high branches of trees earlier, would sound natural coming from the speaker which was on the tree-matted ground alongside the parked truck.

Himself tense and poised for action now, straining to

get at it, he spoke into the mike again, with elaborate forced casualness. "It's been my deal all night, Chief." He could hear his voice, very slightly amplified, mechanically modulated, from the distance. "I stacked the deck, Diehl, and you've been playing the cards just the way I've been dealing them."

The spotlight wheeled to the cab of the truck. There were two more shots, close together, and the sound of glass shattering. He saw the quick flashes at the window of Diehl's car and then he turned his gaze to the windshield of the truck, which in the spotlight's beam, had stellated into a glittering opaque rectangle with two distinct black holes two feet apart.

He waited a second before he laughed again. The sound came from the truck.

"Missed, Diehl. Too bad and fuck you, Theron, *sir,* in your good wife's holy name, amen."

If he hadn't wanted to kill the sniggering little cocksucker, who was obviously a nut, tetched in the head, then why had he blasted away like that? It was that laugh, that obscene mocking delight. As if Ritchie really *were* dealing. As if—

"That's six bullets, Diehl. Out of your trusty old six-shooter."

Still laughing. And still in the truck. Which he could back out and onto the road any time he decided, throw it into reverse, hightail it away—

Without fumbling, his body and mind clenched, Diehl began to reload the Colt with bullets from his gun belt.

"When you get it loaded, Chief, try again."

Exactly what he intended to do. Heedlessly he lowered the window all the way, shoved the revolver out the window, gripped in his left hand, manuevering the searchlight with his right hand. He fixed the light on one tire, but his head all the way out of the window, took aim, squeezed the trigger. At once he turned the beam onto the other front tire of the truck, took diagonal aim, fired again. And once the sound of the reports had deafened him, then petered out into the distance, he could hear the air whistling out of the tires.

Boyd Ritchie wasn't going anywhere. Not tonight. Not in that truck.

He withdrew his head and played the light from one tire to the other, which was now completely flat.

He was picking up the bullhorn when there was another shot. He ducked sideways to the right and down, automatically, fast, but no bullet entered the car. But everything went dark and, through the open window, he could hear the tinkling of broken glass. The bastard had shot out the searchlight.

Quickly then, raising the window with one hand and reaching for the light knob with the other, he straightened, switching on the headlights.

In immediate response there was a barrage. Several shots in quick succession, he couldn't make out from what direction, and then darkness, abrupt and thick and total, closed in.

He was tempted again to call headquarters. But if he summoned help now, cried for it, he'd lose everything. Including that precious and personal thing in a man that he called his pride, maybe his honor. Or his manhood.

Instead, his eyes aching with the strain to penetrate the enveloping dark, he took up the loaded revolver and reached to take the flashlight from its rack on the dashboard. It was a lone hand and he'd play it out to the end.

Boyd Ritchie was running. Luger in his belt, still warm against his flesh. Left arm dangling. The steel trap, set to spring, carefully loose in his right hand. He had let go with the fusillade of shots, all very accurate from long practice, out of a sudden fury, a mounting impatience that he knew he had to stifle. He was running along the line of stone wall in the direction of the pond. He had had to risk Diehl's seeing the flashes from the Luger but he had gambled on the element of surprise. Just as now he was counting on the shock and sudden darkness to allow him to move.

He climbed over the stone wall near the edge of the pond and turned toward the parking area, making his way between the trees, wet branches snapping at his face and his boots sinking into the sodden earth, making squishing sounds as he lifted them. Then he stopped. Christ. How was he going to get out of here afterward? Diehl had flattened the truck's tires and that had angered him—he had *allowed* that to anger him!—into shooting out the police car's lights. And the police car was the only means of escape, afterwards. Christ.

But he couldn't let this stop him. Even this. Or anything.

What the hell was he doing standing here? He had to get behind the cruiser before Diehl got his dim wits together enough to grab his flashlight and throw its beam out the rear window.

Bent low, he moved over the carpet of leaf-covered gravel, approaching the cruiser from behind, crouching so that his figure couldn't be glimpsed out the rear window or in the mirror as it came between the car and the pond which, he saw now as he moved, had a pink glow in the sky beyond it.

Then he heard the bullhorn's blare again: "Ritchie! This here place is surrounded. All I got to do is give the signal, they'll move in."

Oh, shit, yes. All that shooting, especially that last volley by the Luger—if there were any other pigs around, what were they waiting for?

You, Diehl, *sir,* are beginning to crack.

But he couldn't answer Diehl now: he had abandoned the microphone when he began shooting.

Squatting behind the car, head below the rear window, he placed the trap on the ground with delicate care. And listened. The frogs went on raising hell and he heard, or imagined he heard, the first tentative chirping of a bird some distance away. Diehl did not seem to be moving in the front seat.

With his right hand, very slowly, Boyd Ritchie unscrewed the cap from the fuel tank. Then he took a blue bandanna from his pocket, rolled it diagonally with one hand on his bent leg, then placed one end of it as deeply as possible into the tank, left it dangling there to soak. He knew that, once the fumes escaped, the tank would not explode; but if the wick was lit, the car would burn, forcing Diehl to step out.

Theron Diehl knew now that he was definitely trapped in the car. And only himself to blame. His hatred hardened. He had the flashlight in one hand unlit, and his piece in his right, cocked. He knew damn well what would happen if he stepped out: Ritchie would blast away before he could do anything to defend himself. Or worse. Ritchie sure as hell knew how to shoot—he could wound him only, the way he planned to wound Ritchie if he got the chance. To get the bastard at his mercy.

Using his fingers delicately in the dark behind the car, Boyd Ritchie felt for and then picked up the heavy steel-jawed trap, and bending low, he edged along the side of the car, careful not to brush against it, to the front door on the driver's side. Only a few inches of damp air and the thick door separated him from Theron Diehl. He lowered the trap to the ground, and as he did so, his other hand, hanging, came into contact with the gravel. Fresh pain, sudden and intensified, jolted like an electric shock into the exposed flesh and up his arm, and without volition, trying to lock his jaw and teeth around it, he nevertheless uttered a sharp cry.

Rigid and alert in the seat, Theron Diehl heard the sound. At his elbow. On the other side of the door.

He broke his first impulse—to throw open the door

and start shooting. Another trick? But when he heard the animallike scrambling on the pebbles along the side of the car to the rear, he dropped the flashlight to open the window with his left hand, fast, and in the same motion, twisting around, he thrust the long-barreled revolver out the window in a semicircular movement, and then, without aim or hesitation, directing the gun into the darkness along the side of the vehicle, he fired, three times, blindly.

He felt the bullet enter his leg before he heard the report of the gun. It entered somewhere above the knee, white-hot, searing—a thin electric lance. He was lying behind the car, all but under its rear wheels, and he couldn't manage to draw that leg to safety in case Diehl should shoot again. He was certain that the bullet had pierced the flesh of his thigh and emerged, and the hole that was left seemed worse, more terrible and agonizing, than if it had lodged in the flaming muscle or bone.

It was over.

Like that.

A fluke. A goddamn accident. After all his careful planning. All those years.

He could feel wetness on his leg. Blood.

Once the incredible din had cleared, the three shots becoming one and reverberating off and away over the hills, he heard another sound—more wail than whimper, almost a howl. And he realized, with amazement, that it was coming from him. Not from his throat or chest but from much deeper—his guts, his soul.

His stomach was twisting, knotting.

And he was groveling, thrashing about on the wet leaves and pine needles and mud, unable to see but catching the smell of gasoline: his soaked bandanna hanging above him.

All he had to do, he knew what he had to do, all he had to do was flick his lighter, that was all, touch the spark to the wick, but he had lost his lighter, he remembered dropping it someplace, but where, it was very important to remember because he needed it, he could end it all here, here and now, it was all over anyway, over, why not take Diehl along, but then what about Briggs, if only his body would stop twisting and rolling onto his burned hand—

He heard the motor start. He smelled exhaust fumes.

His heart stopped. His cries stopped. He lay still, knowing.

The lights still glowed on the dashboard and on the gearshift indicator, which stood at *P*. But Theron Diehl's hand was on the lever. If he threw it to *R* and gunned the motor, he could wipe out Boyd Ritchie once and for all. Mangle him. Crush him into the earth. Rid the world of him, *now*.

But if he did it that way, it'd be too good for him. Not what the son of a bitch deserved. And they'd blame him, too. Instead of praising him. That's the way they were. They'd ask questions. Say he had no right. Especially since the suspect was already shot. They'd forget damn fast what Boyd Ritchie had done to them, what Theron Diehl had done *for* them.

The howls of pain had stopped. He raced the motor. Let the bastard suffer. If he was still alive, let him think it was going to happen, let him imagine it happening. He pressed the pedal to the floor and heard the motor's thunderous roar. Let him choke on the exhaust, know what's coming.

When he lifted his boot and released the pedal, he listened. And heard a shout. Heard his name. So Ritchie was still alive back there.

Through the open window, without using the bullhorn, he called out: "Y'got some last words t'say to me, Ritchie?"

"You can't kill me, Chief." There was a sob in the voice. "You know your duty." Then a plaintive whine: "You've no right to kill me."

There it was again. Diehl almost laughed, but his

throat locked and a sour taste came into his mouth. Always the same: commit the crime, any crime, then demand legal rights, beg for mercy. He plunged the pedal to the floor again. You got no rights, Ritchie. None.

But he had to use his head here. He couldn't radio in that he'd located the suspect and run him down with a vehicle. Only one way to kill the suspect. With a gun. If he wanted any respect, any thanks at all.

Only . . . only you're not going to get off that light, you perverted little bastard. If you think you're suffering now—

He turned off the ignition. And heard: "Diehl, listen. You got me. I'm wounded." There were tears in the sound. "I'm bleeding to death, man, you got to help me, you got to take me in—"

More orders. More demands. But he called out: "You're right there, Ritchie. You got your rights and that's what you're gonna get." And more. Plenty more. Every muscle in Diehl's body was taut and throbbing and aching for action. "Ritchie?"

"Anything you say. Anything." More whining. "What you want me to do, Chief?"

Diehl relished the moment, turned on the flashlight. "What I want, son, is your gun."

"Sure. Yes, sir. Only . . . I can't find it in the dark."

"Use your flashlight." The bastard had to have a flashlight. "I been screwed the last time, Ritchie. Find it or I'm backing up."

"I got it, I got it, sir! Here—I'll try to throw it over the top of the car." Pain riddled his voice. "I'm throwing it out in front of the car, Chief!"

Diehl was about to instruct him to toss it alongside the car by his door when he heard a thud. Even now the bastard was still calling the shots!

He flicked on his own flashlight, put it out the window, scanned the area between the car and the truck that his headlights would normally have covered. And located the black square-angled ugly-looking gun, pinned it a moment in the beam. Some foreign make, most likely a Luger.

"You see it, sir?"

A Luger. Hadn't Ben Hutchinson reported some time along the way that a search of gun records had revealed that Paul Wharton had a Luger registered in his name? And that no gun had been found in the Wharton house? Well, he'd clean up that little mystery, too: find out what happened at the Whartons'. He had ways of finding out anything. Everything. It'd be a pleasure. Yessir, a real genuine pleasure to solve that little riddle for the records. And he was going to take his time doing it, too.

"I'm bleeding pretty bad, sir. I need help."

"It's coming." He didn't want the psycho-punk to bleed to death. Not yet anyway. "Yessir, help is on its way."

And he unlocked the door, opened it and stepped out.

He heard a sharp metallic snapping. A sound he'd heard years ago when he used to go hunting in Texas. And then he felt the bone of his leg break just above the ankle. And he was falling, aware that he'd been tricked, knowing that he was not afraid to die but that very soon now, very soon, he would wish that he could.

Part Six

It was dawn. The darkness had turned to a faint dull gray.

For a while, a full fifteen minutes by her estimate, after the shooting had stopped in the parklike area by Hanover Pond, she and Gavin had remained in his green VW, which was parked on the shoulder of Echo Valley Road. They had wondered, when they first heard the shots, what they should do, but Gavin had reminded her that Chief Diehl had a radio in his car and if he wanted help, he would call for it. They had agreed that two guns had been involved, in a complex pattern of shooting that they thought had come to a stop with three shots fired close together and after they had waited some long time, debating what to do. But then there had been another report of a gun, a final single shot, and at once the sounds of motors over the hoarse croaking of the frogs and the twittering of birds that had begun on all sides. Then Chief Diehl's dark police car had shot out of the lane and turned onto Echo Valley Road toward town. In the heavy morning dimness she had not been able to see the driver's face, but she had caught a glimpse of the shadow of Chief Diehl's wide-brimmed Western hat and had wondered why he didn't turn on his headlights since it was still dark.

It had been then that Gavin had been convinced that they had been right in following Diehl out from town rather than proceeding, as intended, to the fire, which was being covered by all the media anyway. And it had been then, too, that Gavin had said: "Well, we're in up to our necks now, I think I'll have a look. The big story, as they say, might be right here." But sensing the reluctance in him as he asked for his flashlight from the glove compartment, she was at once tempted to go along and hesitant to do so because it was her idea that Diehl would never leave anyone alive down there by the pond.

Now she sat waiting, realizing that he really might not have needed the light since the sky seemed to be lifting more and more and the new glow dissipated the faint pinkness that she had been watching above the trees. Jerry Gerrard's last word on the car radio had been that the fire appeared to be under control, but that two firemen had been injured as well as the night watchman who had been critically burned and was in intensive care at the hospital; at least fifteen other structures had burned or were burning and the Wharton Manufacturing building itself could not be saved.

She was straining to listen, to see. But the trees were too dense and she was too far away. What if Gavin needed her? She wondered at herself, astonished. She didn't want anything, anything whatever, to happen to this man whom she had met only a few hours ago but felt she had known a lifetime.

Jerry Gerrard on the radio was repeating his request to David Briggs or anyone who might know of his whereabouts: he should not go home but should go to the Tarkington police station and wait. She wondered where Fletcher was and what he was doing now and she only half comprehended the significance, the possible import, of that repeated instruction on the radio. In some odd and mildly disturbing way she had come to feel detached from Fletcher. As if the cool hostility of his daughter, sitting in the station wagon on the Common an hour ago and his angrily muttered "Right!" had together added up to some sort of final rejection. A rejection that now seemed to have little if any meaning for her.

She saw Gavin's figure in among the trees, approaching, the flashlight's beam jerking up and down in the paleness as he hurried, limping. That limp: watching Gavin McQuade move in that way of his stirred a curious sense of compassion in her, something almost—of all the damned things that could happen to her in this world—something almost maternal.

She remembered what Gavin had said on the way out from town as they followed the chief's patrol car: *How do you figure a man like that? His wife's dead, his house burned to the ground, his town threatened—he goes tootling off on his own.* And then he had asked that invisible angel perched on his shoulder—or perhaps he had asked her: *What do you think drives a man like that?* And had added: *I could almost feel sorry for the miserable son of a bitch.* And on impulse, knowing suddenly that Gavin McQuade had admitted to a pity that wounded *him,* she had reached out her hand, again, and had closed it over his hard gnarled knuckles on the knob of the gearshift stick between them.

But even that recollection did not prepare her for the expression in Gavin's eyes when he came around the front of the Volks and arrived at her open window. His face was pale and his mouth was quivering and in his eyes was a torment, a shock, that she had never seen before in anyone. "You drive," he said. "You—" He managed to open the door.

"Gavin, what—"

"Please."

She got out and hurried around to get into the driver's seat and started the motor, conscious of his sitting in the seat beside her, conscious of his body shaking so hard that she could feel its vibrations through the small car. For a second or two she thought he might be going into convulsions.

"Tel . . . telephone," his voice said, with effort, his shoulders heaving spasmodically. "Hur . . . hurry."

She drove. Tempted to stomp on the brake pedal, to take him into her arms, to calm him, to hold him against her, she nevertheless drove, trying to recall where she may have seen a phone booth on the way out, wondering how far it would be to the closest house.

He was sitting stiffly, but trembling, staring ahead, stuttering: "You . . . you call. Police. Tell . . . tell them . . . tell them send help. Farago might still be—"

When he couldn't finish, she remembered that, at Fletcher's suggestion, Gavin had called Dr. Leroy Farago, who had been with Congressman Heckman earlier; he might still be there since Heckman refused to leave the courthouse.

"Ambulance. Christ. Oh, Christ, girl. And tell . . . say Diehl's car stolen. Diehl. . . . Chief not driving. Someone else. Hurry, tell them . . . ambulance, hurry."

She plunged the pedal to the floor, wishing that Gavin would lower his head, would give in, weep or wail or cry out, whatever, and wondering at the same time what impulse on his part had caused him to decide to follow the chief's car when, on the way from the newspaper office to the fire at the Wharton Mills, he had spotted Diehl leaving town in the opposite direction. What strange premonition, or foreboding perhaps, had dictated that decision?

To hell with the goddamn pain, to hell with his burned hand and the hole through his thigh and the blood still seeping out, soaking into the seat of Chief Diehl's nice big hog of a patrol car. Which didn't have the power of the Vega with its X28 engine, but to hell that, too. Who was going to give chase to a car with CHIEF OF POLICE emblazoned on both front doors and driven by someone wearing Diehl's blue tunic and his ten-gallon felt hat? Nor was anyone going to notice the shattered headlights because it was almost light now and no lights were needed and he'd removed all the shards of glass from the rims just in case. He'd thought of everything, as usual, the way he always did, always, even down to knowing that the dawn would break at ten after four—which had given him enough time at the pond to do what he did to Diehl. More than enough time, and he'd taken full advantage of it. And now he was on a narrow unpaved unnumbered side road that circled around town and joined up with Bradford Street, which climbed uphill to the campus and along one side where it crossed Howells Street.

By the time they found Diehl it'd be into the afternoon and by then he'd be finished with what he had to do to the Briggs family one and all, and he'd be long gone. Across the lake in the rowboat, then into the brilliantly painted Ford van, where the bread was, and the ID crap—hell, he'd sail through as many roadblocks the pigs wanted to throw up between here and the Canadian border. With that golden shoulder-length Jesus-freak wig, that beaded headband and Navajo poncho and those leather-thonged sandals—he'd be just another hippie heading for the goddamn wilderness for forty days and forty nights to contemplate his prick. While back here they'd still be scrubbing down the woods and swamp around Hanover Pond.

Nobody knew where he was now. Right here under their noses. *Nobody.*

"Car One, come in, please." The police dispatcher's voice still had that neat crew-cut businesslike shit-ring to it. "Car One, please. Come in."

Car One. This car. He was tempted to pick up the mike and answer. Hell, he could imitate that drawl of Diehl's. That drawl Diehl was not drawling now. Right now Chief Diehl was crying, or whining, or moaning. Or whimpering like some animal caught in a trap. Which he was.

"Car One. Chief Diehl, please answer. It's urgent."

Fuck off. Diehl was in no mood to come in. And who'd made sure of that? Boyd Ritchie. Who'd scraped his raw withered hand on the gravel when he placed the trap on the ground, who'd cried out because he couldn't help it. Which could have licked him, could have ended him then and there if his mind hadn't been working. Boyd Ritchie, even writhing in agony, had kept that mind going. And had used that pain, which was real, to make Diehl believe he was dying. The joker in the deck that he was still dealing. Begging and jawboning—sir, sir, *sir*—and throwing the Luger out in front of the car. And Diehl'd been snowed, just the way everybody had been snowed, and then when he had him in the trap, he'd used the boots—those sharp high-heeled boots like the ones Diehl had used to work on *his* balls. His left hand was no use to him, Diehl's fault, too, he'd burned it at Diehl's house, Diehl's fault, so Diehl got the boots. And he'd used Diehl's own gun, too, the prized old Colt .45. *Open your mouth. Hear me, man? Open it wide.* The end of the barrel driving into the cheek, jabbing. *You want to get your teeth blown off, your jawbone? Wider! Wider, I said.* Lesson learned, Diehl. And he'd broken him. Broken him completely. Till he was pleading, imploring: *Kill me, kill me, please, get it over with, please.* Not a chance, old man, not a chance in hell. But he did oblige, he did do what Diehl had not done seven years ago: he'd pulled the trigger. Not to kill—because if he killed him, how could Diehl live on and remember the way he'd begged to die?

He was on Bradford Street now and he could see people on porches, on the sidewalks and in driveways. Wearing bathrobes, negligees, old slacks. Unshaven, uncombed. Holding small radios at their ears. Staring at the chief's car as it passed slowly by with reassuring dignity. The radio had been repeating an order for several hours: all officers were to calm the citizens, ask them to return to their homes and to stay off the streets. *Instruct them not to panic.* A few waved half-heartedly. Idiots. Havoc. What they deserved. And tomorrow they'd all know who did it to them. Boyd Ritchie. They'd know that name—tomorrow and for weeks and months and maybe years to come. Not only here in this stinking town but all over the country, probably all over the world. Boyd Ritchie. Hell, this was bigger than any skyjacking or kidnapping or any other goddamn caper that anybody'd ever been able to dream up. And all their fault—theirs, not his really, *theirs*. And they'd pay attention, they *were* paying attention now—to him. Boyd Ritchie. He was no longer a nobody, here or anywhere.

"Attention, all patrols. This is a general alert order. Be on the lookout for Car One. Chief Theron Diehl's vehicle. Believed to be stolen. Repeat. All-car alert. Car Number One. Report unverified, but this vehicle is believed stolen by suspect Boyd Ritchie. Approach with extreme caution. Repeat—"

But he was no longer listening. The pain came flooding back. Like a wave breaking. He went faint, mind reeling sickeningly. Disbelief struck with all the power of a blow at the base of his skull and he could feel the blood wet along his leg. How could they know? This soon? How? How, *how?* They couldn't have learned and then made it all the way to the pond this fast, from the Wharton Mills *or* from the courthouse. Then—

He should have killed Diehl. Finished him off. Why hadn't he? Because he wanted some kind of justice. Still wanted it.

But even Diehl couldn't have walked anywhere with that trap on his foot.

What he should have done, he should have cut off Diehl's prick and shoved it down his goddamn throat!

But it couldn't have been Diehl who—

That dark little VW on Echo Valley Road. When he came out from the pond. He'd thought it was abandoned. Or just more fuckers. And it hadn't moved. Or followed. Still, had he seen it there when he turned in toward the pond earlier, to hide the truck in the woods before Diehl arrived? He couldn't remember and suddenly it seemed very important to remember and at the same time he wondered why he had to remember, what the hell good would that do him now?

He'd forgotten something else, too. The wick in the

fuel tank. His bandanna dangling, still hanging there, soaked with gas. How the hell could he—

He wasn't going to make it, after all. He couldn't hack it.

How come, though? Just when it was almost over. *How come?*

He slowed the car. On a hill overlooking the tree-filled campus, the town itself beyond. Red in the sky. He had one chance. One. He could turn around. Take the same road out of town. Drive to the lake, to hell with Briggs now, he could row the boat across, as planned—

But his left hand was hanging along his side—shrunken, withered, charred crisp—the whole arm rigid with pain and useless. Could he row across with one arm?

Yes. He could do anything!

But it was light now. Someone would see him. And what had the radio advised about helicopters being brought in?

And what about the blood he'd lost?

He was done. He'd had it.

It was over.

He felt despair settle through him. Leaving him so spent and weak that he could hardly drive.

Even if he could get across the lake and into the van—all those miles after that. The roadblocks. What had he been thinking? He must have flaked out completely somewhere along the line. How had he ever imagined he could con the state police? Look at him, *look:* burned, bleeding, soaked with blood, even his eyes couldn't focus and—

How could he fool anyone? How could he have fooled himself?

Then he had no choice. All he could do now was finish what he'd started out to do. Because if he didn't finish it, why then everything he had done would go for nothing.

It had always been more important to finish the job. To hell with the bread now—what was ninety thousand dollars if he didn't do what he'd set out to do? What did Canada mean, or Europe, or South America? In a blurring haze of pain and desolation and desperation, he could see very clearly that all that had been only a small part of the dream—the least important part.

And it seemed now that whatever was to happen to him when he'd done the job, whatever happened to Boyd Ritchie himself, had little to do with what he, Boyd Ritchie, had done or was going to do. As if he really was only some kind of tool or weapon. To see that there was justice. After all those years it was as if he himself had not been taken into consideration: some larger and more vital idea had taken over and now, possibly, he was to be one of the victims of that idea that he really didn't understand but that he carried in his mind like the delirium of a disease.

Nothing of what he had already done would have any meaning if he let Briggs off the hook now. Hang onto that now, keep it straight. Hell, Fletcher Briggs was worse than the others, any of them, even Diehl. That's why he'd saved him for last, wasn't it? If Fletcher Briggs wasn't paid off, where was the justice for Boyd Ritchie? *Where?*

He urged the car to the next corner, turned into Howells Street. He could see the high old house with its gables and gingerbread trim. It was dark. With the four of them all snug and safe in their beds.

And if, for any reason or by any chance, Briggs had gotten wise—well, he knew where the professor'd go. Where he'd take his precious family. Boyd Ritchie always had a backup plan. He not only knew the address of Willa Brigg's mother in Boston, but had cased the building; he even knew how to duck security, how to get into the apartment itself.

Boston.

All those miles.

Roadblocks.

Briggs' blue MG was in the driveway, partly on the lawn. The garage door was open.

He edged the police cruiser around the MG and

eased it, slowly, careful to throw it out of gear to idle the motor, into the garage. Then he got out to close the overhead door and his leg caved, but he didn't go down.

If Briggs had made it to Boston, Boyd Ritchie, wincing with pain and hopelessness, knew that he would have to follow, somehow, but he also knew that he would never make it.

All those miles. No way.

If no one was inside the house now, he was done for. *Kaput*.

A thin gray vapor was rising from the black asphalt of the turnpike in front of the station wagon. The sky had been lifting steadily and slowly, but the light was still hazy. He drove at a normal rate of speed, not fast, giving in, now that he felt such a vast and pervasive relief, to what he considered a natural reluctance to face Willa again. He couldn't help recalling the hurt and hate in her eyes and in her voice. Why hadn't he recognized how much she had loved him? Did she still? Would she ever again? And for that matter, why hadn't he himself realized how much he loved her? And Peggy—who was now quiet, perhaps dozing, in the rear seat. And David, who was twisting the radio dial back and forth to listen to the Tarkington station for a few minutes, then to a broadcaster in Boston who was also trying to keep abreast of the happenings in Tarkington. Fletcher was aware of the guilt gnawing at him, the guilt that held the station wagon at its slow pace. How could he have done that to Willa, how in hell? And he was conscious, too, as he listened, of a broader less tangible guilt: that he could feel such relief because *he* had managed to escape with *his* family while back there—

The radio was a steady barrage of reports: killer loose, possibly insane . . . two cold-blooded murders on record already . . . prominent citizens missing . . . including owner of Wharton Manufacturing Company, one of the largest in the state, now in flames . . . fire of suspicious origin . . . night watchman injured and in critical condition . . . many other buildings also burning . . . all state police barracks the New England states alerted . . . airplane standing by to fly investigative team to any spot where suspect may be apprehended—

And then, when David turned the dial again, the by now familiar voice of Jerry Gerrard repeating the appeal for David Briggs to go directly and at once to the Tarkington police station and, in no circumstances, to go home. David had heard it once before. He had made no comment. And he made none now.

Fletcher Briggs had begun to wonder, as he half listened to the voice on the radio, whether it always took some cataclysm of tragedy to shock a man into realizing his life, into defining himself and his values. It was far from an original thought and he probably would have smiled tolerantly, perhaps even cynically, had one of his students expressed it in class, but he had, in the course of the night, come to recognize the sad and terrible truth behind the cliché. And he wondered whether, like most people, he might have arrived at that truth too late.

. . . all citizens requested by authorities to stay in their homes and off the streets . . . some families leaving town regardless of appeals . . . and now, just in, an unsubstantiated report but more than a rumor: the suspect is now believed to be driving the car belonging to the chief of police . . . outrageous and audacious act proving, if anything, that Boyd Ritchie is still in town—

He straightened and pressed harder on the accelerator pedal. The station wagon responded at once. What if Willa was listening? She had never had that much to drink; then she had driven to Boston, her emotions running wild anyway. Now, what if she should hear this? He had to let her know. Now. At once.

"Keep your eyes peeled for a phone booth," he said, "and give me some warning if you can. It's been hours since I talked with your mother." He said no more and had the satisfying impression that there was no need to say more.

Then David, staring ahead into the dusky light, said: "You spent most of the night looking for me, didn't you? That's why it's been so long since you spoke with Mother."

"Well, well," Peggy's voice mocked from behind, "he speaks. He has the gift of tongues after all. Tell me, Daddy, does baby brother still have that foolish beatific grin on his face?"

"I don't think I'm still strung-out, Peg. I've just been sitting here trying to get my head on straight."

"Outtasight," Peggy said. "Far out. You?"

But Fletcher only said: "There are a lot of escape hatches, son." He was thinking of Annette and sex and youth and his own reluctance to accept time and age. And he was thinking of the sanctuary of a campus and he knew now, had learned, that there were no sanctuaries: the assaults of reality could topple the most impregnable ivory tower.

"Plenty of cop-outs," Peggy agreed softly, even a trifle sadly, and Fletcher knew she was thinking of Eric Lindenberg.

OVERLOOK
500 FT. AHEAD

"Slow, man, slow," David said.

And in a few moments the outline of a booth appeared on the right, just off a half-moon of pavement that curved off the highway. He nosed the station wagon toward a low stone barricade that overlooked the distant rolling hills where, now, mist was hanging cloudlike and ethereal in the dim distance. He realized that he had not turned off the headlights although he had not needed them for some time.

He was out of his seat and had taken several strides when he heard David call after him: "Thanks, Dad."

He hesitated but did not stop, or turn. The single word, unspoken until now, said it all. As, in her own way, Peggy had said it earlier. Still, it took his breath and he didn't dare try to reply.

Birds were piping in the trees and fields, chattering and lilting as if delighted by the new day.

In the damp booth with its metallic smell, he realized that, for all the anxiety and terror that had been haunting him through the night, he had not thought of or wanted a drink for hours. Hadn't even thought of one. And he didn't want one now. A fresh sort of relief surged through him—a sharp and satisfying elation, a sense of freedom. Perhaps he was getting his own head on straight. At his age, it was sure as hell about time!

He dialed the operator and placed the call, charging it to his home number, his mind picturing the empty house on Howells Street and then the devastation of the studio on the top floor.

While he waited, he found himself longing, almost painfully, for the sound of her voice, and at the same time, while the distant phone buzzed over and over, he had an absurd sense of anticipation, youthful excitement, boyish eagerness. He had not only to relieve her fears—please don't suffer, darling, don't ever worry again, ever—but he had to shout his love, force her to listen, now at this most unlikely time, in these most unlikely circumstances, while all these horrible things were going on, he had to beg her forgiveness, make her forget, shout, whisper, plead—

"Yes?"

It was not her voice. Her mother's.

"Virginia? This is Fletcher."

"I should have known."

"May I speak with Willa, please?"

"Willa's not here."

"Please, Virginia, she may not want to talk to me. If she's sleeping—"

"My dear boy, you don't *listen*. Willa hasn't come here. I've been expecting her for hours because of your earlier call, but I haven't heard a syllable from her. I'm sure you realize, Fletcher, that if the child has left you at last—"

But he banged the phone onto the hook and looked out through the glass at the lightening hills. He was cold, colder than he'd been all night.

His long, lean body was kneeling and bent double, the face hidden, the top of silver hair touching the gravel, which even in the dim light looked streaked with blood. In the grayness it had been impossible, at first, to determine whether Chief Diehl was dead or alive. But when one of the officers had, impulsively, tried to straighten the body, a deep elongated groan had been torn from the throat, an inhuman sound so chilling and unreal that the officer had stood up and allowed the figure to return to its fetal position. In that moment, though, they had all seen that his two hands were clutching at the groin area, which was like an obscene balloon between his palms.

Staring at it, also hearing the frogs from the pond and the early-morning birds chirping and twittering, Ben Hutchinson forcefully and with an effort of will managed to control the sickening revulsion inside. What he could not fight down, though, was the rage. Quiet and stiff and deadly in him—the hunger for revenge. Much as he had come to despise Theron Diehl and although even now, to his amazement, he could not really feel sorry for the man, he nevertheless felt the call for blood: whoever did this had to be caught and punished. But the feeling, he knew with a tinge of shame, went even deeper: he longed to wreak the vengeance personally. It made no sense. It was as though he couldn't get his own emotions, usually straightforward and uncomplicated, into focus inside himself.

But now he had work to do. And now he'd do it his way and hope he was right. "Confirm the alert on Chief Diehl's vehicle, all units. And give it to the radio station for the general public. But with instructions that no damn fool citizen should do anything but report its location. We don't need anybody playing hero."

"Yes, sir. Right away."

Sir. Well, Diehl *had* put him in charge. Until morning. He still wore his badge—and would wear it, unless he himself decided to chuck it all in the flooding sense of repugnance that was threatening to engulf him. He only wished he'd been in charge all through the night. And as he turned to move away, between the officers who had already begun their meticulous search-down of the area, the ugly irony struck him: if he *had* been in charge, he'd have taken action around ten or so last night when the Congressman and Fletcher Briggs had first demanded to see the court records, and he sure as hell would have acted when they'd come up with the name of Boyd Ritchie. If Diehl had done that, Ritchie probably would have been in custody hours ago and Diehl wouldn't be here on his knees, half-dead, posbly dying.

As he walked toward Echo Valley Road where the green VW was parked, he heard the voices of his fellow officers but did not try to identify the speakers.

"How come he stripped the old man? How come? Top of everything else, he had to rip off his clothes, cut 'em off all except the boots?"

"The hyena's queer, that's why. You heard what he did to that kid. Fancy word's sadistic."

"Might's well be living in the African bush somewheres. Hell, he did everything but tear off his flesh and eat it."

"You see that foot? I'm a hunting man and I seen bears tear off a whole foot trying to get out of one of those things."

"If you know how it works," Ben barked, "get that trap off his ankle, to hell with fingerprints."

And as the officer moved, he said: "One thing sure—the chief won't be walking for a while."

And another man said, "If ever."

"I always heard about beating the shit outta somebody, but Christ, I never saw it before. I never *smelled* it before."

Ben had been spared that: in his nostrils remained the odor of charred wood and smoke and flames. Even with the windows wide open as he sped from the Wharton Mills to Hanover Pond, he had not been able to breathe in the chill morning air without smelling the fumes of destruction back there.

He examined the Datsun half-ton pickup, which had been backed into the woods. The front tires were not only flat but partly shredded and partly off the rim: the truck had been driven on flat tires.

Then, as he continued to explore it—it appeared to be brand-new—he heard a siren in the distance. It was not the ambulance's long wail but the *wow-wow-wow* of a police vehicle. Dr. Farago, he hoped. Just as he hoped that Farago had left Congressman Heckman at the station. Well, at least the doctor could relieve Diehl's pain until the ambulance did arrive—maybe even give an opinion as to whether the old man was going to live or die.

When the reporter named Gavin McQuade, whom he really didn't know, had phoned, asking him to come to the courthouse because Wallace Heckman needed him, Leroy Farago had cursed himself for ever having become a medical doctor, especially a general practitioner. He had been exhausted anyway, having been put through hell at the hospital by Kay Heckman and her concern about their kid, but he had pulled on some slacks and a raincoat and had rushed to the courthouse, realizing along the way that some very damned strange things must be happening in town tonight. And Wally Heckman, who had been in a state of shock just short of the catatonic, had refused to leave police headquarters, had refused all medication and advice, and had said at one point: *You don't think they'll kill him, do you? Before they bring him in here?* To occupy Heckman as much as to satisfy his own curiosity, he had asked for a recounting of the events of the night and had learned that Coralie Wharton and her husband were missing and that there was evidence of some sort of violence at their home, confirmed by a state police investigation. *He did it,* Heckman had said. *Whatever happened there, he did it.* Farago had been able, surreptitiously, to administer a sedative in a glass of water, but that damned sense of duty which, in spite of all his other admitted infractions of medical ethics, had somehow gotten hold of him, then held him at Heckman's side, occasionally begging the patient to accompany him to the hospital. Then, perhaps forty-five minutes or an hour later, another call had come into the station requesting a doctor at Hanover Pond—some girl calling in the name of Gavin McQuade again. Cursing himself but relieved to have an excuse to do something, anything, he had persuaded Wally Heckman that perhaps the suspect had been wounded, and by this ruse he had at least been able to keep Heckman alongside. Judging by the fixed obsessive stillness in his friend's glassy eyes, he knew all the way out from the Common that surveillance might, at some moment, have to become actual restraint.

The action at Hanover Pond had an eerie quality about it in the early-morning grayness, reminding Farago of some scenes he had witnessed in Korea. As the police car came to a halt, the nerve-racking sound of the siren cutting off abruptly, he knew that it would not be possible to keep Heckman in the back seat.

"Don't come with me," he commanded, knowing that Heckman would follow.

But once he had arrived at the circular parking area at the end of the short gravel-covered lane, he could see at once that the naked gray-haired figure bent double over itself was not Boyd Ritchie. But as he hesitated a second, he couldn't recognize who it might be. "Stay here, Wally," he said, and with his bag in hand he stepped through the uniformed figures who stood aside for him.

A yard from the contorted form he stopped again. He'd been an Army medic, true, but that had been years ago. He'd treated victims of automobile accidents at the scene. But he was not prepared for this. Nothing could ever have prepared him for this. "Jesus Christ," he said under his breath, and then he lifted his voice, which sounded odd and dry: "Get an ambulance out here!"

And heard a voice call: "It should be here any minute, Doc."

Still, he remained reluctant to move forward.

As he stepped in, Farago wondered whether an ambulance would really be required. Or whether his help would be. Perhaps he should tell them to notify the medical examiner.

Kneeling, taking a deep breath to combat the queasiness in his stomach, he was struck by the smell. Soaking leaves. Blood. Dew. Human feces.

Death?

Gavin McQuade, leaning against the wet hood of the green Volkswagen, was trying not to retch. He had stopped shaking, but a dangerous and threatening quiver remained inside and kept threatening to attack his flesh. He wanted to go off into the woods alone, just to be alone. He knew Ben Hutchinson, who had joined him on the road, was only doing his duty. And he knew that Annette, very quiet, very kind and considerate and concerned, was still behind the wheel of the little car, listening, observing.

"What I'm asking, Gavin—and I have to ask—" Ben Hutchinson said, "is what you were doing way out here when you heard the shots."

"He was trying to rape me," Annette said from inside the car. "Something always interferes."

Gavin saw a mirthless smile flit along the young officer's lips and he wished that, by some miracle, he could recapture even a little of the old bantering cynicism that had carried him through so many harrowing episodes. But none like this. None, ever. "I followed Diehl out here. It's true my grandparents both were Druids, you know. I suffer forebodings of evil doings." But it was no good. "I just had a hunch Diehl might have a private rendezvous with this Ritchie kid," he confessed flatly.

Ben nodded. "Damned good hunch, you ought to be a cop, McQuade. Ritchie phoned Diehl at police headquarters a few minutes before we got the report of the fire. Gave his name to get through." He turned away to look between the cars toward the activity by the pond.

Beyond the pond, where a heavy cloud of silver mist hung low, McQuade could see a pink radiance above the high pines. Perhaps he only imagined it. Or perhaps it was only the glow from the fire losing its color in the grayness. He could hear radios crackling and growling and still another police car was arriving from town. His stomach was still twisting and he supposed he'd never get rid of that taste in his mouth. Not sour, not exactly bitter—more the taste of chewed rubber. Could it be disgust? With man, the universe?

Ben Hutchinson spoke again, still turned away. "Wanted to play John Wayne all by his lonesome." There was a kind of bewilderment in Ben's tone, wonderment but a lack of bitterness. "Well, who knows, Gavin—maybe you're the hero after all. Maybe you saved his life. If he lives."

And as Ben shook his head but without moving off, Gavin McQuade gave in to his own bafflement. Gave in completely. How could he feel sorry for someone like Theron Diehl? How in *hell?* But he did. And then the nausea took over. He made his way through underbrush, gagging with the effort not to vomit, making hawking sounds, shoulders heaving, until he was deep into the wet clammy gloom of the woods. Hadn't it been Diehl who had fed him the medical report on the Heckman kid, hoping he'd print it? Why? Because Diehl had to settle some small account with Heckman and he'd use any means to do it. Yet he, Gavin

McQuade, the fool, the cynical middle-aged, crippled fool, still felt compassion for the cruel old bastard.

He placed one palm against a wet tree trunk and bent forward and spewed from his innards all the rotten food and lousy liquor and, he hoped, all the poisons of his weakness and humanity so he could from now on begin to rebuild those defenses of detachment and skepticism that had allowed him to survive, in whatever half-ass and often miserable way, until now.

Ben Hutchinson was bending down and looking into the Volkswagen, and Annette, aware that Gavin was alone and sick back there in the woods somewhere, wondered whether she should try to explain that some possibly feminine instinct in her prevented her from joining him, trying to help, that, in fact, much as she herself ached to follow him, she knew that he needed, in this outburst of dismay and aversion, to be alone.

What she said, true to character or true to some phony concept of her own character that she felt somehow obliged to fulfill but which, through the night, she had begun to distrust, even to despise, was: "Does this make you heap big chief now?"

"It makes me the one to ask the questions. What are *you* doing out here at all?"

"You know, Hutchinson, you ask the right questions. The only answer to that one must be I've flipped out, right?"

He shook his head again, sighed, but did not straighten. "Maybe you can be helpful. How many shots did you actually hear?"

"That's an easy one. First, four shots. Then a few minutes later, two more, close together." She was concentrating now, struggling to remember exactly. "Then another two in a very few minutes. They crack like hell through these woods." And then, because it might be important, she added: "All from the same gun."

"Eight shots. That could account for the two tires, the four headlights and two bullets through the windshield of the truck. We've got two shells so far out of the truck, both forty-fives, so we might assume it was Diehl who—" He stopped himself. "Any more?"

"Oh, it was a rooting-tooting gun battle, judging by the noise. A few minutes later there was a single report, but from a different gun. A different kind of crack sound. And right away then, a whole damned bombardment. Like a volley. This also from the second gun. Gavin said it sounded to him like a foreign make of some kind."

"A German Luger maybe?"

"You'll have to ask our Irish expert." She opened her eyes and saw him squinting at her. "Why?"

"There's a Luger missing, that's all. From a house in town." Then quickly: "Any more shots?"

"Four more. Three from the first gun. Close together crack-crack-crack! Some time later, though."

"Yes?"

"Then, even later, quite a few minutes later really, one more shot. Also from the first gun. Just before the chief's car came barreling out and headed for town."

The officer nodded. "That'd be the *coup de grâce*. The one through Diehl's face. There are powder burns on one cheek."

"Nice party, right?"

"Why the hell didn't you report all this as soon as you heard the shooting start?"

She was about to tell him the truth. That it had been Gavin's idea. That Gavin had decided that Diehl wanted to play it out alone and that, by the time any help could be summoned and could arrive from town, it'd be over anyway. But now she knew otherwise: that Gavin had hoped all along that he could be of some damned help. That was why he'd gone down to the pond alone before they located a phone. And, as Hutchinson himself had just said, Gavin may even have saved Diehl's life. So, aware that Hutchinson was waiting, she told what amounted to half a lie only: "Lieutenant, we were scared shitless in no-man's-land with a war going on."

Hutchinson did straighten then. "I'm interested in

those three shots together from the forty-five—well, from what you call the first gun. You're positive about these, are you?"

"I'm interested, too. If we can account for nine out of twelve from the chief's gun, one or more of the other three might be in Ritchie's ass, right?"

"Or they could be in the ground or in the trees around here." He started away, stopped, turned. "By the way, miss—do you have any idea where Professor Briggs might be?"

Startled, she said: "He told Gavin earlier he was leaving town. I assume he's well on his way by now."

"One thing Chief Diehl taught me was: careful about assumptions." He tapped the brim of his cap and walked away.

But he had to make the same assumption himself: that Briggs had lucked out, located his son at the quarry and that he was now well on his way out of the area. But once he was finished here, unless some other outlandish crisis cropped up, Ben Hutchinson decided he'd drive by the Briggs house, possibly only that, just to check out the assumption.

He was striding toward his car, passing Congressman Heckman, who didn't seem to see him, who stood stiff and alone, staring into space. Ben considered speaking to him but knew it would probably be hopeless. And what he had to do now was more important: putting on the air the report that Boyd Ritchie might be wounded. If *that* assumption was accurate, the suspect—who had been a hell of a lot more than a suspect in *his* book for a long time now—could be more desperate and dangerous than ever.

You better come, Briggs. You give a shit about this whore, you better come, fast, man.

Well, he was coming. Decision made, mind clenched, he was returning along the wide rolling empty turnpike at top speed, motor rumbling and vibrating, the whole station wagon straining, shuddering. He was gripping the wheel and leaning forward. Beyond the rim of hills and farmlands to the east there was now a suggestion of pink sky, still very faint. Christ, the night was not yet over. For him perhaps it had just begun.

Back there in the booth, hearing the phone in the house ringing after he had hung up on her mother and dialed his own number in Tarkington, he had cursed himself for having treated Willa as the rational adult she had always been, for failing to consider that she had drugged herself with disillusion and hate and alcohol tonight, for failing to realize for all those hours that she might defy him by refusing to believe him, to do what he had demanded. Or, as the phone buzzed over and over, he had begun to hope that she had gone somewhere else perhaps—

But her voice had stabbed at his ear: *Hello.* If it was her voice: hard, level. *Hello!* it demanded.

Willa?

I told you to leave me alone. The harshness in her tone, the repressed fury, had actually relieved him for a moment. And the chill up and down his body had warmed into sweat. *Stay to hell away from me!* she had cried.

But he was coming; he was on his way now. And each time a car approached, he hoped that it would be a police car, that they'd arrest him for speeding so he could tell them, get help for Willa, but each time he fought down the irrational foolish cowardly hope because he couldn't allow anything to delay him now, even for a few minutes, and above all, he couldn't tell the police. How would that crazed mind react if—

He had tried to tell Willa on the phone, almost overwhelmed at the sound of her voice, thinking at first that she was still angry and that she had been sleeping. They would settle whatever was between them as soon as he could get home, he had been telling her in a rush of relief, when another voice took over, a male voice.

Briggs?

Then the shock had moved in—not slowly, a blow at the base of his skull.

Briggs, where are you, man?

Who's this? Who—

You phony prick, you know who this is . . . sir.

And in the background Willa's voice had screamed: *Don't come, Fletcher. Stay away, don't come here!*

You better come, Briggs. If you give a shit about this whore, you better come fast, man.

How many more miles? How many minutes? Seconds?

And what was happening meanwhile? What of that anguish and horror he had heard in her voice, that wild desperation?

Christ, why had he left her alone? His mistake. His stupid blind trusting mistake. No. His original mistake, for which they were both paying now, was in his own duplicity, treachery—stupidity! Imagining that some other woman, some *child,* could ever—

Willa, Willa, if he—

Smell of leaves. Nostalgia. Another winter. He recalled his discontent of hours ago, days ago, weeks, years—and he gave himself over to cold shame.

No time for that now, he told himself with quiet savagery. No time now to torture himself further by trying to unravel the pattern of chance and weakness and betrayal and blindness that had brought him, had brought her, Willa—

No time for all that, *no time!*

He heard the chopping sound of a helicopter overhead, flying very low. They were watching the roads. They were patrolling the roads while Boyd Ritchie—

And listen, prick. You still on? Bring those kids. Those precious kids of yours.

By then the sweat had frozen all over his body as he clutched the phone, his mind rebelling. But he said, knowing he was lying: *They're with me. I'll bring them.*

Like hell. As soon as he'd come out of the booth afterward, he'd barked his orders: *Get out and hitch a ride to Boston. If the police pick you up, tell them nothing.* Their eyes filling with questions and terror, they had climbed out of the station wagon at once. Their eyes—he ached with love now, every nerve and muscle, his whole being. For both of them. His children, his. Ached.

Not a chance, you bastard, not a chance. No kids.

But he was not bringing the police, either. More compromise? Another half measure?

Listen, prick. No fuzz. We understand each other, don't we? Any pigs come in here, they're going to find a piece of meat. Not your wife, man. A piece of bleeding raw meat.

And when he had been too numb to answer, the voice had snorted a laugh. *We always understood each other, didn't we, Counselor? One cop, just one, and she's dead. Only not just dead. Worse. Like I'm a rapist, you remember me. But I learned new tricks, where I've been. Like old man Stegner. Like little Dennis Heckman. Coralie Wharton. You ponder that. You ponder that all the way—*

Listen! His own shout had filled the booth, piercing his eardrum as it came through the phone. *Now you listen. You touch her, you do anything to her, anything at all—*

And what? I'm done anyway, prick. So you can't do anything to me. Nobody can. It's too late, it's daylight. I'm blood all over, man. Then the voice had erupted into an animal howl: *You can't kill a dead man! I don't care, what can you do about that, I don't care!*

Willa, Willa, Willa, darling. As he drove, his head threatened to split—to explode. Doubts eroded his fixed purpose now. Harrowing doubts. Torture more intense than any physical pain he'd ever known. And he could feel panic prowling like some feral stealthy animal along the edges of his consciousness. What if, what if—

And in his mind he remembered Willa's voice on the phone, close, yelling: *Don't, Fletcher. Fletcher, darling, don't come, please, please, he's insane, don't, please—*

Then there had been two distinct sounds: the thud of a blow followed by a sharp cry of pain. And then the voice was purring: *I touched her, man. I had to touch her. Only not too hard. There're other ways to touch her. I can do worse. Much worse. Think about it.* Then a thunderous yowl: *Bring those kids and get here! Your goddamn phone's outta order! As of now!*

But Fletcher hadn't tried to call back. Now, as he realized that he was approaching the cloverleaf where he had to turn from the turnpike onto the interstate, his mind filled, again, with sickening pictures, hazy but violent and obscene. And he thought of the burning mills, of Diehl's house turned to ashes, of Diehl's wife roasted to death. And he wondered what Ritchie had done to Coralie Wharton and what had become of her husband.

Willa. His love was a wildness in him—so intense and shattering that he was not sure his trembling arms could make the turn ahead. Willa. Where now was all that prattling of self-pity about a candle having gone out? He had never been more quiveringly alive. And he had never been more certain, focused, knowing.

But was it too late? Was it always too late?

He had to clutch the wheel fiercely in a sweaty grip of steel to force the station wagon off the highway and onto the ramp.

Then he saw the flashing lights of a police car in the twilight. There was another parked behind it at the bottom of the ramp.

He was traveling so fast that the rear wheels slipped on the damp pavement and he had to press down on the brake and fight the wheel even more to keep from slithering sideways and to prevent the station wagon from passing the turnoff.

An accident now, any simple sideswipe or dented

fender, an accident or panic—if he lost control of the car, what would happen to Willa then?

As he began to descend in a wide curve, he could see the two state police cars clearly, parked at the bottom, off the pavement, not a roadblock. Two uniformed troopers were leaning against the fender of one vehicle, their attention turned idly on him.

His chance. His only chance. His last—

But what if the police did arrive at the house before he did?

He passed the troopers and the cars and entered the interstate highway. Then he urged the station wagon forward again.

Choice behind him. Decision made.

Another mistake? A tragic one this time? A fatal one?

Afterward—if there was an afterward—a man could be haunted forever, destroyed, by looking back and wondering what might have been if he'd done just this at the proper moment, or that at the crucial time.

His jaws were clamped together so hard that an ache climbed his jawbone, throbbed in the swelling there on one side. Reached his skull. Penetrated. Then sharpened and thrust itself like a spike into his brain.

And his whole body and mind filled with a quiet savage calm. He could feel the weight of the revolver in his pocket, the gun that young Hutchinson had given him back when he had been fairly certain that he would never really need it.

How many miles to Tarkington? Not more than ten minutes to the Tarkington road. Then another ten, or less, into town and up the hill to the house.

It was up to him now.

Him alone.

Everything was up to him.

The ambulance had come and gone, gone with the half-alive burden that had once been Chief Theron Diehl. Wallace Heckman, his mind numb as if he were trapped in a walking trance without any desire to escape, wondered whether Leroy Farago had not slipped him some medicine in some underhanded manner in spite of his wishes. When he had first seen Theron Diehl, naked and mangled and kneeling in the gravel, he had told himself, quite calmly, that he had seen enough, he did not wish to see or hear anymore. Then he had recalled the defendant Boyd Ritchie's charges: that Diehl had beaten him and kicked him before taking him into town naked after making the apprehension in the woods. He had not believed the boy then; now he did. Which was not to say, *ipso facto,* that Ritchie should not be held accountable for what he had done tonight, last night, whenever it was or had been, regardless of whether or not he had been innocent of those original charges. No. Many hours ago now—time was hazy in his mind, but it was almost light, so the night was almost over—Wallace Heckman had made up his mind that, although he couldn't say at precisely which point in time, that he personally would see to that punishment. He could not afford to wait and rely on due judicial process; he'd mete out the only kind of punishment that someone like that degenerate deserved. And as he had listened to the talk of the police officers around him here, he had realized that any one of them would like to get the chance to do the job. Especially after they saw Diehl's foot in that steel trap. Well, he didn't intend to give anyone that opportunity. But he knew, too, that he had to be sly, he had to play a very cautious game.

He was standing quite still, which he knew would fool them all, but he was listening and observing. There was something that he should be doing, he knew he should be somewhere else, but since he didn't know exactly where or even why, he contented himself with listening to Leroy's report to the young officer who had been so kind to him earlier. And then Hutchinson—*that* was his name: Ben Hutchinson!—asked whether the doctor thought Diehl *would* survive. Leroy said that if he were Diehl, he wouldn't want to. He had given orders for the staff to prepare for emergency surgery and now he must phone a certain surgeon to go to the hospital at once.

Leroy only nodded to him as he went by, on his way to the officer's car to make his call—what the hell was that policeman's name and why did he keep forgetting it?—but he didn't mind because he knew that this cataleptic state was only a ruse, only a way to fool everyone so they wouldn't suspect he had the .25 automatic in his pocket.

In the calm dead center of his mind—it was like the still eye at the center of the hurricane—Wallace Heckman held the knowledge, the certainty, that when the time came, he would be the one to do what had to be done. But he was forgetting something else. What?

Where Boyd Ritchie was.

That was it.

He knew, yet he didn't know.

And what could he do if he didn't know where Boyd Ritchie was?

It would come to him. If he was very quiet and still and if he didn't struggle in his mind, it would come to him.

He could hear one of the older officers talking to Ben Hutchinson—now he had the name, he had to hold onto it, for some odd reason it was important that he hold onto that boy's name! They had found most of the chief's clothes, but his Stetson was missing and also the tunic of his uniform. His pearl-handled Colt was also missing and with it the gun belt.

"Now here's a mind bender," the older man said, but Wallace Heckman did not turn around to look; he only waited, staring out over the pond at the cloud of mist that was beginning to lift. "A hand mike and a speaker. The wire was strung in the branches of the trees. Looks to me like it was rigged so somebody over there behind that stone wall, where we found the mike, could talk into it and his voice'd be heard coming out over here in the lane. More goddamned shenanigans, but maybe it worked, who knows? But that's not the half. Look what's in this case from the truck, just look. Wigs, vials of God knows what, mustaches, nitro caps, Christ knows. I ask you, Ben: is there anything our psycho didn't think of?"

But the officer's young voice only replied: "The question is: what will he think of next? Or maybe *who* will he think of next?"

And Wallace Heckman knew. It came to him then, on the instant. Of course. Fletcher Briggs was the only one left.

Ergo.

Ergo, he would go to Briggs' house, as he had done earlier; only this time he would stop and go in.

Only he didn't have his car here. It was parked—where was it parked? He had been driving it earlier. It was a Buick. Last year's model. It was two-tone: gold and black. Or had he, for some reason, been driving Kay's Opel tonight?

Kay. If she had done what he asked her to do, he would not be here. And she would not be where she was. Why hadn't it occurred to him to get a lift back to town in the ambulance? Then he could see Kay. He had to explain, make her understand that there was only one way he could to prove to Dennis—

Dennis. He didn't want to think of Dennis now.

He couldn't bear to think of him or to see him.

But Dennis would know. Dennis would know for all time how much his father really loved him—once he did what he had to do now. If the child had any doubts, ever, he'd know. He'd also know, for all time, the kind of man, real man, his father was. A boy needed that, had to have—

Now he'd lost the thread of thought again. Where *was* he going? Why was he walking away from the pond and up to the road, Echo Valley Road? He'd never get a ride on Echo Valley Road. It ended a few hundred yards farther on the right. And it was miles—

he had no idea how many miles—into Tarkington in the other direction. Who'd pick up a man walking alone on a country road? Tonight. Tonight, of all the nights in the—

Then he saw a car. Not a police vehicle, an ordinary little car, a Volks. But as he quickened his steps, he saw that two people stood beside it. Both short and shadowy and delicate-looking in the thick grayness. And they were holding each other. Not moving. Just standing there locked in an embrace that seemed to have no passion or desire in it—only an ineffable tenderness that caused his throat to close.

But he could not allow this, he could not allow anything to change his mind. His course of action. He had to be cautious, circumspect, otherwise someone, one of those angry officers, would get there first, get where?

He'd remember. He walked along the road, in the direction opposite to the one in which the Volkswagen was headed, along the edge of woods. He had his plan clear in his mind. If he circled the pond, he could cross through a field or two beyond it—oh, he knew this country out here, he'd lived here all his life, after all—and in a brief time he'd arrive on Wooster Road, which also led into town. He turned off and into the woods.

He'd walk. He could do it. Hell, he'd walked farther. And he'd always prided himself on his strength, his stamina, physical and psychological. He didn't want their help. Or need it. Theirs or anyone's. Oh, they'd miss him, back there at the pond, Leroy would miss him first, and they'd wonder, they might even instigate a search, but by then he'd be around the pond and crossing the patterned meadows and fields, he sort of hated doing this, pulling this trick on Leroy, Leroy *had* tried to be kind, but Leroy didn't understand, he wanted to take him into the hospital, he'd nagged him for an hour in the courthouse, not comprehending what had to be done, and of course he couldn't tell him, if anyone knew they'd try to stop him and nobody could stop him now.

He emerged from the woods and paused to listen. The frogs were harrumphing in the pond and birds chattered in the trees and, from a distant meadow, he could make out the friendly greeting of a lark.

Careful to keep the trees between himself and the view from the far end of the pond, he walked on, he had never felt stronger or more at peace, he felt very composed, very still inside, the way he imagined a person in a coma might feel if that person could nevertheless know what he was doing and what was going on around him and what he was going to do.

He climbed a stone wall and started across an expanse of field, feeling the ground beneath his shoes giving way in soggy, sucking softness so that each step made a sound. But he couldn't let this stop him. Not now. It couldn't be more than half a mile to Wooster Road.

But weeds and wetness seemed to gather around his ankles, pulling him down, and when he turned to look back, he could see only the wall of pines between him and the pond, which was some distance away now, and all around him a vapor was rising, a hazy shroud that remained low, like a dense, impenetrable cloud that slowed his body and closed off his view, oppressive, heavy, a weight on his shoulders, a wall of fog that was a solid obstruction against his steps, so that he came to feel giddy, then there followed a moment of panic and the peace inside was shattered, and instead he had the swift onrushing impression that he didn't know where he was, or how or why he had come here, or where he was going, and he couldn't see through the cloud while below his shoes were mired, and now he could hear the buzz of insects, louder than any birds' cries, swarms of insects attacking, buzzing and whizzing and droning, they were on his face, in his eyes, stinging and biting, up his nostrils, in his ears, while all the while he was being sucked down no matter how he braced his legs or set his will, he didn't know where he was and, worse, what direction he should go, if he could go, but he seemed drawn inexorably down and he wasn't moving forward, he was standing, he'd had no idea there was a marsh here, not marsh, no, swamp, there was slimy water over his shoes, sludge around his ankles and he could hear himself trying to breathe as he felt himself going down into the muck, the quagmire of ooze and filth, the primordial slime, and he thought of using the gun then, three shots, SOS the world over, they'd hear and come, but if he fired the gun, then they'd know he had it, they'd take it away, then he couldn't get to Ritchie, the degenerate, no, he refused to fire the gun, he set his will as he had done all his life, he'd get out of this on his own even if his strength was giving out, it was light, it was morning, when had he slept last, his muscles were weak, limp, he hadn't eaten since lunch, it was almost another day, yesterday's lunch, he'd missed dinner, he couldn't remember why, but his mind was made up, he'd get through to Wooster Road and he'd walk all that way and he wouldn't call for help because nobody but Wallace Heckman could do or would do what he had to do alone, if only he could remember what it was now, if only his damned mind wouldn't keep playing these rotten filthy *tricks* on him!

He was on his knees. How had he gone down onto his knees? How long ago? He struggled to stand up. The muck soaked his legs, pulled at them. But hell, anyone could walk through a swamp. It wasn't quicksand.

Only he didn't have the strength.

Perhaps if he waited a few minutes. Perhaps if he rested.

He saw a huge gray stone half-submerged, covered with green slime, but above the wetness. If he could place his head on the rock, only for a few minutes so he could get his breath, allow the strength to seep back into his muscles, into his mind, his will.

Then he heard the crows above the steamy fastness of the enveloping fog: *Cawr-cawr-cawr-cawr*. But he couldn't see them. Or even the sky. *Cawr-cawr-cawr*.

* * *

While she listened to the boy talk, her body huddled on the dusty floor of a corner in her attic studio, Willa Briggs wondered how it could possibly have come about that she had been hurled, with all the incredible shock of a world gone mad, into this alien jungle of blood and guns and absolute horror. Why, she and Fletcher had decided years ago, when they were first married, that they'd never have a gun in the house. Not in this century, in this country—what would be the need? But now there were two: the pistol with the mother-of-pearl handle that the boy held loosely in his right hand—she couldn't bear to look at the left one—and the uglier square-looking black gun lying on the window seat beside him as he sat with his eyes concentrated, for the most part, on the street and lawn and driveway below. He didn't need to point either one of them—had not, in fact, directed either of them at her since she had wakened to find him standing over her bed in the room below. In some contradictory way, his utter casualness with the weapons was more menacing than if he had a barrel leveled at her head.

Yet she was not shaking or quivering—the terror went deeper. It was a paralysis, cold and still, of body and spirit. She held the kimono about herself, legs drawn up beneath her on the gritty floor, the devastation of the large room, itself a result of her earlier shock and fury, seeming now only a part of the pattern of the night.

She was listening. He had taken off the blue police uniform jacket, but he still wore a wide bullet belt and a wide-brimmed cowboy hat tilted back from his face—which, she thought, looked ravaged and tense, drawn and very old in the half-light from the window in the gable. But his tone was cocky and young, blustering in a quiet way, a trifle thin as if the vocal cords were stretched too tight. It demanded attention. He had related what had taken place through the night—a tale of such violence and cruelty, himself always at its core, that her mind recoiled, twisted, struggled to distort what she knew to be true, to convert his boasts into lies, fiction, myth. But a cautious rational part of her mind recalled what Fletcher had told her—or had tried to make her believe, hours ago when she was getting drunk—and she knew that his facts coincided in crucial particulars with certain parts of the boy's story now.

Then, after detailing gruesomely what he had done to the chief of police before stealing that poor man's car to come here, he allowed the stream of words to come to a halt. Willa wondered why he had been so desperate to disgorge them. Then, at once, she knew.

But asked nevertheless: "Why are you telling me all this?"

He glanced at her. Grinned emptily. "You're not interested, ma'am?"

She knew: his ego demanded that someone know the whole story from his view. "If," she said, "you're trying to make sure you get full credit for all your brave acts, that means you won't use one of those guns on me."

The grin flickered. He squinted across and down at her. "Cool bitch."

Not cool—cold. But from fear. Fear she hoped he would not sense: she was *damned* if she'd give him that satisfaction! "Don't fret, little boy, I'll tell your whole filthy little saga to posterity—after you're quite dead."

The grin turned into a scowl. "I mean what I told the hubby on the phone, whore. If the pigs show out there, any red lights or sirens or tear gas before he does, the first bullet's for you. Or . . . or maybe I'll set the house on fire *first*."

He meant it. She had no doubt he meant every syllable. But she said, "Maybe I'm like you, little boy. Maybe *I* don't care, either."

But it was not true. When exactly had she started caring again? Was it when the boy had first demanded in fury, *Where are they? Where're the kids, the profes-*

sor, why aren't they here? In that first minute in the bedroom she had been given strength by her relief: they were not in the house, any of them, so he could not harm anyone but her. She did care. She had cared then, at once, and she still cared now and she knew, too, that when Fletcher came—she had no doubt whatever as to his coming—he would not bring Peggy and David, one or both.

The boy's rage as he had forced her off the bed and up the stairs to the studio so he could get a view of the street in front, had been so terrible and at the same time so pathetic that she had begun to wonder whether he was high on some drug or whether he was, just as possibly, insane. Which was why she had screamed the word to Fletcher on the phone.

The story of the night—along with his insistence on telling it—only hardened her suspicion into conviction. Leaving her where? What weapon was there against madness?

Her front teeth still ached, her puffed lips stung, and she still had the taste of blood on her tongue. He had struck her with the back of his hand—as much, she suspected, because she had called him insane as to prove to Fletcher that he meant business and to terrify him into coming home. She had realized this when she saw him rip the telephone wire from the wall in the upstairs hall and hurl the instrument, base and all, down the stairway to the front hall.

Insane.

What if that possibility had never occurred to him before? What if she had first suggested it, planting the poison of doubt in his mind. Leading to what?

"If you gave yourself up now," she heard her own composed voice saying, "you could probably get off completely, you know." Should she risk it? She said: "By pleading innocence of any crime by virtue of insanity."

He leaped up. He turned from the window. He stepped toward her, fast, and his leg gave way, he dropped to one knee, face contorting, and his eyes lost focus, went rabid, wild.

She glimpsed again the blackened hardened blood on the leg of his mud-splattered dungarees and, in that second, while the gun was pointed to the floor and he seemed oblivious as he writhed with pain, she had two conflicting impulses: to offer some sort of help for the agony he was in and, contrarily, to scramble to her feet, lunge for the black gun on the window seat, turn and fire straight into his head.

The compassion defeated her and she cursed herself for being a woman. His eyes cleared and he was glaring at her. It was too late.

He whispered, harshly: "Stop calling me little boy."

Had he meant to say to stop calling him insane?

He was close now. So close she could see the pallor under the dirt on his face, could see the torment behind the ferocity in his cold blue eyes.

"What," she asked, "do you call yourself, little boy? You don't call yourself a man, do you?"

He stood up, wincing, and hobbled away through the debris. "A free man!" he cried. And as her mind but not her eyes darted again to the odd-looking gun, he whirled to face her. "Free!" he exulted. "And a *man,* yes, only a man, a real man, could do what I did. Only free man alive! You want to know why, whore?" Then he leaned forward, eyes glittering. "Freedom is not giving a shit in hell what happens to you!" His voice dropped into a confidential hiss. "I made myself free. I freed myself, *tonight.*"

For the first time then helplessness—total, profound—took over inside her. And she was quivering, but not outwardly. Was that a form of madness itself—not to care what happened to you? If he didn't, really didn't, then how could Fletcher, the police, anyone, how could, what could—oh, God, if only she'd believed Fletcher, if only she had *listened* to him! She'd be in Boston now. And he—if anything happened to Fletcher now, it would be her fault.

Her head retreated between her folded shoulders. Forlornly, she heard herself ask: "What . . . what are you going to do to us?"

He went to his knees, both knees this time, and tilted his head to one side, the hat throwing a shadow over his face. "That bugs you, doesn't it?" She heard the satisfaction, saw it reflected too in his frenzied gaze as his lips curled into a faint smile. "Not knowing can really blow your mind, can't it?" He sat back on his haunches and she saw the left leg of dungarees redden freshly above the knee, but he ignored the wetness and the blood and the pain. He was too delirious in his power of torment. "Why don't you guess, whore? Take a guess."

She hesitated, considering: the only way she had reached him so far was by suggesting what apparently he had come to fear himself. So she said, quietly, conversationally: "I'm sure I haven't the faintest idea. How should I know how a deranged mind works?"

A moment. His eyes closed. Why was she taunting him? To what end? If she goaded him into shooting her, what then? *Unless we got that straight, you're going to come in here and find a piece of meat*. He had been torturing Fletcher; he had to make Fletcher suffer, too. But, if Fletcher loved her—if, if, if—then coming in to find her dead—oh, hell, she didn't know, anything, whether Fletcher did love her, why he was coming, what would be better or worse, whether her dying might save him, whether he was coming—she was going to pieces, she couldn't go on like this! *"What are you going to do?"* she screamed.

He opened his eyes then, and they looked pleased and gentle. "You're blowing your cool. Ma'am." And then his eyes went sad. "If you don't want to guess, I'll tell you." He took a long deep breath, stood up, limped to the window seat and sat staring out the window and down on the street. "You listen now, please. I'll tell you." His tone became a pleasant singsong, his lips curving around the words. "I'm not going to rape you. Truth is: I don't even *want* to rape you. Even if I am a convicted rapist. What we're going to have here, we're going to have a picnic, ma'am, a family picnic, all-American style. And me—I'm not going to *assault* anyone." He paused and she discovered that her own eyes were fixed on his face, as if mesmerized. "I read a book. I had plenty of time, where I've been. I read a lot of books. Ma'am." He paused without looking at her, but she could not have replied had she wanted to. "They said what every son really wants, ever since those Greeks, is to screw his own mother. I never had a mother, so I don't know. But you must know all this." The lips curled again into another smile. "You've been to college. I almost made it to college once. Something came up." Then his eyes took on a dream-like expression as if his mind were picturing some scene or action unimaginable to her. "Those books also said every father, deep in his inner inner, wants to ball his daughter. Only they lie about it. Deny it. You ever notice that? Everybody lies. Whole world of hypocrites." Her mind flinched away from the scene that had begun to take shape in it. "You've heard the term 'motherfucker,' haven't you? Ma'am? Where I've been, I heard it all the time. Motherfucker."

She had not thought herself capable of more shock. She had been wrong.

"You getting the picture, ma'am? We're all going to sit and watch. Maybe clap our hands if it's a good performance."

He seemed to wait then. When she was capable, she spoke. "No way." It was, she realized, one of Peggy's phrases. "No way."

"Then you die. Ma'am. Anyone doesn't play the game—somebody else dies. Like husband—daughter—son—wife—mother—father—brother—sister. One by one. Now . . . you got the picture? Ma'am?"

She had it. She couldn't move. Or speak again. She had the picture.

"And afterward, whoever's left will remember it all his life. That's why the hubby-daddy's not going to die. He's going to live—to remember."

And she could feel hatred in her bloodstream, throbbing, surging—a poison so virulent and overpowering that it was not human.

She was staring at his face. She was watching his mind, his soul, absorbing the loathing that she knew was on her face, in her eyes. And she realized, as the depths of shock deepened even more inside, that her own expression of horror and hate fed some terrible sick need in him.

Hate.

He demanded it. Consumed it. Devoured it. As if he could never get enough, rouse enough, to satisfy some ferocious hunger that nothing else—kindness or respect or pity or even love—could ever appease.

Against this craving, she was helpless. Against this inhuman subversion of instinct itself, what could she do? Or anyone?

Fletcher, don't come. Please. Don't come.

The blood was thick and red on his leg now. Oozing out again from whatever wound lay beneath the cloth.

She hoped he would lose so much blood that he would pass out.

No. She hoped that sitting there watching her and the street, he would bleed to death.

Die.

Let him.

They were sitting on the half-moon stone parapet at the overlook, their backs to the highway, legs dangling, watching the hazy clouds of steam and fog hanging low and thick in the valleys but lifting off the stone-fenced fields. In the distance, although the sun was not yet showing, the foliage of the hills was beginning to glow yellow and brown and gold.

David had been wishing he had a joint on him, or only a few crumbs of grass, because his nerves had been leaping crazylike ever since their father had driven off, barking orders. At the same time he was sort of relieved that he didn't have anything to smoke. Whatever was to come, he'd probably be better off, like the books and articles and his mother said, facing it straight. He'd begun to wonder whether he could kick that pot scene altogether. Damned if he wanted to turn into a hashhead like some of the dudes and chicks he knew.

"Nobody's going to pick us up for hours," Peggy said. "We'll never make it all the way to Boston."

"You heard what the man said."

"I'm going back."

"Dad told us to—"

"I *know* what he said, David. But I'd go insane in Boston, not knowing what's happening. And all alone in Grandmother's clutches, what big ears you have." She pivoted and lifted her legs and stood up. "You coming?"

Without waiting for his reply, she strode onto the pavement of the highway as he twisted around to look after her. She crossed the curbed grassy island between the traffic lanes and stopped to peer along the road. There were no cars in sight, either direction. He dropped off the parapet and followed. He was glad she'd made the decision; he, too, had to know.

Howells Street.

The station wagon turned the corner.

The radio had announced a short time ago, without giving details, that Boyd Ritchie might be wounded.

There were no police vehicles parked in front of the house or in the driveway. Fletcher Briggs felt a wave of relief break over him, then wondered why. What could he do alone? What could he even hope to do?

Whatever score, real or imagined, that Boyd Ritchie had to settle was with him. Not with Willa. If he could somehow—

1127. The familiar house: old, large, high, gabled, in need of paint. He had never thought of loving a house. Now he did.

Don't, Fletcher. Fletcher, darling, don't come, please, please—

But he was here. He was here because she was here.

Willa. Who loved him. What else did her frantic cry mean?

—please, he's insane, don't—

Insane? Yes. Who but a madman could do what Boyd Ritchie had already done?

He brought the station wagon to a halt in the driveway. Only his little MG was there. The garage doors were closed. He switched off the motor and walked to the garage, aware that he was probably being watched from inside.

I don't care, what can you do about that, I don't care!

He looked through the small front window of the garage. A strange dark car occupied the space. A car with lights perched on its roof and a siren on the side.

You can't kill a dead man!

But as he moved toward the spacious porch, all doubt left his mind: he could kill.

He probably would have to.

He heard the mockingbird in the old elm. Willa's bird. Whose antics gave her such pleasure. Now playfully echoing a two-note chirrup from across the quiet morning street.

On the porch he took the gun from his pocket. Examined it. Flipped off the safety catch. He had told Ben Hutchinson he'd know how to use it if the time should come. But he had wondered then whether he could bring himself to use it.

At the front door, he paused. His tired mind gave in, for what amounted to only a split second, to sheer overwhelming desperation. Not fear: blank utter despair.

Then, with the gun in one hand, he unlocked the door with his own key and pushed it inward, slowly.

The telephone lay on the floor of the front hall in two pieces, its wire like a tangled looped root or thin black snake. Fletcher wondered again: had he been wise to pass those police officers at the roadblocks without stopping?

The gun was in his hand. Heavy. Gripped. Lifted.

He called her name. Once.

As soon as he saw Boyd Ritchie—on the instant of first sight—he would pull the trigger. No talk. No bargaining. He'd pull the trigger over and over, he'd empty the damned gun. And he'd take pleasure in doing it.

He called again: "Willa—"

He recognized the savagery in himself for what it was: the craving in him, the fixed absolute need, for revenge. For all Ritchie had done. For striking Willa. For whatever else—

He shouted: "Willa, are you here?"

He meant: are you alive?

His words rumbled through the house, reverberated back.

Then an empty silence.

"We're up here, prick. In your messy attic, man. Together."

His impulse was to rush up the two flights of stairs at once, charge like a maddened animal in the jungle. But another jungle instinct held him: caution, cunning—a prowling catlike stealth.

"Willa. Are you all right?"

He waited.

And then he heard: "Why don't you come up and see, Briggs?"

He didn't move a muscle. "No point," he called. Knowing that Ritchie would understand, knowing that Ritchie had to guarantee the bait to make the kill.

"Fletcher!" She was alive. "Don't. Don't come up here!"

The note of frenzy in her scream carried him, regardless of will, to the foot of the stairway. Then he began to climb, measuring each step, looking up.

Quiet inside, worn, lifting one tired leg and then the other. Realizing how many steps rose between him and the upstairs hall. How many more between the hall and the studio above it. All thought of retreat had gone from his mind.

With his thumb he pulled back the hammer of the

gun. There was a click. It was the only sound in the house.

At the top of the attic stairs, he came to a stop. If he took another step, his head would appear above the floor of the studio. If Ritchie was waiting to shoot him, it would all be over once he took that step. What then of Willa?

He spoke her name.

He waited.

Then heard: "You may as well come up, Fletch." The note of resignation was strong—and in itself alarming in her. "I don't know what the little boy has in mind, but it's not killing. At least, not yet."

"See, prick? She's convinced. Come into my parlor, Mr. Fly. I don't want to have to kill anybody. Not my style."

Well, if Ritchie didn't want to kill, Fletcher Briggs did. He took the last few steps in two long strides, clutching the gun, turning and directing it at once, and then stood staring.

She was upright in the middle of the long room. Hands tied above her head. She was drawn up by the rope of the block and tackle mechanism he had rigged for her work. And she was naked. Not quite hanging. He caught the fright in her eyes, then he saw blood caked redly at the corner of her mouth, saw the puffed lips. And his gaze searched the large havoc-filled dusty room.

As soon as he saw any movement, he would shoot. He couldn't look at Willa. Didn't dare.

But the movement, when it came, stopped him. A figure stepped from behind her body, stepped defiantly into the clear. Right arm outstretched, almost level with his shoulder. And at the end of that arm, a revolver with a long barrel. The end of the barrel was at her side, its tip buried in the soft fold of flesh at her left breast.

It took all his strength not to blast. But could he be sure, could he shoot the off-balance figure without hitting Willa, was he a good enough shot to—

"It's a forty-five," Boyd Ritchie said, very quietly. "A Colt six-shooter, man. Makes a big hole."

Diehl's. Then Diehl had to be dead. And Ritchie was wearing his hat. And Ritchie's left leg was stiff and soaked with blood. And his left arm dangled. And at the end of it there was a hunk of black charred meat.

"You pull your trigger, prick, and I pull my trigger. What they call a reflex action, man. You can save yourself if you're a good enough shot. But when you kill me, you'll be killing your wife. Got the picture, Counselor?"

Cawr-cawr-cawr-cawr—

Harsh, insistent, nerve-racking. The sound of crows. They seemed to be flying in all directions. He no longer heard the steady shine and buzz of insects, which in a vague way, he knew were attacking him, stinging and biting, but he didn't feel them. And once in a while he could hear, like a cry from another world, the sharp, swift *bob-white* of a quail. Where, though, were the doves? Once there had been mourning doves. He lay limply, still without strength to pull himself up out of the muck and reeds, to stand upright and walk again.

All I got to say is just this, listen. The kid liked it. The sweet little bugger really dug it.

He couldn't let a swamp defeat him. Physical weakness was always only a weakness in the mind. He was tired. Even his mind was tired. But he had to get out of here. So he could kill that lying depraved degenerate. He knew that's what he had to do, but his body wouldn't respond—which meant that his mind was playing tricks again because he had always known and believed that a man was a free agent, all law was based on that, free to choose right from wrong and to determine his own fate, and if he decided wrong, then he must take the consequences. It had always been as simple as that and it was still that simple, damn it, and in a few more minutes, just a very few, he'd pull himself together, clench his mind and pull out of this muck and go to—where had he been going?

He wouldn't have been walking across the fields if he hadn't been heading somewhere.

But where?

It'd come to him.

He was wet all over now. Soaked through. The slimy ooze was inside his suit, in his hair, his nostrils, mouth.

Then if he was soaked, so was the gun in his pocket. His little nickel-plated Smith and Wesson .25 automatic.

He felt an instant's panic. Would it fire? After being submerged in water?

It was damned important that it fire. But at whom was he going to shoot it? Where?

He shut his eyes against the light that seemed to be growing brighter, cutting like slivers of silver through the fog. If only he wasn't so weak—

—The bus was going fast, rocking through the rolling countryside at night, and everyone was singing, it seemed such a long time ago, yet it was now, too, everyone was singing, that was it, he knew, they were celebrating their victory, the last game of the season, at night, under the lights, and he'd made a leaping interception and had run for a touchdown, now they were all full of beer, their voices filling the bus, raucous, masculinely loud and rough and deep as they shouted friendly obscenities across the aisle and down the dim length of the jouncing bus, and Bebe Bartlett was beside him in the rear seat, no one else, only the two of them, and Bebe kept clapping him on the back and drinking more beer and he could hear the tin caps popping up and down the bus, and then he felt something on his leg, inside his thigh, and high, and moving, and he glanced at Bebe, startled, saw Bebe's thick-set brute-jawed face half smiling straight ahead, but the thing remained on his leg, the thing that had to be a hand, and at first he was amazed, he didn't know *what* the hell to do, he couldn't very well just get up and go find another seat, then it was too late anyway because Bebe's arm was around his back, holding hard, no one had ever warned him about Bebe, usually somebody at least warned you, and then they were passing through a small town and there was a great hullabaloo out the window—wake, up, wake up, the British are coming, you sleepy fucking patriots!—and more laughing, but in the passing streetlights he could see Bebe's face, close, and he was not laughing, his eyes hard and intent and very dark and pointed, and the hand down below was on his prong now and Bebe's face was close, and when the dark of the countryside returned, the hand was clasping his dingus, moving up and down, and he was having an erection, with Bebe's handsome, young, athletic-looking face closer still, then Bebe's thick lips closing over his own and the hand moving, oh, God, what was happening, what was he doing, why was he so excited, what the hell was happening, how could he be enjoying this, how could he be opening his mouth, allowing Bebe's tongue to—

Cawr-cawr!

What was that sound? Birds?

Where was he?

He forced his eyes open and twisted his neck. Fog. A thick gray vapor—lifting. He could see it swirling all around him. Like a pall rising.

Then, from the distance, he heard his name being called.

Several voices. From different directions.

He felt something against his hand and looked down. A brown snake slithered by in the brackish water.

He tried to call out. His throat was locked. But he had to shout. They had to hear him. He couldn't stay here. He didn't even know what time it was. He had something to do, somewhere to go. He wasn't sure what or where.

But he could no longer lie here. Remembering.

Remembering what?

It had been a dream.

He'd never been on that bus.

The night he snagged the pass and ran, broken-field and without interference, exactly sixty-three yards for the touchdown that won the championship for Tarkington High.

But that hadn't happened, on the bus; that was only a dream, some distortion in his mind, hallucination. He'd never felt that way about a man, another man, not him, ever, then or since. Then why was he quivering all over, what was he afraid of, what had he always been so afraid of?

He stood up.

And heard a voice. It was not Bebe Bartlett's voice.

Bebe Bartlett had been killed in Korea. He remembered the funeral. It had been snowing.

Then he remembered. Judge T. H. Stuttaford. Who was also dead. His grave.

And now it all came flooding back. Very clear. All that had happened. Including what that deviate had done to poor little Dennis.

He knew, too, what *he* had to do now. In town. On Howells Street.

He called out; this time he heard the sound of his own voice. It was as dry and ugly as the *cawr-cawr* of those damned crows.

But there was a response. Not too far away. He saw shadows moving. Then he recognized the voice. Ben Hutchinson's. He'd been trying to think of that young man's name all morning; now it came to his mind just like that!

"Over here!" he shouted. But it was not really a shout—more of a cry.

He could remember now. His mind had stopped playing tricks, thank God.

But now his voice was failing him.

He had to make them hear him. He tried to call out again. Only a low sound came, as hoarse and harsh as the senseless cawing of the crows wheeling above.

* * *

Looking at her husband's face since he had come up the stairs—haggard, lined, years older—Willa Briggs had felt her heart, already a knot, twisting tighter still as the minutes had passed. There was more, though, in that familiar face now gone unfamiliar: something brutal and pitiless, even savage in those normally gentle, self-mocking eyes. When she first saw him, it had been all she could do to keep from crying out: *Fletcher, what have they done to you?*

But, as if he had plucked it from her mind, that was what he had asked her first—in a tight, low voice packed with pain and anguish and fear. And she had spit blood to the floor and demanded with fury and contempt what a little boy like this could do to anyone. Which had caused the end of the iron gun to prod her breast, to dig into a rib, hard. And had caused Boyd Ritchie to say, *I've done plenty, whore. Ma'am. Last stop right here. You get the honor, Counselor. You and yours.* From what he had told her earlier, she knew why as soon as Fletcher had appeared, he had stepped from behind her dangling form. To hide there for protection would violate that romanticized picture of himself that she had come to realize he carried in that mad brain of his. It would not fit what he called his style.

Then Fletcher had barked: *What do you want of us, Ritchie?*

First, man, like they say in those Western flicks: hand over the shootin' iron, pardner.

A gun. It looked so incongruous and improbable in Fletcher's hand that she wondered how she could have known all along, as she had, that he would not come in without one—if he came at all. Just as she now knew, waiting for his reply, that he would not give it up and place them both completely at the mercy of that sick and cruel mind.

"What makes you think I'm as crazy as you are?" Fletcher asked and extended his arm to look down its length, the revolver not trembling in the slightest.

But she knew the word "crazy" would strike home: she felt the hard, deep thrust of the barrel rim against her breast again and her stomach tightened still more and she went faint. But she refused to flinch, even to turn her head. She kept her eyes, instead, on Fletcher's face over the extended arm. Grim, clenched, it looked implacable with an almost brutish determination. And she felt some small part of herself relax a fraction. Fletcher was here now. Fletcher would do the job.

"I haven't killed anyone yet," the kid named Ritchie said then. "Which doesn't mean I won't, man."

"He's lying," she said quickly, wondering whether she had to warn Fletcher, whether he already knew. "Maybe he hasn't killed anyone himself, but he's forced others to do it for him. He's been boasting about it."

The young man blurted a short laugh with no joy in it, but a bitter satisfaction. "On target, whore-lady. Which doesn't mean I won't. Or can't." This time he prodded her flesh so hard that she saw the action of his arm reflected in the tightening of the lines around Fletcher's eyes. "So . . . hand over the thirty-eight, man."

"You fire, Ritchie," Fletcher said, "and you are dead. Reflex actions work both ways." Then he added, "Man."

"I'm going to die anyway, Briggs. Look at me. Like I told your whore here, I don't give a shit about dying."

"That may be true," she heard herself telling Fletcher swiftly, "but he won't let that happen till he settles his score with you, whatever that is. If killing me would do it, he's had that opportunity for some time now."

"You got yourself a smart-ass wife, Briggs. Pretty, too. Slim and trim." The gun pressed harder, but she refused to twist away. "Some ass. Some cunt. I been that route before you got home, Counselor."

She expected Fletcher's calm to shatter then, but instead he shook his head, once. "You're not going to goad me into shooting you. You're not going to force me to kill my own wife."

The pressure on her breast relaxed. And she was afraid to turn her head as she waited.

Finally Ritchie said, "You're a smart-ass, too." There was a sort of puzzlement in his tone. "You don't want to save your own? All you have to do is pull the trigger, you're home free."

Then her own composure cracked. "Shoot him, Fletcher, kill him, do it, it's the only way, kill him, *now!*"

But even as the echo of her cry died through the house below, she knew he wouldn't. Couldn't. Not if he loved her. And if he did not love her, he would not be here.

"Shh" was all he said, very softly.

Ritchie stepped back, still holding the gun level at her side, and said, "Man, don't you see? If you really love this twat like that, that only makes it better." He almost shouted: *"Wilder!* What're we waiting for? Get those kids up here."

This time her heart stopped. Dead. But only for an instant. Because she knew, without studying Fletcher's face, that he had not brought David and Peggy.

Boyd Ritchie lifted his voice again: "Oh, kiddies, child-*ren!* Time for the picnic and ice cream! Time for fun and games!" Then harshly, low, to Fletcher: "Get them up here, prick!"

"What children?" Fletcher's tone was mild.

And in the stunned silence she asked: "How are they, Fletch?"

His rusty mustache curled up at one end, slightly. "Fine, darling. And miles away."

Then Ritchie's voice spoke. It was a low whisper: "You crossed me again. You did it to me again."

And now she was certain that he would shoot. She braced herself for the thunder and the nothingness, her eyes fixed on Fletcher's, wishing she could thank him and wondering how she could ever have doubted his love.

"You think it's safe, pretty young thing like you hitchhiking this way?" He was a fat man with a pouchy face, high-colored pink, and a bulbous nose set below shrewd beady brown eyes. He had adjusted the rear-view mirror so he could see her in the back seat while he drove. "Bad old man like me loose on the roads this time of morning. Where you two coming from anyway?"

"Boston," Peggy said before David, beside the man in the front seat, could open his mouth and blow it. "Cambridge, actually. Harvard, you know."

"Oh? And where you going *to?*"

"Tarkington."

"Sightseeing?"

"Nothing worth seeing in Tarkington. I've lived there all my life."

"Hell there ain't. That's what I'm doing—sightseeing. If they'll let me in. Heard about all the brouhaha on the TV last night, radio this morning. Thought I'd take a look-see for myself. That what you two up to?"

"Right on," David said. "I'm a fire freak."

"And me," Peggy said, "I'm a bone freak. Once somebody strews bones around, I'd travel a thousand miles to get there. And human bones—wow, that really blows my mind."

"Yeah?"

"Sure. What kind of freak are you?"

"You're putting me on. You're too pretty a gal to put a man like me on. It gives me ideas."

"She's my wife," David said flatly.

"Your?"

"You heard me. She's pregnant, too."

"Twins, we hope," Peggy said.

"Jesus."

"So drive carefully, please," David said.

"Jesus. Listen, if you live in Tarkington, maybe that'd get me in, past the cops. If I'm taking you home."

"Her folks live on Howells Street."

"You tell me where to turn."

"Next exit ramp."

"Fire freak. Bone freak. Jesus, you young people today sure have a way of looking at things."

"That's how we survive," Peggy said.

His whole left side was paralyzed, yet not numb—a mass of throbbing, grinding pain. There was no way now of knowing where the pain from the burned hand stopped and the pain from the bullet wound began. His right leg still supported his weight, but for how long? And his right hand still held the gun, his outstretched right arm aching with tiredness, but he knew what would happen if he lowered the gun or took if off the bitch even for a second. Fletcher Briggs meant business—look at those narrow, burning eyes, bright as blue ice, the bastard.

And he'd done it again, crossed him again, conned him on the phone into thinking he was so scared he'd bring the kids. Just what he'd always done, the prick, what everyone had always done, only he couldn't do it now, wouldn't get away with it, now, right at the end, the final payoff, it couldn't go this way! Not *now!*

The later it got, the more chance the pigs would show. But they'd show anyway, he was done for anyway—

God, it would be so easy to just pull the trigger. Wouldn't that be enough for Briggs—to see his wife blown apart in front of him?

No.

It was not what he'd planned. And it was not enough.

But nothing was going according to plan now. When had it begun to foul up? Why?

Briggs.

"Let her go," Briggs was saying now, and his voice penetrated the pain, "let her go, Ritchie, and I'll give you the gun."

"Fuck off."

Briggs as hero. Briggs as wife lover. Shit.

All the hate of his life had come together in him now. Everything that had happened, all he had become—it all came back to Briggs! And now here he was making suggestions again, trying another snow job—

He had to think of something else. Boyd Ritchie always had a backup plan.

But what? With that black hole of a gun barrel steady on him. Not wavering, not shaking even once, and that arm stretched out with those goddamn wild-beast eyes behind.

And he couldn't take the gun off her, he couldn't even—

It was hopeless. It was all hopeless.

All because Briggs had to prove his lie—prove he loved her. "It's a lie!" he heard that same strange high-pitched voice yelling. "All lies! *Hypocrite!*" He had to break the impulse to turn, go to the window, smash it out, scream down the street, to all of them: "Respectability! Hypocrisy!" Then he realized he'd shouted it anyway, without moving. What he wanted to do, had to do, was finish the job.

But he was trapped. He couldn't even make it to the window. And even if he could, once he was that far, Briggs might take a chance and fire.

Briggs had trapped him.

Now Briggs was just waiting. With those eyes. That black gun fixed on him. Christ, it was enough to make a man break down and cry.

Stymied. Outsmarted. Shafted again.

"You want a way out?" Fletcher Briggs asked then.

The bastard had been reading his mind! "I don't want anything from you!"

"There's a station wagon parked down there. The keys are in it. Take it and go."

You double-faced snaky son of a bitch. "I'm not through here yet."

"I think you are. Finished. And you know it, too."

"I said I'm not through here yet. You haven't had yours!"

But what? Where was the backup?

"For God's sake," the woman shrieked, "oh, for God's sake, haven't you done enough? You're insane. You take pleasure in this, you're crazy, insane, *insane!*"

He lifted the gun and brought it down across her skull. Then he realized he had the aim off her for that one startling instant, so he took a half step to the sagging body, its knees bent so that it was hanging now, unmoving, no longer calling him insane. He fixed the point of the barrel at the temple of the head that had fallen to one side, its black hair already matting with blood on top.

He realized that, even as he acted, he had been expecting to hear an explosion from the other gun. But even now, none came.

"She keeps saying I'm crazy," he told Briggs. "I just wanted to prove it."

And he waited again.

But Briggs said, this time in a rasping whisper: "I told you—you're not going to force me to kill my wife."

"You want to beg? Any bets, you smug, phony motherfucker?"

"Where do you want to take him, Doctor?"

"I know where he belongs, Lieutenant. He's in shock and bitten to hell all over, but—"

"Hospital?"

"I don't think he has a choice now."

"Full speed and siren?"

"No, hell, no. Even in his state he's liable to get up and jump out. And I hope to God I never hear another siren as long as I live."

"Larry, drive the Congressman and Dr. Farago to

the emergency entrance, Memorial Hospital. Fast, but quiet."

"Sure, Ben . . . I mean: yes, sir, right away."

She returned from the dark silent depths into electric brilliance, blinding and startling, a shutter clicking in her mind. She knew at once where she was and why she was hanging here naked, and all the cruel and battering sensations of the morning attacked her in a furious rush. The top of her head felt wet and her whole cranium was slowly filling with a surging pain that was almost blinding. But she could see Fletcher's face: the torture there, the racking indecision, frustration. "I meant it, Fletcher," she said. "Kill the revolting little bastard and get it over with."

And then she realized her mistake: Boyd Ritchie's face, already somewhat misshapen by pain, twisted into a grin. Exactly what he wanted, what he thrived on: her hate. Anyone's hate.

In some obscure crevice of her mind, an idea took vague shape. He needed to die, needed punishment, and he had used his need to punish *them*. To render them helpless against him. Now his fixed and vacant smile reminded her: this was his way to make sure Fletcher lived to suffer the rest of his life. For killing her.

But if it was important, vital, to him, that his victims live in order to look back and suffer, if that's why he had not intentionally killed any of them—then what about himself?

"Go ahead, Fletcher. He'll be dead then, too, and a few people will be alive to hate him, very few and not for long, and he'll be forgotten."

"A few? This whole goddamn town! The world. They'll hate me the way they do right now. The way *you* do!"

Was Fletcher listening? Did he understand?

"What difference," she asked, aware of her own cunning, "if you're not alive to know it?"

And then she heard Fletcher say: "Make no mistake about that, Ritchie. You won't be around to know what happens. You'll be just another two-bit psycho killer in a few newspaper stories, just a *name,* and pretty soon not even that. Because you'll be *dead.* And when you're dead, what kind of satisfaction then, Ritchie?"

Hearing Fletcher's hard and driving voice, she felt herself relax again, just slightly, along the edges. He did understand.

And Ritchie's face, frowning into hers, had lost its grin. "Man, they'll be talking about last night for years. Nobody ever did anything like—" But he broke off and withdrew the point of the gun barrel from her head.

"Maybe," Fletcher said, "maybe. But what good'll that do you? When you're dead, you don't know anything. And if you don't *know,* what the hell good is it all, everything you did last night? Nobody'll give a damn." Then he was hurrying. "Just the work of some nut. No pattern, no reason, he just killed a few people, tortured a few more, went on a rampage, burned down a house, a factory." Contempt colored his tone and she was afraid to look up at him. "Who's going to tell them *why* you did it? Not me. Nobody's figured it out yet, you know. There won't be a damned soul to tell your side of it and you'll be forgotten inside a week. Just another ex-con who blew his top, some smart-ass kid who didn't know what he was doing anyway."

"It's not going to be like that." Ritchie spoke softly and his gaze seemed to go past her, into the distance. "That's not the way—"

She almost allowed her body to sag, to let the rope above support her weakness, when she heard a car door slam outside, then another. And voices.

Whose voices?

She looked across at Fletcher again—and saw an impulse on his face that had not been there before. The impulse to fire now, before Ritchie's gun could move again.

But Ritchie had also sensed this or read it reflected in her face; he jammed the point of the gun into her side again, hard, and held it there.

And she saw the impulse wither in Fletcher's gaze. He swiveled and backed toward the window, not lowering the gun. He glanced out.

And then he did turn away for a split second and smashed a pane high in the window with the barrel of his gun, which he immediately swung back into position. Half-facing the room, he shouted: "Peggy!"

Peggy? Willa stiffened.

"David! Listen to me."

God. Oh, God, no.

Then Ritchie laughed. Gleefully he said: "Picnic after all. Family picnic, fun and games. Get them up here, Briggs!"

Fletcher appeared not to have heard. "David," he called, "listen now. Take your sister and get the hell away from here."

"Screw you, man. If they don't—"

"No questions. Go next door and wait. Nothing else. *Nothing!"*

She watched the indecision distorting Ritchie's face, the wild trapped panic and disbelief. He screeched: "If they don't come up here, you're both dead. *Both!"*

Fletcher glanced out the window, briefly, then turned and his eyes found hers and he nodded. He did not even look at Ritchie.

"Thank God," she heard herself murmur. Then she looked directly into the young man's stunned and frantic face. "Yes. We'll settle for that."

Fletcher returned from the window, the gun lifted and pointed and quivering very slightly. But the expression in his eyes, set in the hard-muscled face, was almost serene. Satisfied.

It was at that moment that the idea came to Boyd Ritchie. Seeing the bastard's face all satisfied, and smug, hearing her soft whisper thanking God, he realized that perhaps they really didn't give a shit what happened to themselves just so long as the kids were safe. Was that possible? Well, he'd change that, fast. It was in his power to change that. He suddenly felt light-headed, even giddy—and not, he knew, from loss of blood alone. It was so simple. He had his backup plan after all. Why the hell hadn't he thought of it before?

The pain didn't recede, but under the pain now there was this great calm. He recalled the way her face had looked earlier when he told her what he'd done to the Cunt. He remembered now, with an intense pleasure, the revulsion gathering in her eyes—the horror and shock. Followed by the naked cold hate.

He wouldn't have to take the gun off the woman for even a second. Just the opposite.

He heard a sound that may have been a laugh. His. "Paul Wharton killed his wife last night," he said, very slowly, looking at Briggs over the black bore of the thirty-eight still leveled at him. "Only . . . before he did, I raped her. That's what rapists do—they rape."

He heard, with a twist of satisfaction under the pain, a gasp at the end of Diehl's Colt .45. But he didn't even bother to glance at her. His interest was in Briggs' face—which had now turned to iron but would not look like iron soon. "I'm going to tell you all about it, Briggs, and you're going to listen."

"Don't," Willa pleaded. "Don't listen, Fletcher."

"You'll listen. It drove her off her nut." Then he did turn his head to look at the woman, his eyes moving down her bare body. "You think I'm insane—this might drive *you* insane. Tit for tat, tit."

He paused then. He was with it again. On top again. Nothing could stop him. Nobody. Pretty soon that frozen pale iron face would shrink into disbelief, then disgust, then loathing. Hate. If Briggs didn't yet hate him enough to pull that trigger, he soon would.

"With that cunt I used a shotgun. Sawed-off. But now all I got is this rooting-tooting cowboy forty-five or the Luger. Whichever has the longer joy stick. Whichever goes farther up the slot—"

In the time they had spent searching the woods and marsh for Wally Heckman—because the girl with that reporter McQuade had told Ben Hutchinson she'd seen the Congressman going into the woods alone—and in the time since he'd seen his patient and friend rising up like some grotesque inhuman monster in the mist over the bog, dripping mud and slime, Leroy Farago had regretted that he had not been more forceful earlier. Wally not only belonged in the hospital, but needed psychiatric care. Now, in the rear seat of the squad car, staring with utter incredulity at the small wet automatic pistol that Wally had pointed at his midsection, below the view of the youthful officer named Larry, who was concentrating on his driving, Leroy Farago was not thinking that his diagnosis was only confirmed by such outlandish behavior; he was wondering whether a gun that had been submersed in swamp water would fire. But when he lifted his gaze to the red-streaked eyes, seeing the quiet, hard, unblinking fixation in them, he decided it wasn't worth taking the chance, even for Wally's health. In his present condition Wally was quite capable of squeezing the trigger.

However, he said, reasonably: "Wally, look at you. You've been through a lot. You've been eaten alive. I can't treat you anywhere but in the hospital."

"Tell him to drive along Howells Street." The voice was flat. "I'll recognize the house."

"Those bites are going to infect as sure as—"

"Tell the driver."

Hell, it wasn't his funeral. He didn't give too much of a damn about living, but why die, absurdly, for nothing, at the hands of a nut who didn't have enough sense left to listen to reason?

"Officer," he said, "I've changed my mind. Congressman Heckman wants to . . . to join his wife at a house on Howells Street. We don't know the street number, but one of us will recognize the house."

"But Ben's orders were—"

"You might radio Lieutenant Hutchinson to meet us there."

"Yes, sir. Siren?"

He glanced at Wally, who spoke, as before: "No siren." Then he said: "Turn right at the next corner. It's only a couple of blocks."

There was a grin on Boyd Ritchie's face, really more of a fixed grimace of delight and satisfaction while he spoke, sparing none of the vivid bloody details. Then he finished: "And you . . . you, man, you get the pleasure of watching."

Fletcher knew that, at whatever cost, he had to conquer, had to choke down and stifle that sick, harrowing fury that threatened to force him to act. *Now!* Knew, too, that he had to be rid of this thing that was not human, this creature from some festering cellar in hell—had to rid the world of it. But he had come this far now; he'd go the route. Up to a point, a certain but as yet unknowable point: perhaps he had arrived at it. He didn't so much as shake his head.

"And, prick, you also get the pleasure of knowing: a forty-five bullet travels just as fast going up straight as it does going straight out."

His nerves were frozen. The appalling picture in his mind held him rigid. While his whole being, mind and body, ached with the craving, the terrible overpowering *need* to kill Boyd Ritchie.

Willa, eyes still shut, didn't appear to be breathing; he could not see her breasts rising and falling.

His hand was wet, his fingers cramped around the trigger.

If he could somehow create a diversion, get that Colt turned away from her body even for the fraction of a second—

His mind was darting desperately. Dangerously. He knew it. He didn't dare panic.

He considered firing. Sighting along his arm and barrel, could he aim carefully enough to put a bullet into Ritchie's left shoulder, spinning his body on the instant before the reflex action—

He could not take that chance. What right had he to make that decision?

Christ.

She lifted her head then. She opened her eyes and stared blindly a second. Then, in a gesture so characteristic that it tore at him like a blade, she shook her dark hair from her face and shoulders.

Willa! It was an inner shout, silent, devastating, shattering.

Then Boyd Ritchie moved. With a low gasp of pain that he probably couldn't contain, he stepped around and in front of her hanging figure, keeping the gun trained on her, and then dropped to his knees and looked up into her blanched and drawn face. Behind the terror in her eyes that were dark and fierce now, there was disgust, unmistakable and defiant.

The Colt was directed at her stomach. Ritchie was contemptuously half turned now so that the brim of the hat hid his face, his streaked and reddened but still glittering eyes.

"Spread your legs, pussy. Spread them."

She did not glance at Fletcher. She did not move at first. Then she brought her two ankles together, tight and close.

Should he fire now? How long could he afford to wait? Wait for what?

Then Willa lifted her head completely. Her eyes, level and bright with decision, met his. "Go ahead, Fletcher." There was no plea in it, only acceptance, finality. No fright, no dread. Very simply she said, "Do it."

Fletcher did not nod, but said, as matter-of-factly as she had spoken: "If he touches you, I will."

And he knew that she had meant what she said and that he had meant what he said, too.

Only Boyd Ritchie was uncertain. He was frowning,

as if in disbelief—as if he really had to test this strange thing that he was, perhaps, just discovering and could not comprehend.

"Ma'am . . . whore . . . bitch," Boyd Ritchie said, very softly, as if pleading very reasonably, "spread your lily-white legs because if you don't, I'll have to put a bullet through the meat. Right here. It'll sting, it might even smart some, but you'll open them then."

Two shots exploded. At first he was certain that the bastard had pulled the trigger. But before he himself could fire, he realized that the sounds had come from below. From outside.

He saw the impulse to rush to the window, pass through Boyd Ritchie's body as it stood up from the floor with stiff difficulty. If he once took that gun off Willa—

But Ritchie stopped himself, turned his face, but not the point of the gun, from Willa and glared at Fletcher. "You had to bring the fuzz, didn't you? You couldn't do what—" He planted his wounded leg at a rigid angle and barked: "Get to that window, prick." And as Fletcher moved, turning and then backing to keep the aim steady on Ritchie: "Tell me who's down there and no lies, no *lies!*"

Fletcher saw the German Luger on the window seat as he bent down to look out, quickly. There was a police car in the driveway. He turned into the room again.

"Well? Well, who's down there?"

His first inclination was to say the house and area were surrounded, but there was no way to predict the consequences of that. How the hell, though, could he describe what he saw? Dr. Farago was crouched behind the rear of the squad car and a uniformed officer whom he did not recognize was stretched out full length on the grass alongside the MG. Both were looking toward the front door of the house—at someone on the porch who was out of his view and who, presumably, had fired the two shots.

Then he heard the front door open and close.

Willa spoke his name.

He faced them, trying to think, breathing hard now.

"Who is it?" Boyd Ritchie demanded, but in a whisper. "Who did the shooting?"

"I don't know."

"Don't con me!" There was a frantic note in his voice as it rose slightly. "Those were shots from an automatic. Who?"

"I said I don't know," Fletcher snarled.

"Then find out! Anyone comes up here—" He stopped. He didn't need to touch the white still flesh with the tip of the Colt. "Anybody's head show up those stairs—"

Quietly then Fletcher said: "If it's true you haven't really murdered anyone yourself, Ritchie, this'd be one hell of a time to start. Now, when you've got a chance?"

Moving toward the stairs, Fletcher spoke flatly, his tone hard. "A chance, I said. But not if you yourself personally kill someone now in cold blood."

"Lay off. More of the same shit! You can't—"

But he was interrupted by a shout from below, inside the house: "Ritchie! I know you're here, Ritchie!"

When the sound had rumbled and echoed through the house, and away, Fletcher glanced at Willa, whose face was a stricken mask, questions in her eyes. "I don't know who it is," he told her, gently. "But I'll make damn sure he doesn't come up." Then to Ritchie: "If I hear a shot up here, or any sound whatever, I'll see you're not arrested. I'll see to it personally that you don't get what you really want."

He turned away and went down the stairs, momentarily gratified by the bewilderment in Boyd's dazed eyes in that pale face that was now contorted by uncertainty, possibly even fear.

There was no one in the downstairs portion of the house. He'd walked through every room. But he knew Ritchie was here. Somewhere. He had to be, that's all.

He'd known where Ritchie would go, all along he'd known. He was climbing the stairs from the basement now. His body itched all over, and his face was so stiff and sore that shouting a few moments ago had caused the dry flesh to feel as if it cracked open in a thousand places. Leroy had argued in the car, all the way, that Boyd Ritchie was hundreds of miles away by now, but when you know a thing, you know it. And when he'd climbed out of the squad car a few minutes ago and had looked through the garage window, and had seen Chief Diehl's car in there, then nobody could stop him, nobody. That's when he'd taken out the automatic because he knew what he had to do, what any man would do. He'd fired those two shots—he couldn't waste more—at Farago and the police officer because they'd tried to stop his coming inside; he couldn't allow anyone to interfere. His mind was fine now, clear, just fine. If it hadn't been for that unfortunate episode in the swamp, he would have been here long ago.

He didn't have much time now because that officer who had been driving would be sending for others and he'd already radioed for Ben Hutchinson to come. He had to reach that young pervert first, before anyone else could—

Boyd Ritchie, weak and faint from the loss of blood, knew that he was not thinking too well. Here he was trapped with the Colt on the whore, so he might as well kill her now and have done with it. He was dead anyway. He had been certain-dead for a long time now and the pain was too much, so why not end it?

Instead, though, after Briggs had gone, he had taken a deep breath and lowered his arm, which felt as if it might break off. Her eyes were shut again, as if she couldn't bear to imagine what might be going on downstairs, tears on her cheeks. He had shoved the Colt into the holster and limped to the window seat. Then he had seen the prowl car. Someone inside it talking into a mike and that prick Farago standing alongside. What the hell was *he* doing here? And if they knew he was inside, why had they sent only one man inside to call his name?

He had sunk down lifelessly to the window seat and now he wondered whether he could ever find the strength to stand up again.

If anyone but Briggs came up to the attic, she was going to die. He had to remember that, his confused mind had to cling to that.

So it was true, wasn't it—that there were certain things that people would rather die than do. He was almost sick with astonishment—incredulity. He'd always thought people, all people, would do anything.

But she would rather have died than let him do to her what he'd done to the Cunt.

And Briggs, too—he would have caused her to die. Like killing her himself.

He still didn't believe it. Couldn't.

And now he'd never be able to even the score with Briggs.

No way.

It was over.

Kaput.

But . . . what was it Briggs had said? That he still had a chance? What did he mean?

"Hey, you," he called across in a loud whisper, "hey. What'd he mean—about he'd see I didn't live to get what I *really* want?"

She didn't open her eyes. "He meant he'd kill you and that once you're dead, you can't enjoy the fruits of your labors. You'll never even know what the newspapers will say."

His mind didn't seem to be clear. Jesus, he was tired.

He picked up the Luger. It was even heavier than the Colt.

They'd hate him for this. The whole motherfucking world. But if he was dead—

He couldn't think straight.

They'd still hate him, but he wouldn't even—

"Briggs!" he yelled. "Briggs, get up here!"

But it was more of a plea than a command. And not loud. He wasn't even sure the prick could hear him. He wasn't really sure he'd yelled out loud.

He looked outside again. But not down. To hell with them.

It was morning. The sun was supposed to come up at five forty-three. He remembered that. And by that time he was supposed to be on his way: all the way across the lake and in the van, driving north, in the van with all that bread in the back of it.

How come he was here when he was supposed to be on his way?

Fletcher had heard the faint cry from above, had heard the frenzied urgency in it and had wondered. But he had no time to think about it because he was standing in the second-floor hall looking down the stairway to the front hallway below as a heavy figure, covered with caked mud and slime, hair matted, arms hanging along its sides, heaved into view like a man sleepwalking. Its face was a brown and red mask, grotesque, unreal. Its eyes were almost swollen shut as it stopped and stood looking up at him.

Wally Heckman? This stolid apparition? Then it had been Heckman who had taken those two shots at either Farago or the police officer or perhaps both. There was a kind of awesome inevitability about Heckman's being here, yet Fletcher remained astounded. The nightmare seemed to have no end. He did not have to ask why Heckman was here or what he wanted. Even the small automatic pistol that was in his hand, pointing to the floor, seemed a natural part of this most unnatural night and morning.

"So," Heckman said, his lips moving stiffly in the frame of mask and his voice as unrecognizable as it had been when he shouted Ritchie's name a few minutes ago, "so—I was right. He is here, isn't he?"

"I'm handling it," Fletcher said. "Go away, Wally."

Then harshly: *"Get the hell out of here!"*

"He's up there."

"So's Willa. So's my wife, Wally."

A moment, the spectral figure still as death. Then: "I'm afraid that's not my concern."

Past astonishment, Fletcher felt a sharp stab of anger. "Well, it's *my* concern."

And Heckman took two steps up.

Christ.

Fletcher lifted the revolver. And held it. It had become a part of his arm and hand, heavy, so heavy that even holding it now became more than he felt capable of doing.

Heckman stopped. His head was back and his eyes were all but lost, slits between puffing scarlet folds of flesh, expressionless. But his voice was sad: "My son's name is Dennis."

More madness. Fletcher understood. The man was beyond reason, crazed, almost catatonic. But dangerous. To Willa.

And all of a sudden Fletcher was pleading, begging Heckman to go away, knowing it was hopeless, even his own voice ringing strange in his ear, and even while he was leaning over the banister, he realized that he was also weeping, there were tears on his face, and he was talking wildly, so wildly that he heard the screech of determination in his tone but could not even make out his own words, the plea then turning into rage: get out, get out or he'd kill him if he had to, he'd kill *anyone* this morning if he had to. And as he spoke, he knew that he was one with Heckman: they'd been brought to the same brink. Only Heckman had stepped over and he didn't dare give in, he couldn't allow himself to—

The shot exploded and rocked through the house and he heard a hissing sound alongside his head, a hissing and a simultaneous thud that stayed in his ears while the reverberation of the report died away.

He went deaf then, as he staggered to one side, knowing why he was staggering, he even uttered a groan, and he made sure his body moved sideways and backward toward the open bedroom door; he had to make Heckman think he'd wounded him, of course, another of the outlandish mad acts that he was forced to do, compelled, he couldn't think of Willa upstairs listening, wondering, he had to make Heckman think he'd—

The slyness took over coldly, completely. He was on the bedroom floor, on his stomach, the gun in hand, arm propped by elbow on the rug, and he was aiming low at the doorway. He heard nothing down below. Or on the stairway.

Stay away, Wally. Go out the front door, leave me alone.

But he knew the other man would not turn away.

He moaned.

If Wally came to help, he'd wing him someway, wasn't that the word, *wing* him so he couldn't move, couldn't climb up that second flight of stairs.

He heard footfalls on the steps now.

If Wally tried to pass the door, he'd fire. He'd fire low although he knew nothing about shooting a gun. He'd shoot to stop him, not to kill, but he'd shoot.

It was too bad that he had been forced to shoot Fletcher Briggs, he wished it hadn't been necessary, but time was running out and if more police officers came, they'd feel it was their duty, not his, to execute the perverted little son of a bitch, so he'd have to pass by Fletcher Briggs, who was groaning audibly in the bedroom off to his right, and hope that he'd be all right, perhaps only a flesh wound, it had not been a very well-aimed shot but the best he could manage in the circumstances, and he hoped it didn't hurt too much but what was pain, he'd heard Ritchie calling from above, higher above, probably the attic, it must have been Ritchie, so after he climbed this flight of stairs, there had to be another to carry him to the attic, he was passing the bedroom door, poor Fletcher, he could see the hall ahead leading to the other stairs, and then he heard something, a violent ear-shattering burst of sound, an explosion, someone was blowing up the house, and then he felt the searing stab, he wasn't sure exactly where, and he was falling, but he mustn't fall, mustn't allow himself, so he straightened, to hell with the pain, he was pain all over anyway, but the walls looked odd, they seemed to be falling in toward him, he had to get away, get out into the air, that explosion, the house was collapsing, that was it, the house itself, but he could make it outside if he turned and retraced his steps, he was at the top of the stairs now, looking down, what a vast expanse down below, but he could make it, nothing was going to defeat him, Wallace Heckman, he could snag a pass and run sixty-three yards, he could make it down any flight of stairs and into the air, odd for a house to blow up, though, he made the first step down, easy, and his leg, the one that really hurt now, as if there was a hot rivet through the calf, that leg went out and down and onto the next step, and then he could feel and see space coming up at him, space itself coming up at him like a solid wall that he was plunging into headfirst.

Even after the second sharp crack of a gun below, Willa kept her eyes closed. She felt Boyd Ritchie leap into place beside her, but the gun barrel did not touch her breast. Had Fletcher fired that shot? Which one? Or had he been killed by one of them? But who would want to kill Fletcher besides this hateful vicious maniac now unbreathing alongside her?

She was giving out. Her mind, stunned by the confusions of the last hour—which seemed more like years!—and by the blow on the head, which left her mind reeling even now, she felt numb. She knew she had to hang on, she couldn't let go, she couldn't let Fletcher down, but the temptation to bend her quivering knees and to hang there loosely, semiconscious, uncaring, was so great and pervasive that, even as she heard the heavy swift tread on the stairs, she wondered whether if Fletcher's head did not appear, she would simply pass out completely, fold, collapse, before the boy could shoot her.

The tread stopped, and into the silence Fletcher's voice, flintlike and ferocious, yet low, said one word: her name. She opened her eyes.

And what she saw there in Fletcher's clenched face and ice-blue eyes—urgency and homicidal fury and barbaric implacability—somehow renewed her. She lifted her head. And felt that same savagery streaming through her, hot and wild.

Ritchie's voice was shrill: "Who was that down there?"

"Wallace Heckman," Fletcher said, his eyes moving from her and hardening. "I shot him. So you've turned me into a murderer. You've had your revenge. If that's not enough, too bad, it's all you're going to get from me."

Congressman Heckman? In her house? Dead. To save her—

Then she was listening to the frigid contempt in Fletcher's voice again, a reckless finality: "No more games now." He had not raised the gun in his hand. "It's over."

"Then I might as well kill her. That what you want, man?"

Fletcher did lift the revolver then. "If you don't want to live to get credit, or blame, for what you've done. If you want to be forgotten in a week, a name in a newspaper. A nobody. Dead and buried in a pauper's grave. *Nothing.*"

She understood then. And waited.

At her shoulder she heard Boyd Ritchie shriek: *"They had it coming, all of them!"*

"Who's going to know that? How? You think I'll tell them for you?" Then he paused, eyes cold and merciless, face stony with scorn and loathing, before he growled: "They'll never know you didn't rape Coralie

Wharton eight years ago. Or why you confessed. They'll never know you were innocent."

"You never thought so! You never believed me!"

"I did my best for you, you bastard, and look where it's got me."

Then Boyd Ritchie was snarling: *"Lies!* More goddamn lies, you're trying to con me again, to save her, this whore, to save—"

But his voice trailed off as the sound of a siren could be heard in the distance: *wow-wow-wow*—

"Damn right," Fletcher barked. "Are you so goddamned stupid you think I'm trying to save *your* life? I'd rather pull this trigger than take my next breath."

Wow-wow-wow-wow—

Hearing the hate in Fletcher's voice, she gave in to her own, on the instant also aware that Boyd Ritchie hungered for it, thrived on it, craved it. "Don't worry about me, Fletch!" she cried. "I don't care what happens to me just so he doesn't live to get satisfaction and revel in what he's done. It's not fair, no justice, for him to wallow in the way everyone in the world will hate him!" She was looking at him and he was staring at Fletcher, his mouth open, a half-smile along his lips. "He should be ripped apart, clawed to strips. His hand should be stomped to pulp, his bullet wound gouged with fire. For God's sake, don't let him live to take pride in what he's done!"

Then, very slowly, Boyd Ritchie turned his head to face her. Under the brim of the hat his eyes looked vague, distant, somehow heavy with a sensual pleasure, satisfaction. With a shock she realized that he looked like a man immediately after an orgasm.

After Ben Hutchinson had learned by radio from headquarters that Officer Larry Scott had relayed a message from Dr. Farago for Ben to meet him on Howells Street and on the fast drive from the area of Hanover Pond into town and up the hills, he could not possibly have imagined what he now discovered as he approached the house.

A heavy mud-splattered figure of a man, whom he recognized even at a distance as Congressman Heckman, was crawling over the grass on two hands and one knee, dragging his other leg, which did not bend and which appeared to be covered with blood. A few observers had gathered and two or three cars had stopped along the street. Before he could reach the scene, Dr. Farago and Larry Scott had rushed to Heckman, lifted him, and they were now half carrying him upright between them to Larry's squad car.

But why the hell had they come here? He'd instructed Larry to take them both to the hospital.

And if Heckman was wounded, it must have happened inside the house.

He flipped off the siren, drew his revolver and stepped from the car.

The siren had stopped outside, close. And Ritchie, although he stood like a man in a stupor, had not lowered the Luger; its end remained two inches from Willa's left side. And Fletcher Briggs could not be sure that his argument had really penetrated. Willa's burst of wrath and repugnance had been a masterstroke, although he sensed that her yearning for revenge was no more feigned than the brutish, barbarous ferocity he felt smoldering volcanically in himself.

"Murder one." At first Fletcher was not absolutely certain that he had heard what Ritchie said. "I'm not going to spend the rest of my life back there in that stinking hole."

"Why the hell should you? You've been too clever to kill anyone yourself." His tone remained flintlike. "But no one'll ever know how damned smart you've been if you don't live to go to trial."

"I told you—"

"I heard you, shut up and listen. You could plead insanity."

Ritchie's arm swung around; the gun was now

pointed at him. And it was quivering at arm's length. He heard Willa gasp his name as she realized his thought: if he fired now, Ritchie could kill only him.

So he shook his head, sharply, and said: "Listen, Ritchie, anyone who could pull off what you have can't be insane." He began to move, walking past Ritchie, past the Luger, ignoring it, to the window, lowering his own gun carelessly. "But a jury could be made to think you are. The average citizen has to think you're nuts—a man'd have to be to do what you've done. They have to believe that. And there's always a shrink around who'll testify that way, too."

"If I thought you were trying to snow me again—"

Aware of the leveled barrel that must have turned as he passed—damned if he'd look at it, though—Fletcher leaned down and looked out. Ben Hutchinson was closing the door of the police cruiser that had been parked there earlier and he could see Heckman's face through the windshield, his eyes wide in a mud-streaked mask. Alive, anyway, thank God. But his hate for Ritchie swelled inside, burning and even more intense.

"I'm talking about *you* conning some stupid psychiatrist. If you think you're shrewd enough." He shrugged and watched the cruiser back out of the driveway. "Rest in some quiet hospital for a year or two, then miraculously recover. Done all the time. Walk out a free man. And famous. *If* you're smart enough."

"Who . . . who's out there, Briggs?"

"Police. Tear gas. Riot guns. Automatic rifles. The works." Again hazarding the lie: the bastard had to be backed against the wall all the way. Then what? "They're setting up blockades on the corner." He straightened and turned. Willa had twisted around; he could feel her eyes on him. "There's a mob of people. Damned quiet. Ritchie, if the cops let them get near you, they'll tear you apart by inches."

Ritchie took two steps toward the window.

"Give me your guns," Fletcher said quietly, and

watched Ritchie stop, stand there, head tilted, injured leg stiff to one side, the Luger shaking visibly now. "I'll see you get protection now and a trial later." Was that uncertainty in those inflamed eyes? Fletcher whirled and called out through the broken windowpane: "Ben. Ben Hutchinson!" Then he saw Ben Hutchinson standing with his own gun in hand, looking up. "Ben. I'm representing Boyd Ritchie. He's here with me and wants to surrender. Can I have your promise that you and your men won't let that mob get to him?"

He saw Ben cast a single glance over his shoulder at the ten or twelve people gathered along the sidewalk, huddled and frightened and curious. Then Ben looked up again and shouted: "You got my word, Counselor."

Then Fletcher stepped back from the window, straightened to his full height and faced Ritchie again. He knew now he'd shot his last bolt. This was it. If Ritchie wheeled and fired at Willa now, Fletcher would try to shoot first. But not to kill. Only to wound. To render the cruel sadistic bastard helpless long enough so that Fletcher could—

Boyd Ritchie did move then. Fast. He drew his arm back and hurled the Luger. Fletcher saw it coming, saw the frenzy, the riot in Ritchie's eyes, ducked to one side in time and heard the gun crashing through the window. Then, with a flourish and a small laugh filled with triumph and relief and delight, Ritchie reached to the holster, extracted the Colt and then threw again. This time Fletcher only stepped aside. The Colt went smashing through the glass, shattering another pane.

Then Ritchie stood there, grinning, revivified—alive and mocking again. "Tell them I'm unarmed," he instructed Fletcher, grinning.

But then whatever he saw in Fletcher's face caused the wild glittering triumph to seep from Boyd Ritchie's overbright eyes, caused them to go dull and cautious at first, then bleak, the grin freezing.

Fletcher glanced beyond the off-kilter figure that waited. Saw Willa slump on the rope, her eyes closing.

He shared that sense of relief and hoped she had fainted.

So she would not witness this.

He stepped toward Boyd Ritchie, the gun directed, pointed until its barrel end was touching his forehead, between the eyes, the vacant glazed eyes. He heard noises from outside. They would be in the house soon.

Too soon.

He didn't have much time.

But enough. Enough.

With the tip of the gun barrel he flipped off the wide-brimmed hat. Then he released the hammer. Then he raised the gun, high. Above the ugly gleaming bald skull.

Boyd Ritchie didn't seem any more surprised than he was. He only waited, knowing.

Before the squad car carrying Congressman Heckman and Dr. Farago had left the driveway for the hospital, Ben Hutchinson had instructed Larry Scott, who was driving, to radio headquarters for more men to be dispatched to this address and to ask that all law enforcement agencies be advised. If the Congressman had been able to talk coherently, Ben might have tried to question him, but all he could get from Heckman was that he had shot Fletcher Briggs. Then, as the vehicle was backing out of the driveway, while he'd been trying to decide whether to go in alone or to wait for reinforcements, there'd been that puzzling shout from above asking him to promise there'd be no mob violence—when, hell, there was no evidence of that possibility anywhere up or down the street. But it had established that Ritchie was inside. And that Fletcher Briggs was still alive.

He had been undecided even then since Briggs seemed to be in control in there, until the two guns came hurtling out the dormer window one after the other. The sight of Diehl's old Colt on the driveway and of the Luger on the grass helped him to make up his mind. He moved toward the wide pleasant front porch, where he could hear a bird trying to imitate a siren: *wow-wow-wow.*

If there was one damned thing he'd learned through the night, it was that indecision could be as destructive as the wrong decision.

As he went up onto the porch, he heard another motor and glimpsed, over his shoulder, McQuade's green VW coming to a stop along the curb across the street and two police vehicles approaching, one from each direction.

Willa had not fainted. She had heard every ugly, crunching blow. The heavy breathing. The grunts. The moans. She could have stopped it at any point, but some cruelty and need in herself held her helpless.

The sounds finally stopped.

She opened her eyes.

Boyd Ritchie was on the floor, curled into a fetal position, his skull a crisscross of ridges and bleeding lacerations, his face hidden, his body still, his wounded leg outstretched and his burned hand, mangled and black-red, like a gruesome shrunken head without features, lying helpless at the end of an outflung arm.

She could not bear to look.

Her eyes then traveled up, along the tall, still figure standing above the fallen boy, past the revolver still clutched in one hand, its barrel red with blood. Her eyes moved up. She saw the savagery in his stance, the pitiless and feral tenseness in his muscles, the heaving of his chest, and her eyes reached his face in profile, the face she knew so well but did not now immediately recognize. His eyes were riveted on the hand on the floor, or what had once been a hand, and she recalled her own shrill barbarous cries earlier: *His hand should be stomped to pulp.* And she understood. Savagery, yes—inhuman, yes. Or human? Very human?

She saw the urge move in his body, she could almost feel it herself: to lift a heavy shoe and to bring it down crushingly, finally.

But horror twisted in her: enough, oh, God, *enough!*

And she did not realize she had made a sound until his face turned to her. She had never seen such ferocity in any face, in any eyes, ever before.

Then, as they stared at each other, hearing voices and motors below, and more sirens, she saw something else replace the bestial, junglelike cruelty on his face, his beloved face. It was rapture, reminding her of that almost ecstatic expression on Boyd Ritchie's face—slack, sated, oddly happy—a short time ago as he had fed on her hate, relished it, devoured it. It was the expression—relief, joy, peace—that she had seen often on Fletcher's face after they had made love. As if he had been purged.

He threw aside the gun which clattered across the gray and dusty floor, slid into the debris of smashed clay. Then he was coming toward her and all the familiar gentleness and compassion returned to his eyes as, in silence, he reached above her head with one hand and placed the other arm, with infinite tenderness, around her bare back so that she felt held and supported and cared for. And she gave herself over.

Gavin McQuade, no longer retching but, at a deeper level, still quivering, himself behind the steering wheel now, watched the police cars gathering, saw the television van and the other cars approaching, stopping, people on front porches now, along the sidewalk, all eyes on the big old Victorian house with the number 1127 above its door. He saw the broken panes of glass on the dormer window on the third floor; otherwise, the house appeared normal.

Then he caught sight of two young people standing together on the sidewalk across the street from the house. The girl had long reddish hair that streamed down her back and she wore a military-type coat to her ankles. He had seen her with Fletcher hours ago in the courthouse. Her companion wore tattered dungarees, dirty tennis shoes, and a sweat shirt with letters on it which Gavin could not read. They stood very quietly, close together, staring across the street. Motionless. They made no effort to cross the street.

Gavin felt the girl beside him, that very strange girl, whom he had met last night in the Colonial Inn, whom he had known for at least a century or so, place her hand over his. Again.

Ben Hutchinson had no use for his gun, so he holstered it.

It was a sort of attic, but of a kind he'd never seen before. And it looked devastated, laid waste.

With a rope dangling. And at the rope, two upright figures, a man and woman. Very still, holding each other. The woman wore a dusty kimono and a man's jacket over her shoulders. The man was Fletcher Briggs, whose eyes were shut tight. They were not clinging to each other. Their faces looked as ravaged as the room. But peaceful, too.

He wondered how long before he could get home to Myra. Where he belonged.

Outside, beyond the smashed window, sirens seemed to be converging, their sound coming from all directions and filling the world.

Then he saw the figure curled on the floor. He crossed through the rubble and looked down.

So that's Boyd Ritchie. He was breathing. He was also bleeding.

Ben went to the window.

Was it over? Was it really over then?

He shouted for an ambulance.

He heard a mockingbird somewhere. Imitating the sound of a siren's wail.

Would it ever really be over?

Morning

She woke early, as usual, and she looked forward to the day ahead, as she always did the last four years. Oh, it might not seem like such an exciting or adventuresome day to some, only small pleasant things and people she enjoyed, but then most people hadn't been married to T. H. Stuttaford for more than fifty very long years. She only hoped they wouldn't bother her again about what had happened last night. It was a nasty sort of prank, true, but once a person's passed on—and his soul's in hell anyway—what does it matter what happens to his bones?

Dr. Wright Scofield had had a busy night, busier than any within memory, and now he had three postmortems to perform in one morning: Vincent Stegner, Mrs. Nell Diehl and Frederick Lansing, who had been night watchman at Wharton Mills. Three in one night and two burned to death. What was the point of going to bed now when he'd have to get up again in a couple of hours? He decided to stay up and have a drink. Maybe two or three drinks.

Dennis Heckman was awake in the strange and sterile hospital room. The pain had gone away—almost. He was glad of that because he didn't want anyone to touch him. The nurses, Dr. Farago, his mother—anyone. Not ever again. He wanted everyone to keep their hands off him, forever and ever, because he hated them all, everyone alive, fuck the world.

* * *

She had been warned that Wally's problem, when he awakened, would be in his mind. Leroy, who looked tired this morning and had begun to show his age, had told her also that, with heavy intravenous sedation, Wally would probably sleep into the afternoon. The bullet had gone through the calf, chipping the bone, but there was no danger, no physical danger. When the psychiatrist came in at nine to speak with Dennis, she'd ask him to return later to see Wally. And Wally would consult with him whether he liked it or not. She didn't hold Wally accountable for all his actions through the night; she knew she couldn't if he was such a sick man. But she only hoped that she could forgive him for his refusal to come to her in that bitter lonely time she had needed him, had begged him. Of course, if he was really sick in that way, then she would have to take over. Make the decisions. Such as the one about Washington, D.C. For the rest of their lives she would simply have to take over. Completely.

In his semicircular office, at his long worktable, Digby Norton finished reading Gavin McQuade's long and detailed story, which was excellent—the complex rendered simple. The account did not include any reference to the indignity suffered by Congressman Heckman's son, but Digby Norton had no doubt that the other news media would. The story did include a statement by Fletcher Briggs that, according to Boyd Ritchie—although this was unconfirmed—Mrs. Coralie Wharton had been murdered by her husband, Paul. Augusta's son. Paul Wharton. And now he also had disappeared completely. Along with his dead wife. Digby Norton wondered silently what the night just passed would have been like if Augie Fuller had decided to marry him instead of Lockridge Wharton. Then there would not have been a Paul Wharton at all. As there might not be now. Yes, the past sure as hell does have a way of catching up. In many ways. He pressed a button on his desk and picked up one of his pipes and thought of the dead and missing and injured, not to mention the property laid waste. As if a small war had been waged right here. It was just as well Augie didn't know what had happened to her town tonight.

"It must be freezing," the girl said. She was huddled in a poncho on one of the gray-stone ledges above the surface of the water. It was still dim this far down in the quarry. "How can you stand it?"

"It blows your mind!" the boy said. She could see only his head, long hair trailing, and he was treading water furiously to keep warm. She knew he had been showing off, for her, and she enjoyed it. "I can't dive to the bottom. No one ever can, I mean never."

Her teeth were chattering and her body was shivering all over. "Thanks, anyway," she said, "For trying." Her mind was still groggy. She'd really been stoned last night. Imagining all sorts of wild things. Like David's father coming. Like seeing the sky burning up. Like hearing a splash in the dark. It had been really hairy. Then. But now it was light again and all she could think about now was what her mother would say when she got home. She hoped she never got old—never, never, never.

Leroy Farago was in a taxi on his way from the hospital to the Common, where he had left his own car parked behind the courthouse. He had heard the report of Coralie Wharton's possible murder, but he didn't believe it. The newspapers and radio reporters always exaggerated everything. But hell, considering everything else, maybe it was true. He thought he should care, he wished he could, but he was losing his sexual powers and prowess anyway, admit it, so what the hell did it really mean to him? That or anything or anyone else. Then why this Hippocratic devotion in a man sick of living? He had assisted in the removal of Theron Diehl's spleen—which was, if he was any judge, an organ that man would most sorely miss—and had aided in an hour's worth of other repairs; later in the day the decision whether to remove the lower left leg altogether would have to be made. And from the look in Diehl's eyes just before the anesthetic was administered, he doubted whether the old man gave much of a damn one way or the other. A broken man. Join the club, Chief.

In recent years, although he was still a good Catholic, Albert P. Gilpin had forgotten how peaceful and soothing a church could be during early-morning mass. Before the priest had reached the consecration, Albert P. Gilpin had made his decision, with the help of the Lord. He must find another job. It was, he acknowledged, still another failure—like his decision that he did not really have a vocation for the priesthood. He knew now that he was not the kind of man to be a parole officer: he was too poor a judge of other men for so responsible a position. Thank you, Lord, for your eternal guidance and forgive me for my trespasses.

She was watching Gavin sleep. He slept quietly, his spare bare chest lifting only slightly with each breath. He was a handsome man, this McQuade, with his lined, gnarled face and mocking, sad-merry eyes—handsome in a strange way that confused her. After they'd made love—yes, not fucked, not screwed, made love—he had said that he was not lonely for the first time in years and that he had not been lonely since eleven o'clock last night. Which was the reason she was lying here next to him, right? Lying here with joy ballooning inside her, and hope. Lying here wondering whether finally Annette Beauchamp, the kid herself, had stumbled across a man who could make her feel whole, and a woman. Lying here making up excuses for cutting her morning classes, right?

* * *

With the cool breeze off the lake blowing against his face, Ben Hutchinson was driving at a leisurely rate of speed and enjoying it. Soon now, very soon, one more job and he'd be home. With Myra and the boys. Once he was with them, he could really put the night behind him. Hearing their voices and their laughter, he could forget, at least for a while. He'd written up his reports; he'd made a lucky guess that the Datsun half-ton might have been stolen from the Datsun dealer's lot and the metallic gray Vega with the souped-up engine had been located there. What bugged him, though, was a feeling he'd had in the Briggs house when he saw Boyd Ritchie lying curled up on the floor of the attic, bleeding. It had been a feeling that had not shocked him at the moment but had haunted him ever since: rage mixed with satisfaction and an urge to finish the job, to finish it personally, or worse. Yes, worse. Like Diehl. That's what bugged him: in time, on this job, was it inevitable that at least some of Diehl's feelings invade every law enforcement officer? But he had to put aside such thoughts now. He was on his way to investigate a van parked in a grove of pines on the far side of the lake. It had been spotted by a helicopter pilot who had been suspicious enough to have it searched, and the search had revealed a large sum of cash concealed in the camping gear behind the driver's seat. The van would not have caught his eye, the pilot reported, if it had not been painted in such brilliant colors and in such a pattern. "Hippie-style" was the way he had described it.

They'd stuffed him with pills, they'd punched him in the arm, shot him in the ass, he had no idea how many goddamn stitches they'd taken, his head was one mass of bandages and they had him trussed up, leg in the air, hand in the air—hell, he wasn't going anywhere. But none of that mattered. He had no pain—only a pleasant floating sensation. Oh, he had his work cut out for him, but he'd have plenty of time. He'd have to do some intense research before he'd be ready to flunk their goddamn sanity tests. Everyone thought he was a maniac anyway, didn't they? Only a lunatic would do what he'd done. Briggs had been right: he'd already heard three of the nurses in the hall agree on that. Then, after some time in a hospital on a nice hill someplace in the country, it'd be even easier to convince the shrinks he was sane again—since the joke was on them, because he really was sane and had been all along. The joke was on them—and Briggs. The prick had outsmarted himself this time—and all the while thinking he was conning Boyd Ritchie. Like that lie about there being a mob outside the house. Well . . . in the center of the drifting floating sensation was peace. To hell with Canada, Europe, South America. Even with the bread, what could he really do in any of those places? Here he knew the next move, and the next, and by then he'd have doped out the next and the moves to follow. First step, a big-lip legal smart-ass but the best, nothing but, somebody like that Bailey bastard—Christ, anyone'd be willing to take on a case like this! He'd refuse to say a word till he talked with his lawyer. But he'd level with him—well, he'd level partway. He'd say he wanted to plead innocent—because in a way he really was. There had to be a trial this time, though. And it was going to be one hell of a trial. He could promise them all they'd get their money's worth. And they'd all sit there hating him. A sea of hate ready to burst over him. They'd all know what he'd done. In detail. With particulars. What they'd all like to do if they had the guts and grit and brains. That's why they hated him so much. There was a tint of gold behind the curtains: sunrise at five forty-three. As he lay bandaged and drugged and strapped and guarded, he never felt more free or more alive. Hell, he was still going to win. This was only the beginning.

The police had gone, old Dr. Toomey had bandaged

Willa's head and prescribed tranquilizers and a vacation for one and all, and the reporters and photographers had taken their television cameras and other equipment off the lawn, and now only a few sightseers lingered outside the house. Neighbors had brought food, reassurances, condolences and advice, and one had left a huge pewter urn of steaming coffee, which now occupied the center of the round kitchen table. When the four were seated around it, Fletcher commented that it certainly took one hell of a lot to get this family down to the table at the same time. And Willa smiled wanly, Peggy winked at her father and David, grinning, lifted his fingers in the peace sign. Then Fletcher asked whether they thought they should take the doctor's advice and go on a vacation, perhaps leaving as soon as they could get packed and ready. But three heads shook and Fletcher shrugged and Willa said she supposed she really should phone her mother. She could tell her, she said, that the reason they hadn't come was that they'd had a guest who had given her one beauty of a headache. At which they all laughed and David said, "Right-on, old girl," and Willa said for him not to call her old girl because she didn't feel old in the slightest. And then Peggy stood up and asked what Noah's daughter would do in the circumstances and answered herself by saying she'd put Noah's pad back into shape. Then David pushed back his chair and said he thought it was Job's son who'd said that. Willa stood up then, a trifle unsteadily. She didn't say anything, though. She looked at Fletcher. She didn't need to say anything. Nor did he.

And, outside, even Hotspur seemed to respect the occasion. He was singing his wildest, sweetest song as if it were the middle of the night.

"Well, friends and neighbors, it's almost six A.M. and you know what that means. Like the cliché says, it's all over but the shouting. And I'll bet some of you felt like Jerry Gerrard from time to time—that the night would never end. . . . Don't forget to tune in at ten tonight and *Tell It to Jerry*. . . . It's a lovely, lovely morning, folks. The sun's broken through and according to the reports, it's going to be a bright pleasant fall day all over New England. Who could ask for anything more?"